# King of Beasts
## DUET

## DIANA A. HICKS

HMG, INC.

# Copyright

This is a work of fiction. Names, characters, places, and incidents are either the product of the author's imagination or are used fictitiously, and any resemblance to actual persons living or dead, business establishments, events, or locales, is entirely coincidental.

**King of Beasts Duet**

COPYRIGHT © 2022 by Diana A. Hicks

Publishing History

Hardback 978-1-949760-58-3

Print ISBN 978-1-949760-53-8

Digital ISBN 978-1-949760-52-1

Credits

Cover Designer: Dar Albert

Editor: Tera Cuskaden and Becky Barney

# Recommended Reading Order

## The Crime Society

Lost Raven - Novella

King of Beasts (Beast Duet #1)

King of Beasts (Beast Duet #2)

Wolf's Lair - Prequel (FREE)

Big Bad Wolf (Wolf Duet #1)

Big Bad Wolf (Wolf Duet #2)

Once Upon A Christmas - Bonus Epilogue

Dark Beauty - Prequel

Fallen Raven (Raven Duet, #1)

Fallen Raven (Raven Duet, #2)

## Steal My Heart Series

Ignite You

Escape You

Escape My Love - Bonus Epilogue

Provoke You

Unravel You

Unleash You

Defy You

**Desert Monsoon Series**

Love Over Lattes

Love Over Time

# Praise for Diana A. Hicks

"Hicks' first installment of her Desert Monsoon series is confident and assured with strong storytelling, nuanced characters, and a dynamic blend of romance and suspense."

**— KIRKUS REVIEWS**

What makes any romance a great read isn't the fact that two hot people meet and fall in love. It is the episodes that bring about the falling in love and the unexpected places the experience takes the characters that make it an enjoyable read. Diana A. Hicks knows just how to make this happen.

**— READERS' FAVORITE**

# About the Author

**Diana A. Hicks** is an award-winning author of dark mafia romance and steamy contemporary romance with a heavy dose of suspense.

When Diana is not writing, she enjoys kickboxing, hot yoga, traveling, and indulging in the simple joys of life like wine and chocolate. She lives in Atlanta and loves spending time with her two children and husband.

Check out my bookstore!

**Don't forget** to sign up to my newsletter to stay up to date on my latest releases, free content, and other news.
Subscribe to my VIP List now!

SINFULLY DARK ROMANCE

Dear Readers,

I'm so happy to share Rex and Caterina's epic love story with you!

King of Beasts is a dark mafia romance that blends in elements of one of my favorite fairytales, Beauty and the Beast and kink.

This book has been on my mind for over a year, and I'm so happy that I finally get to share it with you!!! You're going to love Rex and Caterina's intense love story.

Don't forget to download the totally free bonus novella, featuring Massimo, Caterina's brother.

Lost Raven - Novella (FREE)

Get ready to fall in love with the ruthless men of the Society.

Welcome to The Society!

Diana

# King of Beasts

## BOOK ONE

# CHAPTER 1
## *Do You Have an Invitation?*

CATERINA

"Five more minutes." I hit the screen on my phone to snooze the blaring alarm.

When nothing happened, I opened one eye to make sure I tapped the right button this time. Then I saw Dad's serene face on the incoming call. I scrambled to sit up and quickly pressed the device to my ear.

"Hello? Dad?"

"Caterina, it's me."

"I know, Dad. What's wrong?" I squinted at my watch. "It's one in the morning."

"I know. I'm sorry to wake you, Bells. I need a lift." He puffed out a breath. "You said last week, I could call any time."

My entire body sunk deeper into the mattress. "*I need a lift,*" was code for "*I spent all my money gambling and now I don't even have money for a cab.*" Dad's addiction was getting worse.

"Text me your address. I'll come get you."

"I'm at the Crucible."

I stopped midway with my mouth open and feet hovering over the hardwood floor. *Fuck me.* Why that place? "Okay. I'll, um, I'll be there shortly."

"Thank you. You're the best daughter an old man like me could ask for."

"I'm on my way."

"I am so sorry to do this to you, Bells. You have no idea." His breath rustled on the speaker.

"See you soon, Dad." I tapped on the screen.

These middle-of-the-night calls were getting out of hand. I had a job to go to. I couldn't sit here and listen to Dad drone on about Mom. I was hurting too. A pang of remorse washed over me. I was all the family the old man had left. Dad needed me. And I seriously doubted either of my two brothers would hop on a plane right now, wherever they were, to come to the city and help us out. I had to handle the Crucible all on my own. Putting aside the dread building in the pit of my stomach, I donned a pair of jeans and a white T-shirt.

The Crucible was a super fancy, by-invitation-only, night-club in Midtown Manhattan. It was owned by one of the most ruthless mafia kingpins in the city. It was more than a club. It was a place of debauchery, for lack of a better word, that catered to patrons' deepest and darkest desires. In Dad's case, gambling.

I considered my tennis shoes for a moment, then decided to go with knee-high boots. Literally, the only sexy accessory I owned. While I didn't care what their snooty bouncers thought of me, a nicer outfit might increase my chances of getting in without having to call in a favor.

At this hour, I wasn't sure if I would get a cab quickly, so I decided to get an Uber. As if the universe were trying to reward me for being a good daughter, my assigned driver was only a minute away. I grabbed my keys and headed out to meet him at the curb.

My Chelsea apartment wasn't too far from the Crucible. With light traffic, we made it to the night club in twenty minutes flat. The cool, spring air rustled pollen off the sidewalk. I smiled at the whirlwind and thought of fairy powder. Something like that would come in handy right about now. Dad's gambling addiction was getting so bad, I was willing to give fairy tales a shot.

I blinked to clear a bit of dust that made its way into my eyes and darted inside the high-rise. In the main lobby, a chandelier hovered over my head and cast twinkling lights on the Italian marble. Even though I couldn't exactly hear the music playing a few floors up, the thumping of the DJ beat trembled against the walls and the soles of my boots.

"May I help you, Miss?" The man behind the receptionist desk called after me before I reached the elevator bay.

"I'm just going up to the Crucible." I offered him a friendly smile, trying not to feel so out of place and out of my league.

"Do you have an invitation?"

"No, I'm not here to stay. I'm looking for my father."

An invitation from the Crucible owner wasn't something that was easily obtained. Only the most powerful were allowed in. Dad fell into that category not so long ago. Though in the past couple of years, after Mom passed away, Dad's position and wealth had deteriorated significantly.

I blamed Rex Valentino for all our problems. In so many ways, Rex kept Dad a prisoner in this place. Rex afforded Dad the opportunity to gamble for days at a time. He took advantage of Dad's suffering to suck him dry. Our family money was all but gone.

"I'm sorry, but I can't let you in." He tapped his earpiece as his eyes glazed over me. After a quick nod at the security camera to my right, he smiled at me. "This way, Ms. Alfera."

I opened my mouth to ask how he knew my name, but I already knew the answer. I glared at the camera and imagined the all-powerful Mr. Valentino with his arms over his chest, watching me on his monitors, studying me like I was some kind of bug. I pulled on my coat and fastened the buttons. Rex had a way of making me feel like he could see through my clothes.

Of all the other times when I had come looking for Dad, this was the first time he decided to let me in. Why now? I supposed his reasons didn't matter. I didn't have time to stand here and question his motives. Dad needed my help. When he had called earlier, he sounded sad and defeated, as if he had gone too far this time. Had he?

Given the beast that managed this club, I'd bet he'd encouraged Dad to lose even more money. I didn't have any kind of cash with me. My job as a creative director at A-List, an advertising agency, afforded me a nice apartment in the city and a few luxuries. But it would never be enough to pay for Dad's gambling debts. All I could hope for at this point was to come to some sort of arrangement with Mr. Valentino, so Dad could come home and get the help he needed.

With my heart thumping in my throat, I followed the security guard into the elevator. I had no idea what to expect of the exclusive club that took up most of the forty-story building. I pictured an old school casino with a smoky bar that smelled of bleach and cigars, like something from a goodfella's seventies movie, something cliche and cheesy.

My heart broke thinking how Dad had fallen prey to the release he was offered here. Though, I understood why he kept coming back. Two years was nowhere near enough time to get over Mom. Most days I still picked up my phone to call her. Only to realize that the number on my contacts wasn't hers anymore.

The pressure in my chest tightened like it did every time I thought of her. I inhaled and focused on the task at hand instead. I still had one parent left, and he needed me. Falling apart now wouldn't help either one of us.

"Here we are." The security guard smirked at me as if he knew something I didn't. I ignored him because his smugness was the least of my problems.

"Which way?" I glanced up when the elevator door opened and sucked in a breath. "This doesn't look like the gambling room. My father is Michael Alfera. He asked me to come for him." Somehow, I managed to keep the begging tone out of my words.

A tinge of recognition mixed in with trepidation touched his eyes. When he spoke again, the knowing smirk from before had disappeared. The name dropping had worked. Even if Dad was past his prime, in his time, he had been revered, if not feared, as much as Valentino was now.

He had met Mom when he was in his fifties. For her, Dad turned his life around and became the man she wanted him to be—good and decent and kind.

"Mr. Valentino has asked that you wait at the bar. He will find you," he said over the loud, sensual music while he held the elevator door open.

I turned my attention to the opulent scene in front of me. Not what I had expected from someone as ruthless as Rex. Shimmering chandeliers, set at intervals, hung from high above. I counted twenty of them before I decided it wasn't worth the effort. Their reflection on the massive windows made the warehouse look like it went on forever. The gold and blue accents and high-end finishes were everywhere—from the velvet furnishings and smooth marble floors to the ritzy wallpaper and shiny banister—not a single detail had been spared.

My escort patiently waited for me to peel my gaze away from the velvet sofas and club chairs grouped together where two couples were engaged in a make-out session that was about to become something else. When a nipple popped out in a confusion of arms and legs, I quickly turned away from them.

My gaze landed on the next set of couches where a woman sat seemingly by herself, eyes closed, mouth slack. By the way she kept writhing in her seat, I didn't think she was alone. Every group of people acted like they were in their own living rooms, minus the privacy. I supposed that was the purpose of it all. I wasn't a prude, but this was a bit much for me at two in the morning on a Tuesday. In six more hours, I had to be at work.

"Ms. Alfera." The security guard motioned toward the bar at the far end of the room to get my attention. "This way."

I snapped out of my trance and even managed to follow him without falling on my face. I accepted the bar stool he offered, glad to be away from the sexual commotion on the main floor. What the hell was a seventy-year-old man doing in this place? This wasn't Dad. Or, at least, not the Dad I knew.

"Ms. Alfera." The bartender set a glass of rosé in front of me.

"No, thank you."

"My apologies. I was told this was your drink. I can get you anything you want."

The wine was my go-to whenever I needed a drink, but it wasn't about that. "I'm not here to mingle. And who told you that was my drink?"

"Mr. Valentino always makes sure his guests have everything they need. It makes the experience much more memorable."

I swallowed and then started coughing. With a kind smile, the bartender pushed the glass toward me, and I took it. Maybe a little liquid courage would help. "I'm not here for any kind of experience, or whatever it is you do here." I motioned toward the multiple set of living rooms along the main floor. "I'm here to collect my father. Would you please let Mr. Valentino know I'm tired of waiting?"

"Of course." The bartender nodded and walked away.

"Wait," I called after him, but he was gone.

I fished out my phone from the side pocket of my coat and dialed Dad. After several rings, the call went to his voicemail again. No doubt his moment of clarity was gone, and he was somewhere in this building gambling away what little money he had left.

"Phones are not allowed in the Crucible," a female voice whispered in my ear. "I'm surprised they didn't take it from you on the way in."

"I'm looking for someone." I turned to meet the woman's gaze.

She had that perfect "just been fucked" hair, and her cheeks were a pretty pink. The smile on her face was bright enough to light the room. "I'm Sofie." She offered me her hand.

9

"It's my first time here. Gosh, I feel like I can finally breathe. You know what I mean? That feeling when you just get shit off your chest and then you can truly breathe?"

"I don't, actually." My lungs worked just fine. My sex life, on the other hand, was sort of on hold at the moment. I glanced down at my hands to hide my frown. My entire life had been on hold for the past two years while Mom lost her battle with cancer.

"Hmmm." She leaned on the counter suggestively. "Did you enjoy the show? Earlier?" She pointed at the spot where I was sure I had ogled her for a good five minutes.

"I'm sorry, I didn't mean to...you know. I'm not here for any of that." I shook my head several times.

"That's okay." She beamed at me. "We're moving down to room twenty, if you want to join us." She pointed left to a cluster of deep blue sofas dotted with gold decorative pillows.

My heartbeat spiked at the idea of joining her group. That wasn't me at all.

"Um, no, thanks. I'm good." I reached for my glass and took a big gulp of wine. Where the hell was Dad?

And then I felt it. His presence had a way of sucking all the air out of the room. The hair at the back of my neck prickled. Instinctively, I drew my coat closer and checked the buttons. I lifted my gaze and found his reflection on the mirrored panel behind the bar. His form was no more than a shadow as he approached the top of the grand staircase that led to what I assumed was the VIP loft. He gripped the golden banister and leaned slightly forward as if he were searching the room. Even though it was dark, I swore I could feel his gaze on my back, willing me to face him.

I slid off the barstool. A part of me wanted to run out and never come back, but I still didn't know where Dad was. With a shaky breath, I braced myself and turned around. But when I did, he was gone. Did I imagine the whole thing? I had hated Rex for so long, maybe I was starting to hallucinate about him. Why did he think everyone should bow to him as if he were some kind of king? *He wasn't.* He was a criminal, a nightmare, a heartless thug who didn't care how much he was hurting Dad and me. I wanted to knock some sense into Dad for putting me in this position.

Whatever game Rex thought he had going on was over. I was done sitting around like a good girl, waiting for Dad to magically appear. He was obviously not on this floor. I pushed off the counter in a huff, pissed off that I had let this much time go by. In my defense, it was two in the fucking morning and I was beyond tired—not just from lack of sleep but from my entire life.

Intense heat hovered over me before his hand brushed my lower back. My body jerked in surprise and raw nerves because, this time, I was sure Rex was real and standing right behind me. He'd come out of nowhere and now had me caged in against the barstool. I reached for my wineglass and downed the rest of it. Great, the man had officially driven me to drink.

"Shhh." His long fingers appeared in my peripheral vision. Then the rustle of his dark suit had me thinking he had stuffed his hands in the pockets of his trousers. "Why so jumpy?"

"I'm not." I managed not to slump my shoulders or do anything else that would indicate I was cowering at his mere presence.

"How long are you going to pretend you don't know me,

Caterina?" Rex's smooth, deep voice was loud and clear over the music. When he released a breath, a puff of warm air traveled from the nape of my neck and settled between my legs.

Yet another reason why I hated Rex Valentino so much.

# CHAPTER 2
## Well, That's a Loaded Question

Rex

"What do you want?" She fisted her hands and turned to face me.

Jesus Christ, I had forgotten how beautiful she was. Her long, dark hair fell in messy waves several inches past her shoulders and framed her high cheekbones to perfection. If I had to guess, she had been asleep when the old man called her to get her to come down to the Crucible. I switched my attention to the couple having sex across the way as I considered her question.

"That's a loaded question, love." I had a long list of things I wanted from her. The main one being her tight little body in my bed.

She squinted her eyes at me and followed my line of sight. "In your dreams. You're such a brute."

"You came to me." I raised my voice over the loud music. Maybe bringing her to this section of my nightclub hadn't been the best idea. But when I saw her over the security monitors, I couldn't resist the temptation to show her this room. "I would never make you do anything you don't want."

"I'm looking for Dad. And before you try and tell me he isn't here. You should know he called me. If you don't release him, I'll call the police."

I chuckled. I had always admired her tenacity. How had I managed to stay away from Caterina this long? For the past couple of years, since her mother died, I had tried to do the honorable thing and leave her alone. But desperate times and all that. As much as I needed to stay away from her, I also had to protect my family. And for that, I needed her.

I took in her scent before I raised my gaze to meet hers. The hate I found there wasn't anything new. Caterina Alfera had been my enemy since birth. Our parents had forever been in a constant battle for the seat at the head of the table and the power to control the Society, a hundred-year-old enclave that managed criminal activity all over the country.

"You know very well the police work for me. As for your dad? He chose to be here."

"Why did you bring me here?" She jutted her chin. "Why do you think you own everything?"

That small act of defiance made my blood stir. The urge to make her mine and control every detail of her life rushed to the surface. I reached for her wrist and pinned it to the bar counter. Her slender fingers looked so delicate and fragile under my large hand. Not that my size had ever intimidated this woman. She squared her shoulders, and somehow, her eyes managed to show more hate and disdain for me.

"The fact that I do." I waved in the general direction of the massive room we were in. "And you know why I brought you here. I had expected you earlier. Then you show up in an interesting choice of clothes, which would indicate to me you weren't here for my social function."

"That was today? I forgot." She dropped her gaze from my face down to my tuxedo jacket. "That explains the monkey suit."

"You ignored my invitation."

"I'm not your beck and call girl. You can't just summon me whenever you feel the need to." She jerked her arm away from me, and I tightened my hold on her. "Who died and made you the king?" Her breath hitched. "I'm sorry. I didn't mean that."

"That's a low blow even for you." I cocked my head to look her in the eyes. The hate there had dissipated some, replaced by pity. Caterina understood well what it meant to lose a parent. Dad had passed away last month. Technically, he was shot in the back by a coward. Now it was up to me to ensure the Society survived. "Do you truly not understand how important this is? Our families are in danger, Caterina. You can't keep pretending you don't belong with me." I gritted my teeth. Caterina had a way of putting me on edge. I inhaled and corrected my statement. "You belong with the Society, the same as me. It's time you came home."

"No." She stepped closer to me, jabbing a finger into my chest. "It's time you realize the Society is a thing of the past. Let it go. Dad did."

Something in the air shifted like a rush of raw energy that threatened to consume me. That had always been the case with her. This incessant need I had for her would have to wait though. I needed to focus on the job Dad had entrusted to me. The Society was under attack. And if Dad was right, the person behind his murder was dead set on seeing that our century old legacy died a quick death.

"That's not up for discussion." I released her arm. "You'll join the meeting upstairs."

"And if I don't?"

"I'll make you." I deadpanned. "I've never been a patient man. And you know that."

"I'm not going anywhere with you. Not until I see my father."

If Caterina saw her father now, it would absolutely break her. The old man had lost it after his wife died. His behavior was deplorable and out of control, which was why I had kept him at the Crucible. He couldn't do much harm while he was in my nightclub under my supervision.

"He's been here for the past three days. What makes you think he wants to leave?" I caved into my urge to touch her and brushed the back of my hand over her soft cheek.

"He called and asked me to come here." She slapped my hand away.

"Maybe he remembered I had called for a board meeting with all the families of the Society."

"He wants out. Let him go."

"He came to me. Now he's not going anywhere." I crossed my arms over my chest. "I'll start the meeting in one hour. I expect you and your father to be there. You want to see him? That's where he'll be." I dropped my gaze to her jeans and knee-high boots. What I would give to see her in nothing more than just those boots. "I've arranged for you to change into something more suitable for the occasion."

She huffed. "You have some nerve. I'm not your stupid doll."

"You're in my house. If you scream, no one will help you."

"What the hell does that mean?" She shuffled back.

Any other night, I would have loved to stay here and keep this conversation going with her. But we had more pressing matters to attend to, and Caterina needed to understand that. I bent down and threw her over my shoulder. The impact knocked the wind out of her, and that gave me time to make my way back to the grand staircase before she started kicking and screaming. I tightened my hold over her legs and climbed the steps two at a time. Luckily, the VIP loft on the second floor was mostly empty by now. The few guests that remained didn't even notice us as we crossed the room to the elevator bay in the back.

"When Dad hears about this, he'll want your head on a spike." She pushed against my back.

"I don't think so, love." I moved my hand up an inch, and she froze. "These days, your dad can't see past the blackjack table."

I hit the call button. When the doors slid open, I walked in and released her.

"You can change in the guest room." I inserted my key and pressed the dial for the Penthouse, doing my best not to dwell on the fact that Caterina had never been to my home before. "On the bed, you'll find a dress to wear. Mary Anne, my assistant, will help you."

I texted Mary Anne to confirm she had done as I requested. She responded almost immediately to let me know she had the guest room ready. Caterina spent the entire ride up to the forty-fourth floor glaring at me from her corner of the elevator car. Her cheeks had turned a pretty pink that matched her pouty lips. I shoved my phone inside my jacket and stuffed my hands in the pockets of my trousers.

"You always get your assistant to buy clothes for women you find downstairs and drag up to your fancy penthouse?"

"Yes. That's part of her job description." I had no idea what it meant that she was curious if I brought other women to my home.

She winced. "You're not even kidding."

"Why would I kid about that?"

A pang of excitement rushed through me when the doors slid open again, and I found myself ushering Caterina into my living room. I couldn't remember the last time I brought someone up here. Her gaze followed a path from the marble floors up to the massive fireplace that reached the top of the high ceiling.

"You live here?" She ambled toward the tall windows facing the city lights.

"I can give you a tour of my suite if you'd like." I met her in the middle of the room.

"In your dreams." She puffed out a breath. "Where's the damn dress?"

"Does this mean you're willingly coming to the meeting?"

"Isn't that the deal? I show up and you let me see my father?"

For the first time ever, Caterina and I managed to come to an agreement. The old man was right. Caterina would do anything for him. She came straight here without a second thought to her well-being when he called. She came knowing I would be here, knowing I wouldn't let her leave until I got what I wanted.

"You would do anything for your father, wouldn't you?" I walked a wide circle around her, so I could see her face.

"I'm all he has left." She put her chin in the air with a defiant flare that was so Caterina.

"That's not true."

"If you mean my brothers, you're wrong. I haven't seen them since Mom..." Her eyes filled with tears.

I made to dab her cheek, but she turned away. The late Anna Alfera had been the glue that kept the Alfera family together. Without her, her husband, two sons, and even Caterina had been slowly falling apart. I wanted to tell her that it would all be okay—that as long as she and her dad stayed with me, they'd be safe—but I doubted she would believe it coming from me.

"I thought you were in a hurry to get to this meeting." She faced me. The sadness in those green eyes had been replaced with determination and the usual hate she reserved only for me.

"Yes." I motioned toward the grand staircase. "It's through here."

For whatever reason, she didn't jerk away from me when I took her hand in mine and escorted her up the steps. Caterina's eyebrows shot up in surprise when she reached the landing that opened up to the wide hallway. My chest expanded with pride. I had never been able to impress her with anything until tonight. Her gaze lifted to the row of old, oil paintings lining the corridor walls and the intricate, wood carvings on the decorative pilasters.

I glanced down at her palm and squeezed it before I stopped in front of a large door. If only Michael had had the guts to explain to her why she was really here, we wouldn't be wasting our time with all this preamble. "Mary Anne will help you get ready and then she'll take you to your dad." I let go of her hand, but she stayed close to me. That small gesture unraveled something deep in my chest, even though she wasn't here for me. "You love your father so much you're willing to come all this way, go through all this trouble, just for him?"

"Technically, you dragged me up here. But to answer your question, yes. I would do anything for him."

"Technically, I carried you. What did he ever do to deserve such devotion from you?" Shaking my head, I inserted a gold key into the latch and turned it.

She shrugged and crossed the threshold. I leaned my shoulder on the doorframe and watched her amble toward the bed and the red dress draped over the mattress. When she reached out to touch the silky fabric, Mary Anne barged in from the ensuite bathroom.

"Perfect timing." She beamed at Caterina. "I was just getting your bath ready."

"My what?" She spun around to face me.

I reached for the knob and shut the door. The idea of Caterina naked in my house put me over the edge. I had to get out of here and focus on what I had to do. Tonight, I had to be the leader Dad needed me to be. I had to talk to the board members of the Society—the Dons of the five original crime families. I had to convince them that the only way to survive the threat hanging over our heads was to work together.

Releasing a breath, I headed downstairs, using a secret passage that linked my penthouse to the headquarters of the Society, the same place where the first Dons met for the very first time over a century ago. I played with the ring on my finger, rubbing the lion's face engraved on the platinum. If everything went well tonight, if I secured the backing of all the families, I would be one step closer to making good on the promise I made to Dad—no matter what, save the Society.

If all went well tonight, I would finally get the woman I had wanted most of my adult life. I pushed open the paneled door and strolled into a small room where my bodyguards waited for me.

"Sir," all five men said in unison and stood at attention.

"Will Ms. Alfera be joining you, sir?" Frank, my most trusted bodyguard, stepped forward, ready to escort me to the meeting room down the hall.

"She's getting ready as we speak." A smile pulled at my lips as I adjusted my cufflinks. "Is everyone still in the ante-room?" I moved on to smooth out my tuxedo jacket and a waft of Caterina's perfume clinging to the fabric hit me square in the face. *Fuck. I had to stop thinking about her.*

"Yes, sir. No one dared leave without seeing you first. But they're growing restless." Frank met the men's gazes one by one and they all confirmed with a single nod.

"Let's not make them wait any longer." I gestured for him to get the door. As soon as I walked onto the main corridor, my phone buzzed with a message from Mary Anne.

*Mary Anne: I'm sorry. Ms. Alfera escaped.*

I saw red as I typed a quick response.

*Me: Find her!*

*Son of a bitch.* I should've known Caterina would pull something like this. She would never lift a finger if it meant I would benefit from it. She had gone too far this time. This was too important. If playing the nice guy hadn't worked, now she would have to deal with the ruthless king. I was done asking.

"Bring the old man to me." I practically spat the words. "And then get her."

# CHAPTER 3
## You're Not My Prisoner

CATERINA

After Rex left me in the guest room with his assistant, I had to play along. Though odd and so out of place, the bath was nice. In the short five-minute soak Mary Anne allowed, the essential oils and warm water did wonders for my tired muscles. She was extremely deft and patient as she got me into the dress and ushered me to the vanity seat to work on the updo.

"This quick twist is all we have time for tonight. We can talk about how you like to wear your hair later. I'll be more than happy to help."

The what? Why in the world would I need her to do my hair after tonight? I opened my mouth to ask, but then decided against it. Obviously, Rex had no intention of letting Dad go. And now that I was here, he planned to keep me here too.

"I'll get your shoes." She smiled and returned to the bathroom.

What kind of assistant was she anyway? How did she not

see how weird this whole situation was? I didn't get a chance to ask her any of that because the minute she left me alone, I made a run for it. Without a keycard, the elevators wouldn't work for me, so I headed for the stairwell, which led me to a wide corridor.

My God, this place was a freaking maze. I opened a paneled door that turned out to be just a cubby hole or closet. The Society had built this place to be like a modern-day castle, full of secret doors and passages. Rex's penthouse looked like it had been recently renovated, along with the nightclub floors, but the rest of the property still had that old world feel.

I ran my hands along the faded wallpaper, looking for another way out in this massive corridor. When I made to take another step, my gown caught on a nail sticking out from one of the baseboards. I yanked at the gown and kept going, wishing I'd had time to change back into my jeans before I escaped.

Escaped?

This was always the thing with Rex. Every time I had any kind of interaction with him, my entire life got turned upside down. Three hours ago, I was sleeping in my bed. Now I was on the run from a mafia kingpin, dressed like I was on my way to some fancy ball.

But I didn't have time to worry about my clothes or sleep. I had about a handful of minutes before Rex checked his cameras and figured out exactly where I was. I had to get to Dad and get him out of here. Screw Rex's mobster meeting. Maybe I didn't know Rex all that well, but I knew one thing for sure—everything he did was for him, for some sort of gain.

Rubbing my cold arms, I stopped to try and figure out a plan. The building had seemed so much warmer with Rex next to me. My skin still tingled where he had touched me— so high on the back of my leg. A few more inches, and he would've cupped my butt cheek. Tears stung my eyes.

I hated him. I hated that I couldn't think straight when he was around. I hated how infuriatingly confident he had been that he would get everything he wanted from me tonight—like going to his stupid Society meeting.

A cold draft seeped through the carpeted floor, and my bare feet cramped in protest. I uttered a bunch of profanities directed at Rex as I tried every panel and doorknob along the hallway. I had yet to find the stairs.

From the elevator ride, I knew I was forty-four floors up. It would take a while to get to the street level, but it could be done. I had to find Dad and take him home. This place wasn't for him. He was too old and too sick to be here this long. Hadn't Rex said Dad had been at the Crucible for days?

"Caterina, stop." Rex appeared out of nowhere at the end of the hall. "Why won't you ever listen to me?" He sauntered toward me. When his gaze zeroed in on my feet, he winced. "You'd put yourself in danger just to get away from me?"

"Being barefoot is hardly any danger."

"I wasn't talking about the shoes. I was talking about what's out there, waiting for you. I've told you many times before. I would never hurt you."

"And yet, that's exactly what you're doing by keeping me here."

"What? I merely asked for one hour of your time. You're not my prisoner. And neither is your dad." The edge in his tone told me he was at the end of his rope. Good. Now we could both lose our minds in this crazy labyrinth of secret walls. This was exactly why I stayed away from Rex as much as possible. He wanted to control everything.

"Where is he then?"

"Downstairs. Gambling. I was on my way to get him when I got Mary Anne's text." He reached into his pocket, then put his phone to his ear. "I found her. Take Michael Alfera to the library. We'll meet you there." He didn't wait for confirmation before he tapped on the screen.

When Rex gave orders, he expected them to be obeyed. That small reminder of who I was dealing with sparked a wave of anger that settled in the pit of my stomach. On a normal day, I was what anyone would consider a nice girl. But Rex made this other side of me come to the surface. Even now, all I wanted to do was slap the knowing smile off his face.

"I'll have Mary Anne bring your shoes." He stood inches from me. "You look stunning in that dress."

Prickling goosebumps blossomed across my chest every time Rex puffed warm breath in my direction. Did he run here? Not that I cared. "I look ridiculous." I made to push him out of the way, even though I had no clue how to get to the library.

He grabbed my wrist and slammed my back against his front while his other hand held me by the waist. Raw. Everything about him was just raw—raw energy, raw testosterone, raw want. "I'm trying to be patient for you," he whispered in my ear. "It's just a meeting. I need you here tonight."

"Mary Anne let it slip that I was to stay here for more than just hours. I don't trust you. You're planning to do something with Dad."

I struggled, and that gave him reason to hold me tighter. His lips brushed the side of my cheek, and I squeezed my legs together, trying my best not to melt into him. "You're right. Tonight's meeting is way more than that. This isn't some happy family reunion."

"Dad gave all this up years ago. I live a normal life, Rex." I inhaled. I hadn't meant to say his name aloud. It was like invoking the devil to come to me and give me anything I desired.

Problem was Rex's favors came at a very high price; everyone knew that, which was why I made it a point not to get near him to begin with—let alone ask for his help.

"I have a job. An apartment that's all mine. Friends that don't know that criminal families exist, that you exist. You're pulling us back into something we don't want."

"I know." He exhaled and leaned ever so slightly into me. "I let you be for as long as I did because I knew you didn't want this life. But it's no longer up to me. You're not safe out there. It's time to come home."

"You don't need me. You want me here as some sort of prize. Everything you do, you do for you. I'm not a thing."

"Everything I do, is to keep our families from going extinct." His long fingers cradled my shoulders. "Don't move."

I wanted to get away from him because my body was seriously sending him mixed messages. First, he had to understand that the desire unfurling at my core had nothing to do with him and more to do with general sexual frustration. I was glad he didn't see my eyes flutter closed as I took in his musky scent. Danger, power, and sex oozed from him.

"Ha." I sucked in a breath. When I glanced down, I spotted the sparkling diamond necklace he had rested on my chest. "I don't need a leash. I'll go to your stupid meeting."

His deep chuckle did things to me I wasn't ready to

acknowledge. He gripped my shoulders and made me turn to face him. *Fuck me.* I glared into that intense blue gaze of his under full brows. I'd forgotten how young and beautiful he was. Shit. I shouldn't have made eye contact. When I realized my mouth had been opened this whole time, I swallowed hard and closed it.

"It's just a necklace, love. Jesus, you won't even accept a gift from me?"

"Why would I?"

He inhaled deeply, and his shoulders relaxed a little. "Earlier you said you'd go with me and then you ran off. Can I trust you'll stay put this time?"

"I didn't promise before."

"Are you willing to pinky swear now?" A smile pulled at his lips.

"Will you take me to Dad?"

"How could I not when you ask so nicely?" He shifted the heavy diamonds on my clavicle so they would be centered.

Everything had to be exactly how he said. I had to be dressed in the dress he said. And decorated just like he wanted. And that right there, snapped me out of my trance. I pushed away from him. "Then I promise. Let's go." I gestured to my left. "I'd like to see Dad in this lifetime."

"This way." He motioned to the opposite end. "You were so close to finding the exit."

I rolled my eyes and stalked past him. In two strides, he moved in front of me and opened a hidden door that led to yet another stairwell. My heart drummed faster when I realized that in the half hour I had to escape, I never really left his penthouse.

When we reached the floor below us, his men were

27

waiting for us. One of them nodded to Rex and ushered me down the corridor to a massive double door. This level had more of a mobster feel to it with its carmine silk walls and opulent furnishings.

A long time ago, when I was a teenager, Dad brought me here to meet an old friend, Rex's dad. That single trip had been an exciting adventure to me. I got to see this underworld full of mobsters and kings—a world that, to me, only existed in Dad's bedtime stories.

"Dad." I rushed into the library and hugged him.

"I knew you'd come." He hugged me tight then put me at arm's length. "I'm sorry for putting you through all this tonight."

"What happened, Dad? I thought you said you were done with the families and the Crucible." I gestured toward the elaborate fireplace taking up most of the library, the uphol-stered club chairs, and the chandeliers. Everything in this room screamed mafia. "Were you here gambling?" A part of me wanted him to say no. That he stopped by for a drink and Rex made him stay.

"Rex made me see reason. I have no other recourse. You'll see."

"So, he's making you do this? Did he make you call me to get me here?" I realized I was looking for reasons to blame this whole night on Rex. Anything was better than dealing with Dad's gambling situation.

"I was already downstairs playing." He cleared his throat. "I needed cash. And well, you know how that works."

Of course, the two things were connected. Rex wanted me here to play the ally. Dad wanted money, so Rex was happy to oblige in exchange for a small favor—call me at one in the morning and guilt me into coming here. I should've known.

"Well, I agreed to stay for the Society meeting. But as soon as that's done, we're leaving. I don't care what Rex wants. Can I have your word, please?" I wrapped my arms around his shoulders. The tuxedo he wore was freshly pressed and fit him like a glove. No matter his age, Dad would always have this aura of power around him. If he hadn't retired, he would be at the head of the table tonight, not Rex. "Did Rex send you clothes too?"

"No, I sent for these." He patted my hand. "You worry too much, Bells. Someone your age should be out there having fun in the city."

I glanced down at my hands at the mention of Mom's name for me. She named me Caterina Isabella, only to call me just Bells. I missed her. I missed my brothers. I missed having a family. "Have you heard from Massimo and Enzo?"

"No." He shook his head. "They're still mad at me. I don't think they'll ever forgive me."

"Mom's death wasn't your fault. You did everything you could. And they know that." I offered him a warm smile. "Come sit down. I haven't seen you in days. How are you doing?" I ushered him to a chair facing the roaring fire. Now that I had found Dad, this building was starting to feel familiar, not as cold.

"You know what I've been up to." He pointed toward the wine cart.

I stood and poured him a whiskey neat. "You still haven't said you'll leave with me."

"It's complicated, dear."

"If you're in trouble, you need to tell me." I set his drink on

29

the side table and kneeled next to him. I couldn't lose him too. I'd lost too many people in the last two years.

"I owe the Crucible some money. Nothing I can't handle. I just need a few more days." He took a long sip of liquor.

"The Crucible? You mean Rex." I shot to my feet and paced the length of the small room. "He told me you weren't his prisoner. You can leave if you want."

"I'm more like collateral." He seemed defeated.

Dad wasn't the giving-up type. Our family always stuck together. Massimo and Enzo seemed to have forgotten that, but I still believed we could overcome anything. Whatever the amount, I was sure we could get the money together. The name Alfera still carried weight in this city. I could go to the bank and take a mortgage on the apartment Mom bought for me. That alone would be close to a million, if I really pushed it —begged.

"How much, Dad?"

Earlier tonight, Rex seemed willing to come to some sort of an understanding with me. He had his plate full with whatever the Society was going through. Dad's debt had to be nothing compared to his other problems. If I had to be honest, I had never seen Rex this worried. He was still an insufferable, confident bastard, but something had really disturbed him.

"One million," Dad croaked.

I spun around so fast the room swayed a little. "Tell me you're joking. How is it possible to lose that much?"

"The days are long. Don't worry about that. I'll stay here until I figure something out. I still have a few aces up my sleeve, Bells. Don't let the wrinkles on my face fool you." He raised his glass to me and then knocked it back.

"No. You asked me to come get you. You're coming home

tonight. Rex will have to wait for his money." I paced the room again.

Rex. Always Rex standing in the way, making my life miserable. Why would he let Dad's account run so high? He had to know Dad would have to forfeit on his debt. If Dad was contesting the position of king, I could see why Rex would set this trap for him. Someone as controlling as Rex would want insurance. Was that it? But Dad didn't care about the Society. He left when I was a baby. He did it for Mom. No way would he want to come back now.

"How long do you have to make good on the payment?"

"It was due last month." Dad leaned his elbow on the armrest and pinched the bridge of his nose as if he was too embarrassed to face me.

I couldn't stand to see him like that. "You're ready to stay here as his plaything? Or worse, go to jail? Dad—" My voice quavered. "I won't let him do this to you. I promise you. I'll do anything to bring you home."

## CHAPTER 4
# That's Not Why We're Here

R E X

*Frank: We lost the Alfera brother.*

I squeezed my phone, glaring at my bodyguard's message. I had sent a crew to look for Massimo and Enzo Alfera. They had been recently seen in Ibiza off of the coast of Spain. My men had orders to bring the two of them home. But the Alfera brothers were smart and they didn't want to be found. I had failed in that regard. At least Don Alfera was here. That was all that mattered for tonight's meeting—well, him and his daughter, Caterina.

The hushed voices from the antechamber next door filtered through the thin walls. I smiled at Dad's family ring on my finger. Bringing everyone together here tonight had been hell, but I had done it. The message I had for them was disturbing and almost impossible, but this was the job.

For as long as I could remember, Dad had wanted the Society to be what it once was. We were the protectors of this city. But over time, greed took hold of every member until hate was all that was left. Dad had a plan to make things better. And then he got shot. I ran a hand over the red leather of Dad's old chair and swigged my whiskey. Was he right in thinking Caterina was the key to get what we wanted? Peace.

"Everyone's gathered, sir." Aaron, the bodyguard assigned to Caterina, stepped into my line of sight holding my tuxedo jacket.

"And the Rossis?"

"They're here as well. The woman is pregnant, sir."

I stood and let him help me into my jacket. "Maybe arranged marriages aren't all that bad."

"She hates him."

I chuckled. "Let's get on with it."

Aaron rushed to the door to hold it open for me. I strode across the now empty antechamber and entered the board-room. Everyone froze, and I hoped it was because they understood the gravity of the situation. I called for this assembly because we were under attack.

I glanced around the room to make a quick inventory. All families but the Gallos were here. Santino Buratti was here representing his father tonight since he was too ill to leave his home. Signoria Vittoria Salvatore had brought her niece Giulia. The older woman was as fierce and strong as an ox, but eventually, she would need to find a successor. I doubted the wide-eyed girl clinging to her side was the answer.

On the opposite end of the room, Chase and Mia Rossi stood at attention. They were not part of the five original crime families. Though Chase's grandfather had tried time and time again to be invited to join the Society. No one had ever been invited before because we didn't need to. That changed tonight, and old man Rossi was about to get his wish.

My gaze zeroed in on Dad's chair at the head of the table. The lion's head carved on the crest rail sent a surge of adrenaline through me. If these walls could talk, they would speak of simpler times when mafia families represented something else. I glared at the ashtray sitting on top of the society's crest. Gritting my teeth, I pushed it aside and met Signoria Vittoria's cold stare. She nodded once in understanding.

The emblem representing the five original crime families was carved on the table to remind us of our mission—fac fortia et patere, do brave deeds and endure.

"Where is he?" I asked Aaron.

Without the Alfera family, the assembly couldn't begin.

"He's on his way up. There was a situation downstairs. But it's resolved."

"Is she with him?" I adjusted my watch.

"Yes, sir. Everything is as you requested."

The double doors opened again and they both made their way toward me, to their place at the right side of the table, next to me. When I met Caterina's gaze, she glared at me with renewed hate.

"He's here. I hope you're happy."

I'd thought we had made a bit of progress earlier tonight. She had accepted my gift without complaint, and even put on the high heels that matched her dress. She truly was a vision. Her presence was soothing to me. I no longer cared if I was being a selfish asshole. I needed her here.

"Yes, Caterina. This makes me happy." I waited while she helped the old man into the chair to my left.

I waited another minute until everyone found their assigned seats. The Salvatores at the other end, the Rossis to my left. And the Burattis beside them.

"I believe the first time we were gathered like this; our families were still smuggling rum." I chuckled. "I appreciate you making the time to come here tonight."

"Get on with it, Rex," Signoria Vittoria said in her smoker's voice. "If it'd been up to me, I wouldn't be here, boy."

I clenched my jaw at the off-handed insult. At twenty-eight, I was hardly a boy, but what she meant was that the king's chair was too big for me. "Maybe this will be of interest to you, Signora Vittoria. As of last night, the entire Gallo family has been wiped out. Even the bastards."

"The Big 5 is now down to four." Santino twirled his family ring around his finger. The wolf's head encrusted on the platinum was the only thing that made it different from mine. He rose to his feet. "Is that why we're here, Rex? You could've sent an email and saved us all the aggravation."

"Sit down, Santino." Signora Vittoria's tone was full of warning. Not that Santino cared. He stood his ground as his gaze shifted from hers to mine.

"No, that's not why we're here, Santino. The society has been around for a long time. In one night, we lost the entire Gallo family. I brought you here to call a truce, which will stay in place until we figure out who's trying to wipe us out."

"A truce? Like what? We work together, one big happy family. No, thank you." He leaned on the table, furrowing his brows. "I'll take my chances. I work alone."

The room erupted into a cacophony of angry voices and frantic questions as everyone left their seats and congregated near the door. This was not how I thought this conversation would go. I stormed to my feet and glanced at Caterina. The terror in her eyes made my stomach churn.

The Gallo family was third in line in the Society succession. If someone was planning to take my place, they would come after her family next; even if Michael was now retired, her brothers had never left. Did she even understand the danger they were in?

I wanted to tell her that I would never let anything happen to her, but I doubted she would believe me. Before I could stop myself, I reached for her hand. Her entire body jerked as if I had given her an electric shock, before she yanked her arm away.

"There's a traitor in our midst. If you leave, I'll assume you're it. I'll have no choice but to retaliate. The bylaws are clear on this. Someone betrayed the Society, and I intend to find out who. There are only two sides to this coin. Which side are you on?"

In the next breath, several bodyguards burst through the doors with guns out as they found their bosses. This fucking assembly was over, and I had accomplished exactly nothing—if I assumed inciting panic was nothing.

"I just told you someone wants us dead. And this is your solution? Shoot the remaining Society members?" I nodded to one of my bodyguards.

He immediately left his post protecting me and went to stand next to Chase, while a second guard took Mia through the secret exit behind her to get her out of harm's way. I didn't want the Rossi family shot before they had a chance to hear my proposal. I needed all the allies I could find. Chase and Mia were not part of the five original crime families, but with the Gallos gone, someone had to take on the empty chairs. We still had a fucking business to run.

When I turned my attention to Caterina, she was gone. I grabbed the tumbler in front of me and downed the rest of the whiskey. She didn't trust me, and I couldn't blame her for that. *Fuck me.* I should've told the guards not to let her leave. But she wasn't my prisoner. Why did I think Michael would use the time he had with her in the library to explain things to her? I should've known he would be too much of a coward to tell her the truth.

Chase stayed behind while everyone scattered into the waiting room and then the hallway. I motioned for Aaron to go after Caterina. Now that she knew what was at stake, she had to see that leaving the Crucible was a mistake.

"Where the hell is my wife?" Chase turned to face me.

I nodded to my remaining guard. He promptly left the room and shut the door behind him.

"I read your file. Your grandfather raised you outside of all this. Soon you'll learn that relationships will get you killed." I had assumed Chase and Mia hated each other like Aaron had said. But now I could see how much he cared about her.

"Why did you bring us here? This isn't our fight."

Of course, he wouldn't see it as such. According to what my guys were able to dig up about Chase Rossi, he and his grandfather had recently reconnected. In a matter of days, the old man had arranged a marriage with a crew boss from Jersey, and in doing so, he managed to take control of those crews without bloodshed. Now his grandfather was dead, and Chase was in charge of the family business. I needed to know that the New York and Jersey factions understood they still answered to me.

With Society members turning up dead, I didn't have time to deal with the lower factions. Though I was more than prepared to bring the fight to their back yard if they tried to go off on their own.

"As of tonight, it is."

"What?" His gaze cut to the door, as if he was dying to chase after Mia.

"Isn't this what Jax Rossi, your grandfather, wanted? A seat at the table for the Rossi family?"

"And if I refuse?"

"No one's ever refused." I shrugged.

He didn't need to know that no one had ever gotten this offer before. Keeping the Society in one piece was all I cared about. If that meant making Chase a Don, so be it.

"What exactly are you proposing?"

"Jax had our protection. Whenever things didn't go his way, we'd step in... quietly. We can continue to do that for you. But I need a favor in return. Find the assholes who are doing this to us, the ones who killed the Gallo family."

"Why them and not you?" Chase asked.

He did understand the underlying issue here. Why go after one Don and a bunch of soldiers when they could've come after me and really broken the Society apart? Tonight's shitshow of a meeting showed me how fractured we were.

Each family worked independently and focused only on their particular industry. The Valentino's, my family, was entrusted to run the Society and ensure the Dons acted in a way that benefited all of us. Problem was, they didn't see me as their king, like they did with Dad. The assholes coming after us knew that. Killing me would've gotten them nothing.

"What if I can't find who's trying to kill you all?"

"We all die." I knitted my brows.

"You mean you die. I just got here."

"The Society has been in place this long because even though we hate each other's guts, we understand one thing.

We stand together, or we don't stand at all. Don't let their theatrics fool you. Once they see this for the very real threat that it is, they'll come back."

"That means shit to me. You'll find that my grandfather and I are very different people."

"If I didn't know that already, you wouldn't be here. Jax was never going to be one of us." I ambled to the bar cart near the fireplace, poured two drinks, and set one on the table for him.

"No, thanks." He waved his hand in dismissal.

He didn't want to do this for me because he didn't trust my family. But if trust was the only thing holding him back, that meant he had some sort of clue as to where to begin digging. My life was this side of fucked up if an outsider was the only ally I had left—a reluctant ally, but a friend, nonetheless. I hoped I wasn't wrong about him or his wife.

"You start tomorrow."

"You can't expect me to solve this for you. It doesn't work like that."

"I need people like you and Mia on my side. If the Society goes under, chaos will ensue. This country's economy needs us. It may not be apparent to you, but we're the ones keeping the peace. We're the good guys, Rossi." I stuffed my hands in the pockets of my trousers and let him study me.

"So, you want us to pledge our loyalty to you?"

"That would be step one."

"As long as we can continue to do business, you don't have to worry about the New York or Jersey factions." He met my gaze.

"Good. You'll also need to take over for the Gallos."

He slow-blinked as if this honor I'd just bestowed upon

him was a burden. His grandfather had spent a lifetime begging my dad for this opportunity. Whatever his reasons, I didn't care. The Society was at a pivotal moment. Now more than ever, we had to stick together.

"I'll see you around." He fisted his hands and made his way toward the antechamber.

When the door shut behind him, I grabbed his crystal glass off the table and threw it across the room. It hit the built-in bookcase, and glass splattered all over the antiques and leather-bound books. If Caterina had stood by my side during the assembly like she was supposed to, the outcome would have been much different. Everyone would have seen that we needed to combine our resources and find the sons of bitches doing this to us.

I was done playing nice with Michael. The time for him to hold up his end of the bargain was now.

I grabbed my phone from the inside pocket of my jacket and called Frank. Was I ready for another round of hatred from Caterina? No, I sure as hell wasn't, but we needed to discuss a contingency plan that included some kind of security for her. Whether she liked it or not, she was back into the fold. Maybe she hadn't noticed yet, but her father had already given up. The old man only cared about his own grief.

After the fifth ring, the call went to voicemail. What the fuck? I glared at the screen. Frank would have to be dead not to take my call. My heartbeat picked up the pace as I rushed out the door. A myriad of scenarios went through my head. Most of them included Caterina getting hurt. If that happened, I didn't know what I would do. I took the private elevator to the lobby to see if security there had seen him.

The doors opened, and I immediately found Frank on the

floor with a gash on the side of his head. "Mr. Valentino." He mumbled, sitting up against the wall.

"What the hell happened? Who did this?" I sat on my haunches next to him.

He winced. "She did."

"What do you mean?"

"After the assembly, Ms. Alfera mentioned her Dad wasn't feeling well and that she was taking him home. He looked pale and did look like he needed medical help. I only wanted them to wait a minute so I could consult with you. When I caught up to them, she swung around and hit me with one of the lobby busts. She took me by surprise. She didn't even wait to see what I wanted. I'm sorry." Frank leaned forward like he was about to pass out.

"We'll deal with that later. Let's get you something for that." I pointed to his injury and stood.

Jesus fuck. Was the old man really sick or was he just hoping to delay the inevitable? I fished out my phone and called the number for my security detail to fill them in on what had happened in the lobby. "Get someone to take Frank to the hospital. He's going to need stitches."

"Yes, sir." Aaron answered on the other end of the line. "I'm getting on the elevator now. Should I dispatch a team to Ms. Alfera's apartment?"

"No, leave it to me."

It was painfully obvious that she wanted nothing to do with me or the Society. I was done chasing after her. If I learned anything tonight, it was that Caterina would never be mine. Not in the way I wanted her to be. But this entire situation wasn't about us anymore. The threat hanging over the Society was bigger than all of us.

After I hung up, I called my lawyer. It was high time the Alfera family realized I wasn't playing. My lawyer picked up after the third ring, even though it was close to four in the morning. Shit. At some point, I had to get to bed and sleep. But this couldn't wait.

"Mr. Valentino, how can I help you?" he asked with a tinge of alarm in his tone.

"Michael Alfera broke his end of our agreement." Technically, he had broken more than one contract, but the money he owed the Crucible was the only tangible deal I could act on. "I'm ready to collect on his debt. Make the arrangements. I want this resolved by morning." I considered for a minute how Caterina might react to seeing her father go to jail at his age, then added, "Make sure the police are involved."

# CHAPTER 5
## *You Know How It Is*

CATERINA

"I'm not as ancient as you think. I can walk just fine on my own." Dad motioned for me to lead the way to my Chelsea apartment. For a minute back at the Crucible, I thought he was going to pass out.

At seventy-five, maybe Dad wasn't that old. But he seemed to have aged twenty years since Mom passed away. He stepped onto the curb with his gaze fixed on the front entrance of my building.

The loft style property had once been an olive oil factory that had been renovated into high-end residences. The main lobby had a receptionist desk to the right and a set of elevators on the left. Nothing fancy like Rex's building, but it was home.

Mom had bought me this place for my twenty-first birthday—an over-the-top gift even for the wife of a former mobster, but now I understood why she had done it. She wanted me to have something that was outside Dad's world, something the Society couldn't touch, something that was all my own.

Of course, her efforts had been in vain because now, I was going to have to get a mortgage to pay off Dad's debts. Mom had planned for everything, except how to make Dad want to stay alive after she was gone. I inserted the key and pushed the door opened.

"The spare bedroom is through there." I pointed down the hall on my left. "You remember."

"I do." He patted my cheek, then stalked to the exposed red brick wall with the small window facing the courtyard. The place had an artsy feel to it that reminded me of Mom every day. No doubt Dad felt her presence here too. He turned to face me. "I need to rest tonight, but tomorrow, we need to talk. You and I have a conversation pending that's long over-due." The sadness in his eyes broke my heart in two.

"Dad, I miss her too."

"She wanted something different for you. Better." He smiled at the cozy linen couch and plush pillows.

"I'm happy, Dad. That's all Mom ever wanted for all of us. I have a job I love. Friends."

"I know. And now I've come and ruined all of it."

"You haven't. I can help you. We're still a family." Even if it was down to just the two of us. "Let me help you. I was thinking about maybe talking to Rex. I was going to do it tonight, but then the assembly happened, and you got sick. How are you feeling?"

"Better. We'll talk about it in the morning. Right now, I need to sleep." He ambled over to the bedroom.

Numb, I made my way to the sofa and collapsed in a heap of tired bones and red fabric. What an insane night. My eyes fluttered closed, and instantly images of Rex's intense blue eyes flooded my mind. What a hateful man to think he could keep Dad in his nightclub like some kind of expensive necklace.

"Arggh." I screamed into the decorative pillow. How the hell was I going to get the money Dad needed to free himself of Rex? Reaching behind me, I pulled down the zipper of my gown. Oxygen rushed to my lungs, and that was all my body needed to fall asleep.

After what felt like a minute later, a bang on the door startled me awake. I scrambled on the sofa, trying to get my bearings and find my phone. Shit. It was nine in the morning. I hurried to my bedroom while I texted my boss to let her know I would be late to work.

"Ms. Alfera, it's the police." A voice rumbled out in the hallway.

My head snapped up. Rex. He called the police on us? No, he wouldn't do that. Not without talking to Dad first. Dad and I hadn't talked about the particulars of his deal with Rex. All I knew was that after almost two years of incessant gambling, he had managed to burn through millions of dollars. I personally could not wrap my head around that amount. But Dad had grown up in a mobster family where excess was a way of life.

When I was born, Mom made him leave it all behind. For twenty-five years, they had been happy together. Now that she was gone, he had returned to the only thing he knew—a mobster life. Except now, he wasn't a Don.

Rex had always had a vendetta against my family. Who the hell knew why? Maybe he hated Dad for leaving the Society, something no one had ever done before. Maybe he felt threatened by Dad because he was the only one who could unseat

Rex and take over the Society. Or maybe he just wanted to make my life miserable.

Growing up, I knew of Dad's old life because he never tried to hide it. The five original families attended functions together and interacted outside of the Society. Rex was the same age as my brother, Enzo, so I got to hear all the stories. How he acted like he owned everything, even when we were in school.

I supposed knowing he'd be king one day, that he would take over the reins of the Society, went to his head. He became especially ruthless after his mother died when he was eighteen. He held a special kind of hate for me then. I never understood why. Though it was all too easy for me to return the sentiment.

By the time he finished college, he had become the Rex I knew today, powerful, merciless, and unyielding—a beast. I called him that once.

My uninvited guest knocked on the door again. My body jerked when he called my name again. Jesus. I donned a pair of jeans and a T-shirt and headed to the door before the cop woke Dad and my neighbors.

"Good morning, officer." I used my calm, business tone.

"Good morning, Ms. Alfera." A man in a worn suit and greasy head stepped in front of the cop. "I'm Jack Smith, Mr. Valentino's attorney."

Jack Smith didn't sound like a real name. I didn't care. "What is this about?"

"I'm here to ensure Mr. Valentino's assets are secured. That is, to make sure your father doesn't leave the country."

I rolled my eyes. "We both know there isn't a corner in this world where Rex wouldn't be able to find Dad. His money is safe. He will get it as soon as I can get an appointment at the bank."

Jack raised both eyebrows in surprise, as if he hadn't expected us to have a plan. He exchanged a nervous look with the cop. "I'm afraid I was not told of an extension. We're here to take Mr. Alfera into custody until payment is made."

"Do you have a warrant?"

"He doesn't need one." The cop finally spoke. "We heard complaints from your neighbors. I have reason to believe someone might be in danger."

"Ah good. You're a crooked cop. Of course." I gripped the edge of the door as I considered what a trip to the police station would do to Dad. I mean they couldn't really take him to jail for owing money. They intended to humiliate him. This level of disrespect toward Dad was uncalled for. Being a retired Don had to count for something.

"Bells. It's okay." Dad came out of the bedroom fully dressed. He looked pale and tired, like he hadn't slept all night. "Jack. Good to see you, old friend."

"Michael." Jack nodded once with reverence. "You know how it is."

"I do." A half-smile pulled at Dad's lips. He winced and his Adam's apple bobbed a few times. When he cleared his throat, he braced a hand on the hallway wall and leaned forward.

"Dad." I dropped to my knees to catch his head before it hit the hardwood floor. "Omigod." I turned to Jack. "Call 911. I think he's having a heart attack."

"Son of a bitch." Jack reached inside his coat. To my disbelief, the asshole called Rex instead.

"What the hell is wrong with you?" I ran to my room and grabbed my mobile.

The operator answered on the third ring. I gave her a quick recount of the night before and today, leaving out the fact that Dad's stress and anxiety was due to the fact that he owed a shit ton of money to the mob and that one of their lackeys was standing just outside my door ready to collect.

I spent the next twenty minutes trying to keep Dad comfortable and making sure he was still breathing. When the paramedics arrived, I went into auto pilot, nodding to their instructions and following them to where they said for me to go.

From the back of the ambulance, I called Enzo, but it went to voicemail almost immediately. Why would he not want to talk to me? We hadn't spoken since Mom's funeral. He would have to know that if I was calling, it was for a good goddamn reason. I got that they were hurting too.

Seeing Mom lose her battle with cancer took a toll on all of us. But they couldn't just leave us like this. I wiped my cheeks and started a text thread with him and Massimo. I glared at the screen while tears pelted on my words—Dad's on the way to the hospital. Please call me.

It was one thing to tell myself that Dad and I were alone in this. But knowing for sure was like a kick to the stomach. When we arrived at the hospital, the paramedics, more or less, shoved me aside while they took Dad inside. I stood there at the canopy entrance, feeling more forsaken than ever.

"Are you with Mr. Alfera?" a nurse asked me.

When I turned to face him, the sun shined in my face and blinded me. Here I had thought I would go back to my normal life after we escaped Rex's place. "Yeah."

"Is he on any medication? For his heart condition?"

His what? I didn't know Dad had a heart condition. "I don't know. He didn't say," I mumbled. A pang of remorse gnawed at my insides. Dad had sought out the Crucible because he was hurting, and I wasn't there for him long enough to even ask about his health.

"That's okay." He motioned for me to go inside the hospital. "The waiting room is through the double doors on your right. I'll come find you when we have an update."

The stench of bleach and sweat evoked a bunch of old memories from two years ago when Mom was here. I couldn't lose Dad too. I pressed a hand to my forehead and found an empty seat out in the hallway. A few minutes later, my phone rang. My pulse quickened as I put the device to my ear.

"Hello?"

"Omigod, Caterina. Are you okay? How's your Dad?" Sarah panted into the speakerphone as if she were walking and talking. Like me, she was a creative director at A-List.

"I don't know." I sobbed into the phone. Relieved to know I wasn't as alone as I had thought.

"Okay. Don't worry about the boss. She said you could take the day off. And as many days as you need to." She blew out a breath. "Jeez, I'm so out of shape. Anyway, I'm crossing the parking lot now. I'll be there shortly."

"Oh Sarah. You didn't have to come down."

"You know I did. Don't give me that. See you in a bit." She hung up.

I laughed, shaking my head at the phone. As much as I didn't want to be an imposition, it would be nice to have someone here to help keep me calm. This waiting had my nerves on edge. I had never been a patient woman, and with Dad in the mix, I was about to explode.

*"I'm trying to be patient for you."*

Rex's words flashed in my mind. Of course, he wasn't. If he were, he never would've sent his crooked lawyer and cop to fetch Dad. And then Dad wouldn't be at the hospital. I stormed to my feet, wishing Rex was here so I could punch him in the face.

The double doors at the end of the white corridor creaked opened. I turned around to welcome Sarah but met Rex's intense blue gaze instead. Glaring at him, I fisted my hands and I waited as he sauntered toward me with his entourage behind him. He looked even taller in the light of day—taller and lethal. When he stopped a few feet away from me, my back tensed with a mix of fear and sheer rage.

"Don't you think you've done enough?" I whisper shouted.

"I'm here to help." He stepped closer, and I got a blast of his signature scent.

Everything about him screamed confidence. Even now he stood there, looking at me as if he could patch up Dad's heart and make everything better. He should know better than anyone that power and money meant nothing in this place. Mom had had the best treatment money could buy, and it hadn't been enough. Wasn't that how it had happened with his own mother?

"You mean you came here to help yourself?" I pointed at his bodyguards. "Came to make sure Dad didn't escape the country while convalescing?"

"No. They're here for Michael's protection. He's vulnerable right now. We need to make sure no one gets any wicked ideas." He gripped my elbow, clenching his jaw. "Why did you leave?"

"You said we weren't your prisoners. Did you lie?"

"People lie when they're afraid. I don't lie, Caterina. Ever." He cocked his head to look me in the eyes. "My men will stay until your father is ready to come home. I've arranged for him to be moved to a private room."

"We don't need you." I gritted my teeth. Mainly because I knew that was a big fat lie.

"Yes, you do." He took a strand of stray hair off my face and fixed it behind my ear.

I wished I could do the same for Dad and fix his situation with Rex. Wouldn't that be a great surprise for him? To wake up and know he no longer owed Rex anything. We could be a family again. I met Rex's gaze and opened my mouth to speak, but no words came out. What would I say to him? Help us. Make Dad's debt go away. Would that be enough? Knowing Rex, he would ask for way more than a simple gesture.

"If you need anything, call me." He nodded to his men, and they dispersed.

I could only assume they had gone to guard Dad, wherever he was in this massive hospital. Of course, they knew where to find him. Of course, they had access, and I didn't. Of course, I needed Rex. He turned to leave. In a few strides, he was halfway down to the exit. It was now or never.

"Rex." I called after him.

He stopped and glanced upward. His broad shoulders in that dark suit were so out of place in the stark white hallway. When he turned, he had a satisfied look on his face. My blood boiled, and I almost told him to go to hell. But Dad's livelihood was on the line.

"Could we talk?" I stood a little straighter.

He cocked an eyebrow. "We're talking now."

"No, I mean. In private. Can I come see you sometime?" I cleared my throat and corrected myself because our conversation couldn't wait. "I mean, can I see you tonight?"

"You know where I live." He met my gaze, and my pulse quickened.

"Ms. Alfera?" the nurse from before called after me.

"Yeah." I practically spun around to face him. For whatever reason, I was out of breath.

"Mr. Alfera is awake and wants to see you." He offered a kind smile.

"Thank you." I sighed in relief.

When I turned to find Rex, he was gone.

CHAPTER 6

# You Look Like a Million Bucks

CATERINA

"Were you just talking to that guy?" Sarah walked in as Rex crossed the threshold. She stared at the double doors, mouth hanging open and eyes wide. "Jeez, I think I'm pregnant."

"What?" I laughed.

"From the blast of testosterone. Wow." She pulled me into a hug, shooting glances at the empty hallway where Rex had been. "How are you doing, girl?"

"I'm good." And that was the truth. I was glad she had come here to sit with me. "Dad wants to see me. So, I think that means we're making progress."

"I'm sure it does. Go see, I'll wait here."

On the way to Dad's room, Nurse Sam explained Dad's situation. He was stable but would need open heart surgery to address the clogged arteries. I vaguely paid attention to the details of the procedure after he uttered the words "open heart."

"I'm sorry. Did you say Cabbage?" I stopped in front of Dad's window. He seemed so peaceful yet, somehow older.

"Coronary artery bypass graft, C-A-B-G." He stuffed his hands in his white coat. "Don't worry. There won't be a test on it later. All you need to know is your dad is in good hands. Mr. Valentino has already taken care of all the arrangements."

I gritted my teeth at the mention of Rex's name. I hadn't asked him for help yet. He didn't need to be interfering in my life like this—like he owned Dad. How did Rex even know who to talk to in this hospital? Dad wasn't completely ruined, living out on the street. We could hold our own. Couldn't we? Now wasn't the time to bother Dad with money questions, but we definitely needed to have that conversation. Did I need to sell my apartment? Did he still have his penthouse? Shit.

"Mr. Valentino is one of our most generous donors, we're always happy to oblige whenever possible." He motioned toward the state-of-the-art suite Dad was in.

"I'm sorry. He was restless. I had to give him a mild sedative." Another nurse came out of the room. She was an older woman in a tight gray hair bun. The kindness in her eyes put me at ease almost instantly. "The stress he's under is making things worse. Try not to wake him." She smiled. "You have a few minutes before we have to take him to run a few tests. Go home and rest. We'll text with updates." She nodded to Nurse Sam.

"We will." Nurse Sam dipped his head in agreement.

"Thank you."

"Recovery shouldn't be a problem. If we don't encounter any complications, he should be back to normal in three to four months. Let us know if you need anything. We'll be around."

They both left. I turned my attention back to Dad, bracing my hand on the window.

*If.*

That was a huge *if* that Mom hadn't survived. The more reason to have Dad's Rex-problem resolved by the time he came out of surgery. All I had to do was walk back into the lion's den. When I asked Rex for a private appointment, I had hoped he'd suggest we meet at his office not his home.

"He looks good." Sarah pressed a cup of coffee in my hand. "Drink."

"Thanks. How did you get in here?"

"They let me in." She winked.

"Can I ask you a super personal question?" I reached for Dad's door and shut it.

"Yeah. What's going on?" She cocked her head. The sadness in her eyes wasn't for Dad; it was for me.

Sarah couldn't possibly have the right answer for me, but I figured it would help to say the words aloud. To see if what I was planning was as crazy as I thought. Or maybe I was putting way too much stock into my own worth. Technically, I was betting on Rex's desire to see me beg and grovel. He seemed to get a lot of enjoyment out of that.

"Have you ever slept with someone for money?" I winced, bracing myself for an over-the-top reaction.

"Wait." Her eyes went wide as she pointed toward the waiting room. "Holy shit, no way. The guy from before? Did he try to hire you?"

I chuckled. "No, not at all. Of course he didn't. It was just a crazy thought."

"Do you need money, sweetie? I have some stashed away.

It won't pay for the medical bills, but it'll get you by for a few months." She wrapped her arm around me.

"We're fine. Forget I said anything." My plan was as stupid as it sounded.

She bumped her shoulder against mine. "When I was in college, I gave my boyfriend a blow job for helping me move. Does that count?" She shrugged.

"I don't know what I'm saying." I touched a hand to my forehead.

For a moment, I wanted to tell her everything—about who Dad really was, about Rex, and about the indescribably difficult situation I found myself in. But I couldn't do it. I was afraid she would get hurt for knowing too much. She was my closest friend. But this thing with Rex, I had to face it alone.

"Hey, so I have to go home and get some stuff for Dad. But thanks for stopping by. I was freaking out before."

"Don't mention it. I'm gonna get back to the office. Text if you need anything." She hugged my neck and then took off.

I sat with Dad until the nurses came in and got him. The tests needed before surgery were going to take hours, which gave me some time to get away. I walked through the maze of hallways, following the signs to the waiting room. From there, I was pretty sure I could find the way out. When I reached the ER entrance, I spotted Aaron, one of Rex's bodyguards. As soon as he saw me, he jerked into action, heading my way.

"Ms. Alfera. Mr. Valentino asked me to stay behind and drive you home."

"Of course he did." I considered making a point and tell him no. But then I would have to walk all around the medical campus to hail a cab and waste precious time. "Lead the way."

"Just here." He pointed at the black SUV parked behind an ambulance.

I climbed in the back and relaxed on the soft leather. I must've dozed off because when I opened my eyes again, we were pulling up to my building. "I'll be just a few minutes."

If Rex had bothered to send a car, I could only assume he meant for Aaron to drive me to the Crucible.

"I'll be here. Take your time." He hopped out and opened my door.

My blood pumped hard and fast through me as I rushed upstairs to get ready for my appointment with Rex. Based on what I saw at the assembly with the Society members, I could tell Rex appreciated formality and decorum. Normally, I wouldn't give a damn what he liked, but today I aimed to please him. I showered quickly and blow-dried my hair. After playing around with the tresses framing my face, I decided to use a curling iron to add a few messy waves.

I slipped into a black, cocktail dress that didn't require a bra. It was sexy without showing too much cleavage, since the spaghetti straps were adjustable. When it was all said and done, I stared at my reflection in the mirror, and my resolve crumbled. Who in their right mind would pay to have sex with me? Jesus, what the hell was I doing? I sat on the bed and dropped my head into my hands.

But then I thought about how Rex made me spend almost an hour in a room full of strangers having sex. If anything, Rex Valentino enjoyed seeing me squirm and suffer. I shot to my feet. This *had* to work. Maybe he wouldn't pardon Dad's entire debt, but enough that we could come up with a payment plan that didn't include Dad going to jail or spending any more time in the Crucible under Rex's thumb.

I painted my lips red, added a pair of lacy pumps and headed out to meet Aaron. The minute I stepped out of the building, he climbed out of the SUV and opened the door for me. "Mr. Rex will be meeting you in the boardroom tonight."

"Thanks."

Glancing out the window, I imagined Rex perched at the head of the long table in the ornate red leather chair that had to be as old as the Society was. I thought of him in his pristine tuxedo with his hand casually resting on the armrest. Before I knew it, I saw him shirtless. I blinked a few times to erase the image from my mind. I didn't even know what he looked like under his designer clothes. My pulse spiked below my navel, and I squeezed my legs together. What the hell was wrong with me? No matter what, I still hated Rex. He was cruel and ruthless and...I wasn't here for me. I was here for Dad, to solve the very real threat hanging over his head.

"Here we are." Aaron said for the second time tonight.

Like before, I jerked back into reality. Jesus, we got here fast. I shifted my body to see where we were. We had gone in through a rear entrance. The garage was fairly empty except for several racer cars and other shiny brands I didn't even recognize. At the far end, the car rolled to a stop in front of a large set of glass double doors. Inside, a huge chandelier hung from the high ceiling and sparkled on the marble floors.

"Is this Rex's private access?"

"It is." He unbuckled his seat and helped me out of the SUV. "You want the forty-third floor." He motioned for me to go ahead.

I swallowed and ambled toward the elevator bay. The ride upstairs dragged on. Every time the numbers on the screen changed, the pressure on my chest increased. This would be over soon. Whatever Rex wanted from me, he would tire quickly and then Dad and I could go back to our normal lives. And who knew, maybe one day my brothers would come around.

The elevator finally arrived, and the doors slid open. As soon as I stepped onto the carpeted hallway, Rex's voice filled the air. He was on a call. A work call? I glanced around, looking for a receptionist or someone to tell me where to wait until he was finished.

"I understand your predicament. But the purchase of that company needs to go through before the end of the month. I don't care if you have to work through the weekend to finish your due diligence. Make it happen." He tapped on the phone and then threw it on the massive wooden table in front of him.

I pushed the door to open it all the way, just as he started typing on his laptop. His long fingers hit every key with purpose and some of that impatience I had come to associate with Rex's overall demeanor. When he stopped, he reached for a manila folder, then glanced up. The look in his eyes should have sent me running, but I had come this far. I couldn't back down.

He stood. To my surprise, his tie was undone and hung loosely around his collar. His crisp white shirt was unbuttoned halfway, and his sleeves were rolled up. My gaze immediately fell to the patch of light hair showing through his undershirt. I tried not to think about the fact that I might get to see more of that tonight. Seeing him like this, he looked more like the CEO and less the ruthless, mafia king.

"Caterina. You look stunning." He stepped toward me. "One could say you look like a million bucks."

I fisted my hands. He knew exactly why I had come here

today. Why did he make me meet him here? To rub it in? His crude comment knocked sense back into me. He was right. This was a business transaction.

"How about a drink?" He motioned for me to sit to his right, the same seat I had occupied last night during the assembly. "What would you like?"

"Whatever you're having."

"Whiskey." He showed me a bottle I didn't recognize. Mainly because I knew nothing about liquor. I preferred wine.

"Sure."

He poured the amber liquid in two tumblers and stalked over to me. "How's Michael doing?"

The question threw me off because he sounded genuinely concerned about Dad's well-being. "He's going to need open heart surgery."

"I know that. I meant, how is he really doing?" He sat the glass in front of me and returned to his chair or throne, whatever he called it these days.

"He's tired." I took a long swig of whiskey.

"The last two years have been taxing for everyone." He braced an ankle over his knee and let his long fingers hang over the armrest.

His gaze stayed on me. I didn't dare look up. My brain got fuzzy every time I made eye contact with him. The minutes ticked by as I continued to sip fire water and he kept on staring. How would one start a conversation such as this? I glanced down at my freshly shaven legs and thought about how hard I had scrubbed my skin in the shower trying to feel clean again.

"Caterina."

That single sound filled the room with an electric charge. Sarah had called it a blast of testosterone. Either way, my name on his lips made my head snap up. And damn if he didn't have the bluest eyes I had ever seen. And a perfect nose to go with that chiseled jaw. And...my gaze dropped to his chest again.

He chuckled.

Crap. I glared at him.

"You asked for this meeting." He gestured for me to go on.

"Right." I stood and pretended I was at work presenting a new ad campaign to a very demanding and cruel client. "As you know, my father is in the hospital, and um, he, he doesn't have your money."

"This is not new information." He slid his elbow back on the armrest, so he could rest his temple on two fingers. The odd angle allowed him to look me up and down without moving his head.

"Right. Um." I felt naked standing in front of him like this, hoping he would put me out of my misery and just take me already. But this was part of his game. He wanted me to grovel, beg. I took another swig from my glass. When I swallowed nothing but air, I put the empty tumbler back on the table with a loud thud. "The thing is, I thought maybe you could give us an extension or reduce the amount."

"Why would I do that? I'm running a business here, love, not a charity. You know that."

"I thought we could make a deal."

A surge of courage burned through me, or maybe that was the whiskey, but somehow, I found the will to step into his circle. With shaky hands, I slipped my thumbs under the spaghetti straps of my dress, rolled them off my shoulders and let the rest of the fabric drop to the floor.

## CHAPTER 7
# I Don't Pay for Sex

CATERINA

His breath hitched. And then he chuckled. A deep, lewd sound that set my skin on fire, and not in a good way. I was embarrassed for thinking Rex might want to pay a million dollars to be with me. I was embarrassed because I thought he actually cared and would make an exception for us. He uncrossed his legs and spread them wide. From where he sat, he remained at eye level with my breasts.

A decent man, who had no interest in making this kind of deal with a desperate woman, would look away. Instead, he licked his lips as his gaze shifted from one mound to the other and then down to the triangle between my legs. The way he looked at me, I had to glance down to make sure I was still wearing underwear. They were still on, and to add to my disgrace, I could see the wet seeping through. Could he see it on the dark fabric?

He gripped the armrests with both hands and shook his head. There was my answer. He had seen all I had to offer, and it hadn't been enough. No doubt he had at least ten other women with way sweeter dispositions waiting for him downstairs.

"You're a real beast. I hate you." I said in a shaky voice and bent down to pick up my dress.

In a swift movement, he was out of his chair and had both my hands pinned behind me on the tabletop. The softness of his dress shirt rubbed against my taut nipples, while his hot breath traveled down my back.

He cocked his head to look me in the eyes. This close, I could see how clear and almost luminescent his eyes were. That had to be the lighting playing tricks on me. In the next beat, his pupils dilated to where almost all the blue in his irises was gone.

"So, let me get this straight." He panted a breath in my face. The whiskey lingered in the air between us. "If I were to rip your thong off of you and flip you on this table, you'd let me?"

I hadn't considered what he would do to me if he agreed to our deal. When I thought about sex, I figured it would be in a bedroom and over quickly. We couldn't possibly do something like that here where the Society members met.

"Answer."

"If that's what it would take. I'm willing to do anything to save Dad."

"Yes or no?"

I imagined him doing exactly what he had said. The images played in my mind like a runaway reel. Rex forcing me out of the one garment I had left and then pressing my chest on the cold table, while he entered me from behind. I would shut my eyes and take every one of his thrusts. Why did I not think of this before? Somewhere in the unwanted fantasy he had planted in my head, I also imagined him dotting my spine with gentle kisses.

"Answer." He repeated, his voice sounded deeper and strained. "I see I have my work cut out for me. We'll have to work on your responses."

"Yes." I said louder than I meant to.

He reached for the lacey string of my underwear and pulled until it dug into my skin on the other side. All the while he kept both my hands pinned to the table. "You'll let me fuck that pretty ass into oblivion?"

I gasped. Again, another thing I hadn't considered. He leaned into me, not touching me still, but every time his chest rose and fell along with his breaths, his shirt rubbed my front. My nipples couldn't take any more of that. I was way out of my depth when it came to Rex. I was mad at myself for rushing into this and not thinking about all the things he would do to me if he had me naked and all alone in a century-old board-room built specifically for a bunch of mobsters.

"Answer me. Yes or no?" He ghosted his lips over my shoulder. "Those are your only choices today."

"Yes." I squeezed my eyes shut, and hot tears streamed down my cheeks. He didn't have to be so crude.

"Such a devoted daughter. To give up the virginity you have held on to for this long just to save your deadbeat of a father." He released a breath. "He doesn't deserve what you're doing for him."

"He's not a deadbeat." I glared at him. Then his words fully registered. How the hell did he know I was still a virgin? I wasn't a prude or anything. But before I went to college, I promised Mom I would wait for the right guy. I looked long and hard for someone decent, and that someone never came. Then Mom got sick and time got away from me. Ironically, it seemed I was never destined to have my first time with an honorable man. I jutted my chin up to show Rex I wasn't afraid of him. "I'm not a virgin. I'm twenty-five years old. I've done it many times. Where did you get that ridiculous idea?"

He knitted his brows. Finally, I had won a round. My answer cut him. With a loud sigh, he bent over and picked up my dress by the straps. Slowly, his gaze covered every plane of my body as he raised the fabric over me like a shield.

When he brushed the back of his fingers over my nipples, heat sprung from my belly and shot straight to my clit. It happened so fast I wasn't sure if he had really fondled me there. Up until now, he'd only touched my wrists. I took over. He didn't make room for me to cover up, not even when I elbowed him a few times trying to adjust the ties.

"I suppose there's only one way to find out." He wrapped his arms around me and pressed his lips to my neck. "You're so fucking gorgeous. And I would love nothing more than to fuck you for days until you can't walk anymore, until all you know is my name." He sucked hard on the length of my cord with uneven breaths. "I'm sure there are a lot of men out there who would gladly throw a million dollars your way just to have you for one night. But here's the problem, love. I don't pay for sex."

He ambled back to the bar cart and poured whiskey into two fresh glasses while I stood there, gasping for air and shivering now that he had removed the warmth of his body from mine. "You made me believe this is what you wanted. Was this just another one of your games? To make me suffer? Why do you hate me so much? What did I ever do to you?"

"I don't hate you." He furrowed his brows and his gaze

intensified. "I truly did not think this—" he pointed at me and the table as reference to what almost happened. "—would be your next move. I have to admit, I'm pleasantly surprised."

"Fuck off, Rex." I darted toward the entrance. This meeting had not gone how I had expected at all. If anything, and as naïve as that sounded, I thought we'd be done with the whole sex thing by now.

"No." He slammed his hand on the door and shut it with a loud thud.

I could scream for help. But who was I kidding? I was in his house. It was as he had said last night, no one would help me. I was alone in this.

When I didn't move, he continued. "You came here to make a deal with the devil. Don't back down now. Let's make a deal."

I stared him down. Though all I wanted to do was run out and crawl under my bed. Rex didn't want me. All those innuendos about sleeping with me were nothing more than lewd comments to harass me and make me feel uncomfortable.

"I have nothing else to offer you."

"That's where you're wrong. Sit down. I'm going to make you an offer that, believe it or not, you can refuse. But know that once you agree to my terms, there's no going back." He motioned for me to go on and take a seat. "So, think long and hard before you answer."

I considered my non-options. I was already here. And I had made a fool of myself in the most spectacular way. There wasn't anything he could do to embarrass me further. To be honest, I was intrigued. What could he possibly want from me? I had no money or high-end properties, which of course he knew if he also knew I was a virgin.

"Please have a seat. I have no intention of letting you leave until I show you what I really want from you."

"Show me?" My nipples perked up at his words. Apparently, my body hadn't received the memo that sex with Rex was off the table. Literally.

He glanced down at my chest and smiled. "The sooner you sit down and listen to me, the sooner you can go home and take care of things."

That set me right. *Asshole.* I shoved him away from me and strode back to my chair. Why did he have to be so hot and cold? I'd been in this room for all of ten minutes and I was already dizzy and confused. I turned to face the grandfather clock near the door and realized, I'd been here with Rex for almost two hours. What? How?

"Enough with the games. Just tell me what the fuck you want so Dad and I can get on with our lives." I sat up straight in my seat, grateful that he didn't know how uncomfortable the throbbing and wetness between my legs had become.

He sauntered to the bar cart and picked up a tumbler then a manila folder off the table and slid one item at a time across the table. I went for the drink first. All this preamble had my nerves on edge—just how Rex liked it.

"All I want from you—" he pointed a lazy finger at the file, "—is your complete surrender."

"What the hell does that even mean?" I flipped open the page and gasped.

I saw red for several beats before I recovered and stormed to my feet. Rex did too. He probably thought I was going to try and run out the door again, which I definitely wanted to do. What the fuck?

"What the fuck? I thought you didn't pay for sex."

"This practice isn't about sex." He cocked an eyebrow. "As you can see."

I didn't want to see. "Is this for real or another one of your games?"

"This is what kept me going after Mom died. After I found out about all the things I was expected to do for the Society. It helped me cope. And I think it might do the same for you. Michael is being selfish."

"Yeah, and you're more than willing to stand here and take advantage of it. How noble of you."

Rex moved my drink aside, emptied out the manila folder on the table and then spread out every single picture for me to see. I glanced upward feeling like a peeping Tom. The rest of the images were not as shocking as the first one. He had done that on purpose to get a rise out of me. Once my pulse returned to normal, I was able to see what was in front of me for what it was. A kink. More specifically, Rex's kink.

He relaxed his hip on the edge of the table and smiled. A gesture that melted the lump churning in my stomach. He tapped a finger at a page. "She asked for this. I would never ask you to do more than you can handle. This process is about trust."

I laughed. "Something you and I will never have."

"Not if we don't try." He motioned for me to look, to really look.

I reached for my tumbler and knocked it back. The burn helped me find my bearings again. For once, Rex decided not to rush me as I scanned every page. He patiently waited until one caught my eye, and I picked it up. "Tell me about this one."

"The practice is called kinbaku. It's an ancient Japanese form of bondage. It technically means tight tie, and it sort of implies *with connection*." He lifted an eyebrow at me as if the word should mean something to me, which it didn't. "There are several terms to learn but for now, this is all you need to know."

"Kinbaku." I repeated the word.

My gaze dropped to the woman in the picture, her round hips and voluptuous breasts. I glanced down at myself and what I had recently offered Rex. No wonder he wasn't interested. My eyes watered when I realized how far off the mark I had been. The blonde looking up at me oozed confidence and a sense of peace. The rope binding her legs together had an intricate series of flowers all from the same tie. In truth, it was a work of art that must have taken hours to do.

"You did this?" I ran a finger over the sequences stacked between her legs that met at her apex. For lack of a better word, they were perfect in execution. Something that struck me as so Rex. He was exactly this, a perfectionist, and a control freak.

"I did."

"How long did it take?"

"Two hours." He raised his hand before I could protest. "Not what I'm expecting you to do. These women have been practicing for years. It's a skill." The half-grin that touched his lips made him look younger. And like the women in the pictures, he appeared content and at peace when he spoke.

"Why me?" I lifted my head toward him.

He perched a leg on the table and crossed his arms over his chest. Oh, he was enjoying this. His gaze found mine. I stood my ground and stared back for what felt like hours. And just when I thought I couldn't handle any more of his scrutiny, he answered.

"I think your surrender would be sweet. The fire in your eyes begs me to put you at ease. I can do that for you. If you can find a way to trust me."

"You're doing this for me now?" I braced my hands on my hips.

That small gesture made him lean forward and regard me with intensity in his eyes. Shit. That was it. Every time I defied him, he thought it was a direct assault. He thought that was me daring him to control me. I was a challenge for him. What could be more satisfying than to tie down the only daughter of his enemy? My father, the man who at any point could unseat Rex from his so-called throne.

"For the both of us. So, here's the deal I'm willing to make with you. And all you have to do is say yes." He rose to his feet and closed the space between us. "I will pardon your father's debt and even recover all the properties he has lost in the past year. He will have the freedom to come back to the Society or not. His choice—for real this time."

"And in return?"

"You become mine. All mine." He placed his large palm on the woman in the photo, the red head with stars in her eyes. "I want your complete and utter surrender."

"For how long?"

# CHAPTER 8
## Did That Hurt?

Rex

"The terms of your stay are negotiable." I stuffed my hands in the pockets of my trousers while I tried to reel in my shallow breathing to regain control. I had to stay focused and not give into all the things I wanted to do to her.

*Jesus Christ.* Caterina had a way of unhinging me. The hate and the fire in her green gaze had haunted me for years. Now I also had to contend with her perfect tits and those mouth-watering nipples begging to be sucked.

Why would she go there? When she asked for this private meeting, I had assumed she was ready to do whatever I asked. I should've known she would come prepared with an offer of her own. And fuck me, if I didn't want to send it all to hell and take her up on it.

For all my honorable intentions, if I could call them that, I hadn't resisted the urge to peek inside her panties. Something I realized now was a complete mistake because I couldn't stop thinking about her bare sex, the smell of her arousal, and her

71

plump outer lips. If she asked me for sex again, I didn't know if I would have the strength to refuse her again. I still couldn't figure out how I had managed it before. Her pussy was like a ripe fruit, and I wanted nothing more than to...

"As in a contract?" The quiver in her voice stopped me from spiraling down into yet another Caterina fantasy.

She ventured another step toward the table and then squeezed her legs together. Staying away from her would be hell, especially after she moved in with me. But this was too important for me to taint it with a tumble around a boardroom table. I rubbed the stubble on my cheek to hide my smile and chase the filthy images flooding my mind.

"Yes, but before I show you." I walked around the table and picked up my portfolio. "We'll both sign a non-disclosure agreement." I shuffled through my folders until I found the one with Caterina's name on it.

"If you're so embarrassed about your kink, maybe you should, you know, not do it." She glared at the papers I set in front of her.

"I'm the owner of a sex club, Caterina. This agreement is for your protection. And the peace of mind of all my clients." I waved in the general direction of the photos I had chosen to show her.

Her lips parted slightly. "These women paid you to do this to them?"

"Of course not. At the time these pictures were taken, they were my submissives." I sat down and motioned for her to do the same. She seemed more at ease when we were at eye level. "A lot of them are still members of the Crucible. They're no longer with me, but they continue to, for all intents and purposes, be my clients."

I refilled her glass, and she sipped from it absently as she read the non-disclosure agreement. Since I took over as leader of the Society, I had closed many deals. None of them were as important as this one.

If Caterina said yes tonight, I would finally have everything I ever wanted within reach. With her by my side, the Society could not only survive its current threat, but also thrive and flourish as something new, something more relevant to the current times.

"What would we tell people?" She glanced up. "The families are going to think something is up if all of the sudden I move into your palace." She waved her hand in the general direction of the built-in cases.

"They can think whatever they want. As long as you don't tell them what you're here to do." I leaned forward and braced my arms on my knees. "What we do behind closed doors is none of their business."

"What am I going to tell my friends? I have a job to go to."

"You can quit."

"What a chauvinistic thing to say. I'm not going to drop my entire life just to please you. I'm not a toy." She glared daggers at me.

The urge to take her upstairs and tie her down rushed through me. I wasn't lying before when I said I was doing this for both of us. I needed her to give into me. I needed her to be mine. I needed to control everything in her life. That was on me. Kinbaku afforded me a way to do it that wouldn't be harmful to her. If I could just have her for one hour a day, this incessant need I had of her would subside to a manageable level.

"I never said I was prince charming. I know what I'm

asking is beyond anything a person should ask of another, which is why I need your consent—in writing. I promise I will not make you agree to anything you can't handle."

"I can deal with not telling people. I could make up some story about moving in with my estranged cousin." She sat back, looking satisfied with herself.

"We're not telling people we're related because we're not. I don't lie, remember?"

"No, you don't. You're just asking me to lie on your behalf."

"I'm asking you not to divulge the details of our sessions."

"Sessions? That's what we're calling them?" She brushed her hand over one of the photos, then took it away with a tinge of fear in her eyes.

I wanted to hold her and tell her there was nothing to be afraid of. But until she learned to trust me, no number of words or holding would convince her of anything different. This was Caterina Alfera after all. The most stubborn and indelible woman I had ever met.

But tonight, all I had on my side was hope and I had to go with that. I reached inside the pocket of my briefcase and retrieved a three-foot rope. I figured anything longer would scare her off.

Her body jerked in surprise. "Do you carry that stuff on you at all times in case of a bondage emergency?"

"No." I cocked an eyebrow, rising to my feet. When I sat on the table next to her, she didn't flinch. Progress. "I brought this for you." I showed her my palm, feeling much like a magician about to do a trick for his audience. "Give me your hand." I slowly made two loops, twisted them inwards, and created a cuff with a pretty braid.

She held her breath as I slid it down her hand and onto her wrist. When I pulled in the tail end of the rope in the opposite direction, she automatically squeezed the smooth strands and let my fingers wrap around her wrist. The soft skin there prickled with goosebumps.

Caterina could be so alluring when she wasn't throwing insults at me or running away. Her breathing was even as she watched me gently pull, leading her toward me. I had never had to start this way with a rope bottom. It was way more satisfying than I thought it would be.

*Say yes to me.*

"Did that hurt?"

She glowered at me then blinked a few times. "No."

"Can you get out of it?"

She stripped the jute off her and sat back. "Yeah."

Her fingers released their hold on the rope and fell gently into mine. We had never held hands before. If she realized it, she didn't show it. We stayed like this—her bright, green gaze glued to mine, our bodies close, breathing the same air.

"Sign and then I'll answer all your questions," I whispered.

Her nipples perked up under the thin fabric of her dress, and she leaned into me. As usual, the spell never lasted very long with her. She shook her head as if to clear her thoughts and yanked her hand away from me.

"There." She quickly scribbled her name and shoved the paper toward me. "Let me see the contract. If you're trying to dissuade me from helping Dad, it's not going to work. I've made up my mind."

"I want this more than you know. But I need you to come to me with your eyes wide open." I reached behind me and grabbed her folder.

"Do all your submissives get a folder?"

"Rope bottoms. Yes."

She gasped. "That many?"

"I've been doing this for a long while. I like things to be in order."

"Did you have sex with all of them?" She asked casually while she opened the manila.

"How is that relevant to our arrangement?" A half-smile pulled at my lips.

"I guess it isn't." She shrugged, while her gaze stayed glued to the page. After a few beats, she shot to her feet. "I can't read while you're hovering over me with your broody stare." She glanced over at the grandfather clock by the entrance. "Omigod. How did it get to be this late? I have to get back to the hospital."

Shit. I had hoped to start tonight. Although, she would need more time to digest everything I had just thrown her way. I didn't like disappointment though. "Aaron will drive you. I expect an answer tomorrow."

"Tomorrow? Dad is in the hospital. I can't move all my stuff here and do what you want." The fear in her eyes dissipated and was replaced with determination. She was in her professional, get-it-done mode.

I could only hope that meant she was ready to agree to my terms. She raked a hand through her loose curls. Christ, I ached to bury my fingers in her hair, take in her scent, and kiss her. One more night. I could handle one more night without her.

"You will not need your things."

She furrowed her brows at me. "This is too much. I have to see Dad and then Google the heck out of this."

"I expected no less. You'll find everything you need in that folder."

She collected her papers and slowed down when she got to the photos. With a quick glance at me, she picked up those too and shoved them in her folder. *Good girl.* I walked behind her as she made her way to the double doors. The pressure in my chest grew with every step. As if I knew that if she left tonight, I would lose her forever.

I braced my hand on the wooden panel. When she spun around to glare at me, I caged her in. "If you and Michael leave the country, just know that there isn't a single corner on this Earth where you can hide from me."

Her cleavage rose and fell as she labored to catch her breath. The red in her cheeks was such a fucking turn on, I couldn't stand it anymore. I leaned in to take in her perfume and revel in her energy. When I made to step back, she jutted her chin upward.

"I see. So, this trust thing is a one-way deal. I need to surrender to you, but you can't even give me this small freedom of seeing Dad?" She pushed at my chest once, before sliding her hands down to my pecs.

Could she feel my heart racing underneath her palm? The awestruck look in her eyes told me she did. *We're done pretending, love. Aren't we?* I wracked my brain for a good reason why Caterina and I couldn't have this. Just this once. The plan was the plan. A kiss couldn't ruin that.

I pressed my thigh to her core. She rewarded me with a small sigh of pleasure and my name on her lips. "Rex." Her eyes fluttered closed. Caterina needed this as much as I did.

"You can go. But tomorrow I get my answer."

The look she gave me was of pure desire and raw need. A

hint of her scent sparked a flame below my navel. Suddenly, the room was too quiet, the air thick and hot, and my pulse out of control. Like water going fast down the drain, my restraint shot away from me—farther and farther, until I couldn't get it back.

Our gazes locked. She was so beautiful, and for once, she wasn't looking daggers at me. Oh, fuck it. I captured her mouth with mine, thrusting my tongue past her lips, while I cupped her cheek to keep her in place. All the pent-up frustration came gushing out of me in that kiss. All the times she told me she hated me, and all the times she recoiled from me. I took everything from her now, pressing my body to her soft flesh. Jesus, I ached to bury myself inside of her. She called for me again, rubbing her wet spot on my pants.

I could take her now, but where would that leave us? Me paying for sex? Her using her virginity to save her father? She had denied being a virgin before. But I knew the truth. I knew she had saved herself for someone good. That had been her mother's influence, and she'd been right. Someone like Caterina deserved so much more. She deserved a man who could give her all those things she wanted, like a home and a family. I wasn't that man. But I had other things to offer her.

I drank from her lips hungrily, even after I had decided I needed to stop. It took a few more minutes to give up on this fantasy, where Caterina had her arms around my neck, kissing me as if she had never been kissed before. I deepened the kiss and then pulled away. Her breath hitched from the abrupt change now that she no longer had my body supporting all of her weight against the door.

If she didn't have a reason to hate me before, she did now. The fire in her eyes told me she didn't get off. The frustration brought tears to her eyes. I shouldn't have done that. Our relationship was too fragile for this kind of added confusion.

"Aaron will drive you home so you can change out of that dress before you see Michael." I pointed at the wet spots all over her skirt.

I tried not to think of her pretty pussy all swollen for me, waiting. Instead, I imagined her going home and touching herself. A smirk pulled at my lips. For the first time ever, I knew without a shadow of a doubt that Caterina would be thinking of me the next time she climaxed.

"You're an asshole." She smoothed out the fabric. When she felt the moisture there, her cheeks turned a bright red. Pursing her lips, she turned on her heel and scrambled out of the room.

I took two strides and stopped before I made things worse. Before I sent it all to hell and fucked her into next week on the boardroom table. For Christ's sake, she had already said yes to that. I raked both hands through my hair and sauntered back to my chair.

*Me: She's on her way. Take her home.*

*Aaron: She's in the car.*

*Me: Don't leave her side.*

*Aaron: Yes, sir.*

I touched the faded white stain on my trousers and brought my fingers to my nose and mouth. *Tomorrow. We start tomorrow.*

# CHAPTER 9
## Letters of Bottoms Past

CATERINA

God, I hated him. I grabbed the bottle of water Aaron had left for me in the backseat beverage tray and chugged it. What exactly had happened? I went to Rex to ask for a favor and give him the one thing I thought he wanted, but then he refused me and counter-offered with something much, much worse than sex.

I glanced down at my dress. Heat rushed to my cheeks. Never in a million years would I have guessed Rex would have this effect on me. Everything he did tonight was a huge turn-on. How was that even possible? I had always thought he was attractive, well no, more like crazy hot with a devilish face that made him dangerous. I had never been touched like that before. My skin still burned in the places his strong hands had been.

And Jesus, that kiss!

In college, I fooled around plenty. Even if I never went all the way, I had gotten pretty close. I had kissed at least five

80

guys. But none of them made me feel like Rex. He took control and devoured me. I shivered against the cool air. Now that I had several miles between us, my body temperature declined drastically.

I brought my fingers to my lips and let my head rest on the window. The memory of Rex sent more flutters to my pussy. They hadn't stopped since he wedged his thigh between my legs and pressed against my core. I had been so close to coming in front of him. What the hell was wrong with me? I drank more of the water and looked out just as Aaron pulled up to my building. I hadn't asked him to bring me here. No doubt he was following Rex's orders. I let it go because I did need to change before going back to the hospital to check in on Dad.

He should be done with all his tests by now. Hugging the folder close to my chest, I climbed out of the car as soon as we stopped and headed straight to my apartment, hoping I wouldn't run into any of my neighbors. They weren't noisy or anything, but I was just too frazzled right now to have a civilized conversation with another person.

I walked in the door and went straight to the shower to wash Rex's scent off of me and our entire interaction, really. After I got cleaned up, I dressed in a pair of jeans and T-shirt. When I sat down to put on my boots, I spotted the manila folder on the bed. My pulse quickened immediately. The contract was a thick document. I couldn't even begin to imagine what kind of terms Rex would have for me. Shit. I didn't have time for this. I had to see Dad. Rising to my feet, I grabbed my big purse and stuffed the papers inside it.

Aaron was on his phone when I walked up to him. He put it away immediately and did that thing where he moved quickly to let me in the car. Again, I didn't have to tell him where I was going. He knew I needed to see Dad.

"Thank you." I met his gaze in the rearview mirror.

"Just doing my job." He dipped his head.

At the hospital, Aaron dropped me off at the front entrance where Nurse Sam came out to greet me. If this was Rex's way of smoothing things over with me, I supposed it was working. I was a ball of nerves waiting to hear about Dad's tests and surgery.

"Ms. Alfera, I was told you were on your way here. Mr. Alfera is awake. His tests are in good shape. He's scheduled for surgery first thing in the morning." He ushered me down the hallway to the elevator bay.

I counted at least five of Rex's guys along the way. They were by the main lobby, the elevators, the nurses' station, and two near Dad's room. When we were kids, Dad insisted we keep a security detail. Overtime, he got used to the idea of being a regular citizen and gave up on the strict precautions. Now that he was under Rex's protection, it seemed the bodyguards were needed again.

"Thank you. Would I be able to stay with him?" I asked Nurse Sam when he opened the door to Dad's private room.

"Of course. I'll get you some blankets and a pillow." He smiled and left the way we had come.

Dad's room smelled of disinfectant and new plastic. But for a hospital room, it was nice. The large windows at the far end let in plenty of light and offered a great view of the city. Seeing Dad like this broke my heart, and it also scared the shit out of me. I couldn't lose him too. I ambled over to his bed. As soon as I placed a hand on his blanketed foot, he opened his eyes.

"Hey, Bells. I was hoping you'd stay home for tonight." He patted my hand.

"I can't do that knowing you're here."

"Such a fuss. These doctors ought to know you can't mend a broken heart." He gestured to the machines hooked up to his arm. "You don't need to worry about me."

"I'm doing it anyway." I gave him what I hoped was a happy smile. My heart hurt for him. "So big day tomorrow?"

"I suppose." He shrugged. "I'm tired. Maybe if they stopped prodding and let me sleep, I would get better faster."

"Did you eat?"

"I did." He deadpanned.

"Want to watch TV?"

"That sounds nice." The sadness in his eyes was unbearable.

I knew what he wanted to say—that he didn't need heart surgery. He needed Mom back. Blinking away tears, I busied myself with the remote. I scrolled through the guide until I found a documentary on lions living in sub-Saharan Africa. Within minutes, Dad's breathing settled into an even rhythm. His weak heart had to do with how tired he felt. Until his surgery, there wasn't much else the doctors could do to help him.

Nurse Sam returned with a set of pillows and a blue blanket, and then gave me a quick rundown of what to expect in the morning. When he left, I settled into the oversized lazy boy near the window. I propped my bag on the side of the chair and stopped with my hand hovering over the contract.

I thought of Rex and all the photos he had shown me. Photos I had brought with me. Blood rushed through me as my head snapped up to Dad. He was fast asleep with his face tilted away from me. Somehow that felt like I had a bit of privacy.

Letting out a long breath, I reached for the folder and set it on my lap. I flipped through the pages without really reading anything in particular. When I got to the end, I noticed a set of handwritten notes. The cover page had Rex's letterhead. I rubbed my clammy hands on my pants and picked the letter. His tone was business like and polite, which made me wonder if these were his own words. In real life, he was dourer and demanding.

I focused on the last paragraph.

*Caterina,*

*You can do your own research on kinbaku or shibari, but you won't find what you're looking for. Which is why I have included three testimonials from women who have partnered with me. They know about you and have graciously volunteered to answer all your questions. I do hope you take them up on their offer.*

*Rex*

Was he fucking kidding me? His contract included letters of bottoms past? I supposed he wasn't all that wrong. I didn't need to know where kinbaku came from or what it entailed. I needed to hear from women who had done it. More specifically, I wanted to know what kind of Dom Rex was. Was he cruel? Was he rough and impatient like his kiss had been? I squirmed in my seat at the thought that maybe our sessions might include more kisses like that.

I shook my head to clear my thoughts and opened the first note, furrowing my brows at her bubbly tone. Violet was excited I had decided to take Rex up on his offer. She assured me she had tried to get back on his schedule for the past two years and hadn't had any luck. I rolled my eyes every time she called me a lucky girl. I stopped counting at five. Violet had a few tips on floor exercises to do to stay flexible and promote body awareness. What the fuck? She ended her testimonial by offering one last piece of advice.

*Enjoy your time. But whatever you do, don't fall for him. You'll be alone in that effort. Rex's heart doesn't work that way.*

Lucky for me, I already hated the guy. My problem would be not scratching his eyes out during one of our bondage sessions. I dropped my head in my hands. Thanks to Rex, bondage session was now in my vocabulary. I hated him all right. I threw the covers aside and ambled toward the body-guard outside. Aaron had also joined the crew. He wasn't here for Dad. He was here for me. Jeez whatever for? To make sure I didn't leave the country?

"Could you put his number in my phone?" I gave him my mobile.

"Of course." He didn't even ask whose number I wanted. Everything in our world revolved around Rex.

"Thanks." I turned around and returned to my makeshift bed. My heart raced a little knowing I had Rex's number now.

I thought about what I would say to him. More like, I fantasized about calling him to tell him the whole thing was off. That I would find another way to get him his money. But all the scenarios that played in my head were nothing more than a pretend world where I called the shots instead of Rex. I glared at the screen, my forefinger hovering over his name, while I imagined him sitting at the head of the table in the boardroom with his ankle braced on his knee. After several minutes, I closed my eyes. When his impossibly beautiful face appeared in my mind's eye, I didn't chase it away. I hugged the contract to my chest along with my phone and let myself drift off to sleep.

The next morning, my day started with a whirlwind of nurses and doctors taking Dad away for his surgery. Nurse Sam promised to give me updates via text and recommended I go home since the surgery and recovery would take hours. Numb, I did as he asked. But after several minutes of pacing up and down my apartment, I decided to go to work instead. I needed the distraction, not to mention, I had several projects pending that required my attention.

I hopped in the shower and donned a pant suit in a peachy color. The outfit had the desired effect of making me feel like I was in control of my life. Of course, some of that went away when I met up with Aaron outside my building, and he promptly informed me he had orders to stay with me all day. I opened my mouth to tell him I didn't need a babysitter, but then decided it would be easier just to let him tag along.

"Hey, Cat." Sarah knitted her brows from behind her desk when she saw me outside her office.

"Hey." I leaned on the doorframe.

"How's your dad? What are you doing here?"

"He's in surgery right now. I was going crazy at my place waiting for news."

"Well, I'm not gonna send you home. We need the help." She pointed toward the set of cubicles in the middle of the floor and the commotion of voices, phones ringing, and keyboards clicking. "Some big wig investor is coming over to see how we're doing. The boss is beside herself trying to get statuses on all projects and financials."

"I better get to work then." I waved and headed to my office at the end of the hall.

I sat on my chair and fired up my computer. This normalcy was exactly what I needed today. I smoothed out the soft fabric of my trousers, and Rex's voice echoed in my mind. "You will not need your things." What had he meant by that? I stole a quick glance to the chaos outside my door then grabbed Rex's contract from my purse.

Flipping through the pages, I got to the section titled: Living Arrangements. He expected me to live in his penthouse, wear the clothes he would choose for me every day, and basically be his pet. Why would anyone with a choice want to do this? Pursing my lips, I grabbed a red pen and started crossing out items I didn't agree with. I wasn't going to let Rex bully me into any of this crap.

Suddenly, the air shifted in the room. Out on the floor, the staff members had stopped their chattering and typing. I walked around my desk to see what had happened. When Rex turned the corner at the end of the hallway, adrenaline shot through me. He took long, confident strides across the way and headed straight for my boss's corner office. What the hell was he doing here? I hid behind my door, while my heart thrashed in my ears.

"Hello?" Sarah rapped on the window.

"Yeah." My body jerked in surprise. Maybe I had imagined the whole thing. I took in a breath and opened the door. "What's going on?"

"Did you see the email? Impromptu meeting in five."

"No, I didn't see it." I checked my watch. Apparently, I had spent the last two hours revising Rex's contract. "I wonder what this is about." I grabbed my iPad and motioned for her to lead the way.

"It's probably about that big wig I told you about."

Our company leased the entire tenth floor, but we shared conference room space with other tenants two floors up. To get to the elevator bay, we had to walk by the corner office. I stole a few glances at him while Sarah pressed the call button a few times. From where I stood, I could only see the back of the man in there. But it was definitely Rex.

"Are you coming?" Sarah waved a hand in front of me to get my attention.

"What? I mean yes." I hopped on the car and the doors slid closed.

As soon as we started moving, I relaxed against the mirrored wall. Rex just had a way to put me on edge. What the hell was he doing here? He couldn't possibly be expecting me to go with him today. I had barely finished going through the entirety of the document he wanted me to sign. And I had a ton of changes he needed to make.

I followed Sarah into the conference room and found a seat at the far end of the table. When I looked up, I met Rex's gaze on the other side of the glass wall. He was with my boss, who was practically sprinting to keep up with his pace while she talked with exaggerated hand gestures. Wait, what? This was his meeting?

# CHAPTER 10
## Can't Stand the Wait

CATERINA

"Jesus fuck." Sarah gripped my forearm and leaned in toward me to mouth. "Is that the Adonis from the hospital?"

"I don't know." I shrugged. "Is he?"

Sarah squinted at me in disbelief. As if anyone could meet Rex and then forget about him, his face, or the raw charge that trailed behind him wherever he went. As soon as he sauntered in, a stillness spread across the conference room table. Rex's gaze cut away from me as he went to stand at the front of the room. I tried really hard not to roll my eyes at that. He couldn't barge in and start acting like he owned A-List or this building. In spite of what he believed; he wasn't the king of everything.

He seemed so out of place here surrounded by cheap office furniture and bad overhead lighting. Rex Valentino was the king of a century old underground criminal society. Power and money had been part of his upbringing. He had been groomed to rule. Thinking of him perched on his high-back leather chair, next to old books, mahogany, and whiskey made more sense than this stuffy conference room.

My boss, Jill, joined him with a nervous smile and apologetic eyes, as if asking him for permission to be that close to him or to take over the meeting.

"Thank you everyone for joining us on such short notice. Mr. Valentino is here to learn more about our firm and see how we do things. So, he'll be sitting in on our weekly status meeting today. Which I realize is a day early." She put up her hand when other staff members exchanged concerned glances.

Rex shifted his weight and stuffed his hands in his trousers. Next to me, Sarah squeezed her legs together and let out a little sigh. I couldn't blame her. Rex in a dark-tailored suit was an aphrodisiac. I quickly scanned the room. Everyone was more or less in the same trance, even the men. Could they sense it? Did they know what Rex was? A ruthless mobster.

When I turned my attention back to Rex, his intense gaze zeroed in on me. A spark fluttered in my belly right before my imagination flashed a series of warped memories—a mix of the events from last night and the fantasies he planted in my head. I should be afraid. Where the hell was my sense of self-preservation?

"Pretend I'm not here." A half-smirk pulled at his lips, then he motioned for Jill to go on with the meeting.

Had he meant that for me? A little inside joke? Ignoring him had been so much easier before he kissed me, before he almost made me come with just the brush of his thigh.

I busied myself with my notes while he stared at me. I didn't have to look up to know he was doing exactly that. He was here to intimidate me and torture me like always.

Except, this time, he had gone too far. When he played the

part of predator in his own mafia world, it was like it was contained in the pages of a dark fairytale book. But here? At my work, my world? I realized he was very real and so was his offer to make me his rope bottom—for the small price of one million dollars. To me, it was way more than that. This arrangement between us was to save Dad.

I glanced up and met his gaze. He didn't look away. He didn't smile either. He simply stared at me as if he owned me, as if he wanted to remind me of that fact. The contract waiting downstairs in my office was merely a formality, our terms of engagement. But the part where my body and soul now belonged to him—that was sealed the minute I stumbled into his boardroom.

Jill did her best to conduct our status meeting like she would any other day—mafia king aside. I managed to keep it together until she called on me to report on the campaigns I was working on and also the new clients I had been courting. Next to her, Rex knitted his brows. Why? In disbelief? What did he think I did for a living? Got Jill coffee and donuts?

Slowly, I rose to my feet and tapped on my iPad to bring up the numbers I had put together last week. I didn't care what Rex thought of me—if he thought I was smart or capable. None of it mattered, not for what he wanted me for.

"Go on, Cat." Jill motioned for me to start.

"Thank you." I looked away from him and focused on my boss instead. Over the years, I had gotten really good at pretending he didn't exist. His kiss burned on my lips, but I quickly wiped it off with the back of my hand and moved on to the task at hand. My top three projects were ahead of schedule, which put a big smile on Jill's face. "On the new accounts, I met with Mr. Suede, and he's agreed to let us take a stab at his new campaign. As far as Mr. Ricci, I've yet to get a hold of him. I know he's been meeting with other agencies. I just need to get him on the phone."

"Thomas?" Rex asked and suddenly the temperature in the room shot up to a million degrees. "Thomas Ricci is a good friend. I can get you a meeting."

"I don't think that's necessary," I fired back.

"Cat." Jill's gaze darted between me and Rex.

"Anyway, that's all I have. Thanks." I sat, looking daggers at him, while hot blood rushed through me. He had no right to come here and interfere.

"Let me know if you change your mind." He flashed me a smile that made Sarah squeak next to me.

As soon as Jill ended the meeting, I shot to my feet and scurried out of there. I needed the safety of my office, where Rex couldn't get to me. Sarah caught up to me near the elevators. She rushed in front of me and hit the call button.

"My ovaries are shot." She stepped into the car and leaned on the mirror wall. "I think I'm pregnant."

Across the way, through the glass wall, Rex stood in the middle of the conference room talking to Jill. Right before the doors slid closed, his gaze cut to me. My breath hitched, and I stepped back, closer to Sarah.

"Do you think we'll see more of Rex if he decides to invest? I wouldn't mind the daily dose of eye candy." Sarah held onto the rail as the old elevator clanked and whined on its way down.

"No idea. I'll see you later, okay?" I hugged my iPad and stepped out.

"Yeah, bye."

I shut my office door and leaned against it. Why did I let

him get to me? My heart pumped hard for at least another minute before it settled into a normal rhythm. Aahh! I fisted my hands and walked around my desk to get back to work. My first order of business would be to get a meeting scheduled with Mr. Ricci. That account would be a huge win for the agency. But I wanted to do it without Rex's help. I already owed him too much. What would he ask of me in return for that small favor? I shivered at the idea that Rex would want more from me apart from my complete surrender. What else was there for me to give to him?

"That was a good meeting." His voice startled me back to reality.

Rex Valentino in my office space was a new kind of torture.

"What do you want, Rex?" I glowered at him. "I didn't think you ever left your lair."

He glanced up, as if asking the heavens for patience. Then with two long strides, he reached for my door, shut it, then locked it. We were alone. If I screamed, would anyone come to help me?

"You know what I want." He let the blinds fall over the only window in the room, then turned to face me.

My gaze fell to the folder sitting on my desk. He followed the line of sight and smirked. "Ah. There it is."

He took the chair across from me, undoing his jacket before he reached for the contract. "Do you have any questions?" His eyebrows shot up in surprise when he flipped through the red-inked pages. I was sure at some point he smiled at the small devil I had drawn on the corner of the page and labeled Rex. "A month?" He raised an eyebrow.

He meant the section where it stated that our arrangement

would be for a year. A whole fucking year. "I can't pause my life for longer than that. I have twenty days of vacation time. That's all I can give you."

"That's nowhere near enough time to cover Michael's debt. Six months."

"Three."

"Six." He braced his arms on his knees. "May I remind you that you have no leverage here?"

"I can't take that much time off."

"Jill is very supportive of her staff working from home. For as long as the agency is still hers anyway." He scratched the stubble on his jaw.

Jill? He said her name with such familiarity, I had to wonder if they knew each other from before. Did they? I shook my head to stay focused on the second part of his statement. *"For as long as the agency is still hers"* sounded like our days in this office were numbered.

"What is that supposed to mean? Wait. Are you buying A-List? Why? What do you want with an advertising firm?"

"It's good business."

"Since when are you in the advertising business? What exactly are you planning to do with us?"

Rex's bread and butter was crime. It was how the Society had amassed billions in the last hundred years. Whatever Rex was thinking, it had to be illegal. Or at the very least, not good for the company. What would he do? Take it apart and sell it by the pound? Because that was the only way for him to make money off of us. He couldn't do this to me.

"Don't do this."

"I'm not running a charity, love. Don't tell me how to run my own company." His hard stern tone told me how serious he was about this transaction and how little he cared about my opinion or my feelings.

"You're despicable. You stood in our meeting for an hour, looked everyone in the eye, knowing you were here to destroy their livelihoods. Don't you have a heart?"

"No, I don't. I thought we had already established that." He turned his attention back to the contract. "The living arrangements are non-negotiable. You will live with me for the duration of the contract, and you will wear what I decide."

I blinked fast, unable to meet his dark gaze. This wasn't the Rex who had kissed me in the boardroom. The man sitting in front of me was the cruel mobster I knew him to be. He was here to collect on Dad's debt in the form of that contract. I had been naive to think I had a say in what our agreement would look like.

"I do need time to make sure Dad is okay. He can't be alone all that time."

"He won't be. I've arranged for a nurse to go home with him. He will be taken care of. I promise you that." He said it all while still reviewing my changes. "The body awareness sessions are for your benefit. Without them, you could get hurt. You will do them." He slow-blinked, and then blew out a breath. Was he trying to be patient with me? "Caterina, this contract is for your own good. It's what other bottoms have agreed to because it works. As your rigger, my job is to do anything in my power to ensure you're safe." His tone had a different quality to it, somehow kinder and understanding.

"I don't know what half of that stuff is." I pointed at the pages in his hands. "What the hell is a reverse shrimp? And gagging? Hair binding? How is that even a thing?"

"Gyaku Ebi." He pronounced the words I had left out perfectly. "I will teach you."

"Those letters from your previous clients? That was a farce. I'd like to read the one-star raters." I crossed my arms over my chest.

Amusement registered in his eyes. "You just have to trust me."

"And you decided the best way to earn my trust is to tear apart the company I work for."

"Those two things are mutually exclusive."

"What? How? This is my job. You're taking it away just because you want me to be your pet." I hated how he made my voice tremble so much when he was around.

"Pet is the wrong term." He sat back calmly. We were in my office and still, he looked like he owned this place, like he owned me. "This practice will be more enlightening if you don't fight it. Don't fight me on this, love." His eyes softened along with his features. He felt familiar when he did that—when he regarded me as if we were complicit, partners in crime, equals. "I can't stand the wait."

A ribbon of desire swirled in my core. This version of Rex was so much harder to repudiate. Did he know that? Did he know how he affected me when he wasn't being a complete asshole? He had to know.

"Have dinner with me tonight." It wasn't a question.

"My father is in surgery as we speak. I don't have time for dates."

"It's not a date. It's a business meeting." He tossed the contract on my desk. "To finalize our terms. You will sign the agreement tonight." When I didn't move, he cleared his throat and nodded once. "Aaron will take you to see Michael. Dinner is at eight. My place."

"Don't you get tired of bossing people around?" I stood and braced my hands on my desk.

Slowly, he rose to his feet while he swept his gaze over my body. Heat rushed to my cheeks as images of his kiss flooded my mind. Also, I couldn't help but be painfully aware that he had seen me naked. And more than that, he had almost seen me come. My nipples hardened at the memory of Rex's suit rubbing against my chest.

He leaned forward until his face was inches from mine. "No, I don't. I'm very much looking forward to the day when you do exactly as I say." His warm breath brushed my face. He smelled so good, a mix of mahogany and Rex's signature musk. "Eight o'clock. Wear the dress."

"What dress?" I furrowed my brows in confusion.

He glanced down at his phone with a satisfied smirk then braced his palms on my desk. "The one being delivered to your apartment as we speak."

He reached for my chin, and I jerked my head away from him. His smile faded some, and that gave me a surge of satisfaction. I hadn't exactly won this round, but anything that wiped that infuriating smirk off his face was a win for me. Though something told me he would make me pay for it later.

# CHAPTER 11
## *Leave It to Me*

Rex

"Home, sir?" Frank, my driver and bodyguard, met my gaze in the rearview mirror.

"No, I just got a text from Michael's nurse. He's awake."

"Yes, sir." He put the car in gear and peeled off the curb to merge into the incoming traffic.

I settled into the back seat of my SUV and worked on getting my breath under control. When it came to Caterina, nothing was ever straight forward, nothing ever went the way I wanted it to, and I was losing patience. Though I could see she had come to terms with the fact that there was no way out for her. If she wanted to keep her dad out of jail, she would have to say yes to me.

My hand pressed on the manila folder. Smiling, I flipped through the pages layered in red ink. She had read every single clause and had countered with something different, which meant she was willing to make this work. I had hoped she would stay home with me tonight, but she needed more time. I had already waited two years for this, I could wait another day or so.

At the hospital, I entered through a private entrance in the parking garage and took the elevator to the third floor. Something felt off. But no one could be stupid enough to mount an attack on the Society in broad daylight and in a public building. As I made my way down the sterile corridor, the hair at the nape of my neck prickled, and I couldn't ignore my instincts any longer. I reached inside my jacket, flipped the safety strap on my shoulder holster and wrapped my fingers around the grip of my nine-millimeter.

When I turned the corner at the end of the hallway, I found three of my men unconscious on the floor. I rushed to them and checked their pulses. Joey and Mike were still alive. Marco was dead. Mother fucker. Who had the guts to come to a crowded place and do this to us? I got on my phone and called Frank, who picked up on the first ring.

"Get a cleaning crew in here."

"Jesus Christ. Right away."

Tossing my phone in my pocket, I darted toward Michael's room. My heart pumped hard and fast. The steady rhythm cleared my thoughts and allowed me to focus on what I had to do next. I pulled out my gun and pressed my back against the wall. While I listened for any movement inside the room, I threaded a silencer onto the barrel. Then I peeked inside. Sure as fuck, there was a man there shoving a pillow over Michael's face with his back to me. I exhaled and stepped into his line of sight. A single shot was all I allowed myself. We were in a hospital for Christ's sake.

I got him in the knee cap. *Dead men don't tell tales.* He spun around with a confused look on his face. His gaze darted from his knee and up to me as if he couldn't figure out what had happened to him. The shock of being in pain wore off and he limped to the edge of the bed. I had him cornered. If he wanted to leave the room, he'd have to go through me.

"Do you know who this is?" I jerked my chin toward Michael, who seemed to be unconscious.

"A fucking criminal," the man spat.

"Who sent you?"

The man swayed and put his hands up in the air. He hadn't lost so much blood that he'd be dizzy. I furrowed my brows and aimed my firearm at him again as he stepped back toward the open window. In the next breath, while I finally realized what he was about to do, he let himself drop. I rushed toward him, but it was too late. No way he could survive a three-story fall. I squinted and searched for him on the rooftop below me, but he was gone. Jumping out the window had been his exit strategy. This man wasn't some random asshole. *He was a professional.*

After I made sure we were alone, I hit the call button for the nurses' station. Sam darted into the room, his eyes wide in surprise.

"What the hell?" He frowned at the splattered blood on the floor, while he checked Michael's vitals and placed an oxygen mask over his mouth.

"I know. This was a gutsy move." I unscrewed the silencer and holstered my gun.

Sam was one of ours. In our line of work, having a medical professional with access to a hospital was an invaluable asset. He was the best we had, which was why he had been assigned to take care of Caterina's dad.

"Is he okay?" My chest tightened at the idea of having to

tell Caterina that her dad was killed. That would be on me if that happened.

"Yeah, the old man is tougher than we all think."

"Don't let the wrinkles on my face fool you, I'm not that easy to kill." Michael pulled the mask off and coughed. I chose not to mention that, when I walked in, Michael had not tried to fight back. He hadn't moved at all. His gaze bore into mine for a long minute before he conceded with a nod. "You saved my life. Why?"

"We're family. I need you alive."

"Is the throne giving you hemorrhoids already?" He chuckled at his own joke.

There was a time when his smoker's voice terrified me. There was a time when I looked up to him like an uncle. But that was before he abdicated, before he left the Society for good. Michael was a coward who didn't deserve his daughter's sacrifice.

"You would know, wouldn't you?" I stuffed my hands in my pockets. "Once again, you owe Caterina your life." That got me the desired reaction. His murky eyes watered, and he squeezed them tight. He had lost his wife and was about to lose his only daughter. "That asshole trying to kill you was a professional."

"Hired guns don't use pillows." Sam replaced Michael's saline bag then examined the needles in his hand.

"They do if they're trying to hide what they are." I met Michael's gaze. "The question is, is that asshole trying to kill Michael Alfera over old grievances, or was he simply going after a member of the Society."

"The latter." Michael placed a hand on his forehead.

The fear that registered in his eyes sent a shock of adrenaline through me. If someone out there had orders to execute our members, that meant we were all at risk, that our identity had been discovered. If whoever this asshole was knew about Michael, he knew about Massimo, Enzo...and Caterina.

"Now you see Dad was right. The Society is under attack. Someone knows we're still here. And they're hell bent on eliminating us one by one."

The motives could be anything—revenge, money, someone wanted to take over the Society, or they just wanted us gone.

"I didn't think that was possible," Michael croaked.

"Sam, give us a minute." I motioned for Sam to leave the room.

With a nod, he quickly made his way out and shut the door behind him. Last night, I had called for an extraordinary assembly of all members of the Society because the families needed a truce. We needed to join our resources and go after the son of a bitch who killed the Gallos and Dad. If Michael had sided with me, they all would've fallen in line. I needed to make them understand the threat was real.

"Did he say anything to you?" I pointed toward the window, a reference to his would-be killer.

"The usual." He snorted. "That I was going to die like the pig I am." He squinted at the wall, as if trying to recall the details of the assault. "Maybe, I saw a badge inside his jacket. I don't know. You know in all my years in the mob, there was only one group of people concerned with pigs and how they die."

"The cops."

He shook his forefinger at me. "More specifically, FBI."

"You have proof? The badge could've been fake." I

stepped toward him. For the first time since Dad died, I felt like I was making progress on the promise I made to him.

"Maybe."

"What else did he say?"

"Nothing more. He wasn't after revenge. I can tell you that much." He placed the oxygen mask over his mouth. After a few breaths, he went on. "In my time, I had to take care of many fathers, mothers, sisters, brothers. Every time, their family members would come for me with a shaky pistol in their hands and hatred in their eyes. They could never just shoot me. They wanted me to know why I was dying by their hand. They'd give me a whole sob story about who their loved ones were, what they meant to them, how I robbed them of someone they cared for." His voice trailed off as he struggled to inhale.

I stepped toward him and helped him with the mask. His eyes cut to me as if asking, "do you get my meaning?" A smirk played on his lips as if he found the irony of it all amusing. The old man truly believed he was hard to kill. Maybe he was right. The real irony was that Michael had lost the will to live, and yet he lived on. He had survived long enough to know the pain of losing someone he loved. For all his money and power, he couldn't save his wife.

"He called you a fucking criminal. If this isn't about revenge, then that only leaves duty. The asshole who tried to kill you is a fed? A fucking uniform?" I chuckled, rubbing the stubble on my face. "A pig."

"Find my sons," Michael begged.

Seeing him like this, defeated and alone, made my stomach churn. He had selfishly turned our world upside down to be with Caterina's mom. And for what? Nothing he did changed anything. He and his entire family were back in the thick of it.

As it always played out, an innocent like Caterina would have to pay for Michael's mistakes.

"Please."

"I already know where they are. It's time they come home."

"Yes, it is." The old man sighed in relief. "And Caterina?"

"Thanks to you. She's mine to keep."

"Her brothers won't stand for it." He glowered at me. "She doesn't deserve this. She's good."

"It's not up to them. Just like it's not up to you anymore."

The old man was right. Caterina was good. But our enemies didn't care who or what she was. They intended to destroy our way of life and she was a huge part of that equation. She was mine to protect. "She'll be safe with me. You trusted my father once with the reins of the Society. I need you to trust me now."

Almost thirty years ago, Michael Alfera fell in love with an artist. He lost all reason and sense of allegiance. He was the king of everything, but for his wife Anna, he chose to leave the Society and leave Dad in charge. A decision that eventually put me on my current path. I had never wanted to be king. But duty came first. It was high time Michael remembered that.

He nodded. "What do you need?"

"Call Signoria Vittoria and tell her this truce needs to happen. If the families don't fall in line, we won't survive this thing coming for us."

"And in return, you'll keep my family safe?"

"You have my word." I offered him my hand.

He glared at it for a several breaths and then accepted it with a weak shake. "What happens now? Your father and I made a lot of enemies in the eighties. The FBI has been at our heels since forever. And sure, they have so much red tape to go through, they can't get to us. That has played in our favor for decades. But don't make the mistake of underestimating them. That's not how you stay alive."

"Leave it to me."

Frank caught up with me outside Michael's room. "It's all taken care of. We lost Marco." He pursed his lips. "Those sons of bitches can't keep doing this to us."

"Agreed."

"What do we do, boss?"

"Have you heard from Aaron?" A ribbon of adrenaline fluttered in my stomach. Who knew how determined the asshole who tried to off Michael was? Did he go after Caterina as soon as he jumped out the window? I had no doubt he had survived the fall.

"Not yet. I've tried a few times. Should I go to Ms. Alfera's home?"

"No. I got it. I need you to stay on this asshole's trail—see if anyone checks in at a hospital or clinic with a broken leg or a shot to the knee or both." I squeezed Frank's shoulder. "He won't get away with it. You have my word."

"You can't go alone."

"I won't." I pointed at two of my guys. "You're with me." Then I turned to Frank. "I need Michael alive. Get more men in here. Get a whole fucking army if you need to."

"Yes, sir."

I strode out of the hospital with my men close behind me. My hand rested on the gun holstered inside my suit jacket. Caterina had stayed in her office after I left her. Aaron was with her, but if he hadn't touched base with us, it was because something had gone wrong. I stopped at the entrance to the hospital and waited for my guys to do their checks. When they nodded, I darted to the SUV and climbed in the backseat.

"We're going back to Madison to pick up Caterina." I fished my mobile out of my pocket and called Aaron. My pulse spiked as I waited ring after ring. When he didn't answer, I uttered a string of profanities then left him a message to warn him.

"Floor it. He's not picking up."

Michael had warned me not to underestimate the FBI. Well, the uniforms had made that mistake today. This attack on Michael in broad daylight, while he was still at the hospital, was a direct insult to me. It said they thought I would stand back and let them fuck us over.

Two good things had come out of this incident with the alleged feds, though. One, I had an idea of who was after the Society. And two, I had made up my mind about my arrangement with Caterina.

Before, I was willing to go at the pace she needed because I knew it was all too much to digest in one night, because I knew she was worried about her father. But now that her life was at risk and she needed me, I couldn't wait any longer. Caterina wasn't leaving my high-rise after tonight.

# CHAPTER 12
## Tie Me Up, Tie Me Down

REX

Red spots clouded my vision as my driver ran the light to get ahead of traffic. The fast beating of my heart had turned into an odd buzzing in my head, like the bombinating of a thousand bees. I didn't mind the pain in my chest. It gave me focus. All I could wish for was that this ache wouldn't be permanent. When I lost Mom, I went to a very dark place, a state of mind that I never thought I'd recover from until I began studying kinbaku.

My driver weaved through traffic in a chaos of screeching tires and honking horns. When we rounded the corner and her building came into view, I swallowed hard and focused on getting control of my breathing again. If the FBI went after Caterina tonight, I would have no choice but to retaliate in a way they had never seen before.

The Society had gone underground shortly after the Great Depression. The families found that dealing in secrecy was much more efficient than having to butt heads with the feds at every turn. Every now and then, the FBI would come close to uncovering who we were and how we operated. But all those times, after they spun their wheels and exhausted their resources, they got nothing but smoke.

As far as loyalties went, I didn't trust Michael one bit. Back when he ran the Society, everything he did was to serve himself. I didn't give a fuck if he now considered himself reformed, simply because he found love and got himself a family. He acted like he was the first man to ever earn all that bliss.

I would be an idiot if I didn't take his warning seriously, though. He had no proof the uniforms were after us. In my world, everyone was guilty until proven otherwise. No way in hell was this happening on my watch. I wasn't about to let the pigs kill us all off one by one.

"Keep the car running." I tapped my driver on the shoulder and then turned to my other guy. "Check the perimeter."

I darted to the front entrance. By some miracle, the doors to the elevator car slid open as soon as I reached it. I hopped on and hit the call button for Caterina's floor. For the second time today, I unholstered my firearm, but kept it hidden inside my suit jacket in case I ran into one of Caterina's neighbors. Civilians had a thing about calling the cops whenever they were spooked. If I thought the cops could handle this matter for us, I would've called them myself.

After what felt like an eternity of hotel lobby music, the car stopped. I inhaled, and in the next breath, I stepped out and silently made my way to Caterina's door. Her furious voice filtered through the walls in a whirling of furniture getting knocked over and muffled whimpers. I didn't allow myself time to check in with my guy. This was Caterina in danger. I had to save her.

I gripped my gun and barged in. My body temperature went from cold to hot as I ambled toward Caterina holding a butcher's knife to Aaron's throat.

"What the hell is going on?" I slammed the door shut. The apartment shook, and I winced. So much for keeping her neighbors out of this.

"Are you kidding me right now?" She shot me a glare that actually made me step back. "There's a fucking stranger in my home. A stranger that you—" she waved the blade in my direction, which gave Aaron the opportunity to get away from her, "—sent to spy on me. I'm the one who should be asking what the hell is going on in that thick head of yours?"

I inhaled and held my breath until my brain processed the fact that Caterina was safe. Pissed off as all fuck, but alive and well. With all the patience I could muster, because I knew this misunderstanding had not been his fault, I holstered my gun and shifted my gaze toward Aaron. "We called and you didn't answer. You know the rules."

His cheeks and ears turned red. If he was angry or embarrassed, I couldn't tell. I would be both if a woman had bested me the way Caterina had fought him off. He had been trained to handle any kind of situation. "She tossed my phone out the window."

"Why?" I pinched my nose.

"I wanted him out of my apartment." She braced her hands on her hips, and my hand itched for a bit of rope.

"I got the message about the clean-up crew. I figured it would be safer if I kept my eyes on her."

"While I got dressed?"

"I wasn't going to look." Aaron's eyes went wide in panic. He knew what Caterina meant to me. He knew what the punishment would be if he so much as touched her.

I put my hand up to get him to stop. "I understand. Did you clear the apartment?"

"Yes, sir."

"You did the right thing. Go find your goddamn phone." I gestured toward the door. When it shut behind him, I turned my attention to Caterina. Her cheeks were flushed while she stood at the ready with a big ass knife in her hand. With my hands up in surrender, I stalked toward her. "I get that you don't trust me, but you put yourself in danger today with your antics."

"I get that you think you own me because of my dad's debt, but you don't. And you don't get to send random guys to barge into my home. Come to think of it, you don't get to barge in either." She raised her arm higher as if aiming for my face, rather than my gut.

"Jesus fuck. We don't have time for this." The bombinating in my head returned and all I could think of was getting her to a safe place. I closed the space between us, grabbed her wrist and squeezed it until she let go with a whimper. "Your life is in danger. We need to go."

"Get out of my house. Our dinner is off." She shoved at my chest. "You think everyone is after you."

"That's because they are." I bent down, wrapped my arm around the back of her legs and hoisted her over my shoulder.

"Have you lost your mind?" She fisted my suit jacket.

When she realized she had access to my weapon, her body twisted as her hands roamed my back.

If she weren't trying to shoot me, I would've enjoyed her touch. "Don't even think about it." I darted toward the elevators. The digital screen on the side panel showed it was two floors down.

"Then put me down." She went limp on my shoulder, then started screaming and kicking. "Help."

I set her down and clamped my hand over her mouth. My phone vibrated with a message, and just because this night had gone all wrong, I knew it wasn't good news. "I need to get that," I whispered in her ear. "If you run or scream again, our deal is off."

She stiffened in my arms, then nodded. As soon as she did, I fished my phone out of my pocket. "Son of a bitch."

"Having a bad day?" She smirked.

"No, love. You're having a bad day. I'm trying to fucking help you." I grabbed her arm, possibly a little harder than needed, and headed for the stairwell. Aaron had found one of my guys knocked out in the courtyard behind her building. That could only mean one thing. The feds had come for her too. While we rushed to the garage level, I called Aaron. "Where are you?"

"Courtyard. The two men went inside. It's safe to come out."

"Got it. We'll meet you there." I hung up and turned to Caterina, who had finally realized this wasn't a game. "What's the best way to get to the back entrance?"

"Through the garage. There's an access door on the far end."

"Go." I motioned for her to lead.

The terror in her eyes told me she had a million questions running through her mind. But she knew she needed to get to safety now and figure out the rest later. She picked up the pace, holding on to the rail for balance until she reached the bottom floor. Gasping for air, she pushed the door and pointed toward the other end.

I nodded and took the lead from there. Shielding her with my body, I ushered her toward the back. We came up to an alley that smelled of trash and had a few cars parked to the side. That was a good thing because that meant Aaron had a way to get to us.

In the next beat, my SUV turned the corner with wheels screeching. Who knew if Caterina ever had any kind of training, but even now that she knew she was in danger, she remained calm, and to my satisfaction, she obeyed my orders.

"Get in." I opened the door when the car jerked to a stop in front of us. She did as I asked and even made room for me in the backseat. "Go." I tapped Aaron's shoulder. "Where are the others?"

"I put them in a taxi. They're on their way to the Crucible."

"Good." I sat back and released a breath before I reached for Caterina's cold hand. "Are you okay?"

"Yeah." She pulled away from me as if my touch repulsed her.

I swallowed the insult and focused on what we needed to do instead. We would deal with our contract later. We rode in silence the rest of the way. I relaxed my tensed muscles as soon as we crossed the entrance to my private garage. We'd made it. Caterina was safe. As long as she remained here, she would be okay, just like I had promised.

For tonight, I had hoped for a different kind of dinner for us, more like a date and less like an arrangement. But our run-in with possibly the FBI ruined my plans. She didn't get to change into her dress. I fisted my hands. Why was it that when it came to Caterina, nothing ever went the way I wanted it? Everything she touched had the ability to spin out of my control.

"Where are we going?" She finally spoke when we walked into the elevator car.

"Earlier today, we didn't get to finish our conversation."

When the doors slid open, I ushered her down the carmine corridor. The old building smell soothed me and helped me find my center again. Next to me, Caterina fidgeted as we walked toward the boardroom. Good, she remembered this room. The last time she had been here, she offered herself to me. I swallowed and put the erotic images of her out of my mind.

"What do you want from me?" She headed for her chair at the table, as if the piece of furniture could save her from me.

I ambled around her and found my seat. Bracing my hands on the new manila folder, I leaned toward her and smiled. She was finally here. "Here's a revised copy of the contract."

"Wait. What?" She knitted her brows in disapproval or confusion. Who the hell knew? "We got chased out of my apartment by someone who possibly wanted to hurt me. And all you can think about is getting your stupid contract signed?"

"I wanted to give you more time. But that's not going to happen now. This part of our deal needs to be done."

"Why?"

"Because you're not leaving here tonight. Not for a long time."

"What?"

"You're staying. And I don't think I can stand sleeping in the room next to you until we hash out our terms."

"You're insane."

"The fact remains." I pushed the papers toward her. "I need you to sign."

She thumbed through the pages. Every time she stopped at a particular page, she would purse her lips and shake her head. I leaned back and crossed my ankle over my leg. After a long while, she closed the folder and glanced up at me. "You literally only changed two things."

"I conceded plenty on a lot of things."

She shook her head, and my heart raced. Was she going to say no?

"What happened today? Who was after me?"

"You don't need to concern yourself with that."

She rolled her eyes. "I can handle my own. I'm not your fragile pet." She motioned toward the contract. "Tell me. I won't sign until you do."

"I'm handling it."

She rose to her feet and headed toward the door. Jesus. I chased after her and slammed the door shut before she crossed the threshold.

"This is a familiar place." I cocked my head to look her in the eyes. "Maybe you'd like to make a different kind of deal."

My cock sure as hell wanted to. I braced my hands on either side of her head, pressing hard against the door to steel myself. She was such a distraction.

"What happened today? And don't lie."

"I don't lie." I stepped back. "Someone tried to kill Michael today. I got there just in time and shot the assailant in the knee. He got away."

"How's Dad?"

"He's fine. He's tougher than you think." I released a breath. Telling her about the incident made me feel lighter. "I called my personal bodyguard to send a cleaning crew to the hospital. Aaron saw the request, and thankfully, thought to stay closer to you to protect you until I got there. He did the right thing."

She stared at me with a blank expression. "I tossed his phone out the window and told him to go fetch." She tapped her head to the door, then her body jerked. "I need to see Dad."

"Not until we figure this out."

"You can't keep me here." She stood taller, glowering at me.

"I told you the truth." I extended my arm toward the table. "Or were you lying about signing after I told you what happened?"

"This is ridiculous." She practically stomped back to her chair. Her eyes watered as she picked up the pen I had left there for her and signed.

Hot adrenaline rushed through me. Suddenly, the air felt lighter, tasted sweeter. She was finally here. After two years, Caterina had agreed to come to me. She'd agreed to be mine. Yeah, the world was falling apart outside these walls. But at least now, we had each other.

"Why would you want your enemy living under your roof?" She surveyed the library on the other side of the room. "Tie me up. Tie me down. Nothing will change between us."

"We were never enemies, love."

"Yes, we are." She shot to her feet. "You're about to find out just how much. Because nowhere in that stupid contract does it say that I have to be nice to you."

I rubbed the stubble on my cheek. "Today was a long, fucked-up day. Let's end it right. My assistant will help you get ready."

## CHAPTER 13

# If You Want, We Could Make It Real

CATERINA

I had signed the contract. As of now, I was Rex's plaything for the next six months. He had agreed to reduce the time of our arrangement, but he didn't concede on letting me return to the office. Not that it mattered if he was getting ready to buy the company and sell it for parts. At least now I could talk to Dad and tell him he was free of Rex. The stress of his debt was literally killing him.

"I want to see Dad."

"Do you understand what's happening?"

"Sure I do. I'm not an idiot. Somehow, the Society is under attack. And even though Dad and I have nothing to do with it, we're being targeted just the same."

He prowled closer to me, and I crossed my arms in front of me. Tonight, his smell had an added hint of danger and sweat. And damn if that wasn't intoxicating and distracting. Holding my breath, I stepped away, but all he had to do was reach out to bring me back into his circle. How was I going to survive six months of him being this close?

"That's correct. Except for one thing." He brushed a strand of hair away from my cheek. "You have everything to do with the Society."

I glared at him, hoping he could see how much I despised him. "It's all because of you. This is all your doing."

"If you need to pretend Michael had nothing to do with your current predicament, fine. I'll let you be." His sexy stubble made a scratchy noise when he rubbed his fingers along his jaw. "Are you hungry?"

"No."

He rolled his eyes. "You will join me for dinner later."

"I don't think so. Meals were not in the contract."

A small win. If I could call it that. But something in his infuriating smirk made want to hurt him with pettiness. He grabbed his phone off the table and tapped on it. "How's this for items not in the contract?" He showed me the screen. When Nurse Sam appeared, I reached for the device, but he held it at arm's length. "Your time with me can be as hard or as pleasurable as you make it. Just remember that."

"Why do you hate Dad so much? I know you're doing this to hurt him." I jerked my chin toward the stupid contract.

"I don't hate him." His eyes softened. "Not anymore."

"Ms. Alfera. How are you?" Sam waved at me from the screen and saved me from yet another argument with Rex.

"How is he?" I stepped closer to him, or Rex really, since he was still holding the phone.

"Much better. Do you want to talk to him?"

I nodded with tears brimming my eyes. "Yes, please."

"Bells, are you okay?" Dad touched a hand to the device. I

imagined him brushing my cheek to soothe me. He didn't look like someone who had almost been murdered. "Sam says the surgery went well. But I still have a long road ahead before I'm back to normal."

"That's great, Dad." I beamed at him, wiping my face.

"Bells, don't worry about me. I'm well taken care of here."

I opened my mouth to remind him that someone had managed to sneak into his room earlier today, but instead, I glanced up at Rex, silently asking the question—was he safe? How did we know we wouldn't have a repeat of today's incident?

"He's at a private clinic nearby. Sam and twelve of my most trusted men are with him."

"Thank you," I mumbled. Having Dad wedged between us added a layer of awkwardness to our already unorthodox arrangement. For Dad's sake, I felt like I needed to be nice to Rex.

"Please remind Rex of the promise he made to me. I'll see you soon. Okay?"

"What promise?" I asked, but Dad was already gone. I shifted my gaze to Rex's. "What promise? And don't tell me you don't want me to worry my little head with details. If it has to do with Dad, I need to know."

"Fine." He motioned for me to sit down then lowered himself on his high-back chair.

He fit so well perched on his throne in this old-world room. When he hesitated again, I braced myself for the worse. "I can handle it. Whatever it is."

"Michael is sure that whoever is after him will come for his family too." He inhaled. "I think we can all agree he's right in that, given what happened at your place. He wants me to find your brothers."

I beamed at him. Enzo and Massimo had been gone for two years since Mom passed away. "Don't waste your time." I took a seat. "I tried calling them when Dad had the heart attack. I got nothing. They don't care."

"I'll make them care." He reached for my hand.

His soft caress unraveled something inside me. I supposed if anyone could bring my brothers back to New York, it would be the all-powerful Rex. "Why would you do that?"

"I made a promise." He smiled at our intertwined fingers. "I'll need one thing in return."

I pulled away from him, but he tightened his grip. He already had a signed contract that made me his plaything for half a year. What else could he want? Sex? He had said he didn't pay for sex, but technically finding my brothers was more of a favor. I squeezed my legs together, hating my body for the way it responded, the way it melted every time Rex was near. Did it not understand Rex was bad for our health?

He chuckled, jerking me back to reality before my imagination flashed more images of the last time Rex kissed me. "I know what you're thinking. But it isn't that." He tugged at the hem of my shirt and my nipples perked up. "I want your help."

"What?" I furrowed my brows. "What could I possibly do for you?"

"It seems that after today's attack, you and I have a common goal." He shot a glance toward the ceiling as if looking for the right words. "Even if Michael made a deal with the devil to leave the Society, you're still part of it. Your brothers too. Because whoever is after us, didn't get the memo that your family bailed."

"What do you want from me?"

"Join me. Publicly. Show the other families that the Alferas have agreed to a truce with me. I need us to work together. I can't be watching my back while fighting off the FBI."

"The FBI tried to kill Dad?" I placed a hand over my mouth. They were supposed to be the good guys. How could they try to assassinate an old man who had just had surgery?

"It's all speculation at this point. But we need to operate under that assumption until we prove otherwise. I need you." He squeezed my fingers.

For the first time since I met Rex, he was asking instead of demanding. The simple gesture warmed me to my core. But beyond that, he was right. Whether we considered ourselves part of this mafia family or not, my family was implicated in this new war with the FBI. If I wanted us to survive, I had to agree to Rex's request for a truce.

"Okay. I'll do whatever you want."

He sat back in his chair and puffed out a breath. "I have a few guests coming today. All you have to do is make an appearance with me."

"Are you serious? Do you ever sleep?" I checked the time on the grandfather clock behind me. "We're well into the evening."

"Did you think mobsters kept office hours?"

"I don't know what I thought." I rose to my feet. "Is this what I'm to expect? A run in with the FBI in the morning, then sex parties at night?"

He fisted his hands and stood. The look in his eyes said he was more determined than mad. "There's someone I want you to meet. I want her to see us together."

121

"I thought you said you didn't lie." I braced my hands on my hips just because I knew that rubbed him the wrong way. "You know for someone who doesn't lie, you sure spend a lot of time manipulating the truth. Which you ought to know is the same as lying."

In two strides, he closed the space between us and wrapped his arm around my waist. My body more or less slammed against his hard chest. "Rex." I panted a breath and slightly pushed away at his shoulders.

"If you want, we could make it real." He ghosted my lips, then moved over to my cheek and went on. "Every time you say my name, my resolve goes out the window."

His hands lingered on my lower back for several beats as if he were trying to decide if he wanted to take me on the table like he had said before or not. Or maybe he was waiting for me to make the first move. Meanwhile, my throbbing clit had already come up with a bunch of bad ideas—like what would happen if I shifted half an inch and let him kiss me again? I inhaled, and he dropped his hands so fast I thought maybe someone had come in. But when I checked, we were still alone.

"You hanging from my arm should do the trick." He lowered his gaze down to my core for a split second before he added, "You'll need to change."

"I didn't bring any clothes."

He smiled. A genuine gesture that made the temperature in the room go up several degrees. "You'll find what you need in your room. I'll walk you." He ambled toward the door and swung it open.

Outside in the vestibule, he let out a breath while he surveyed the end of the hallway as if considering something. I had been in this part of the building a few times now. I knew the elevator bay up to his penthouse was straight ahead.

"I think it'll be a good idea for you to learn where the secret passages are. There's a door through there." He pointed at the far corner of the antechamber. "The stairs will take you up to the penthouse."

"Okay."

"Let's go through there now."

He pushed on the wooden panel, and a skinny door swung open. The stairwell went up and down. I knew he was two floors up, so I headed that way. The cement steps and steel rails were a stark contrast to the room we had left behind with its silk wallpaper, huge fireplace, and antique looking furniture. This section of the building was meant as an escape route, not to impress guests.

When we reached Rex's floor, he punched in a number in the security keypad and then pulled on the door. On the other side of the wall, we were in a small lobby with a shimmering chandelier hanging overhead. Here, we were back in modern-day times with a decor that was fresh and sleek with beige walls and shiny marble floors. I followed him to the massive double doors on the left.

This had to be the front entrance to his penthouse. "Do I get a key?"

"No." He deadpanned and pushed the door open.

The elevator we had used yesterday was to my right, facing the grand staircase that led to the upper bedrooms. My heart rate spiked when I realized that the gray and beige color scheme of his living room, the marble fireplace, and the city view felt familiar to me.

"You'll be staying in the same room as before." He

motioned toward the steps. "It should be unlocked." He stayed close to me as we went up the steps and down the wide corridor adorned with tall mirrors and fresh floral arrangements. "I'm right next to you. I'll come and knock in half an hour."

I stood there and watched him go into his own suite. At least he wasn't expecting me to share a bed with him. That would've been creepy. And agonizing for me. Shaking my head to clear my dirty thoughts of Rex sleeping next to me, I strode inside the bedroom. Everything looked exactly as before with the bed on one side and a seating area on the other. The sofa and bedding decor were posh, done in creams and grays.

Making my way to the bathroom, I half-expected Rex's assistant to jump out. She didn't, and I was grateful for that. I didn't need any witnesses tonight watching me officially become Rex's mafia doll. He hadn't even flinched or shown a modicum of contrition when he said he just wanted me to hang from his arm.

Like last night, I showered quickly and slipped into a fluffy bathrobe. There was no escaping for me tonight. It occurred to me that, that was probably why Mary Anne hadn't been here. Rex knew I wasn't going to run away from him this time.

I put my hair up in a loose side French braid and made use of the toiletries and makeup in the vanity, before I headed to the adjacent room to pick something to wear. Since my power suit from work wasn't good enough for Rex and his guests, I had to assume he wanted me in a cocktail dress. I ambled into the walk-in closet and froze, glaring at the single garment hanging there, a corseted dress in a rust color.

The sheer top fit tight around the waist while the skirt was feathery and flowy with a slit that went up to my crotch. Luckily, the outfit came with matching underwear. It was a sexy number. I had to give him that. I puffed out a breath and donned the dress, the matching Jimmy Choos and the diamond bracelet. Basically, every item found in the closet.

Twenty-nine minutes and fifty seconds later, Rex knocked on my door. Pacing the room, I fidgeted with my attire, knowing I was being petty for making him wait. It was his own party. He could be late if he wanted. He rapped again. Harder this time.

"Caterina." He called for me, and I stood my ground. "Jesus fuck, Caterina. If she left, I swear…"

A string of profanities in Italian echoed out in the hallway. I didn't speak the language, but I knew a few of those words. He slammed his hand on the door one more time right before he barged in with a wild look in his eyes. When he saw me standing in the middle of the room, he stopped in his tracks and raked a hand over his perfectly styled hair. The man should not be allowed to wear a tuxedo. It wasn't fair how it made his blue eyes look even bluer, deeper, and more intense.

"I'm ready." I pointed at the dress suddenly regretting my pettiness. "This was all I found in there."

Slowly, he prowled toward me and cradled my neck. "Beautiful."

My toes curled when his hot breath fluttered on my face and deep down into my cleavage. Rex's world was unfamiliar, layered with danger and mystery. Everything about this place made me want to run out and never look back. But his touch made me feel like I could do this. I felt safe here with him.

I caught a glimpse of my reflection in the full-size mirror by the bathroom door. How the hell was I going to survive six months of this? More importantly, how was I supposed to help

Dad and my brothers, while still keeping my sanity and my sense of self? Because one thing was for certain, when Rex asked for my utter surrender, he not only meant my body and mind. By the way his gaze roamed every inch of me now, I knew he meant to unequivocally claim my heart and soul too.

# CHAPTER 14
## Bunny, Bun, Hun

CATERINA

Rex ushered me to his private elevator. As we made our way down to the Crucible level, I braced myself for another round of Rex's sex club. But when the car door slid open, we were on a different floor. The warehouse style room had floor-to-ceiling windows that offered a fantastic view of the city. Not that any of the patrons noticed it as they kept their gazes glued to their cards. This had to be the place where Dad lost millions of dollars gambling.

The music played in the background, but not too loud that it was impossible to carry a conversation. Not that Rex had anything to say to me after he found me in my suite. The whole way here, he kept his hand firmly on my waist, as if he were afraid I might take off if he didn't. He expertly maneuvered me through the gaming tables and sitting areas until we reached the bar, which covered the entire length of the room.

"Is she here yet?" His long fingers tapped on the counter as he waited impatiently for the bartender to turn around and answer. He had leaned away from me, but his arm stayed tightly wrapped around me.

"Yes, sir. She was here a minute ago."

"Good." Rex returned his attention to me. His gaze dropped to my cleavage then up to my lips before he pressed his mouth to my temple. "You really do look stunning in that dress."

"Rex." I wedged my arm between us. His proximity and soft tone were a huge turn on. Why?

He groaned and pulled me even closer to him. "Don't say my name unless you mean it."

"What am I supposed to call you?" I fired back. "My liege?"

"That has a nice ring to it coming from your lips." He slid his thumb across my cheek.

A spark of heat unraveled below my navel. Was this him pretending we were together? Or was this just another game of his to torture me? My body didn't care either way. Real or not, I melted into him and got lost in the gleam of his eyes. The man was infuriatingly hot.

His hand slid down to cover the column of my neck. "I'm very much looking forward to our first session later tonight."

What? The room swayed a few times as the words fully registered in my mind. He had meant a bondage session. He meant to do all those things from the pictures to me in a few hours. Suddenly, I couldn't breathe as I imagined myself in those photos. Tightly roped with my arms behind my back, suspended several feet off the ground. My body twirling round and round in a dark room.

"Shh." Rex cradled my face as he ghosted my slack mouth. "Don't be afraid."

"So, the rumors are true." A woman with a deep smoker's voice appeared in my peripheral vision. "Caterina Alfera has come home."

The middle-aged woman adjusted the mink shawl over her proud shoulders as she studied me with curiosity. She wore a black sequined floor-length gown that made her look ten feet tall. Her gray hair was twisted into a chignon. It sat on her head like some sort of crown. Everything about her, her presence, her energy, and even the way she held her hands screamed power and old money.

A wicked smile pulled on Rex's lips before he turned to face her. "Signoria Vittoria. I'm glad you could make it." He glanced down at me. "I don't believe you have been properly introduced."

"Caterina. This is Vittoria Salvatore." He offered her a curt nod. "She represents the Salvatore family."

The woman was a Don.

"È un piacere conoscerti, dolce bambina." She took my hand in hers as her gaze bore into mine, as if trying to look into my soul or maybe drink from it.

Vittoria scared the crap out of me.

"Nice to me you too," I replied in English.

Even though I understood a few words, I didn't really speak Italian. Dad was fluent, but he never spoke the language around the house. I supposed that was his way of letting go of this mafia world, to prove to Mom he was really out. Though, now that I had met Rex and Vittoria, I could see that whatever Dad and Mom thought they had outside of the Society was just an illusion.

"I never thought I'd see the day. I'm happy to be proven wrong." She squeezed Rex's arm and smiled. A gesture that had a tinge of warmth to it. Of course, the older lady had a soft spot for Rex. "My niece will be devastated."

"Which reminds me. Last night you left in such a hurry, we didn't get to finish our conversation." Rex motioned toward the grand staircase behind her.

The upper-level loft offered a view of the entire floor. But more importantly, it was private—for very important people only. I tried to remain cool, but this was too much for me. Rex wanted my help. But if he wanted me to talk to Vittoria or convince her of anything, he had the wrong girl.

"I believe you're right." She smirked at me.

Rex placed his hand on the bar, and that was all the bartender needed to rush toward us. "Caterina will have a glass of rosé. Send a bottle of Macallan upstairs."

When he faced me, he removed his arm from around my waist. Losing his support made me feel lost and cold.

"I had hoped to leave you in good company." He scanned the room and pursed his lips. "I'm sorry." He brushed my cheek with his lips. "Stay here. I'll find you when I'm finished with Vittoria."

Finished? Something twisted in my gut. I knitted my brows at him in confusion. No, I wasn't jealous, of course not. But if he was supposed to be here with me, I was curious to know what kind of business he had to finish with Vittoria and a bottle of expensive whiskey in the VIP loft.

"Take all the time you need." I took the wine the bartender set in front of me and took a long swig.

"I like this look on you." He flashed me a knowing smile as he brought my fingers to his wet lips.

"Get over yourself."

Whatever he thought was going on, he was dead wrong. I

watched him as he escorted Vittoria to the empty and dim-lit loft. I spun to face the bar and drank some more, glaring at my reflection in the mirror wall. My eyes watered, and I swallowed. This place wasn't for me. This wasn't my world. I belonged out there where the real people lived. This twisted and dark fairytale world was more than I could handle. No wonder Mom couldn't wait to get out—why she did everything she could to make sure we would never need a favor from the mob.

"There you are."

I glanced up and spotted a face in the mirror just over my shoulder. She seemed familiar, but I couldn't quite place her face. "Hi, I'm Violet." She plopped herself on the barstool next to mine. "You're Caterina?"

Shit. Rex's former bottom. The five-star rater. The one who wrote me a two-page letter on how great Rex was at being a top.

"Rex asked me to talk to you." She beamed at me.

I shifted my body to get a better look of the VIP section. Rex appeared at the top of the stairs with his phone pressed to his ear. Right away, Violet's phone rang in her purse. Her cheeks flushed as she pulled out her mobile and faced Rex.

"Hey." She nodded, turned to me, and handed me the phone. "He wants you."

Shit. I had let Rex bring me here and didn't even think to ask him for my phone. Come to think of it, I hadn't even brought my bag with me. "I left my stuff at my apartment." I spoke into the speaker.

"I know. Aaron will get it for you." He took a long pause while he watched me from the loft. "I'd like for you to spend some time with Violet. Would you do it?"

"Why?" My gaze shifted from Rex's tall form to Violet's eager face.

"I don't want you to be scared about tonight." He said matter-of-factly.

"Oh. Um. Fine."

What choice did I really have?

As soon as I agreed to his request, he hung up. I tilted my head in his direction, but he was already gone. I let out a breath. Between sleeping at the hospital, working, and spending hours going through Rex's contract, I was beyond exhausted. Didn't he feel tired too? He had spent his afternoon chasing bad guys. How was he still in the mood for kink?

"Hey, bunny." Violet bumped her shoulder against mine. When I rose both eyebrows in surprise, she clicked her teeth. "Bunny, bun...hun. I'll just call you hun."

"Caterina works."

"I was just trying to break the ice. I can see you're nervous. Don't be. Rex is the best rigger I've ever had." She beamed at me. "I was honored when he asked me to help you out."

"What exactly are you helping me with?" I sipped my wine.

"Like I said in my letter." She jumped off her seat and went to stand behind me. "Face the mirror." She pointed toward the wall lined with liquor bottles then started massaging my neck. "Relax."

I made to push her hand away. It was eerie to have a complete stranger touch me with such familiarity in a public place. But then she hit a particularly tight knot along my shoulder, and I loosened up, practically melted into her.

"Rex was right. You carry the weight of the world on your shoulders." She bent her head to meet my gaze in the mirror. "I bet your hips are super tight too." She swapped hands so her left fingers rubbed the bundle of nerves near my spine while her other hand kneaded my hip.

Again, if we weren't in a gambling house, all of this would've been heaven. She worked her magic until I remembered where we were. A cold shiver ran through me at the thought that other people might know who Violet was. If they did, they would guess why I was here and what Rex planned to do to me later on.

"Whoa." She pulled away. "You're making yourself all stiff for no reason. We'll keep working on that in the morning." She patted my shoulder blades then hopped on the barstool. "What are you worried about? Talk to me."

"Fine. You want to know?" I shot a glance behind me. "It's humiliating. He's doing this to punish me. He hates me, my family, my father more than anyone."

"Oh, hun." She rubbed my cold arm a few times. "He's doing this for you. Not to you. Humiliation has nothing to do with it." Her kind smile was full of pity. As if I were some lost girl who needed someone like Rex to save me. "Give him a chance."

"Do you know what he is?" I cleared my throat. "I mean apart from his kink. Do you know what he does for a living?"

She needed to understand Rex wasn't some nice guy who wanted to help me. He had literally paid a million dollars to get me to take off my clothes and let him tie me up into a pretzel. Or whatever those positions were on the pictures he showed me.

"What does one thing have to do with the other?" She furrowed her brows at me. "I see he has his work cut out for him. Here's my advice. Go to him with an open mind. We'll talk again tomorrow."

"Tomorrow? Why?"

"I'm going to be your body awareness instructor. Did he not tell you that?"

"No. He didn't. Or maybe he did. I don't know." I rubbed my temples to ease the avalanche of scary images flooding my mind. Six months was a fucking long time.

The bartender brought me another glass of wine. When I reached for it, Rex's hand appeared out of nowhere and slid it away from me. "I think one glass is enough for tonight."

"Excuse me." I pursed my lips and shot him a nasty glance. It was one thing to tell me what to wear, but to tell me how much I could or couldn't drink, that was my absolute limit.

"I need you sober for later." He didn't even try to lower his voice, so Violet wouldn't hear him.

"Why?"

"I can't have your consent while you're impaired. Did you ladies have a good talk?" He directed his question at Violet.

"We did." Violet took my hand in hers. "You're right. She's so tense. Her whole right side is one big knot."

"Yes, she is." He met my gaze.

"What does that even mean?" Acid burned at the pit of my stomach at the idea that Rex had talked to Violet about me and what he thought of my body.

"I'll explain everything in the morning." She patted my wrist and slid off her barstool. "I'll see you bright and early tomorrow."

"Yeah, okay." I watched her as she planted a kiss on Rex's cheek, and then, disappeared into the crowd.

"Are you ready to go?" Rex wrapped his arm around my waist and pulled me off the seat.

Heat rushed to my cheeks at the huge implication of his question. Was I ready for a session with him? Hell no. But also, I didn't want to stay here and risk running into another one of his friends. How many ex-bottoms did he plan to bring in to teach me?

"I thought you said later." I wedged my hand between us, putting emphasis on the later part of my comment. I hoped my scowl reminded him of how much I despised him, how much I didn't want to be here with him, how much he was hurting me. "I think I want to stay. I mean, I would love to meet more of your girlfriends."

"I know what I said. But I can't wait any longer." He bent down and brushed his nose to mine. "And for the record, Vittoria and Violet are not my girlfriends, or ex-girlfriends for that matter. At least not in the sense your tone implied." He chuckled. "I'm sure Vittoria would get a kick out of that."

"I can't do this." I pressed my hand to my forehead, while my heart threatened to break my ribs. "Don't make me do this."

Rex wrapped his arms around me until he was supporting most of my weight. "Walk," he ordered as he ushered me through the crowd. Prada pumps and expensive Italian leather shoes whooshed in and out of my line of sight until they became a blur. I squeezed my eyes shut and focused on breathing or rather on the fact that I couldn't breathe. Before I knew it, we were back upstairs in Rex's penthouse. And I was all alone.

I crossed the threshold with his body close behind me. I turned around and held his gaze. His features relaxed as he reached for my cheek. Was that a smile? He had thought he had won, which technically he had, but did he have to be so smug about it?

"Rex." I snaked my hand inside his tuxedo jacket.

My fingers touched the cold handle of his gun, and I lost it. In a moment of pure insanity and a lame attempt to remain in control, I grabbed his weapon and aimed at his heart.

# CHAPTER 15
## Face the Mirror

Rex

"What do you plan to do with that?" I put my hands up in surrender.

My heart pumped hard with exasperation and desire. That was how Caterina made me feel all the goddamn time. Why did she refuse to listen to me? Trust me? Why couldn't I stop wanting her? There were literally a dozen women downstairs waiting for me to invite them up to my penthouse. My life would be so much easier if I could stop thinking about Caterina Alfera.

"Let me go. Now."

"You know I can't do that." I stalked toward her. "One, there's a target on your back. You wouldn't last a day out there. And two, your father hasn't paid his debt."

"I don't care." She gritted her teeth, treating me to one of her "I hate you" glares.

"You're not the first one to pull a gun on me. Or shoot me for that matter." I stepped into her personal space, and she pressed the barrel of my gun to my chest. "You don't want to kill me. I can see it in your beautiful green eyes."

"Rex." She backed away, still holding my firearm but with less conviction than before.

"This is about the rope session. You're afraid you might enjoy it."

She shook her head.

"You're afraid you might like me. You're afraid that maybe you don't hate me as much as you say." I ghosted her lips. A beat later, she melted into me, and I pressed on. "You're ready."

"Rex."

"Stop saying my name." Really, every time she uttered that one word, I felt my resolve fading and giving in to her.

She braced her hand on my pecs, pushing me away but also digging her nails in. I bet she was wet and ready for me. When I didn't bend down to kiss, her cheeks flushed a bright red. The disappointment in her eyes cut me. It disarmed me. She disarmed me.

*Fuck it.*

I crushed my mouth to hers. She opened slightly with a quiet moan and grazed her teeth over my bottom lip. The taste of wine on her tongue sent me on a downward spiral. My thigh rubbed against her core as I walked her backward, slowly, until the sofa cut us off. Caging her with my body, I gripped her wrist and peeled the gun from her fingers.

"I need you," I whispered and deepened the kiss. "You need me too. Don't lie."

In my mind, I had already turned her around and undone her dress. I had kissed her mouth and neck until she begged me to fuck her hard. If she asked me, if she said those two little words...fuck me...I knew I wouldn't be able to say no. Jesus Christ, I had to get her upstairs before all my plans went to hell.

I pulled away, panting to catch my breath. "There's a change of clothes waiting for you in your suite. You have ten minutes. Leave your hair the way it is." It physically hurt to step back and drop my hands to my sides. "Go."

"You're such a jerk." She snatched the skirt of her gown from between my legs and darted to the grand staircase.

I stood there filled with anticipation as she disappeared in the hallway beyond the landing. Savoring the moment, I followed her. This had always been our dance. Ever since we reconnected after I came back from college. The push and pull of her feelings toward me were maddening.

She wanted me. That much I knew. But her instincts told her any kind of relationship with me would be bad for her. She wasn't wrong. All that was about to change. Because now, I had a way to communicate with her. Really speak to her outside of what our lives were supposed to be—outside of our obligation to the Society.

I shortened my gait in front of her door. The flutters in my chest threatened to spin out of control. So much was riding on this first session. If I could get Caterina to understand this new language, we might stand a chance. Smiling, I rushed to my own bedroom next door to hers and quickly removed my tuxedo, shoes, and socks. I donned a pair of grey sweats and nothing else, then paced the length of the room while I waited another minute to go see her.

At exactly ten minutes, I rapped on her door. This time, she didn't make me wait like before. She had finally understood that all the petty tantrums in the world could not change my plans for her. Not tonight. *Not ever.*

She stood at the threshold, proud and incredibly sexy in those tight, black yoga shorts and cami. Her cheeks blushed a pretty red. And in that moment, I decided we would start with a champagne, rose color rope to match her sun-kissed skin.

"We're not going far." I motioned toward the door across the hallway.

"I didn't think we would." She ogled me, blinking fast several times. "I'd never seen you this casual."

"I'm dressed for the occasion." I beamed at her.

"Can we just get this over with?" She side-stepped me to make sure she didn't touch me.

"What happened? First you want to leave. Now you're in a hurry to get tied up?"

She stopped in front of the rope room. "You enjoy the chase. I decided not to give you that anymore. Do your worst."

I dug a gold key out of my pocket and slipped it into the lock. When the door swung open, she knitted her brows at me.

"I think you made up a whole story in your head about what rope sessions are. Are you disappointed?" I ushered her into the mostly bare suite.

"No bed?"

"We won't need it." I sauntered to the side wall where I kept bundles of coiled rope and grabbed the pale rose one. I took my time to give her time to explore the room.

"Is that Central Park?" She walked to the tall windows, rubbing her arm.

"Yes." I inhaled the sweetgrass scented air and stood on the yoga mat positioned in front of the floor-length framed mirror. "Get on your knees."

She spun around, pursing her lips. "Yes sir." She rolled her eyes. "Is that what I'm supposed to call you?"

"Rex is fine."

"I thought you didn't like me using your name." Her bare feet slapped on the warm hardwood floors as she ambled toward me.

"I'm in control in this room. And starting now, you will only speak when I ask you a direct question. On your knees." I gestured toward the mat.

Her gaze shifted to the floor. After a few erratic breaths, she kneeled facing me. Under the soft flickers of the chandelier, her skin shimmered like the city lights beyond the windows. She was such a distraction. I had to call on my extensive training to control my breathing and focus on our session.

I fisted her hair at the nape of her neck and pulled gently to make her meet my eyes. Yeah, the fire and the hate were still there. "Face the mirror."

When she shifted her body, I dropped to my knees and cuddled her from behind, watching her reaction across the way. Her chest rose and fell as she waited for my next move. I sat on my ankles and pulled on her waist to gently invite her to do the same. She obeyed with a big exhale, as if she had been afraid we would explode if our bare skin touched.

Her smooth skin on my chest was everything I thought it would be. Normally, at this point of the session, I would ask my partner to close her eyes and focus on her breathing. But I couldn't do that just yet with Caterina. I craved for her to look at me in this setting. I needed to see that she wasn't scared of me, and what I was. She knew I was a mobster, a beast in a world of criminals. And in a way, she understood I had to be this way.

But rope practice was a completely different matter because she didn't know how I had ended up here—why kinbaku had become integral to my survival.

I dug into my pocket and removed my phone, a pair of rope shears, and an hourglass timer. When I glanced up at her reflection, her eyes were big, and she had stopped breathing.

"These items—" I slid everything to the top of the mat, away from us but still within reach, "—are for your safety. Our hour starts now. You move when I move you and you breathe when I say, how I say. Let me do the thinking for you. Whatever is waiting for you outside this room, it'll be there when you wake up. Do you understand? Yes or no."

She met my gaze in the mirror, then glanced down at the jute snaking down her leg. I pressed on her hip, and her lips parted, but no words came out. We sat at a standoff for a few beats before she finally conceded.

"Yes." She let her side rest on my forearm, melting into me, all smooth skin and soft heartbeats.

That was it.

I had her.

She was mine.

Placing my palm across her clavicle, I flipped the hourglass with my free hand. "Take a deep breath and hold it. Keep it there."

When she released a bit of air, I held her tighter and let the tail ends of the rope fall on her bare thighs again, a little forceful this time.

"Exhale and close your eyes."

My hand trembled in anticipation as I held her wrists and quickly did a single-column bind on them. While I used my whole body to keep her contained, I brought her hands together against her sternum. "Match your inhales to mine."

Her head lulled to the side and rested on the curve of my neck and shoulder. I filled my lungs with air, and she did the same. That was my cue to add more intensity to our session. Using my whole body to box her in, I wound the rope around her body twice, tight and fast. I knotted the jute at the center of her back and used the remaining rope to add her foot to the bind. All the while, I varied the rhythm like a dance—quick, quick, slow, quick, quick, slow—to keep her guessing, to keep her mind on me and no one else—not Michael, her brothers, or her dead mother—just me.

In this moment, I was the only one who existed in her world. A surge of adrenaline washed over me. Having this much control over Caterina Alfera made me feel like I could take over the world. All my worries, all the people dying around me, all the chaos was muted and minimized by this power spiraling through me.

All my fantasies of Caterina in this very pose paled in comparison to the real thing. Her body heat and the scent of her arousal were something I hadn't considered. My heartbeat spiked as desire unfurled below my navel. I had to use all my training to reel it in and calm the fuck down.

I gripped her French braid, nudging my arm along her spine to push her away from me. The cold air that brushed between us helped me regain control. She was a vision in this pose, her neck long and silky, her chest heaving, and brows furrowed. She leaned back, looking for my body heat, but I held her in place, wedging my elbow into the middle of her spine. I wanted her to experience this sensation on her own.

The bind of the jute on her skin combined with the stretch

was a delicious kind of pain that I knew she would enjoy. Even if she refused to admit it, Caterina and I were so much alike. She needed this as much as I did. Her whole body screamed exactly that.

I flipped the rope over her shoulder and ran it just below her jaw. Pressing my lips to her skin, I exhaled a hot breath on her cheek. When she breathed exactly like me, I released the cord off her throat. The fact that she didn't flinch with the slight choke of the bind meant she trusted me completely.

Jesus fuck, now that I had her surrender, I wanted more of her. I wanted to bury my cock deep inside her and show her all the things we could have together. I wanted to make her come while she said my name over and over. I moved her head to the side and ghosted her lips. She squeezed her legs together, mouthing, "Rex."

"I'm right here." I wrapped one arm around her, unraveled the rope, and let it cascade around her. "I've always been here...Wake up," I whispered in her ear.

Her eyes flew open. When she met my gaze in the mirror, she blinked a few times, then shot a glance toward the hourglass. Our time was up, and it had been everything I thought it would be with her. Now I had no doubt she was my queen. Even though we were thrown together by circumstance, we were always meant for each other. The biggest question now was—did she agree?

She shifted her body away from me and turned to face me. Even though she was free to go, she remained on her knees with her hands planted firmly on the floor as if she were afraid that if she let go, she would fall. Her eyes watered and slowly filled up with the usual anger and hate. If she had shot me downstairs with my own gun, it would've been less painful.

"You can go." I stood with my arms crossed tight over my chest.

She opened her mouth to speak but no words came out. Instead, she glowered at me with a slight tremble to her lip. I could see she had a million things going through her mind. No doubt half of those were insults she wanted to hurl my way.

"Breathe, Caterina." I reached for her, but she recoiled away from me.

"I hate you." She scrambled to her feet and ran out of the room.

I raked a hand through my hair and stared at the door. A part of me wanted to chase after her, but what good would it do? She had seen the real me and now there was no going back. Maybe I was wrong, and Caterina didn't have the ability to put her hate aside. All this time, I thought I could change her mind. I thought I could make her face her feelings and see we could make something whole out of our broken pieces.

How could I have been so wrong about her?

# CHAPTER 16
## *His Heart Doesn't Work That Way*

CATERINA

So that was his fucking plan? Make me want him only to show me how much he didn't want me back? I slammed the door shut behind me, relieved that he wasn't following me, that he was done torturing me for the night. I stomped to the middle of the room, facing the city lights.

Wait. What? I hugged my waist. When had I decided I wanted sex with Rex? Anger bubbled in the pit of my stomach. From the moment he said he wanted my surrender, when he kissed me, when he held my hand, he had planted that seed. But he never had any intention to go through with it and put out this fire burning in my core.

I sat on the bed, not bothering with the lights. A small shiver went through me, and slowly the hour I had spent with Rex came rushing back. The sultry music and his touch were tattooed on my skin now. It'd been hypnotic the way he moved me and made me feel complete, lighter, and without a care in the world. I let myself fall on the mattress. As disappointed and hurt as I felt when he dismissed me like I was nothing, I didn't want the feeling to go away. I wanted his body close to mine. I wanted *him*.

There had been a point in the session when I thought he was going to fuck me right on that mat in that empty, dim-lit room. My clit throbbed so painfully. If I had not been tightly bound, I would have thrown myself at him and begged him to take me already. What was wrong with me? He was the reason Dad was in the hospital—why my family was ruined.

I rolled into a fetal position and slipped my hand inside my pants. Burying my face on the pillow, I moaned at the sweet relief. Tears streamed down my cheeks as I conceded to the fantasy brewing in my head—his wide chest and slim hips became a bright image in my mind. He was all smooth skin and hard muscle. Just like I had done in the rope room, I surrendered my body to Rex, letting the memories of him and everything he did to me flood my senses all over again. His hot breath brushed my neck and rushed to where my fingers moved in a circular motion around my folds.

"Rex." I called for him in defiance. He didn't like me saying his name. So, I said it over and over.

I imagined his intense gaze on my sex while he rubbed me near my aching bud, but not quite giving me what I wanted. I thought about how he would be cruel in bed like that. How he would make me want him until I felt like I was going to explode. How he would touch every inch of me like he did before and kiss me until he left me breathless. And then, just when I couldn't take any more of that sweet torture, I knew he would palm my sex and bring me to orgasm. I did exactly that. With rough strokes, I pleasured myself until I came.

The release was over quickly, like striking a match that gets put out almost immediately by a gust of wind. Argh. I screamed into my pillow in exasperation. How could Rex toy with me like this? And how was it that in spite of how cruel and dismissive he could be, I still wanted him. My tears left wet spots on the pillow. I wanted to flip it over, but I was too exhausted to move. Instead, I squeezed my eyes shut and yelped into it. *Go to sleep. Go to sleep.* I tried to lull myself to go to sleep.

"My beautiful Caterina." Rex's voice echoed in the dark room as the mattress dipped under his weight.

My body jolted awake or back to full awareness. I tried to twist my body to get away from him, but he held me tight.

"What do you want?" I hardly recognized my hoarse voice.

"I heard screams. I wanted to make sure you weren't hurt." His arms felt so good around me.

He smelled of incense, the same woodsy smell from the rope room, and his own manly musk. Did he hear me come? Had I really screamed loud enough for him to catch me saying his name? Heat washed over me, followed by cold sweat. Had he seen me too?

"You're not alone, Caterina."

If that were the case, I wouldn't be here. I clung to his body, gripped his T-shirt and buried my face in his chest. And now my humiliation was complete. He had my surrender. And he knew exactly how much I wanted him. My eyes fluttered closed, while he caressed my jaw and neck.

---

"WAKE UP, HUN." Violet's voice startled me awake.

What? I glanced down at the pillow where I was fisting the

sheets. Did Rex come to my room last night? Or did I dream the whole thing? I pressed a hand to my forehead. Jesus, the man was driving me crazy.

The bright sunlight seemed to be everywhere in the room, and it hurt my eyes. "What time is it?" I threw the covers over my head. Apparently at some point during the night, I had gotten under the bedding. Or did Rex tuck me in before he left?

"It's noon. Do you always sleep this late?" She set a tray of food on the side table. The coffee smelled amazing and made my belly rumble with hunger for the fluffy omelet on the plate.

"No, I actually never do." I reached for the mug and sipped. "Ah, thank you. What are you doing here?"

"Our body awareness session started two hours ago. You forgot, didn't you?" She plopped herself on the bed, beaming at me. "How was your first session?"

"Hmm...don't ask." My cheeks flushed at the way I had lusted over Rex last night. Heat rushed through me when I recalled that in my frenzy, I had masturbated to Rex, and that there was a huge possibility I had done it while he watched.

"That good." She laughed.

"Did you ever have sex with him?" I blurted out, then winced. "I'm sorry. That's none of my business."

"Once." She shrugged and slowly her smile faded. "It was a mistake. I got all confused and thought I was in love with him."

"What happened?" I grabbed the tray and started eating.

"Just that. One night he was at the Crucible. I went up to the VIP loft and begged him to take me. He did. But then told me we were done. He said he couldn't love me. Remember what I said in my letter? Enjoy your time with him, but understand love isn't on the menu. His heart doesn't work that way. He was honest about that since the beginning."

"Why are you here then? Doesn't it bother you to be around him?" My anger returned. How could Rex toy with her emotions that way?

"That was over two years ago. I'm over it. I was in a really dark place when he met me. I owe him my life. My time with Rex healed me. Shibari was a huge part of that. He's just a beautiful memory. Not to mention, I'm with someone new. He loves me and I love him. So no, it doesn't bother me to see him. I'm here because I love the idea of introducing a new bunny to the community. I told you. I was honored that he asked me to help you."

"Shibari?"

"Oh, it's just another term for erotic rope bondage." She picked up a strawberry off the tray and fed it to me. "Finish up and we'll get started."

I finished my breakfast and darted to the bathroom to shower and brush my teeth. As much as I didn't want to do the training session for Rex, Violet's energy was infectious. I was curious to learn what she had to teach me. In the walk-in closet, I found a change of clothes—a buttery soft bodysuit that was basically tight short, shorts and a halter-top.

"Who brings in these outfits?" I met Violet out on the terrace.

I had been in the suite several times now and hadn't noticed the outdoor space before. Violet regarded the sunny view while she sat on an outdoor chaise with white sand cushions. She smiled at me when I joined her. "Mary Anne. She's very sneaky that one." She winked.

"I bet." So Violet knew Rex's assistant whose sole job

appeared to be to take care of his bottoms. "Was this your bedroom?"

"What do you mean, hun?"

"Before when um..." I trailed off.

It felt wrong to say, "when you were his." I didn't like the lump that churned in my stomach when I pictured the two of them together. And then I pictured piles and piles of manila folders and all the women he had invited to his rope room, all the women he had cuddled and tied up the way he had done with me. My body temperature went up a few degrees while I imagined doing another session and going through all those sensations all over again. I shook my head to clear my thoughts and focus on Violet.

"Oh no, hun. I went home every day." She cocked her head to meet my eyes. "Rex is very protective of his privacy."

"He helped me find a place not too far from here. He also got me a job. A good job."

Rex had helped her. As much as I liked to paint him as the villain, Violet's words didn't feel at odds with the man I had come to know. I could see him doing all those things for her. "What kind of trouble were you in before?"

"You know the usual, sex, drugs." She glanced down at her hands, shaking her head. "He dismantled one of those brothels. You know what I mean?"

I nodded.

"I had been working there for a year when he found me. I watched him kill a man that day...my pimp, I guess is the word." Her head snapped up at me. "Rex was kind to me, though. Like I said, he saved me."

"I'm so sorry." I wrapped my arm around her. "I'm glad he found you."

"Me too. I've been sober for three years now." She beamed at me. "Are you ready to get started?"

"Sure. Where do you want me?"

"Right here." She patted the seat. "I'm going to map your shoulders. It'll help you figure out how to breathe and where to position your arms during the binds."

I let out a breath, rubbing my temple. "I still can't get used to that terminology. Normal people don't use those words on a daily basis. Certainly not right after breakfast."

"Just keep an open mind." She chuckled.

Getting used to the idea of being Rex's bottom wasn't the problem. The real issue was my body thinking that Rex was on the menu. Twice, Violet had warned me against this. Rex could've asked any of his past bottoms to help him out. I was sure he had chosen Violet because of her experience with him. I needed to listen to her and stop wanting him this way. I had to remember that the rope sessions were just a kink to him, a game with his new plaything.

I spent the rest of the day with Violet doing hip flexor stretches and talking like we were old girlfriends. She was beautiful and funny. Every time she would crack a joke that had me in stitches, I couldn't help but wonder why Rex couldn't fall in love with her.

A soft knock on the door sent a rush of adrenaline through my body. I hadn't seen Rex since last night. I wasn't sure how I was going to face him again. "Come in." I shifted my weight on the mattress with my heart drumming in my throat.

Mary Anne strolled in with the outfit du jour for me, and I sat back on the pillows like a deflated balloon.

"Mr. Valentino would like for you to join him for dinner

tonight." She lifted the dress to eye level before she arranged the items on the upholstered chair near the window.

The last time we saw each other, I had been nice to her but only so she would let down her guard. I hoped my little escape stunt that night didn't get her in trouble. "I'm sorry about before." I glanced over at Violet sitting on the bed next to me with her legs stretched out in front of her.

"You were scared." She smiled at me with kindness in her eyes and shrugged, as if Rex brought frightened girls to his penthouse all the time. "Dinner is in an hour."

"Dinner? Omigod. I didn't realize it was so late." Violet scrambled across the bed and jumped to her feet. "I have to go."

"Why don't you stay?" I met Violet halfway to the door as soon as Mary Anne disappeared into the bathroom. "I would love the company."

She laughed. "I wish I could stay, but I have to go. I'll see you tomorrow." She threw an arm around my neck. "Be kind to yourself." She waved a finger to my eyebrows. "Even now I can see you're overthinking everything. Rex is offering you a gift, an escape of sorts. Take it." She kissed my cheek and left.

Blowing out a breath, I collapsed on the bed. I wasn't ready to see Rex again or to be in his arms. I flipped onto my belly to take a look at the clothes Rex had sent. It was a backless sheath dress with spaghetti straps. It reminded me of the cocktail number I wore when I threw myself at Rex the first time. Anger and shame fluttered in my gut at the memory. That night I had convinced myself I was doing it to save Dad from jail. And yeah, that part was true. But I would be lying to myself if I didn't admit that I had also been turned on by the idea of having sex with Rex, the ruthless mafia king who hated Dad.

"I can help you get ready." Mary Anne stood by the foot of the bed.

"No, thank you." I let my bare feet drop to the plush area rug beneath the bed. "I won't be needing help. Please let Mr. Valentino know I will not be joining him for dinner. I'm not hungry."

Mary Anne's eyes went wide in surprise. "Are you sure you want me to say that?"

"I am."

"I'll let him know." She gave me a quick nod and walked out.

The suite felt too quiet and too empty when the door shut behind her. I curled up on the bed and thought of Dad all alone in a hospital bed. Had Massimo and Enzo responded to my messages? Where the hell were they? Dad needed them. I needed them. Hot tears stung my eyes.

"You need to eat." Rex's voice jerked me back to reality.

"I'm not hungry." I rolled off the bed so I could glower at him properly. "You let Violet go home." I cringed at the whiny tone in my voice.

"She didn't have a target on her back like you do. You're here for your own safety." He closed the space between us and effectively sucked all the oxygen out of my lungs. "You will join me for dinner."

"And if I don't?" I met his gaze.

"We'll have to find a way to work up your appetite." He ghosted his lips along my jaw. His hot breath seeped down into my sports bra and then my pants. And just like that, I was wet and ready for him. He snaked his arm around my waist and whispered in my ear. "You still owe me an hour for today."

A raw charge sparked at the apex of my sex, and I melted into him. "Rex." I gripped the front of his T-shirt, and then, I realized he was dressed in a pair of dark gray sweats and no shoes.

"I tried to stay away. I swear I did." He wedged his thigh in between mine and walked me backward. "You should've said yes to dinner instead."

Before my brain could figure out what he was doing, I was in the middle of the hallway waiting for him to unlock the door to the rope room.

# CHAPTER 17
## He's Not on The Menu

CATERINA

*He's not on the menu.*

I repeated it several times in my head until the ruckus in my chest settled down. Warmth seeped through my bare feet as I padded across the heated hardwood floors. Behind me, Rex shut the door and walked over to the rope wall. I rubbed my temples and tried not to overthink things. Yeah, the man had a rope wall. That was normal in his world because he was Rex Valentino and that meant he could do whatever he damn well pleased.

I ambled toward a chic armless chaise, upholstered in dark blue velvet. On the gold side table, a dish with two incense sticks fused the air with an earthy scent. Had this piece of furniture been here before? I ran my hand over the smooth fabric. It had to have been because it all felt familiar. Last night I had been too nervous and too angry to really absorb all the details, though the sweetgrass scent had stayed with me for hours—on my skin and in my hair.

I turned around, and my gaze zeroed in on the floor-length mirror. That part I hadn't missed. Heat flushed across my skin as memories of what I saw in there last night reeled through my mind. We were about to do it all over again.

When I faced Rex, he reached behind him and pulled on his T-shirt. The city lights illuminated every plane on his chest and abs. Jesus, the man had the body of an Adonis. And now I knew how hard his pecs were. I knew how well I fit in his arms.

"On your knees." His commanding tone sent rays of want through me.

I closed the space between us. Something about being in a semi-dark room emboldened me. "What do you get out of this? I get it's a control thing for you. But if you plan on doing this to me for the next six months, you have to know how this makes me feel. Or is that it? You get your kicks by getting women to want you just so you can reject them?"

"Go on." He gestured toward the thick mat, ignoring my question.

In this room, his intense blue eyes were more serene and bright. He was in control of his emotions and my body. I hated that he could make me squirm with desire, while he remained unaffected by all of it.

"I forgot. No talking." I dropped to my knees.

"That's right."

The sequence of his movements was the same as last night. He kneeled behind me, then removed his phone, the hourglass, and a pair of shears from the pocket of his sweatpants and placed them on top of the mat. The soft hair on his chest bristled across my back. I softened my body, molding myself to him—my head and hips and legs, they gently nestled into his space. Whatever happened an hour from now or in six months, I didn't care. I craved to feel alive again.

In the next beat, a slow piano tune began to play, and suddenly I was aware of his hands on my shoulders softly kneading and applying pressure below my shoulder blades. "Take a deep breath and hold it." His lips brushed the soft spot behind my ear and then went on. "Your skin is so soft, like velvet."

A slight burn gripped my chest, but I didn't dare let go of my breath. Not until he told me to.

"What do I get out of this? I get you, Caterina. All of you." He wrapped his arms around me and then guided my legs to crisscross in front of me as if I were his doll.

I supposed at this point in the session, I was his doll, his rope bottom, just his.

"Empty out your lungs...slowly...sweetly."

We did a few more rounds of breathing until it felt natural that our inhales and exhales kept the same rhythm. The tempo of the song increased, and a woman quietly sang in Italian. It was too fast for me to understand, but she sounded lonely. Rex snapped the coiled rope and let it fall on my leg. The hard feel of the jute on my thigh effectively stopped my mind from wandering off.

"Let me do the thinking for you." He brought my hands behind my back until my wrists crossed right in the middle. "Close your eyes."

The feel of the polished rope on my skin, the sound of it hitting the mat combined with the vibrations of it against my torso as he pulled the line through was a sensation like no other. And that was all my body and mind needed to surrender to Rex's wicked game. I watched in the mirror as he carefully wrapped the jute around my chest, then leaned into me while he kept his gaze glued to mine. He commanded the attention of all my senses in a way that was so erotic to me and a huge turn on.

He continued working on the tie, using a single hand to knot a second rope to the one he had going. Violet had given me instruction on a few simple harnesses. Rex had decided to do a box tie or takate kote tonight. I knew what was coming.

By the time he was ready, my shorts were drenched with want and anticipation. He paused for a breath, then firmly cupped my breast to secure the rope where he wanted it. A raw charge sparked at my core in response. His large hands fit perfectly around each mound as he repeated the process twice more. When he finished, my heart thrashed in my ears.

"Rex."

The name had become synonymous with "Please, I want you." Tears stung my eyes with frustration. But that didn't stop me from letting my mind wander to the place where Violet had warned me not to go.

"I know." With rough tugs and pulls, he secured the rope behind me. The stretch felt good on my arms, but the part that enclosed my breasts was agony. I wanted more than the pressure. I wanted his hands on me again. Instead of giving me what I needed, he yanked until my whole torso rested on his thighs and my tits were practically on display for him.

My aching nipples begged for his touch. If the smirk that played on his lips was any indication, he knew exactly how he affected me. "The scent of your arousal has become a drug to me." He snaked more cord in front of me, right over my taut peaks and then between my legs. "Why is it that with you, things never turn out the way I planned them?"

"Maybe because you made me come here. You made me your prisoner just to hurt me and..." I meant to say Dad. But in truth, he had no clue what I was going through, or all the things Rex had made me do to settle his debt. This thing was only between Rex and me. It was about us and no one else.

"And are you in pain right now?" He gripped my bound wrists and did another loop over my throbbing pussy.

When I realized I was so close to coming, a wave of heat rushed through me. It was a mix of shame and unadulterated desire.

"Answer."

"No." I panted a breath. "Please." I wanted to buck my hips toward his hand, but the position I was in made it so only he could move me. He decided how much sensation to give me and how much to take away. "Rex."

"I'm right here. And I'm not going anywhere." He rose to his knees and brought me up with him to face the mirror. I gasped and shut my eyes. I didn't want to see what I had become in his hands. "I want to see your green eyes when you climax. It'll be a nice change of pace from the usual hate they spew my way every time I get near you."

I shook my head. Everything with Rex had a price. The price of my release right now was my humiliation. He wanted me to watch him while he made me come. My clit screamed at me to say yes. Just this one time. Who cared if Rex won this round? Wasn't that always the case with him anyway? He always got what he wanted. It was why I was here, forty-five floors over Manhattan, literally trapped in an ivory tower.

"Open your eyes," he whispered. His hot breath scurried down my arm and made my sex pulse a little harder.

The woman in the mirror wasn't me. I didn't recognize the

wild look in her gaze or the messy waves cascading over her shoulders. My rib cage expanded with a rugged breath and made the tie rub over my nipples. I did it again to soothe me, and then again. It was a small act of defiance to sit here and pleasure myself when Rex refused to.

"What do you want me to do?" I asked when he didn't move.

"Just look at me."

I did. At this point I was so turned on and hot for him, it only took three strokes before my core exploded into a bouquet of hot waves that ravished every part of me. And it was like nothing I had ever felt. He continued to work me until every last bit of my orgasm was spent. The whole time, his gaze stayed locked onto mine. My bright eyes in the mirror betrayed me, offering him a glance of gratitude. I collapsed backward on his chest while tiny convulsions gripped my pussy and shot up into my breasts. Just then, Rex pulled at the rope around my wrists and the entire harness unraveled over my shoulders. For a second, an odd panic washed over me as I recalled Violet's words when I asked her if she'd had sex with Rex.

*"His Heart Doesn't Work That Way"*

I scrambled to my knees and turned to face him. Being this far from him hurt. The room was suddenly too cold and too empty. Would he leave now? Or tell me he was done with me? My eyes watered at the realization that I wanted Rex with me, that if he left now my heart would break in two.

"You're so fucking perfect." He cradled my cheek and crushed his mouth to mine.

He kissed me hard and desperately while I ran my hands over his chest and into his soft hair. Without asking or easing into it, he thrust his tongue past my lips, tasting me and egging me to do the same. I took what he offered because I knew it wouldn't last. Per his rules, this arrangement was over.

His skin smelled of incense and mint. I wanted all of him, but in the back of my mind, I steeled myself for what I was sure would come next. The hourglass was empty, and our time was up. He pulled away first and flashed me a knowing smile that made me want to slap him and then kiss him again.

"What happens now?" I pulled the collapsed harness over my head. After he had sex with Violet, he sent her away right after. Or at least, I imagined that was how it had happened since she didn't exactly elaborate. She did say, they only had done it once. "Is your little experiment over? Violet told me what happened with her."

"I figured she might." He rose to his feet. I supposed he wanted to hover over me so he could throw me out properly.

"I went too far." I licked my lips. Certainly, Rex watching me come on his rope counted as sex. I stood, though my stance didn't have the strength I had hoped for. For one, I had been tied down for almost an hour. And two, my clit was overly sensitive, like it expected another round—or two. I ran a hand through my hair to clear my thoughts. "I broke your rule."

He chuckled, rubbing the stubble on his cheek. "My little virgin. If you thought that was sex, you have much to learn." He stalked closer to me. "When you and I have sex, you won't have a single doubt that we indeed had sex. Now that you're here, I'm not letting you go. When are you going to understand that?"

When? Why did it seem like he had said sex a hundred times?

"Stop saying that word." I made to leave, but he gripped

my elbow. I should've known he'd use his no-sex rule to play yet another mind game with me.

"Wait." He glanced up and released a breath. "We're getting side-tracked again. I thought the orgasm might put you in a better mood."

"I wasn't...I don't need you doing me any favors. I can manage on my own just fine." I shoved him out of the way. I didn't need to be pacified.

"Oh? Is that so?"

"You're an asshole." I strode out of the room.

After being in a dim-lit room for so long, the lights in the hallway hurt my eyes. I blinked fast and didn't stop until I was safe in my room. Of course, Rex followed me there too.

"For the record." He slammed the door behind him. "All I wanted tonight was a dinner. But you threw my kind invitation back in my face."

"What?" I braced my hands on my hips. "That wasn't even remotely close to an invitation. It was a rude command. You can't just snap your fingers and expect people to do your bidding."

He shrugged and slowly folded his arms over his chest. Because of course, in his world, all he had to do was wave a hand and things would happen exactly as he said.

"Point taken." He stepped toward me. "Can we start over? I need to talk to you. Jesus Christ, we can't even have a civilized conversation. I've never had to deal with this."

I sat on the bed, feeling drained. The good news was Rex just wanted to talk. He wasn't throwing me out. Wait. What? I dropped my head into my hands. No, the good news would be me going home and taking care of Dad. Or, at the very least, I should be looking for my brothers. They were in danger too.

The mattress dipped, and the warmth of his body enclosed me like a cocoon. "Have dinner with me. Please."

"What do you want from me?"

There was enough ceremony in the rope room that I could pretend I was someone else—someone who lusted over a mafia king, someone who sold six months of her life to save her dad. I told myself that the woman in the mirror wasn't me at all. But sharing a meal and conversation was a different matter. I turned to meet his impossibly blue eyes. Rex and I were not friends.

"There are many things I want from you. But for tonight, I'd like to talk about what Michael asked us to do. I trust you haven't forgotten."

I shot to my feet. "You mean find Massimo and Enzo."

"Yes."

"You know where they are?"

"Yes and no." He reached for my hand and pulled me toward him. "I've been keeping tabs on them. But they're smart. They don't want to be found. I think if we tried, we would make a good team."

"Why in the world did you not lead with that an hour ago?" I glanced down at his fingers playing with mine.

"Probably for the same reason you couldn't agree to a simple meal with me." A smirk pulled at his lips. "Are you ready to do that now?"

"You're intolerable."

"I'll take that as a yes. Be ready in half an hour." He sauntered out of the suite, leaving me utterly confused about our arrangement, the non-sex we had, and now this idea that we could work together to find my brothers.

# CHAPTER 18
## No Rest for The Wicked

REX

I shut the door behind me and collapsed against the wall. Caterina Alfera was going to be death of me. How could she pull my strings like that? The more important question was how the fuck was I going to keep my hands off her while we worked together to find her brothers. As much as I wanted her, sex between us could get complicated. And I wasn't ready for that.

I sauntered to my suite next door and headed straight for the shower. Though it would take more than a good scrub to get Caterina's scent off of me. She wasn't wrong when she said we had gone too far. If this had been a session with any of my other partners, I would've ended the relationship. Sex wasn't what I needed from those hours. I needed the escape and the sense that I had control. Even if most of it was contrived, it still worked for me. *It kept me sane.*

But with Caterina, I was afraid the line between desire and rope practice had gotten blurred since she dropped her dress in the boardroom and offered herself to me. I had watched her become the woman she was now for over two years, since before her mother died.

In that time, I had developed feelings for her that up until now I was sure they would dissipate with six months of her in my penthouse. But the more I had of her, the more I wanted her. This was exactly the opposite of what I had promised her mom. I had truly made a mess of things.

I ran the cold water and stepped in. But after a few minutes, the spray did nothing to cool my desire. No matter how hard I tried, my mind played Caterina's spectacular climax on repeat. The raspy tone of her voice when she said my name made me rock hard all over again.

Bracing a hand on the marble tile, I considered my options, which were few. Since Michael had come to see me for help, I had not been able to stop thinking about Caterina and the very real possibility that she would come to live with me. That added up to one thing—I couldn't see myself fucking anyone but her.

I gripped my erection and tugged at the tip. It was either this or barge into Caterina's room and throw our contract out the window. I smiled and stroked a few more times. Knowing that she wouldn't say no to sex with me made my cock steel even more. Jesus fuck, the woman was a beautiful contradiction. I pictured her long neck as she lay on my thigh, panting from want. Her perfect tits had looked so proud bound in layers of jute while she begged for release.

"Caterina."

I pumped harder. As my heart increased the drumming in my chest, I let my brain add the final, and most perfect detail—my name on her lips over and over, while she rubbed her pretty pussy alone in her bed. I shot off onto the wall as an orgasm ripped through me. Stroking a few more times, I waited until the last wave of pleasure wore off and Caterina's green eyes faded into the background of my mind.

"Fuck me," I muttered and finished washing off.

Now that I didn't feel so on edge, I could focus on what I had to do tonight. I needed to find Massimo and Enzo, but for that, I needed to earn Caterina's trust. That whole shitshow from before was proof that neither one of us knew how to communicate with the other. Every time we spoke, it was like a damn game of Chinese whispers.

Smiling at the idiot in the tall vanity mirror, I donned the navy suit I had planned to wear to our dinner before Mary Anne delivered the news that Caterina wasn't joining me. Maybe now that we had both gotten a sort of release, our conversation would go a lot smoother. Highly unlikely, but I had to try. I headed out of the room and straight to her suite. I knocked once. And to my shock, she opened the door immediately, brows knitted.

"I come in peace." I put up my hands in surrender.

"I seriously doubt that." She glanced down at her sheath dress and Prada pumps.

So what if it resembled the hot number she wore the day she came to make a deal with me? Why would that upset her? Probably because everything I did revved her the wrong way.

"You look beautiful." I smiled and then I remembered. Shit.

I purposely did not include under garments for her tonight. Not that I had planned anything. I simply wanted to see her reaction. I wanted her to think of her bare pussy during dinner. I wanted her to think of me. But that was before we called a truce of sorts. Or rather, before I realized I needed to call for one.

"Are you ready?" I motioned toward the landing. "We're eating in."

Lips pursed, she sauntered in front of me. I caught up to her with a couple of long strides and placed my hand on her lower back. Her eyes went up in surprise when I ushered her toward the elevator bay, but other than that, she didn't object, as if she was trying extremely hard not to pick a fight with me.

I had no misplaced illusions that she was doing it for me. To Caterina, family was everything. She was here because she wanted to find her brothers. She was here because she promised Michael.

We rode the elevator car in silence to the rooftop. The city lights were the perfect backdrop for a date with Caterina. If this was such a thing, of course.

"It's beautiful up here." She strolled to the large table set up in the middle of the roof garden.

"Yeah. I had forgotten about that. I don't come up often." This place had been Mom's oasis. "I thought you might enjoy the fresh air." I pulled up the chair next to mine.

"You know it's like almost midnight? Do you ever sleep? Or keep normal business hours?" She blurted out as soon as her heart-shaped ass touched the seat. When her skirt rode up her leg, she froze. No doubt she had remembered she wasn't wearing underwear. Her legs pressed together, and my cock twitched. If that wasn't the definition of irony, I didn't know what would be.

"No rest for the wicked, I guess." I cleared my throat and moved to my seat. "We have work to do."

"So, what's the plan to find my brothers? That's why we're here, right?"

"It is." I waved toward the door to get Mary Anne's attention.

She darted toward us and placed a set of manila folders between us. "Dinner is on the way as well, sir."

"Thank you. We can take it from here."

As soon as she was out of earshot, I flipped open the file and turned it so Caterina could read it. While she busied herself catching up on every piece of information I had collected on her brothers since her mom passed away, the chef came in with our covered plates. I had wanted to keep the meal simple, the way I ate every night.

"Mangia benne." He removed the cover and took off.

"Thank you." Caterina stared at the pan seared Bronzino and roasted vegetables. "I thought you ate caviar and washed it down with the blood of your enemies?"

"That sounds like a recipe for indigestion." I sat back to meet her eyes. "I'm not the beast you think I am."

"No? Just a run of the mill health nut? Huh?" She chuckled, shaking her head at the work of art the chef had prepared for us.

"Ramen noodle packs are not good for you." I motioned for her to eat.

"I love Ramen. Don't knock it 'til you try it. Wait. Is that in my file?" She cocked her head. "You know what? Don't answer that."

"It is." I poured wine into her glass. "You should really cut back on sodium and junk food."

"You should really mind your own business." She inhaled deeply over her meal as she placed a napkin on her lap. "This is my favorite." She took a forkful of the fish, then moaned. "Except better."

"She approves." I took a long sip from my glass. "So, what do you think? I lost track of both your brothers about a month ago. Where should I look next? I let it go before because I hadn't confirmed the FBI was a real threat to us. But now every minute they spend out of my reach, where I can't protect them, they're sitting ducks."

"I can't believe this is happening. Isn't the job of the FBI to put you in jail and call for a fair trial?"

"They like to think so. But this thing with the Society, it has always been sort of personal. I think it started with Dad and Michael. My grandfather used to tell me stories of a time when government officials would come to us for help. We used to maintain the peace out on the streets. We protected our own."

"I know. Dad used to tell me stories too." She offered me a genuine smile.

"We won't let them win. Whatever their reasons for coming after us, whether it's personal or they just want a shiny badge for catching a big whale, the end game is the same. They want us all dead. I can't let them do that."

"Why haven't they come after you?"

"I'm not sure." I shrugged. "They either don't know who I am, or they have something bigger planned. Jesus, I can't even say for sure this is the FBI's doing. I'm running blind here."

"All this killing doesn't make sense. Don't they have laws for that? Maybe an agent gone rogue?" She put down her fork and leaned forward. "If we find my brothers, maybe they can help."

"That's what I'm hoping for. We need a truce so we can combine our resources and figure this out."

The pressure on my chest lifted some. Caterina finally understood the kind of danger we were all in. With Michael's support, and now Vittoria's, we had a shot at getting the son of a bitch who dared come after the families.

We finished our dinner in silence. From the deep V between Caterina's brows, I could tell she was really trying to figure out where she could find her brothers. Her phone had led us nowhere. Even though she had texted them multiple times, they had been smart not to respond. I reached inside the pocket of my suit coat.

"You can have this back." I placed her mobile on the table. "We've added a few security protocols to it. You can use it to call Michael now."

"Thank you." She beamed at me then glanced down at the screen. After a while, her smile faded. No surprise there. Her brothers hadn't reached out. "They're ignoring me. Dad could've died."

"Do you know any of their friends in Ibiza? Anyone who could give us a clue where Massimo took off to? He was there for a long time then disappeared."

"Not really." She sucked in a breath with recognition in her eyes. "Your file didn't say anything about Enzo's yacht, the Lady Anna." Her gaze lowered to her glass. "He named it after Mom. Anyway, he keeps it at Port d'Eivissa."

"We checked with the port authorities, but they said they didn't know anything about them. But of course, Enzo could've paid them off to buy their silence." I grabbed my own phone and texted my security detail. I had sent a crew there a few weeks back to make contact. They should still be there.

Before we had no reason to believe the port authorities would lie to us. But now that we knew Enzo had a connection to the marina there, it would be easy to go back, offer enough motivation, and then ask the right questions. Was it as simple as that? Enzo and Massimo seemingly fell off the face of the Earth because they had been out to sea this whole time?

"If they sailed their boat somewhere near Ibiza, we'll find out soon." I reached for her hand, half-expecting for her to pull back. When she didn't, my heart skipped a beat. Jesus, my fingers itched to reach up her thigh. Would she let me rub her pussy again? *Fuck me.* I shook my head and grabbed the bottle of wine. "You should see the view from the other side. Come on."

When I pulled on her fingers, she stood and followed me to the seating area facing Central Park, which was a stunning sight this time of night. She ambled toward the cinderblock wall with her mouth slightly open.

"If I lived here, I would spend my days in this very spot."

"You're here for the next six months. The place is yours." I handed her a fresh glass of wine. "The roof garden belonged to my mother. Call it a peace offering."

"You've never mentioned her before." She took the globe and drank.

I pursed my lips and shook my head once, a silent request to leave it alone.

"What happens now?"

"We wait for news." I closed the space between us. It was getting harder and harder to keep my hands off her. Especially when she looked at me with so much awe in those gorgeous eyes. "What we do with our time is up to us."

"Rex."

My breath hitched. "Don't say my name unless you mean it." I wrapped my arms around her waist.

"What am I doing here?" She placed her hand inside my jacket, right over my heart.

"I thought the contract was very clear."

"You damn well know what I mean. Why the dinner? Why this view? Why am I here without underwear or a bra?"

"I don't know." I pressed my forehead to hers.

"You just like messing with me, don't you?" She molded her body to mine, pressing her sex on my thigh. The thin fabric of her dress was soaked through. "Admit it."

"I feel alive when I'm with you. When you shoot daggers at me, all I want to do is—"

My Goddamn phone decided to ring just then. It was probably for the best. I tapped on the screen. "You got something, Frank?"

"I do, boss."

I met Caterina's gaze, and she stood at attention. She knew this was about her brothers. Knowing I would probably regret it later, I put the call on speakerphone. "Go ahead."

"Massimo spent the last month on his brother's yacht. But he took a jet back to the States this morning."

"He's coming to New York." Caterina covered her mouth.

"No, he's not. He's headed for Atlanta."

"Atlanta?" We asked in unison. "What the fuck is in Atlanta?"

"Dunno. You need me to set up a team, boss?"

"Yes. We leave in the morning." I hung up the phone and glanced up at Caterina.

Her eyes were wet with tears. Suddenly, she didn't look so defeated as before when she had come to me to save her dad.

Having a brother in town could really throw a wrench in all the plans I had for her.

Caterina had signed a non-disclosure agreement, so I was certain she wouldn't divulge the particulars of our arrangement. The problem was her brothers hated me as much as she did. If they found out she was living with me, they might start a war, which was the last thing I needed with the Feds riding our asses.

So, the one-million-dollar question was—how in the hell was I going to save the Alfera brothers from getting slaughtered, and at the same time, keep Caterina with me? The click clacks of her pumps caught my attention. She was leaving.

"Where are you going?" I darted toward her and gripped her elbow before she reached the elevator.

"To get my things." She yanked at her arm.

"Why?" I towered over her. And just like that, we were back to square one.

"Because I'm coming with you."

"Absolutely not."

# CHAPTER 19
## My Little Virgin

CATERINA

"You don't get to tell me that I can't go." I stepped back. Not because I was afraid of Rex, but because I needed space, distance to think clearly. "You asked for my help. Remember?"

"I know."

"If it hadn't been for me, you never would've thought to go back to Ibiza and dig deeper."

"I know that too." His shoulders relaxed. "You're so stubborn."

The deep, velvety tone of his voice lulled my senses. When he reached for my cheek, getting away from him didn't even occur to me. This entire day had been surreal. I had spent the better part of it learning about Kinbaku. Then because my life was this side of crazy, I let him tie me up and get me off. The memory of that orgasm washed over me as he skimmed a hand down my lower back. At first, shame flickered in my belly, but then it turned into something else, something like yearning and desire all meshed together.

"I appreciate the help. But we don't know why Massimo is going to Atlanta. We don't know if he's alone or with someone else. We don't know if he's being chased." He brought me closer to him. "The only thing we know for sure is that we're flying blind. I don't want you in the middle of all that. It's too dangerous."

"I get that." I wedged my hand between us. "But you brought me into this, this mafia world of yours. You can't keep me tucked away. It doesn't work that way."

He tilted my chin up to meet my gaze. At first, I thought he was going to kiss me again. The stubborn part of me immediately decided to let him. But when he didn't move, I realized he was trying to sort it all out. Did Rex care about me? He cared what I thought? About my safety?

"I suppose it comes down to this." I inched closer to him. "How badly do you want to find my brother? If he finds out I'm with you, he'll think twice about running off again."

That was a long shot because, technically, Massimo had already left me when I needed him the most. In the last two years, he never reached out to me, not even to see if the pain of losing Mom had killed me already. My eyes watered like they always did when I thought of my broken family. I braced myself for the avalanche of emotions that tended to follow—the sorrow, the self-pity, and all the regret. But Rex held me tighter. He didn't move or try to tell me some cliché line, like time heals all wounds. We both knew it didn't.

"I know it hurts," he whispered after a long while.

"Let me come with you. I promise I'll do anything you say."

He hissed and buried his nose in my hair. "Now that's something I'd like to see happen at least once before I die."

"Is that a yes? You're letting me join your team?" I beamed at him. "Operation: Get Massimo?"

"Yes, I think you're right. Massimo might hear me out, if you're with me." He bent down and pressed his lips to mine.

The act felt so intimate and normal, as if we were a couple, which we weren't. We were just two people playing rope, and now playing detectives.

"Did it ever occur to you that you could, I don't know, call the police?" I meant it as a cute joke. But Rex didn't laugh. Instead, he dropped his hands away from me, knitting his brows.

"If I thought they could help, I would. But the incident with Michael has me questioning everything. For now, we can only trust our own." He glanced down at my dress. "You should get some rest. Tomorrow is going to be a long day."

"Yeah, I should go pack." I started toward the elevator, then stopped to face him. "I have nothing to pack."

He smirked, and I had to bite my tongue not to lash out. After all, he had agreed to let me go with him. He reached into his coat and pulled out his phone. "Mary Anne, Ms. Alfera and I are traveling tomorrow. Could you pack two bags?" He listened to her response, then continued, "Yes, that'll do."

"Thanks." I rolled my eyes. "One day you'll have to tell me what this whole clothes thing is about."

"Yes, I suppose, one day I'll have to." He motioned toward the elevator. "I'll walk you back to your room."

"That won't be necessary."

"No, but it's what I want to do."

His gaze was so full of indecent promises and really bad ideas. I broke away first and headed out. He stayed silent as we rode the car back downstairs and then strolled up the grand staircase. I imagined this was what a date night would be with Rex—stunning views, expensive wine, and dinner with a side of *mobstering*. I had no doubt in my mind that because of me someone thousands of miles away, in Ibiza, got a good beating for lying. And then another round so he would tell the truth about my brother. How was I ever going to date regular men after meeting someone like Rex? And more importantly, why was I not scared out of my wits right now?

We stopped at my door and he pushed it open for me. "Good night, Caterina."

"Good night." I stepped away from him, and he gripped my upper arm.

"No matter what happens tomorrow, I need you to remember our agreement because I have zero intention of letting you go. Your brothers be damned."

"Good night, Rex." I pulled my arm away and shut the door in his face.

What the hell did that mean? That I wasn't allowed to tell my brothers about the contract I signed? I already knew that. For one, I didn't want to break our deal and watch Dad go to jail. But more than anything, I didn't want Enzo and Massimo to know how far Dad had spiraled downward since Mom died. Dad would probably have another heart attack out of shame if my brothers found out about his gambling addiction. Michael Alfera was a proud man. Dad would hate for his sons to see this weaker side of him.

I ambled toward the bed, where Mary Anne had laid out a set of pajamas, underwear included. Shaking my head, I donned the fresh clothes and climbed into bed. Tomorrow, my brother was coming home.

Hours later, I woke up with a startle. I sat up and listened for sounds in the dark room. My phone said it was five in the morning. With my heart beating fast, I threw the covers off me. As soon as my feet hit the floor, Mary Anne stepped out of the ensuite bathroom.

"Jesus, you scared the hell out of me." I pressed a cold hand to my forehead. "Do you ever sleep? What in the world?"

"I'm sorry. Mr. Valentino asked me to make sure you were ready for your trip." She pointed toward the steamy room behind her. "Your bath is ready. I can wait and do your hair."

"Our trip?" Between the scare and my sleepy brain, her words hadn't fully registered. "Omigod, we're flying soon?"

"Yes." She put up her hands. "You have an hour. No rush. All your things are packed and loaded in the car."

I rubbed my face with both hands. My things? What things? "You don't have to stay. I can manage. A bath actually sounds like a good idea. Thanks." I padded to the bathroom and shut the door.

While I got ready, Mary Anne had come in with breakfast. She stood there until I finished the fruit and scrambled eggs—Rex's orders. She then proceeded to rush me into a mini dress with a side long sleeve. The powder blue georgette fabric was soft and very flattering on me, which was a good thing since I didn't have underwear to wear with it.

Just as Rex had said, we pulled out of his private garage exactly an hour later.

Jesus, if it wasn't for the fact that Massimo was waiting for me on the other side of this flight, I would be so annoyed to be hurried like this. It wasn't like we were late to catch a flight. We were flying Rex's Gulfstream. The whole ride to La Guardia, Rex stayed on his phone giving instructions to the different crews. He had stayed in touch with the men in Ibiza.

And now he had people in Atlanta. Did he sleep at all last night? Not that it showed. He looked as he always did—in control, powerful, hot. His wet hair and body wash scent stirred butterflies in my stomach.

He hadn't looked at me at all since we left the penthouse. For some stupid reason, that hurt my feelings. I had gotten so used to his attention and the way he ogled me. Yeah, it was crude and disrespectful. So why the hell was I missing it today? When did I become so addicted to his touch and his ministrations?

As soon as we pulled into the hangar, Rex climbed out and walked around the car to escort me to the plane. He ushered me to the big leather seat in the first row and bent over to help me with the buckle. For the first time this morning, his gaze found mine. The way his fingers lingered over my legs made all my frustration go away.

"The dress suits you."

"Bite me." I pursed my lips.

I meant it as an insult for the way he rushed me out of the house, for ignoring me the whole way here, and for the whole no-underwear thing. But of course, that didn't hurt him in the least. Instead, he smirked at me as if my bad mood amused him.

"Maybe later." He sat across the aisle with a smug smile on his face.

I glared at him, shaking my head. He was fucking messing with me. I opened my mouth to tell him no, but the flight attendant blocked my view. Maybe that was for the best. Rex and I needed to be a team today. All this petty back and forth wasn't helping my cause.

"Can I get you a drink, Rex?" she asked him with her back to me.

Rex? Okay.

"No, I'm good." He reclined on the headrest to find my gaze again.

"How about you, hun? Can I get you a glass of rosé?" The flight attendant shifted to her right to face me, though her body stayed closer to Rex.

Violet called me Hun. It was her own short version of bunny, which I was pretty sure had to do with being a rope bottom. Did everyone on the plane know what I was to Rex? My cheeks flushed. "No, thanks."

I glanced out the window and did my best to ignore Rex's eyes on me. After a while, he reached across the aisle and brushed the back of his forefinger along my forearm. That was all it took for my body to melt into the seat. I squeezed my eyes closed, hating how much Rex could affect my moods.

"I thought the trip would put you in a nicer disposition."

Why was there humor in his voice?

"I'm fine."

"I didn't ask." He cocked an eyebrow, then his gaze shifted toward the front of the plane. He made a gesture with his head that apparently meant "leave us alone" because the two flight attendants disappeared immediately behind the galley curtains. "Come on." He offered me his hand as he stood.

"Where are we going?" My heart raced with anticipation. By now, I recognized that look in his eyes. He couldn't possibly mean to tie me up here with everyone hiding just a few feet away. "No."

"I'm not asking." With a half-smirk pulling at his lips, he gripped my elbow and hoisted me off my seat.

"Do they know? About me? You know." I couldn't even say the words aloud. Did they freaking know I was his rope bottom?

"Do you care what they think?" He cocked his head to look me in the eyes.

"Yeah, I do. She called me hun."

"She calls everyone that."

"Not everyone. She called you Rex."

"Hmm...so that's what this is about?" He released a breath and flashed me a charming smile. "They don't know."

"She was so friendly. I thought maybe she was an ex or something."

"I like this look on you." He gripped my waist and pressed his forehead to mine. "I could have anyone I want, including her. But for some reason beyond my comprehension, it's you I can't stop thinking about. I want you so damn much, it hurts."

"Rex." I took in his scent, and a ribbon of desire coiled itself around my clit. He had no right to look this good in a tailored suit, and then say those things to me.

"I'm right here." He cradled my cheek and slowly stalked toward the suite in the rear of the plane, pulling me with him. "Jesus, you're already wet and ready for me. My little virgin." He nuzzled my neck, then bit me gently.

Somewhere in the back of my mind, a tiny voice told me to refuse and return to my seat. But I didn't listen. His intense look was hypnotizing as he opened the door and ushered me inside the luxurious bedroom. A double bed dotted with gold and navy-blue pillows faced a large, shiny desk on the other side of the cabin. With my heart in my throat, I waited as he ambled toward the table and pulled a coiled rope from the drawer.

"You gotta be kidding me?" I panted a breath. If I had been turned on before, the cord put me over the edge.

"I'm not." He raised a brow, sucking in his bottom lip. His gaze darted between the small, carpeted space in front of me and the mattress. "Let's try the bed."

I shook my head no, but I did as he asked anyway and kneeled on top of the plush comforter, facing the headboard. His hands found my neck and started kneading gently until I relaxed against his chest. The silky-smooth fabric of his coat rubbed against my bare shoulder and sent a flutter across my navel. I was already wet for him. Not that it mattered. This session wasn't about sex. Rex was too cruel to give me that kind of relief. I ached for him to fill me, to put out this fire between my legs.

"Paying for sex doesn't seem like such a bad idea right about now." His lips ghosted the side of my mouth.

His erection pressed against my ass, and a shock of adrenaline rushed through me. Was he seriously considering throwing out his own rule to not pay for sex? Heat rushed to my core and cheeks at the realization that if he tried, I wouldn't say no.

# CHAPTER 20
## Sitting Ducks

CATERINA

"You're always so tense," he whispered on the column of my neck while he removed his jacket and dress shirt.

"It's kind of difficult to relax around you."

"Take a deep breath and hold it."

By the time he asked me to exhale, his commanding voice was the only thing in my head and my hands were tied in front of me. He picked them up over my head then pulled them toward him so my wrists would cross on the nape of my neck. The effort stretched the top of my dress across my breasts, and my skirt lifted to just below my bare pussy.

"So beautiful." His hot breath traveled down my back as he wound the rope under my boobs and over them.

"What is this called?"

"What?" He stopped to study my profile.

"I know they have names. What's the name of this tie?"

In my peripheral vision, he grinned at me as he slid his fingers down my underarm. "Wakizarashi Shibari because of the exposure of the armpits. In Japanese culture, showing them is considered shameful." He ran his forefinger up to my elbow then planted a soft kiss there. "In English, it's just called a simple bunny tie because your elbows make it look like you have bunny ears."

Bunny, bun, hun. I thought of Violet and her cute name. Oddly enough, though, shame wasn't what I was feeling right about now. Especially not with Rex's hot breath on the nape of my neck, and his deep voice so close to my ear.

"I'm glad you're taking an interest in the study." He brushed his knuckles along the side of my body, all the way to my thigh.

Only Rex would talk about bondage like it was this everyday thing. For crying out loud, we were rope playing thousands of feet off the ground. Rex lived in his own world where time and place didn't matter, where dinners at midnight and flights at dawn were a thing. He tugged at the rope behind me until my head rested on his shoulder. The bed wasn't as firm as a mat. I had to spread my knees farther apart to keep my balance.

In this room, he had no music playing, but he still seemed to move to a certain rhythm as if he could hear a tune in his head. The soft pressure of his hand guided me to double over and rest my chest on my thighs. He climbed on the bed. Every breath of mine was aligned with his measured movements until he sat across from me, legs stretched out on either side of me.

I lifted my torso and got a good look at him. Jesus, the man was beautiful. I wanted to touch all that hot skin over defined abs and chest. When I exhaled, he gripped my waist and brought me closer to him. I landed with my tits in his face, straddling his thigh. The sensation of my throbbing clit against his dress pants was more than I could bear. I let out a moan that if it weren't for the booming hum of the jet engine, I was sure everyone in the cockpit would've heard.

"Shhh." He clamped a hand over my mouth. "I want to see you come."

My eyes widened in surprise. How the hell was I supposed to do that with my arms tied over my head and down my back. I could hardly move or breathe.

"Now, Caterina." His gaze dropped to my bare pussy. The dress had ridden so far up, I could only imagine the view he had of me and my wet folds, grinding on his muscular thigh through the fabric of his pants. But there was nothing I could do to help it. In this position, he controlled my entire body. "We haven't much time." He slid his free hand down to my hip and softly kneaded it.

Shame washed over me when I realized that not only could I come like this, but that I also wanted to. I dug my knees into the mattress and quickly settled into a gyrating pace. I panted into the warm confinement of his palm while he technically forced me to watch him, watch me. The way he looked at me like I was dessert or the last meal on Earth was a huge turn on.

"I'm close." The muffled words didn't sound like me.

He lifted his leg and that was all I needed to get me over the edge. The raw bundle of nerves at the apex of my sex exploded into tiny sparks of fire and burned through me fast. I kept at it, trying to ride every last wave of sensation. It all ended much too quickly, like something was left out of the equation. I met Rex's gaze.

"Soon," he whispered, as if he could read my thoughts,

then reached behind me and unraveled the rope. Gently, he brought my arms down to rest on my lap. I brought my legs together and stayed in his arms like that while he brushed his fingers across my cheek. "We'll be landing in a few minutes. You'll find what you need in the bathroom."

I stretched my legs and let them drop on the side of the bed, feeling cold and confused. "I thought you wanted me."

"I do. But not like this. Not while Michael's debt is hanging over our heads." He rose to his feet and headed to the small closet next to his desk, where he had a fresh suit waiting for him.

And just like that, he was done with me. I strode to the bathroom and shut the door behind me. Tears of frustration rolled down my cheeks. Rex was impossible. I wiped my face and reached for the carry-on bag. Mary Anne had packed toiletries for me, including a mineral water facial spray and underwear. I could only imagine the kind of conversations Rex and she had about me.

"Are you ready?" Rex rapped on the door.

"One second." I made use of the Evian bottle to soothe my puffy eyes and donned the panties. When I opened the door, I felt more like myself. I couldn't let Rex get in my head like that. I had to stay focused on getting my family back together. They were the only reason I was here.

When we landed, the flight attendant opened the plane door and Rex's crew boarded. I turned to Rex with furrowed brows. "We're not leaving?"

"Not yet. I need a full debriefing first and a solid plan."

His private jet basically became a war room of sorts. Rex went back to his business persona. He ignored me while he shook hands with the crew in Atlanta and got the latest update. Except this time, he included me in the conversation to make sure everyone knew I was there to help. It was better, but I still felt like I shouldn't be here, like I was being an imposition.

The day wore on while they finalized their plan and security. I tried not to dwell too much on the fact that we were here hunting my brother. But one thing was for sure, if we were here looking for him, there was a good chance the FBI was too. According to Rex's guy, the Bureau's resources were limitless. After a late lunch in the main cabin, Rex finally decided it was time to head to the hotel and settle in for the night.

Thirty minutes later, we pulled up to the front door of the Four Seasons in Midtown. The executive suite Rex escorted me to was exactly what I thought Rex would go for, a luxury room with a living area, a fireplace, and a butler. According to Frank, we hadn't managed to reserve the whole floor on such short notice, but we did have the entire corridor all to ourselves. Rex seemed satisfied with that answer as he ushered me into what would be our bedroom. We could barely make it through a ninety-minute flight from New York City to Atlanta. I couldn't even imagine what this new setup would mean for us.

"Where are you going to sleep?" I turned to face him after his guys dropped our bags and left.

"Here."

"With me?"

"I'm not letting you out of my sight."

"I can take the couch." I exhaled and inhaled evenly, the way he had shown me during our sessions. Leveling my breathing on my own wasn't as easy without Rex guiding me through it, though.

"You're sleeping on the bed." He deadpanned.

"Well, there's always the terrace."

"I'll think about it." He stalked toward me. "You should get something to eat. The bar downstairs offers a decent menu."

Who had time for food? I opened my mouth to object, but then Frank barged in with a wild look on his face. My heart beat spiked, while I expected the worse. Were we too late? Was Massimo hurt?

"He called in." He stopped in his tracks a few feet from Rex.

"What did he want?"

"A favor." His smile stretched from ear to ear.

This was the best news he could deliver to his boss. If Massimo needed something bad enough to call Rex's crew, then he was in such deep shit, he would be willing to do anything Rex asked. Wasn't that how he got me to become his rope plaything?

"Give him whatever he wants."

"We're on it. And then?" Frank exchanged a meaningful look with Rex. "Where do we take him?"

"Bring him to me." He glanced at me, then shook his head. "On second thought, I'll go to him. Let me know when you have an address for him."

Frank nodded then left in a hurry. As soon as the door shut behind him, the air shifted. It was lighter and less murderous. I didn't want to think that Rex would order my brother's execution just because he refused to do what we needed him to do. I shook my head to clear my thoughts. Rex wasn't that guy. He would never do that to his own family. That much I knew for certain about him—Rex thought of everyone in the Society as his family.

189

"What happens now?" I sat on the upholstered chair by the balcony.

Now that the immediate danger was over, I was able to take the time and take in the room. The entire decor was centered around plush and elegance. All done in creams, yellows, and powder blues.

"We wait for Massimo to make his next move." Rex ambled over to me and sat on the four-poster bed across from me.

The act was so intimate and friendly, I didn't know how to respond. Mainly, because the last time Rex and I had a few hours to kill, it ended with me riding his leg until I came. Fuck. I needed to stop thinking about that and focus.

"Too bad I already used up my hour for the day." He smiled at me, then glanced down at his phone. His shoulders stiffened instantly.

"What is it?" I shot to my feet.

"Nothing." He shook his head.

"I thought you said you didn't lie."

"Fine." He blew out a breath while his gaze darted from his bags to me. "I'm sorry." He picked up his suitcase and plopped it on the mattress.

"Sorry about what? What's going on with Massimo?" I leaned on the footboard with my heart thrashing in my ears. "We're a team, remember? You can tell me. I'm not some fragile flower."

He placed a hand over mine and met my gaze. In the next beat, the cold steel of his handcuffs hit my wrists with a sharp flick. "Sorry about this. But we're flying blind here. I can't let you come with us. Not yet."

"Where are you going?"

"Massimo had dinner at the St. Regis, about four miles from here. Sounds like he left in a hurry before he even finished his meal. Shortly after that, he called Vittoria asking for a favor to help a woman. Vittoria just sent me the details."

"You're going there now?"

"Yes. Turns out he's staying there too."

"You're gonna ambush him when he comes home?" I yanked at the chains, scowling at him. "I can talk to him. Let me come with you."

"No." He put up his hands as if he meant me no harm and shuffled away from me. "As soon as it's safe, I'll come for you."

"For the record, this is why I don't trust you," I called after him.

He paused at the door for a moment, but then took off. Damn him.

I got that the FBI had put a target on our backs. But shackling me to a post was overkill. It wasn't like the feds were in a hurry to make a huge scene at a luxury hotel this far from New York City. Massimo didn't trust Rex. The second he got wind Rex was on his tail, he was going to disappear again. Massimo was ignoring my calls, but I was sure he wouldn't turn me down in person. We were family.

If Rex thought I would stay here like some puppy and wait for him to return with news, he had another thing coming. I glanced around the room for a way out. The room phone was on the other side of the bed. I winced at the idea of having to explain my predicament to the concierge. It wasn't like I could lie about it. What could I possibly say that wasn't utterly mortifying?

"Hello?" I shouted at the shut door. "Anyone there?"

When I didn't get a response, I plopped myself on the bed

and dropped my head into my free hand. No doubt Rex left a whole team right outside my door. So even if I could get the cuffs off, I would still need to deal with them.

The minutes ticked by while I stared at the empty suite. Then it hit me. Rex had to have a key somewhere in here as a safety precaution. Wasn't that why he always had rope shears within reach when he tied me up? I grabbed his bag and dumped the contents on the comforter, then rummaged through all the small pockets. Sure enough, he had the keys in there. No doubt he did that on purpose. He didn't mean to keep me chained to the bed all night. Just long enough so he could go after my brother. The pressure on my chest lifted as I made quick work of the lock to free myself.

I darted to my bag sitting on the sofa and fished out my phone. How long ago had Rex left? Maybe an hour? If I called a car service now, I might still get to Massimo in time. Wishing I was wearing better clothes for this mission, I tiptoed to the door and pressed my ear to it. The commotion on the other side sent my pulse into overdrive—several men were talking fast and at the same time, I couldn't really make anything out. Something was wrong.

Did the FBI send someone after me again?

I listened harder as a table got knocked over, and Frank called for help. The fear in his tone compelled me to swing the door open and rush into the living room, just in time to see Rex, the invincible king, fall to his knees in the middle of the foyer.

"What the hell happened?" I kneeled next to Rex, ready to catch him, though I knew that if he passed out on me, I wouldn't be able to hold him.

"Long story." Frank appeared in my line of sight with a medical kit. "He got shot."

Adrenaline rushed through me as I took inventory of the amount of blood on his suit coat and dripping down his fingers. Rex couldn't die like this. I fisted my hands to warm them up and exhaled. This wasn't the time to lose my shit. "We need to call an ambulance."

"No hospital," Rex mumbled, "I'll be a sitting duck."

"Okay. Um. Let's bring him into the bedroom. He can't stay on the floor."

Rex needed a doctor. Where the hell were we going to get one? If we were in New York, we'd have access to his own network of people, but out here in Atlanta, we were, as he'd said, sitting ducks.

## CHAPTER 21
## *Mobsters or Doctors?*

REX

*Fuck me.* Between the sleepless night, the flight here, and the altercation with what I was certain was an FBI agent gone rogue, I was starting to think my luck had run out. The searing pain in my shoulder kept me lucid, but I had lost too much blood on the way to the hotel. Ironically, the face-off had happened at a hospital nearby, but it was like I had said, without the proper contacts, I couldn't risk letting one of the doctors treat me. They were required to report all gunshot wounds. The FBI would take all of two seconds to connect the dots and find their way to me.

"Bed sounds like a good idea." I let Frank hoist me up and half-carry me to the bedroom where Caterina had already tossed all the bedding aside and covered the mattress with bath towels.

"Why are you smiling?" She shoved a strand of hair away from her face and reached for my suit jacket.

"You're worried about me." I winced while she removed my clothes, including my pants, shoes, and socks. Not how I had envisioned our night would go.

"I'm worried my brother did this to you." Her eyes softened. "Did he? Did Massimo shoot you?"

"No." I sat on the edge of the bed, angling my neck to check the wound. "Looks like my luck hasn't quite left me yet."

"Your shoulder is split open. How is this good news?" She wedged herself between my thighs and pressed a clean kitchen towel to the area. "I think you're supposed to keep pressure on it until it stops bleeding. Or at least, that's what I've heard, I don't even know if that's true." Her lip trembled.

The deep V between her brows told me she cared more about my well-being than keeping her distance. She hovered her fingers near the gash then took the hydrogen peroxide from Frank and squirted it all over my left side.

"Fuck." The burn intensified as froth built around the injury. When the room swayed a few rounds, I squeezed my eyes shut.

To my surprise, Caterina cradled my cheek and spoke in a gentle tone I had only heard her use with Michael. "You should've let me come with you."

"And risk you being the one sitting here, wounded? Absolutely not." I swallowed against the pain. "How is it?"

"It looks like the bullet went through your muscle." She squinted while she assessed the damage. "He's going to need stitches. A lot of them," she said to Frank.

"Everything you need should be in the medical kit." He presented the bag like it was a peace offering of sorts. "I have sausages for fingers. I can't." Frank put up his arms as proof.

Next to Caterina's delicate features, his hands looked like dust pans.

"So, I have smaller appendages and automatically I'm supposed to know how to sew?" Her gaze darted between Frank's and mine. "I don't like needles."

"No, but if I have the choice, I'd rather have a delicate touch tending to my wounds." I reached for her wrist and kissed the inside of it. "I trust you. The sooner you patch me up, the sooner we can go home."

"We can go home." She echoed my words, pressing a hand to her forehead. "Fine. I need to call Sam first. You stand a better chance if someone walks me through it."

"That's a good idea." I lay down on the pillow. The soft bed felt good, and suddenly my body weighed a ton.

"I got it." Frank stepped away as he reached into the pocket of his trousers.

"This is the craziest thing I have ever done." Caterina cleared the bedside table and dumped all the contents of the first aid kit onto it. "This is why Mom refused to be part of this mafia world. She hated the idea of Dad coming home bleeding like this." She waved a hand toward me.

"You're mumbling." I reached for her waist and got her to sit next to me. "I'm fine. I just need a few sutures and a shot of whiskey."

"Tell me the truth. Did my brother...?" She trailed off.

"No, he didn't. Massimo and I had a relatively civilized conversation. He's not happy, but he's willing to come home. He was with Mikey Gallo."

"Gallo? I thought the entire family had been wiped out."

"We thought so too. Massimo has been hiding him this

whole time. But now because of Gallo, they, the feds, or whoever tried to kill us tonight, also know about Massimo."

"What do you mean?"

"Gallo wanted to start a street racing business here in Atlanta. Long story short, the locals didn't like it. He retaliated by kidnapping one of their own. Massimo and I went to Mikey to talk some sense into him and ended up getting mixed up in a shoot-out. I got a good look at one of the guys. He smelled like a pig."

"You think he was FBI?"

"He had that look in his eyes." I nodded.

"Where's Massimo? Is he okay?"

"He is. He said he had something he needed to handle first, but that he would meet us in New York." I blinked slowly to chase the shadows creeping on the edges of my eyes. "I trust him. You'll see your brother soon. Once he's home. He'll be safe. I promise."

Tears spilled down her pink cheeks. "Thank you."

Frank came back with Nurse Sam on the phone. "He wants to see your arm."

I nodded and scooted up the bed to let them do their thing. Caterina jumped to her feet and grabbed the device from Frank. If she was still afraid for my life, she didn't show it. She talked fast as she explained in detail how bad the injury was. Apparently, a mild infection had already settled in. Sam walked her through the process of checking for bone damage, and to see if the lacerations and skin tags were clear of debris before she started sewing me back up.

While she listened intently to Sam's instructions, Frank left the room, then returned with a bottle of Bourbon. He poured three shots and offered one to Caterina. "Nothing can hurt at this point." He shrugged.

"You're right." She took the glass from him and knocked it back. Wincing, she covered her mouth. After she recovered from the lingering burn of the liquor, she shook her hands out and turned to me. "Okay, keep adding pressure. I think I can do this. But I need to practice a few times."

"There's peaches in the kitchen." Frank refilled my empty tumbler. "I'll get them."

"Let me see." She removed the cloth from my shoulder to take a look. "How do people do this for a living?"

"You mean mobsters or doctors?"

"I guess both." She knitted her brows, angling her head one way and then the other to get a better view.

"At home, Sam would've handled this."

"She can do it." Sam's voice boomed from the bedside table.

Frank returned with three choices of fruit for Caterina. My fingers had already gone numb from the aching pain, but watching Caterina practice her stabbing motions on an orange and then a peach kept my mind off the fucked-up situation we were in. I smiled at her profile, noting how she sucked on her bottom lip every time she delivered a measured blow.

"Are you ready?" She glanced up at me from her mangled fruit.

"You're the one doing all the work." I relaxed my body and focused on her scent while she rinsed the affected area again.

The first stitch hurt like a mother fucker, but as she went along, her touch became more assured and precise. At some point, the whole thing became a series of tiny burns. Some areas felt so hot, I didn't even feel the piercing of the needle.

Either the pain was manageable now, or the Bourbon had already kicked in.

"Stay with me," she said urgently. "He's burning up."

In the background, a cacophony of loud voices and phones ringing turned into a deafening echo in my head until Caterina's call for me became a faraway dream. My eyes fluttered closed. The desperate clanking in the room ceased, along with the bright lights, Caterina's touch, and the pain—right before I passed out.

The next morning, I woke up feeling like I had been hit by a truck. Most of my aches and pains wore off the minute I noticed Caterina curled up next to me. She had changed into pajamas shorts and a tank top and her hair was up in a pony-tail. Her form looked so small and delicate next to me. I wanted nothing more than to pick her up and kiss her until she begged me to take her.

My cock steeled under my boxer briefs. Fuck me. If I hadn't gotten shot last night, I might've spent the night buried deep inside her—our contract, her dad, and brothers be damned. Why did she stay with me? Any one of my guys could've slept on the couch to keep an eye on me. Playing doctor was definitely not part of our agreement.

A low moan escaped her lips as she stirred next to me. I could only hope her dreams were just as haunted as mine. Every night, I thought of nothing and no one else but her. I outlined the curve of her hip with my forefinger, remembering how soft her skin was there when she let me touch her on the plane ride here. My gaze settled on the bow of her mouth. God how I wanted to fuck that mouth. I had been so close to doing just that yesterday before I realized we were due to land in a few minutes.

When she nuzzled her face against me, I hovered my fingers over hers and watched her while she stretched her legs out and ran her hands all over my abs and chest. Her puffy eyes and lips made her look so young and so innocent. I took in her flowery scent and the warmth of her body flushed against mine.

Over the years, I had learned so much about Caterina Alfera—everything from her grades in college or her favorite wine, to how many strokes of my rope it took to make her come. But I had no idea what she looked like in the morning after she woke up. Yeah, I could get used to this kind of bliss with her. In the next breath, she sat up with a wild look in her eyes.

"Oh, um, I'm so sorry. I fell asleep." She scooted away from me.

"Don't be. You look good in my bed." I reached for her but caught only empty sheets.

Her gaze dropped to the bulge in my underwear, and her brows shot up in surprise. "You're unbelievable."

"I never said I was a saint. Anyone waking up to a beautiful woman sleeping next to him would've had the same reaction."

"You almost died."

"It was just a scratch."

"You passed out from it. The fever spiked so fast and so high, we had to pump you full of antibiotics."

"I don't understand. Are you mad at me because I find you irresistible or because I almost died?"

"You scared me." She inched closer to me.

"Thank you for helping me. You know you didn't have to. Most people would've left their enemy to die. Why didn't you?

This could've been your way out." My chest tightened at the idea that maybe Caterina Alfera didn't hate me after all. I wanted to hear her say the words—I don't hate you. "I thought you hated me."

She relaxed against the pillows next to mine, suddenly intrigued by her palm lines. Like last night, she gently nibbled on her bottom lip, as if the answer to my question required serious effort.

"I thought I did too." She glanced up at me with tears brimming her eyes. "I don't hate you, Rex."

"Hey." I pulled her toward me until she rested her head on my chest.

"How do you feel?" She pointed her chin at my poorly bandaged arm. "I'm so sorry about all this."

"I'm fine. You never have to worry about me." I buried my fingers in her hair, wishing we were back in my penthouse.

"I was afraid I'd never see you again." She brushed her finger over my brows. "Or talk to you." She panted a breath, and the green in her eyes darkened.

Jesus, I knew that look. She hoisted herself up and kissed me on the lips, soft and tentative at first. But when I cradled the nape of her neck, she completely let her guard down. She thrusted her tongue past my teeth, rubbing those gorgeous tits all over me.

"Fuck." I groaned.

"Did I hurt you?" She pulled away to look at me. Her cheeks burned a bright red, and her eyes showed the level of surprise I had felt at her sudden display of affection.

"God, no." I gripped her waist with my good hand. "You've never kissed me before."

"Yes, I have." She brought her knees in and settled against my side.

"You've kissed me back, but never..." I swiped the pad of my thumb over her lips. "Never this."

Our gazes locked.

*Well, who needs a convoluted plan when you have blind luck?*

I had been trying to get close to Caterina for years, but the hate she had for my family was too great and she couldn't see past who I was—a beast, she'd called me once. "After all this time, you're telling me that all I had to do to gain your favor was get shot?"

"This isn't that." She climbed out of the bed.

I made to get up, but pain shot up my arm like wildfire. "Jesus." I fell back on the pillow. "Don't go."

She stood in the middle of the room, as if weighing her options. The worry and agony I had seen in her eyes last night was back. A knock on the door saved her from having to make a choice. Blowing out a breath, she fixed her tank top and pajama pants and swung the door open.

"Sorry to bother you." Frank's voice boomed across the room. "Is he up? It's about Massimo."

"Come in," I called and threw the covers over my boxer briefs. Not for me, but I figured Caterina wouldn't want my guys knowing our business. "What is it?"

"Massimo couldn't find Mikey. But he's headed for New York in a few hours."

"There's nothing keeping us here anymore. Get the plane ready. I'd like to go home."

"You got it, boss." He gave me and Caterina a quick nod and took off.

"We're going home?" Caterina padded over to me.

I nodded.

The word on her lips sent a shock through me. She'd said we. Gunshot wound aside, our trip to Atlanta had been more or less a success—Mikey Gallo was still alive. Massimo had agreed to return to the fold, and more importantly, Caterina no longer considered me her enemy. More than that, I believed she cared about me.

## CHAPTER 22
# You Don't Even Know Me

CATERINA

The flight home turned out to be a whirlwind of getting rushed from one place to another. For whatever reason, Rex wanted to keep his injury a secret. We didn't check out of the hotel. Frank found a private charter plane to fly us out of a smaller airport in Atlanta straight into Teterboro. He even left a few of the guys behind to keep up the charade that he was staying in Atlanta for a couple of weeks, which was the minimum amount of time Sam had said Rex would need to recover.

As soon as we landed, Frank and his team rushed Rex to an ambulance, while I was escorted to an SUV. A tight pressure gripped my chest as my car pulled away, leaving a convalescing Rex behind. He had seemed fine earlier this morning when we kissed. But after all this cloak and dagger, I couldn't help but feel like maybe something was wrong, that I had messed up the sutures somehow.

My driver made record time to Rex's penthouse. When he

pulled up to the private entrance, I didn't wait for him to open the door for me. I climbed out and darted toward the elevator bay. Of course, they knew I was coming. The minute I reached the end of the lobby, a guard appeared to escort me upstairs.

The penthouse was a madhouse. And it was just then when I realized what a huge deal Rex's incident had been. He was the head of the Society. No one was allowed to move a finger unless they had his approval first. As much as the families didn't agree on things, they all conceded that Rex was in charge. If something happened to him, who would take over? I had been so afraid for his life for my own selfish reasons, I hadn't considered what his death would mean for everyone else. What a sad existence, if he couldn't even show a little bit of weakness, not even after getting shot.

I darted up the grand staircase. Out in the hallway, a bunch of people in white coats seemed to be having some sort of conference. I adjusted my gait and slowly made my way toward them. A woman in a tight ballerina bun that reminded me of a much younger version of Signoria Vittoria broke away from the group, waving a hand to get my attention.

"Hi, I'm Dr. Salvatore. I assume you're Caterina?" She offered me her hand, and I shook it. So, she and Vittoria Salvatore were related. I supposed it paid to have a medical doctor in the family. There was so much I didn't know about Rex's world—our world.

"I am." I opened my mouth to ask how he was, but the words didn't come out.

"He's fine. All this is routine to make sure he doesn't lose a limb over this." She cocked an eyebrow. "You did a decent job. He'll have a scar, but hey, at least he gets to keep the pretty face." She laughed at her own joke.

"Yeah, I guess. Can I see him?"

"Maybe later. Right now, he needs to rest. You do too." She stepped closer to look into my eyes.

"I'm fine." I blinked several times to regain focus. "I'll just wait in my..." Shit. I couldn't tell her I was staying in the room next door. Would she know that meant I was Rex's latest resident bottom? "I'll wait in the kitchen."

I turned to leave, but she stopped me. "Caterina, wait." The amusement in her voice pissed me off. She knew. She fucking knew.

"Everyone here is here because Rex trusts them." She pointed at my door. "Get some rest. I'll let Rex know you're home."

I swallowed my pride. One, because I was extremely tired. And two, because it shouldn't matter what Dr. Salvatore thought of me. Though I did hate that she knew so much about me and I knew nothing about her. Why did Rex tell her about me?

"Okay." I strode to my suite with as much dignity as I could muster, locked the door behind me, and face planted on my bed.

The next morning, I woke up to Mary Anne drawing a bath for me. Of course she had a key. I rolled my eyes at her back. "Good morning," I called out.

"Good morning." She smiled. "Welcome home. I brought you some breakfast and fresh clothes."

"Thanks."

Right. I had forgotten this wasn't really home. If it were, I would have my things with me and the key to my own lock. A swirl of bitterness settled in my stomach. I let it stew until I was ready to admit that the real reason I was annoyed with Mary Anne was because I wasn't allowed to see Rex.

"How is he?" I asked on my way to the bathroom.

"Better. He wants to see you."

"Oh." Those five little words shouldn't have made me so happy. "I'll get ready."

I showered and blow-dried my hair as quickly as I could then donned the romper Mary Anne had laid out on the bed before she left. The soft blue and mint green fabric clung to me like a second skin. It was flirty and comfortable and kind of perfect. I ate my breakfast, feeling nervous about seeing him again.

Yesterday, we had left things at a really awkward standoff. Mainly because I wasn't sure what I wanted from Rex. Yeah, sure, every time he was near, I wanted him in my bed. But apart from a physical relationship, I knew there couldn't be more. So, what the hell was I doing here?

I finished my coffee, and after a few calming breaths, I strode over to Rex's room. My heart beat fast against my ribs. And why did this even mean anything to me right now? I was just here to make sure he was fine. As any decent person would do. I rapped on the door and stepped back.

The door swung open, and the stupid grin on my face froze at a weird angle. I bet Dr. Salvatore thought it was terrifying. "Good morning." I used my business voice. "I stopped by to see how the patient was doing."

"He's sleeping," she whispered. "Maybe come back later."

"Oh. Of course. Later." I nodded several times like an idiot. This woman, like Signoria Vittoria, intimidated me. Something about her screamed power and danger. And it was so obvious she didn't like me. Or maybe she just didn't like me near Rex. Did she have a thing for him? I mean, who would blame her?

"She can come in, Donata." Rex's voice boomed inside.

"Come in." She waved me in.

I did my best to keep my gait even and not rush to Rex's California king-size bed on the far end, overlooking the terrace. Rex's suite was as big as my apartment, with a spectacular view of Central Park. The fireplace in the middle of the room made the space seem inviting and calming. Just like downstairs, the color palette followed the same tones of navy blue, grays and browns.

He sat on his bed wearing nothing but sweatpants. His wet hair smelled of body wash as if he had just taken a shower. A pang of jealousy ripped through me before I could stop it. Did Donata help him with that? I shook my head and forced all the sexy images out of my mind. Rex wasn't mine. We weren't even sleeping together.

"How are you?" My voice was barely audible over his fast and furious typing. After a few seconds, he stopped and closed his laptop.

"Good as new." He beamed at me.

"He still needs more days of rest." Donata walked past me and sat at the foot of the bed.

"Your bandages look way better." I pointed at his chest. When I had tried it before I couldn't exactly get the wrap to comfortably go over his shoulder and around his chest, so I coiled it around his arm. Sam had said that it just had to be tight, not pretty. "I um—"

He raised his hand to me then turned to the goddess sitting at his feet. "Donata, can you give us a minute?"

"Of course, dear. Text me if you need anything." She stood

and offered me a smile. "No strenuous exercise for at least a week."

"Okay." I watched her leave and slowly shut the door behind her.

"Come here." Rex offered me his hand.

My body started moving toward him before I could mentally react to his command. I stopped and glared at him. "Is she Vittoria's niece?"

"She is. How did you know?"

"The last name. Is she the niece that's going to be devasted?"

He chuckled. "What do you mean?"

"Vittoria said that when she met me. That her niece was going to be devasted because I was here." What did it matter?

"Come here. Don't make me ask again. We're past all this pretense, aren't we?" His tone was low and layered with sinful promises. "I've been dying to kiss you all day." His extended fingers were like a magnet to mine.

I slid my hand into his and let him pull me on top of him. With our bodies fused together, he kissed me hard until I melted into him. This was always the thing with Rex. He made me throw logic out the window and forget how cold and lonely this place was without him. He made me forget about the gunshot wound I had sewn, but more importantly, he made me forget about Donata.

"Jesus Christ. You have no idea how much I want you."

"I kind of do." I pressed my hips to his massive erection, running my hand up his chest and into his hair. The wet strands brought up images of Rex and Donata in the shower together. "Rex, stop." I muttered, hoping he didn't hear the hitch in my voice.

"What is it?" His eyes searched mine.

"Did she help you with your shower?" I gritted my teeth to stop myself from saying more. That was something a jealous girlfriend would ask, and I was neither.

"No. Why would you think that?" He laughed.

"I'm glad I amuse you." I made to get away from him, but he held me tight. Even in this state, he was still in control. He still held all the power.

"Donata is just one of my doctors and a friend. Nothing more. I promise, I managed the shower all by myself." A sexy grin pulled at his lips. "Maybe you can help me with that tomorrow." He inched his hand from my waist up into the side of my breast.

"Does she know about me?"

He blew out air and that was all the answer I needed.

"I can't believe you. You make me sign a NDA and then you turn around and tell everyone that I'm your plaything." That speech would have been more effective if I was standing on my own two legs and not rubbing myself all over his abs. "I can't keep doing this. It's humiliating."

The smile faded from his face and he loosened his grip on me. "Apart from Violet, who graciously agreed to help guide you through the process, no one knows you're my rope bottom. Those sessions are between you and me and no one else. Do you understand?"

"She knew I was sleeping next door." I raised my voice to make my point.

"She does know about that."

"Why did you tell her?"

"I didn't. Her aunt did." He glanced upward, as if searching for the right words. At this point, there wasn't much he could say to put out this anger I felt in the pit of my belly. "She also told her about how I feel about you."

"Well, that's nothing new. Everyone knows how you hate my family." I sat on the mattress next to him.

A cold shiver ran down my spine when he didn't try to keep me close to him. When I met his gaze, the intense and oh so intimidating fire I found there shocked me out of my moment of insanity. What was I thinking? That I could just climb into bed with Rex Valentino and then what? How was I going to explain to Dad that I slept with his enemy? What would people like Donata and Vittoria think? They belonged here. They understood Rex's world because it was theirs too.

"Last night, I thought we had agreed to stop pretending. I thought you understood." He twisted his body to face me and winced.

"Don't move. You'll hurt yourself." I braced my hand on his chest, so he'd lie down again.

He did, but then brought my lips to his again and kissed me with a hunger that left me breathless. "How is it that everyone can see how I feel about you, except you? All this time. Don't you get it? I want you. It's more than that." He furrowed his brows, staring at me with pursed lips, as if the thing he needed to say next hurt him as much as the gunshot wound on his shoulder. "I love you."

"Violet said you couldn't love. That your heart didn't work that way."

"Now you know why. It's because of you. It's always been you."

My lips parted. How was this even possible? "You don't even know me."

"I know enough. And I've known it for a long time." He

kept his bandaged arm to his side while his fingers massaged the nape of my neck. "Yesterday, I was too high on meds and too much in pain to finish our conversation."

"Rex."

"Let me finish. I know you want me. That much has always been clear to me. What I didn't know was if you could ever stop hating me for just one minute, just long enough to see the real me. To see the man, and not the ruthless king." He puffed out a breath. "Last night, you said you didn't hate me."

I stared at his beautiful face and the softness in his eyes. I thought of our sessions, his gentle touch, and how much I craved him. No one could kiss like that unless they actually felt something. No one could kiss back, unless...

"Say something."

"I don't hate you."

"I know." He pulled me toward him until our foreheads touched. "I'm not asking you to love me."

"What are you asking then?"

His phone rang just then, and he cursed under his breath. Yeah, that was the worst possible timing. Rex Valentino had just confessed the mother of all confessions. The last thing we needed was someone barging in again. He picked up the device and sent the call away. Three seconds later, the screen lit up with a text.

*Mary Anne: The Alfera brothers are here. And they're demanding to see their sister.*

"Fuck me." He gripped the mobile in his hand.

In an instant, he became the ruthless king everyone feared. The one who never bothered to ask and simply took. This time, I was that something or someone. Massimo and Enzo were probably thinking that same thing. That I was here against my will, which I wasn't. Rex and I made a deal. At first, I had thought he only meant to humiliate me, but I was wrong. He never did anything to bring me shame. Heat rose to my cheeks when I thought about all the times he had made me come because I begged him to. That was all on me.

Rex *loved* me.

My eyes traveled down from his face to my arm, where I was sure his fingers would leave a mark. "My brothers are here?" I pushed away from him, but he held me tighter with both hands this time. "You're staying right here."

"I have to see them. Rex, they've been gone for two years." I struggled until my arms ached under his iron grip.

"No."

"Why not?"

"Because they won't understand what we have."

# CHAPTER 23

# We Don't Need to Be Out of Time

Rex

"Rex." Her gorgeous lips found mine again.

I had finally told her the truth, and she hadn't taken off. She hadn't said I was out of my mind for thinking she could love me, for thinking she could love a beast. Why couldn't her brothers have waited one more night before they decided they wanted to play the heroes. They left Caterina all alone. All this time, she'd had to deal with Michael on her own. Now they show up thinking they can take her away from me. Not bloody likely.

"You can't keep me from seeing my brothers." She rubbed her nose against mine, letting her body be heavy on top of mine. "Do you hear how insane that sounds?"

"I'm crazy for you." I sucked on the column of her neck until bit by bit, the pieces fell into place and my brain caught on to the fact that she was right. Sooner or later, she had to see Enzo and Massimo. Honestly, I had hoped for later, much, much later. I nibbled farther down to her chest until a button blocked my path. "Do you remember the day you came to see me?"

"Hmmm."

"Your tits have haunted me every night since then."

"I offered myself to you. Technically, served myself up on a platter for you." She let her head fall back. "Why did you refuse me?"

"An irrational sense of duty?" My lips curved over the silky fabric of her romper and her hardened nipples.

"I thought maybe I wasn't your type."

"You're so fucking beautiful. That would be impossible." I kissed across to her other breast, mentally kicking myself for not choosing something for her to wear that showed more cleavage. Earlier, I figured a long sleeve romper would be the safest thing for the type of conversation we had pending for today. "Take it off. Take it all off. I want to see you naked like that day." The commanding tone in my voice made her shiver in my arms. "I bet you're ready for me too. Wet and tight. My little virgin," I whispered in her ear.

"You can't keep doing this to me." She pulled back, panting a breath. "You make everything so fuzzy and tingly and so fucking good."

"Then stay."

"Gosh, you have the worst timing ever. Of everyone I have ever met."

"Seems we're always running out of time." I let my head fall back on the pillow.

"Our deal is our deal." She smiled at me, running her fingers over the fabric to right her clothes. "I'm a woman of my word. I'm staying with you. Massimo and Enzo don't need to get involved. Beyond breathing life back into Dad by just being here, that is. He'll be so happy to see them." She kicked her legs over the side of the bed and padded around to say goodbye.

If she thought I was going to let her go by herself, she didn't know me at all. I exhaled all the air out of my lungs until it burned. Then I inhaled, hoping to find the physical strength for what I had to do next—take Caterina downstairs and somehow not lose her forever.

My phone went off again. I picked up this time. "Tell them we're on our way. And get Frank." I dropped my device in the pocket of my pants.

"You can't walk like this."

"You wanted to see your brothers. Let's go."

I grabbed my T-shirt off the upholstered chair facing the fireplace. For a second, I considered not wearing it just to spite them, to throw them off their game. But then decided against it. When it came to Caterina, I wanted to do things right. Not to mention, it would be better if they didn't find out about my incident in Atlanta. Slowly, I sat on the couch and put on my shoes. Of all the days to only have one good arm, why did it have to be today? Caterina tried to help me, but I waved her away.

"It's okay to ask for help."

I stopped halfway to glance up at her. "You don't think I know that? Why do you think I wanted to see Massimo this week?"

"I was talking about the shoes, but okay."

"I'm sorry." I rose to my feet. "I promise. It may not look like it, but I am trying to do the right thing."

She cradled my neck. "If it weren't for you, I'd be a mess right about now."

"Why do you care what they think?"

"They're my family."

I bit my tongue and decided not to point out the fact that Enzo and Massimo weren't here for her. Michael was up to something. Why else would he send his sons here to retrieve Caterina when he was the one who orchestrated this whole plan? Somehow, I knew that whatever he was scheming, she'd be caught in the middle of it again. Whatever it was, the old man wasn't going to get away with it.

I reached for her hand and pulled her closer to me. I hadn't meant to do much else, but my mouth found hers and I couldn't stop tasting her. Especially after she hung from my neck and deepened the kiss.

"Relax. This is your family. You owe them nothing."

"I know. I just haven't seen them since Mom. And now they're here of all places because of me." She sighed.

"You mean, in their enemy's lair?"

"Don't make fun of me." She slapped my chest, then covered her mouth. "I'm sorry."

"Breathe, Caterina." I turned her around and pressed my lips to her ear, the way I had done our first time in the rope room. "Take a big gulp of air. Fill up. And hold it."

She did as I asked without question. We'd come so far in this regard. I held her for a few more counts and then exhaled along with her.

"Thanks." She smiled at me. "Mom would be so sad to see how disconnected from each other we had become. This isn't us. We're a family. I missed having a family."

The pink had returned to her pretty cheeks and she seemed more in control. She cared about what they thought of her, and that made my insides twist with guilt. If she hadn't been concerned about her dad, she wouldn't be here with me. I wanted to say I was sorry for the deceit. But I knew she wouldn't understand. Not yet. Goddammit, we needed more time.

From the top of the stairs, I spied Enzo and Massimo near the fireplace. Tall and dark was how anyone would describe the brothers. If Caterina was an angel lost in my world, the Alfera brothers were quite the opposite. Because unlike Caterina and her mother, Anna, Michael and his sons never left the Society, not really. For Anna's sake, they all pretended and lied.

"Massimo." Caterina practically ran into her brother's arms.

I let them have their moment while I texted Frank and asked him to be ready. He promptly responded to let me know he had twenty men just outside the front door and another crew downstairs. Unless Enzo was ready for a war, Caterina wasn't going anywhere tonight.

"Are you okay? You look...older." He furrowed his dark brows as he inspected his little sister.

"It's been two years, you asshole." She hit him square in the chest.

I would've gone with a right hook.

Enzo and Massimo towered over her by at least seven inches, same as me. But just how she had never been intimidated by me, she didn't take shit from them either. She gave them an earful on how selfish they had been for taking off and then ignoring all her calls.

"I know." Enzo cut her off in the middle of her speech to pull her into a bear hug. "We were idiots. We messed up.

That's why we're here. We're taking you home. You don't owe him anything."

"It's good to see you boys." I crossed my arms over my chest and immediately regretted it as the pain shot through me.

Enzo glared at me. If they weren't trying to take Caterina away from me, I would've laughed at how familiar that scowl now was to me. Enzo and I were friends a long time ago. Before our parents dropped a bomb on us with their bullshit talk about duty, honor, and doing right by our families. They turned our lives upside down that day. After that night, Enzo and I slowly began to drift apart until our friendship became nothing but rivalry and hate.

"I can take care of myself, Enzo." She glanced my way for a beat then returned her attention to both her brothers. "Actually, I did need you a few days ago, but luckily, Rex was there to save me. He brought me here to protect me. The Society is under attack."

"And you believe that? You don't think this is all just to make himself look the hero?" Enzo advanced toward me, but Caterina cut him off.

"He's telling the truth. Someone came after Dad and me."

"Someone came after Mikey too. When we were in Atlanta." Massimo shrugged as if saying, "they're not lying."

But beyond that, he didn't bother to set Enzo straight, which meant they had come here with a plan. I stayed focused on my breathing, willing the pain in my shoulder away. Not much I could do about the ache in my heart.

"What do you want? I have a hard time believing you're here to check in on your little sister after all this time."

Pursing his lips, Enzo reached inside his suit jacket and retrieved a piece of paper. Caterina took it from him. From where I stood, all I could see was the emblem from the Crucible. It was a statement. If I had to guess, it was Michael's account statement from the Crucible.

Caterina crumbled the sheet in her hand and turned to me with glossy eyes. "Dad's debt."

I wanted to hold her and tell her it was all right. That her Dad didn't deserve all this pity and loyalty. "How did you get that?" I asked Enzo.

"We know why Caterina is here." Massimo cocked an eyebrow to emphasize his meaning.

The assholes thought I had paid for sex. I was okay with them thinking that. "I can't control your dad's actions. No more than you can." I stuffed my hands in my pockets to keep me from reaching out to Caterina. She seemed so alone and so hurt. "Get to the point."

"Did you tell Dad?" Caterina sucked in a breath. "Does he know?"

"Jesus, Caterina. Do you think he's an idiot? He told us. He sent us for you." After Enzo's stentorian revelation, the room fell eerily quiet.

"How did Dad find out?" She turned to me.

"Isn't it obvious?" I reached for her hand. "He sent you to me."

"Rex, you know I came to you of my own volition."

"That's not what I meant." This was the worst timing.

"What's done is done." Massimo stepped in. "His debt is settled."

"I don't believe you." A shock of adrenaline ran through me. Now I was afraid—afraid I was losing her.

"It's true." Caterina turned to face me. "The statement has been paid. How?"

"I had the money." Enzo shrugged. "When Dad explained, we came straight here."

Fuck my luck. From the moment Caterina signed our contract, I knew it would end sooner than I'd hoped it would. But I always assumed it would be after I had time to make her see we belonged together. After she had time to get to see that we weren't much different. That destiny had brought us together for a reason. The Society was still under attack. I needed her and I needed the Alfera family to back me up. What happened? Why did the old man change his mind about helping me?

"That's all fine. But Caterina and I still have a deal. Our agreement doesn't end until I say so." I stepped toward her, but both brothers stood at attention.

"You mean until the debt was paid." Caterina shot me a look of daggers.

"You read the contract. What did it say?"

She opened her mouth to speak. As the realization that we never discussed a way out of the contract by paying off Michael's debt, her eyes grew wider. The anger that registered there was enough to wipe the smirk off my face. It had a been a low blow to only put a timeline on the page, and not a form of payoff. But I never cared about the money. I cared about spending six months with her.

"You tricked me?" She finally snapped out of her bewilderment.

Well, it was more than that. She was, rightfully so, pissed off at me all over again. The million-dollar question was, would Caterina call my bluff? I was willing to push her to the limit, but I wasn't going to call the damn cops on her for refusing to honor a contract that was meant to serve as a conduit of trust more than a legal document.

"Seems we're at an impasse." I hit send on my phone. Before Caterina could think of any other insult, my guys barged in. "Caterina stays."

"Fuck off." Massimo fisted his hands. "Last night, I thought you wanted to help make a difference."

"I still do." Was I being the asshole? Absolutely. But Caterina would've stayed with me, if Enzo and Massimo hadn't come in here with their proverbial guns blazing, shaming her for what she did to save her dad. I met her gaze. She felt so far away. And to think that just minutes ago, she was in my arms calling for me. "Caterina, we don't need to be out of time. We belong together."

"You should've thought about that when you orchestrated this whole entrapment. I trusted you. I thought..."

"Enough." Enzo took the statement from her and stuffed it back in his coat. "We're going home right now. Get your things."

"I didn't bring anything with me." She scowled at me.

I bet they were both thinking the worst right about now. Fine. That one I did deserve. When she walked past me, I gripped her wrist. Her flowery scent was a shock to my senses. I had so much to say, but the right words didn't come to me. Instead, I thought of her tied up in my arms in complete surrender. "You're making a mistake."

"You lied."

"You know I don't do that." I pursed my lips.

"Oh no. I forgot. You bend the truth to suit you. Jesus, Rex. That's lying. I came here because of Dad. I think it's fitting that I leave here because of him, too." She yanked her arm away. "He needs me. They all do."

I need you. I wanted to say, but not here, not with her brothers watching us.

"Tell your men to step aside." Enzo wedged himself between me and Caterina.

I was taller than him and more than willing to fight back. But that would solve nothing. For the good of the Society, our families, I had to let her go. I had to forget about her and move on.

"Let them through," I said through gritted teeth.

Rage surged through me, hot and thick, until all I saw was red as both Enzo and Massimo escorted Caterina out the door. She crossed the threshold, and I held my breath, waiting for her to turn back and tell me she didn't want to go, to make her stay.

She made it all the way to the elevators before she turned to me with tears in her eyes. All that planning. In the end, I only managed to hurt her deeply.

"I'm sorry." I mouthed before the elevator's doors slid closed all the way.

# CHAPTER 24
## The King's Back

REX

I slammed the front door and headed upstairs. My head swam, and all I could hear was the regret in Caterina's voice. Jesus Christ, I almost had her. She was in my arms and ready for me. Would it have made any difference for her if we'd had sex? Probably not. She had been so hurt and angry when she left. That was on me. I'd been so afraid to lose her. I lied to keep her and lost her anyway.

Halfway up the steps, my damn shoulder decided to act up and discharge a shock of pain down my back.

"Mother fucker." I leaned against the wall for support and slipped all the way to the floor. The cool marble brought some relief to my shoulder, which seemed to be bleeding again. Black spots hovered in front of my eyes and blocked my view of a pair of legs in high heels. "Caterina." I reached for her.

"For crying out loud. I knew this little experiment of yours wouldn't end well."

My eyes flew open and focused on Donata's face. I winced and glanced at my arm. "I think I passed out for a minute."

"You think? A chunk of your shoulder is trying to put itself back together. What part of stay in bed is so hard to understand?" She shook her head and hooked her arm around my waist to help me up. "Can you walk, or should I call your guys?"

"No. I can manage." I trudged to my suite and settled on the sofa facing the fireplace.

"You should lie down." Donata ambled to the side table and prepared a syringe, then sat next to me.

"I'm tired of the fucking bed." I waved her hand away. "No drugs. They make me stupid. Right now, I need to think."

I rested my head on the cushion and glared at the crown molding on the ceiling. What the hell had happened? In one fell swoop, I lost Caterina and the support of the Alfera family. No matter how hard I tried, I seemed to keep going backward instead of forward. I shot to my feet and strode to the bar cart to pour myself a whiskey.

"As your doctor, I'd like to point out that drinking in your condition is a bad idea." Donata strolled over to me and picked up a tumbler.

"As my doctor, are you going to stop me?" I filled her cup.

"Even as you are, I don't think I could." She clinked my glass. "Cheers."

She ushered me to the bed. I let her take off my shoes and fluff my pillows. When she was finished, she leaned her thigh on the side of the mattress, resting her drink against her chest. She studied me for a while, then finally spoke. "I heard everything."

"I'm sure you did. The Alfera brothers weren't exactly quiet."

"What do you see in her? I mean, sure, she's pretty. But she's afraid of her own shadow." She furrowed her brows.

Of course Donata would see Caterina's fear as a weakness. But the thing was, Caterina wasn't afraid for herself, she was afraid for her family. I valued that in her. Even if that was the very thing that separated us today.

"She cares about her family."

"I'm sure." She chuckled. "The old man must've done a number on her. What happens now, Rex? The old man seems to have changed his mind."

"It seems he has." I took a long swig of whiskey. "I believe he means to wage war on me to get his throne back."

"What a week you've had." She inhaled. "First you win the favor of the sweet princess. Then you get shot trying to help her brother. Then the other brother swoops in and rescues her." She pointed a long finger at me, looking up as if trying to remember all the fucked-up events of the past several days. "And now she hates you again. You should've married me when you had the chance."

"We would've killed each other in the first week." I barked out a laugh.

"For sure."

"As my doctor, shouldn't you be trying to make me feel better? Or at least give me some sound advice. I don't need a reminder of the shitshow my life has become."

She finished the rest of her whiskey and ambled back to the coffee table in the living area. When she returned, she had a syringe in her hand. "As your doctor, I recommend you take the goddamn meds and rest so you can heal."

"And as a friend?"

"Well." She offered me a one-shoulder shrug with a smug smile on her face. "As your friend, I suggest you take the fucking meds, rest so you can heal, and then give the old man a run for his money. He doesn't get to have his cake and eat it too."

"You're starting to sound like Vittoria."

"My aunt is a lot of terrible things. But she's rarely wrong." She sat next to me. "Rex, for once, my family and yours want the same thing. There's a cancer in the Society. We need to cut it out."

"Michael said the exact same thing." At the time, all I could think of was that Caterina could only be safe with me. I had my head so far up my ass, I didn't see through the old man's half-truths.

"You have my family's backing. But you know that in our world, friends are hard to come by. And even harder to keep." She braced her hands on her hips. "Desperate men will do and say anything."

"I know."

"Choose wisely, Rex."

I stared at the city lights beyond the tall windows. She was right. Donata understood this mafia world as well as me. She had her father's sister to teach her. I had Dad. Since I left Atlanta, two things didn't add up for me—one, how was Mikey Gallo able to escape two murder attempts in which his entire family ended up dead? Mikey wasn't that smart or lucky. And two, how was it that Michael, without proof, knew exactly who attacked him?

He was so quick to blame the FBI. And I fell for it. Michael knew I would know about Dad's history with the feds.

Yeah, they hated us, and we hated them right back. But wiping out an entire mafia family required resources and a shit-ton of knowledge. Secret information that only the board had.

Son of a bitch. Michael Alfera had gone too far this time.

"He's using her again. This time, he's using her to get to me." I fisted my hand in anger and my shoulder promptly protested. "She's an innocent. She doesn't deserve this."

"You want to live? Stay away from her. It's the only chance you have to win this fight with her father." Donata's eyes softened. She really wanted me to survive this. "You know I'm right."

"I do. But here's the thing. She was promised to me. She's mine."

"How did I know you were going to say that?" She puffed out a breath. "Michael thinks she makes you weak. Honestly, we all do."

"He wants ruthless. Fine."

I had failed today. Royally. But that didn't mean I was ready to give up on the promise I made to Dad. I swore to save the Society, reunite the families, and honor our code to protect our people. I wasn't about to give up just because some greedy, old man had decided he wanted to play king again.

This was far from over. I had been patient with Michael because of his long-standing friendship with Dad. But enough was enough. Fuck my luck. I knew what I had to do. And I was sure Caterina was going to hate me for it. For real this time.

I fished my phone out of the pocket of my sweats and called Frank. As usual he picked up on the first ring. I didn't wait for pleasantries. "Get my plane ready. We leave in the morning."

"You got it, boss. Where to?"

"Ibiza. Don't tell the onsite team we're coming."

"On it." Static filled the air, and I could tell he wanted to ask if Caterina was coming too.

"You and I are handling this alone. Make sure Caterina's security detail stays with her. I don't trust Michael."

"Yes, sir."

I hung up and glanced up at Donata, who had the biggest smile on her face.

"The king is back."

"I'm following your advice." I pointed at the syringe.

"What's in Ibiza?" She pumped me chockfull of pain killers, a cocktail of her own design.

"A hunch," I mumbled.

Up until now, I had been working under a shit-ton of assumptions and gut feelings. I needed proof now. I needed all the fucking names spelled out. For Caterina's sake, I hoped her father's wasn't on that list. The Society had very specific rules on this. And it forgave no one.

My mind slowly began to drift off, until the throbbing subsided. I closed my eyes and let the images of Caterina play in my head like a movie. At least I had that much. I had real memories of her. I knew how her skin smelled and what she tasted like. And that would have to be enough. Too many lives were at stake.

I couldn't afford to be weak. I had to let her go.

# King of Beasts

BOOK TWO

# CHAPTER 1
## Assholes with Guns

Rex

Caterina Alfera was safe at home. She stayed in her brother's apartment in the upper east side for the most part and only went to work twice a week, properly escorted. I re-read the daily account of Caterina's comings and goings until the letters blurred and ran into each other. Then I switched to the set of images of her.

I glared at the different stills of her eating lunch with a co-worker, shopping for flowers, getting a latte, and a bunch of other mundane things normal people did—as if the time we had spent together hadn't happened. A whole month had passed since I left New York City—since she left me. And I'd yet to figure out how to let her go. I shut the iPad screen and pushed it away.

Through the yacht window, the moonlight rays slanted across the oversize cabin. I imagined Caterina sitting on her

233

heels in the pool of light on the floor. And fuck me if my entire body didn't ache to have her like that again. Caterina was my rope bottom for another five months. One way or another, I would get her to finish her contract with me. For now, I had to stay away from her.

For her own safety, I needed Michael to think he had won this round. Technically, he had. He took Caterina away from me, and I still had no clue who was killing Society members. The old man had covered his tracks well. In all the weeks I had been in Ibiza, I didn't find anything that would indicate he was behind the assassination of the Gallo family. I also had no proof that the FBI was behind it all, or that he was the rat who sold us out. Because of him, the Society was about to be wiped out for good. I couldn't let that happen. I made a promise to Dad, and I intended to keep it.

"Permission to come aboard, Captain." Santino Buratti leaned on the door frame. His mussed hair and undone tie told me he had been out partying all night.

"Way to keep a low profile." I glanced at the clock on the mantel. It was three in the morning. Out of habit, I subtracted six hours to calculate the time in New York City. "You're here to help me find Mikey Gallo, not spend your nights drinking yourself stupid." I rose to my feet and walked around the desk.

The Buratti family was one of the five original families of the Society. An attempt on Santino's father's life made them realize that we were all in danger—that whoever killed the Gallos was coming for us next. When Santino found out I had traveled to follow a clue, he reached out to my guys and offered his help.

Together, we had been tracking Mikey's associates in Ibiza, but every bit of information so far had gotten us nowhere. I was beginning to think my gut had led me astray. I had been so sure that Mikey hadn't survived the attacks on his family because he was that lucky—that he was alive because he'd cut a deal. I had hoped someone in Ibiza would know who was behind it all. I needed a fucking name—or names. Because I was certain Michael wasn't acting alone.

"I'll have you know," he put up a finger and stumbled to a club chair, "I was out chasing a lead."

"And?"

"Another dead end." He shrugged and extended his legs out in front of him.

"I'm so tired of chasing smoke." I paced the length of the room, taking in the salty breeze wafting across the marina and the open windows below deck.

"I'm done with this bullshit trip too. It's time we go home, Rex." He shot a glance toward the door. "Which is why I did something you're not gonna like."

He waved a hand, and five guys barged in with their weapons pointed at my head. The son of a bitch sold me out. I glared at Santino. Blood pumped fast and hard through me while I considered my options. If I started shooting, I would get gunned down before I made it off the boat. *Fuck me.* My only way out was to get Santino to reconsider, to think about what his actions meant for the Society, and his family.

"We want the same thing, Santino. If I go down, we all go down. You just signed your own death warrant."

"Maybe." He perched his hip on the edge of the desk. "We've been trying to talk to these guys for weeks. They don't know anything. They're just assholes with guns."

"We have orders to bring him in." One of the men spoke

up as he stepped toward me. By the tinge of fear in his eyes, I had to assume he knew exactly who I was.

"See? Now you get to meet their boss." He cocked his eyebrow as if he were waiting for me to congratulate him for his brilliant plan.

"You served me up as bait."

"Caterina is messing with your ability to do your job, Rex. Don't pretend. We all know about you and her. Your relationship with her has gone beyond a business one. And not only that, but Michael Alfera has decided he no longer needs to uphold his end of the deal with your family."

I pursed my lips, wishing I could tell him he was wrong.

"You said you came here to get a name, find out who's after us. But I think you came here to prove Caterina's father is innocent in all this. When you know damn well that old man would sell his own flesh and blood to get what he wants. Because of Caterina, you're afraid to find out the truth, which is why all this time you haven't made a modicum of progress. You wanted the Buratti's family help? Here we are. Progress." He turned to the crew. "What the fuck are you waiting for? His permission? Take him."

In the next beat, all five men rushed me. I punched one of them square on the jaw, and then his gut. The effort didn't help my case. Without Santino's help, I had no shot at getting out. He stood back while the crew brought me down and let their leader put me in a chokehold. The last thing I saw before I blacked out was Mikey Gallo's face. *Son of a bitch.*

When I woke up, the sun was high up in the sky. Shimmering blue water sloshed against the yacht. In the distance, a sliver of land appeared. I squinted at it as I tried to catch my bearings. We were out to sea with not a single boat in sight. If

Mikey wanted to kill me, this would be the perfect spot to do it. Easy clean up too since all he would have to do would be to shove me off the deck.

"You had it all. What did the FBI offer you that you didn't already have?" I scowled at Mikey.

Other than Michael Alfera's suppositions, I had no proof that the FBI was behind the killings, but Mikey didn't know that. Even if I didn't make it out of this one, I still wanted to know who betrayed us. Would Santino take that information back to his family and make things right? He'd always been somewhat of a lone wolf. I should've known he'd go off on his own to get answers.

"They offered me my life and freedom." He crossed his arms over his chest. "And a seat at the table. Something my own goddamned family never thought to offer me."

The circles under his eyes were more pronounced than they had been since I last saw him in Atlanta. That night I had gotten shot trying to help him. "The crew in Atlanta. They weren't after you, were they?"

"No. They were there for Massimo. But then you showed up."

"You betrayed your own best friend." I barked out a laugh. "Massimo spent days looking for you. He was worried about you. All the while, you didn't think twice to drag him all the way to Atlanta just to get him killed."

"I'm tired of living in the shadows. Living on the run. I love Massimo. But I love myself more. In the end, it all worked out. Massimo's still alive."

"You're a fucking coward. He could've been killed. How long do you think before the FBI decides they no longer need you? What do you think is going to happen then?"

"What do you care? You won't be here to see it." An older man strode on deck. The greasy hair and cheap suit were a dead giveaway. He was an agent.

"Who the fuck are you?" I met his gaze.

"I'm the hero. The one here to save the day." He glowered at me with so much hate and greed in his eyes, I could only assume he had been waiting for this day for a long time. The man had to be in his late sixties, which meant that at some point he had been chasing Dad too.

"Does our hero have a name?" I shifted my weight against the two men holding me down. The chair inched forward, and the pig shuffled back as if he were afraid of me—coward.

"Special Agent in Charge, Clifton." He offered me his hand, then chuckled. "I see you're tied up at the moment."

"Get on with it. What are you waiting for, Clifton?" I challenged him to make his move.

"I want to savor this moment. Michael didn't think I could do this. He thought you'd be harder to catch. Look at you. I'm not impressed." He pointed at the zip tie around my wrists.

"You didn't make a deal with Michael. What could you possibly offer Michael Alfera?"

"I have plenty to offer." He pointed a finger at me. "A new Society, for example."

*Jesus Christ.*

Made sense. I would bet the heads of all five Dons would earn Clifton a bunch of shiny medals within the bureau. With the board gone, Michael would have the opportunity to come in and build something new, completely under his command.

Where the hell was Santino? Did Clifton really let him go? Or was he dead? Santino was next in line to represent his family. He was already running most of the Buratti businesses.

If Clifton was looking to catch big whales, Santino would be one of them—unless the asshole betrayed us too.

"I came to Ibiza to get a name." I slanted a glance behind me and spotted two men next to Gallo. "And now I have three. I won't stop until you, Mikey, and Michael pay for what you did."

"Enough." Mikey strode into my line of sight. "Throw him overboard already. We're sitting ducks out here."

I peeked at the chopper headed our way, approaching fast. "Yes, you are."

The helicopter circled around us while bullets pelted relentlessly on the polished cockpit. In a matter of seconds, the yacht began to creak and slowly tilt. I stormed to my feet to take cover because the asshole shooting at us didn't seem to care who got hit. He continued to spray the boat with lead until I was the last one left on the foredeck with nowhere to go.

As soon as the machine gun stopped, fucking Santino lowered himself to the landing skid and threw me a fire escape rope ladder. Clifton and his men had disappeared. With the wreckage going under, I didn't have time to go look for them. Mikey had stayed behind, cowering by the closed door that led below deck. Clifton bailed on him.

I flipped over one of the men on the floor and took his weapon. "Fac Fortia et Patere." Do brave things and endure. I reminded Mikey of our mandate as members of the Society. "You betrayed your family," I yelled over the loud hum of the propellers, wincing against the strong wind and debris.

Mikey put up his hands and opened his mouth. I shot him before he had time to think of another lie to save his skin. The Society's by-laws were clear on this. Treason was punishable by death. I dropped the gun and released a breath.

"We don't have time for a memorial," Santino called over the loudspeaker.

*Shit.* I darted toward the chopper, but two steps in, the deck gave out from under me. Fuck my luck. I inhaled and waited for the sea water to drag me under. When I resurfaced, I spotted Santino's rope ladder dangling a few feet away, and swam toward it.

"Hold on." He shouted a bunch of instructions I didn't quite hear over the loud screeching of the boat sinking several feet away.

Kicking hard with my legs, I hooked my elbows around the top step and let Santino and his men pull me up. As soon as I landed inside the cockpit, we veered away from the wreckage.

"You fucking asshole!" I shot to my feet and shoved him onto the seat. "I could've been killed."

"I told you, you were not gonna like my plan." He sat back on his captain chair with a wolfish grin on his face. "Did you get us a name?"

"I did."

"I may not agree with you on a lot of things, Rex. But we're family. Whether we like it or not. We stick together. Mikey Gallo forgot that. And now he's dead."

"Yeah." I nodded while he cut the zip tie around my wrists. "And Clifton?"

"I have a cleanup crew on their way to scour what's left of the yacht. We'll know soon. You got a name?" He cocked his head to look me in the eye. "I gotta hear you say it."

"Michael Alfera," I confirmed the name for him.

Michael Alfera, Caterina's dad, was working with the FBI to wipe us all out. Of course, I had to assume that, at some point, the old man was thinking about betraying the FBI too. It was obvious to me that the only reason he aligned himself with someone like Clifton was because he wanted to come out of retirement and be king again. Except, that position was already taken—I was the king.

"Alfera betrayed us. The by-laws are clear on this, Rex."

"Yes, they are. Michael will answer for what he did. I'll make sure of that."

"You're thinking about his daughter? Jesus, fuck!" He threw his hands up in frustration. "This is why marriages within the families are forbidden."

"More like frowned upon."

"Your dad made a mistake agreeing to Alfera's deal. And now, here we are dealing with the consequences of his actions. But here's the thing, I don't give a shit about what Caterina wants. She'll have to get on board. As for you, you need to stop thinking with your dick and start acting like a king." He winced and swallowed hard.

"I recognize that look on your face." I pointed at his side. "You got hit."

Jesus Christ, Clifton's men were so busy shooting at the chopper, they didn't think to kill me. Santino had taken a huge risk using us both as bait. A risk that had paid off. So, I couldn't be all that pissed off at him, especially since he had been right in his assumptions. A part of me had hoped to find evidence that Caterina's dad wasn't involved with the FBI.

"It's just a scratch." He winced.

I chuckled thinking of how mangled my shoulder had been the last time a bullet grazed me. The wound had taken weeks to heal, mostly because the muscle was shredded in different spots. I tapped the pilot on the shoulder. "How close can you get us to the hospital?"

"Absolutely not," Santino blurted out.

"I have an arrangement with the local doctor. She'll patch you up." I helped him out of his suit jacket. Sure enough, the sleeve of his dress shirt was soaked in blood. "You'll have to wait until we're back in New York to get one of Donata's reviving cocktails."

"You're stalling." He met my gaze. "If you fail to deliver on this, the other families will find a way to unseat you."

"I'm well aware of what's at stake here. And I know what I have to do."

Within the Society, treason was punishable by death. Michael Alfera had crossed the line when he cut a deal with a pig. If left unchecked, he would continue to murder key members of the board, starting with me, Signora Vittoria, and Santino's dad. I had to order Michael's execution. But Santino was right. I was thinking about Caterina and how losing more family would kill her. I was thinking about how much she would hate me for doing my job. I was thinking about how if I went through with it, she would never love me.

But what choice did I have?

## CHAPTER 2
### Back in The Fold

CATERINA

Four weeks, five days, and three hours had gone by since I had left Rex's penthouse. Massimo and Enzo hadn't lied about Dad telling them the whole truth about what I had done to save him from jail. Dad knew. He knew that a couple of months ago, I had gone to Rex and asked for a favor—I'd asked him to forgive dad's debt. Rex had agreed to help. As payment, I became his rope bottom. Dad thought the worst of Rex and me. Except he couldn't possibly know what the worst part was. He imagined Rex kept me in some dungeon, where he had sex with me day and night.

No, Rex didn't do that. What he did was far more intimate than sex and far worse. He got under my skin, into my head, and into every breath I took. And now he was everywhere. I saw him in my dreams and in the sea of faces on the street. On really bad days, I even saw him wandering the halls at work.

Rex Valentino *ruined* me.

I glanced out the window of Massimo's penthouse. The

rain clouds had moved in since mid-afternoon and hadn't let up. In the distance, pedestrians went about their lives in spite of the torrential showers. Or at least, they seemed to be. It was hard to tell from this high up.

My brothers had come to rescue me from Rex. But all they did was change the cage. I still wasn't allowed to go outside or even sleep in my own apartment. Massimo had agreed to drive me to work twice a week so that helped break the routine and this sense of aimlessness.

"Are you ready?" Massimo walked into my line of sight in the living room. "Let me rephrase that. Why are you not ready?" He pointed at my pajama shorts.

"I'm really not in the mood for parties."

"I'm not either. But we have to go and make an appearance. You'll get used to the politics of it all." He sat on the sofa armrest across from me. "Dad wants to show the Society members that the Alfera family is still going strong."

"Mom worked so hard to keep us away from this world." I shook my head. "Why does Dad want to go back to that?"

"To protect us. Things aren't always what they seem." He rubbed the stubble on his cheek.

"What are they really, then?"

"It's not up to me to tell you about all this. You need to talk to Dad." He cocked his head to meet my eyes. "Dad doesn't care about what happened with Rex."

And there it was. The pity. They thought I was some victim who survived something terrible. How could I explain that it wasn't what they thought? That I wasn't hurting or feeling used because of what happened. How could I explain anything if I didn't understand it myself?

"Being a member of the Society isn't as bad as you think. I

244

talked to Rex. He has the right idea. We lost our way over the years, but our priority still is to protect our city, our people."

The mention of Rex's name was like a shock to my system. Suddenly, the light in the room shone brighter. And my body tingled all over. I leaned against the pillow, looking away from Massimo. When the doorbell rang, he stared at me for a few beats, then got up to answer it.

"Oh, I'm sorry. I didn't know you were busy." A female voice boomed out in the hallway. "I'll just go."

I twisted my body to see who it was. The woman at the door was a beautiful blonde in tight jeans, a cropped top, and boots.

"Hi." I rose to my feet and waved to her on my way to my bedroom.

She was obviously here for Massimo. In school, I always had girls being super nice to me. The minute I started talking to them, the conversation quickly turned either toward Massimo or Enzo. Massimo was the smooth one, so the talks were mostly about him.

"Hey, I'm your new neighbor." She stepped toward me; cheeks flushed. "I live two floors down. Mom and I moved in a few days ago. Just needed some sugar." She smiled at Massimo, then quickly turned her attention back to me. "No, I mean, Mom's baking and we're out of sugar."

She rambled on for another minute about mince pies and her mom. The whole time my brother stood there watching her with stars in his eyes and a huge smile. He chuckled and reached for her elbow as she turned to leave. "EJ, why don't you come in and meet my little sister?"

EJ's eyebrows shot up in surprise. "Of course, she's your sister. Look at her."

"Nice to meet you, EJ. I'm Caterina." I offered her my hand, and she shook it. "I live here, too, though I hope it's temporary."

"It's great to meet Massimo's family." She stuffed her hands in the pockets of her jeans, biting her lip as she exchanged a look with Massimo. "I'll talk to you later."

"Yeah, I'll walk you." He winked at me and closed the door behind him.

I couldn't even begin to imagine having such an easy-going relationship with Rex. Even the day he showed up at my work, he seemed so out of place, like a character from some fairy tale who had taken a wrong turn and ended up in my world. My eyes fluttered closed, and my mind quickly unfurled a long sequence of images of all the time I'd spent in his rope room.

"No." I shot to my feet and shook my hands out to clear my thoughts. "Don't go there."

The door opened again, and Massimo walked in with the biggest smile on his face. It seemed EJ had done the impossible. Massimo was happy. I never thought I would get my brother back—the fun, loving brother, the one I had before Mom got sick and Dad started spiraling into a world of depression and gambling.

"Could it be possible?" I laughed. "The great Massimo is in love?"

"Honestly, I don't know what the hell this is. But I've wasted enough time already since Mom. I want to see where it goes. EJ just moved to the city." He managed to say all that without losing his grin.

"Yeah, I got that. Oh wait, she forgot her sugar," I teased.

"That's later." He winked.

"I don't need details."

"Then stop poking." He released a long breath. "Every time she smiles, I get a surge of hope. Like this thing with the Society and Dad, it all seems doable when she's around. I can live this life Dad wants for us, but only if she's in it."

"What does Dad want from you?"

"Bells, you're a smart girl. Now that Mom is gone, Dad wants back into this mafia life. He doesn't just want a say in the day-to-day operations, he wants to sit at the head of the table again." He paused for a few beats as if waiting for me to digest this information. "From the get-go, I told him no. That's why I took off. But now I see how we can use our resources to do good. Rex believes that too. We all want the same thing."

"Dad can't do that to Mom. She fought so hard to keep us all away from his mobster way of life."

"She did. But now she isn't here to talk him out of it." He wrapped his arms around me and let me rest my head on his shoulder.

I missed having Massimo around. I missed how everything was before Mom died. Now that we were all back together, I had hoped that maybe we could be a family again, like we were before. Not exactly as before, obviously, but content enough. I couldn't let Dad ruin that for us. He had already made both my brothers spend a million dollars to bail him out and get me out of Rex's contract. All I could hope for was that Dad wouldn't think to make a deal with Rex like I had. All of Rex's favors came with a high price tag. Surely, Dad knew that.

"I wish I could help you. Now that you're back, maybe we can be a family again. Like before."

"I'm not the one who needs help, Bells." He beamed at me. "I'm happy."

"And I'm happy for you." I plopped myself on the sofa and

patted the cushion next to me. Massimo's good energy was contagious. I would bet anything EJ was behind it all. "Is this the friend you went to Atlanta for? She's got a bit of a southern accent. Doesn't she?"

He braced his hands on his hips, shooting me one of his dour looks.

"You said I could talk to you." I retaliated with an innocent glance.

"Yeah, I meant about your problems. Not my love life."

"Ah, so you do love her?"

He surveyed my face as if considering his options. He knew I wasn't going to let this juicy news go. After a few seconds, he finally conceded and sat. "I met her in Atlanta last month." He shrugged. "She loves cars like me. Actually, she more than loves cars, she builds them. Anyway, she needed a favor for her mom. I helped."

"Hmmm...you're a real-life knight in shining armor, aren't you?" I quipped. "Has she seen your sword?"

The thing about Massimo was, he actually did have one. We all did. Dad had a bit of an obsession with all kinds of weapons. Swords were the only thing Mom allowed us to play with. Somehow, they were a better choice than guns. Jeez, why did I ever think our family was normal? We were far from it.

"You're such a brat. Maybe later we can go upstairs to the gym and I can show you a few moves and wipe that smirk off your face," he teased.

"You know what?" I sat up straighter. "That actually sounds like a good idea. I need to do something. You won't even let me go for a walk."

"That's for your safety and you know that. Something's out there waiting for us. I can feel it. It's hard to explain." He shook his head and reached for my hand. "You told me Rex got hurt in Atlanta, right?"

I nodded.

"He got shot helping Mikey and me. We were ambushed at the hospital where EJ's mom was doing cancer treatments. EJ was there too. I'm going to regret saying this, but Rex is one of the good ones, Bells. His dad did a number on him. I can see why he's so intense and unyielding with everything. But his head and his gut are in the right place." He rolled his eyes. "Not sure about the rest of him though."

"You say that because he was raised to be king of a secret Society?"

"Yeah, among other things. Jesus, Bells, just talk to Dad."

"Okay. I'll do that tomorrow."

"Good. Because he asked me to take you to the Hamptons in the morning."

"The Hamptons? I thought Dad had lost the beach house in one of his gambling stunts."

I coiled myself tighter around the pillow in my arms and tried not to think about where Dad's addiction had led me. I tried not to think of Rex and all the things we did together. Because no matter how much I tried to deny it, I had consented to everything he did to me. And not only that, but I also wanted it. I still did, which was what pissed me off the most. I craved Rex every minute of every day.

"You can ask him about the beach house tomorrow."

"Fine. It's all done anyway. I can wait. Right now, I have to get ready for some bullshit party." I groaned into the decorative pillow. "Rex is going to be there, isn't he?"

"I doubt it. I talked to him last night and he was still in Ibiza." He rose to his feet and pulled me up to stand. "I'll stay with you the whole time. We'll have a few drinks, shake a few hands, tell everyone how Dad is as strong as an ox and that the heart surgery was a minor thing. Then we can come home. You can go back to your sulking." He pressed a hand to his chest. "And I shall go back to the pretty blonde waiting for me downstairs."

"Wait. What? He's not in the city?" I didn't recognize the shriek in my voice. For weeks, I had been agonizing about going to see him. I'd been angry and disappointed that he hadn't tried to reach out to me to talk things through. I hated how we had left things the last time we saw each other. We didn't even say goodbye. "Why didn't you tell me he was gone? What's in Ibiza?"

"Slow down." He put up his hands. "I didn't think you wanted to know. You didn't ask. He went to Ibiza to check on a lead. It seems the trouble that tailed Mikey and me to Atlanta started there."

"Why didn't you go with him? Someone is trying to wipe out the entire Society. All the families. He needs our help."

"I know. I didn't go with Rex because he asked me to look after you." He brushed a strand of hair away from my face. "Man, you have it bad for him."

"I hate him."

He laughed. "Wow. You're in love with him?"

I glared at him.

"Madly in love with him." He blew out a breath in that older brother way that said little sisters could be so annoyingly obstinate. "I can always tell when you're lying. You're so bad at it. Why are you so mad at him? What did he do, Bells?"

The list was long because, as Rex had said, he wasn't a saint. He could've given Dad more time to pay off his debt;

instead, he made me his rope bottom. I was practically a prisoner in his house. And then when my brothers showed up to pay him off, I found out there was no way out of the contract I signed for him.

That was the thing with Rex, everything was a manipulation of sorts, a game. He always held all the power. I hated how weak I was around him—how easily he controlled me. I thought of all the times he tied me up, all the times he made me climax. The images immediately flooded my mind. And as always, in a single breath, I was hungry for him all over again. *Fuck me.* I really, really hated him.

I turned away from Massimo, shaking my arms out to clearly state we were done talking. "I'm getting in the shower."

"Oh, I almost forgot. Your dress came. I left it on the bed for you." He picked up his phone and started texting.

"Thanks." I took a couple of steps, then stopped. Swallowing my tears, I charged him and hugged him tightly. "I'm glad you're home."

"Me too."

An hour later, Massimo, Enzo and I were in a limo headed for the Crucible. The butterflies in my stomach were fluttering something fierce. Not even the breathing techniques I learned from Rex were working. I spent the ride fidgeting with the velvet fabric of the dress Massimo had gotten for me. The strapless bodice of it pushed up my boobs higher than normal, but overall, it fit me like a glove.

"Did EJ help you pick out this dress?"

"What?" Massimo pulled his gaze away from the window to squint at me. "I didn't get that for you."

"Then who did?" My heartbeat picked up the pace. I only

knew one other person who liked to buy me dresses. "You left the box in my room."

"Yes, because I answered the door when the package was delivered. I thought you had bought it."

"I didn't." I blew out a breath. Shit. Shit. Now I was going to spend the entire evening looking over my shoulder, wondering if Rex was there.

"We're here," Enzo deadpanned from his seat across from me. "Let's get this over with."

We pulled up at the front of Rex's building in Midtown, and Aaron rushed to open my door. "Ms. Alfera. Welcome back." He motioned toward the door as if I were a long-time friend. I wasn't. The last time I was here, I was Rex's prisoner.

# CHAPTER 3
## You Ruined Me

CATERINA

Massimo stayed true to his word and didn't leave my side as Aaron escorted us to the gambling floor. The place looked exactly as it had last month when I was here. Why did I think it would look different? Because I felt different? My life hadn't changed much since then. So that made absolutely no sense.

Aaron left us at the bar, then talked into his sleeve. Security was always tight at Rex's parties. With the feds following everyone's steps so closely, it was a huge risk to have all the family members together under one roof. I sipped from the glass of wine Massimo shoved in my hand and scanned the room. Okay, yeah, I was looking for Rex, even though he was thousands of miles away. Maybe he had decided to show up at the last minute. Why else throw a party if he wasn't even going to attend? I supposed Rex skipping his own shindig sounded like something he would totally do. The man could be so infuriatingly enigmatic.

"Drink." Massimo tipped my hand toward my mouth. "You're so tense. And Signora Vittoria is headed this way."

"The woman terrifies me."

"You don't get to be Don by knitting all day."

"When did you meet her?"

"Oh. Dad introduced us." He clinked his glass to mine and laughed just as she strode within earshot of us. Massimo was a natural at this. "Signora Vittoria. Ciao." He kissed both of her cheeks.

"Seems I owe someone a Louis Vuitton." She chuckled as she pressed a cheek to mine. "I didn't think you'd come back. After what happened."

"What happened exactly?" I should've known rumors about Rex and me would spread quickly. Why did I think Enzo and Massimo would keep Dad's debt situation a secret? I made a mental note to give them an earful about airing the family dirty laundry later.

"The attempt on your father's life, of course. Michael's not used to our way of life anymore. I was certain that after what happened, he would change his mind about letting his children be part of the Society. How is he doing? I trust his surgery went okay? You must send him my regards." She surveyed my face with curiosity.

"Well, you know the old man." Massimo leaned casually on the counter of the bar. "He's strong as an ox. The heart thing was nothing."

When I met his gaze, he winked at me. He wasn't intimidated by Vittoria's blank stare at all. I supposed when you were in love, you really did start seeing the world through rose-colored glasses. *Lucky him.*

"I was hoping to see him tonight before my trip. Maybe

next time." She adjusted the mink shawl around her shoulders. Her gaze stayed on me for a beat before she continued, "I'm meeting my niece in Ibiza tomorrow. She's been there for a while taking a well-deserved vacation."

Adrenaline rushed through me. Donata was in Ibiza too. Was she there with Rex? In my mind's eye, I immediately saw them together on a sandy beach, half-naked, and drinking fruity drinks. I wasn't jealous. It wasn't like Rex and I were together. Our contract didn't stipulate that he couldn't see other women. I swallowed the lump in my throat and somehow managed to plaster a smile on my face.

"Ibiza sounds lovely. Safe travels." I gripped the back of Massimo's tuxedo jacket. By the look of pity he gave me, I could only assume that my attempt at playing coy hadn't worked. Why did Vittoria want me to know that her niece was with Rex? To make sure I left him alone? He wasn't even here.

"Signora Vittoria, it was a pleasure to see you again. Now if you'll excuse us. I promised my little sister the next dance." He offered me his hand and I took it.

"Of course, dear." She stepped aside in that regal way of hers. "Do give your father my regards."

I let Massimo usher me away from her. My heart thrashed so hard in my ears; I could hardly catch his words. He kept talking in a soothing tone, until I calmed down. "Anyway, one dance and then we can get out of here. We delivered Dad's message. Vittoria and the other families have no doubt the Alfera family is as strong as ever."

Massimo ushered me through the crowd, smiling at the happy faces turning his way. "I really wish I could have brought EJ to this party." He steered the conversation into a different, more pleasant, direction.

"Why didn't you?" I went with it because I figured this wasn't the time nor the place to talk about what Dad wanted.

"It's too dangerous. I don't want her to get caught up in all this bullshit. Well, no more than she already has because of Gallo." He shook his head. "It's better this way."

"Yeah, it's a good thing she's not here to fend off all these women." I pointed my chin to the group across the way.

I got that we were the gossip du jour, but the glances we were getting on our way to the dance floor were just ridiculous. Correction: the attention my brother was getting was ridiculous. It was like being in high school all over again.

"The mobster ladies love you." I laughed.

"Not interested." He twirled me twice then settled into an easy fox-trot.

Suddenly, the energy in the room shifted. The place got hotter, and somehow, quieter, still. When I glanced away from Massimo's face, my heart spiraled out of my chest and into my throat. Rex stood overlooking the main level, up in the VIP loft, in his usual spot with both hands gripping the banister.

"You told me he was out of the country."

"He was last night." He shrugged.

Rex kept his intense gaze on me as I continued to dance with my brother. Well, Massimo was dancing, I was just getting dragged across the floor because I couldn't get my legs to work properly. I inhaled a long sip of air and focused on the jazzy tune instead of Rex. After a while, my body relaxed enough that I didn't feel like the tin man trying to sway.

Even after Massimo had told me Rex was out of the country, a part of me had fantasized about what it would be like to see him again. Now that we were here, I didn't know what I wanted. I craved his touch. I craved his voice in my ear ordering me to breathe. But if we caved, where would that leave us? We weren't in any type of relationship like Massimo and EJ. Rex wasn't exactly the boyfriend type.

"May I cut in?" A man about Massimo's age and height tapped Massimo on the shoulder. "I don't believe we've been properly introduced."

"There's a reason for that." Massimo tensed next to me.

His reaction shot my heart rate into overdrive. Something about this newcomer felt dangerous. When I glanced up toward the VIP loft, Rex leaned forward. And even though I couldn't exactly see his eyes, I knew he was shooting daggers our way. Massimo stood his ground with his grip firmly on my arm while he stared at the man waiting to see if my brother would let him dance with me. The angry quality in the man's voice was familiar, but I couldn't think of where I had heard it or seen him.

"Caterina." My brother finally conceded after a few seconds. "This is Santino Buratti."

As soon as Massimo said the name, I remembered where I had met Santino before. He had been at Rex's board meeting over a month ago. That night Rex brought all the Dons together to tell them that the entire Gallo family had been wiped out. He called a truce between families, so they could all work together to figure out who was after the Society.

Santino had sat across the table from Dad and me. He was one of the first ones to tell Rex he had no interest in combining resources to face a common enemy. That night, I got the sense that, like Rex, Santino was one of those lone wolf types. This mafia world could be such a lonely place. No wonder Massimo was afraid to get his new girlfriend mixed up in all this. She was his light in this land of darkness.

"We've met before." I shook his hand. "Upstairs."

"That's right. The board meeting." He smirked at me. "You were there with your father. How's the old man doing? Is he here?"

"No, he stayed home." Massimo stepped closer to Santino.

"Right." Santino nodded. "I forgot. The man is as strong as an ox. The heart thing was nothing."

"That's right." I smiled at Massimo, then turned to meet Santino's hazel eyes.

I didn't care about his handsome face, especially when he looked at me as if he could see into my soul. Something about the man scared me. Goosebumps fluttered down my spine. At first, I figured my body was having a fearful reaction to Santino's cold demeanor.

But then a familiar hand settled on my lower back. "How long are you going to keep pretending you don't know me, Caterina?" he whispered in my ear so only I could hear him.

His voice sparked a tiny flame at my core.

"Are you okay?" Massimo squeezed my arm gently. What he meant was—Was I okay being this close to Rex? Did he need to take me away from him again?

"No," I blurted out as my body drifted away from Massimo and toward Rex. My brother had been the only anchor I'd had all night. The fact that I'd let go of my safety net the minute Rex showed up, said so much about the dichotomy in my head. Rex was bad for my health. It didn't matter how good he felt. It was why I couldn't make myself look at him. "I mean yes. I'm fine."

"Are you sure?" Rex slid his thumb over the dip of my waist. "From where I stood, it looked like Santino was overstaying his welcome."

For whatever stupid reason, I thought of his rope room, his hands on my skin, and the way he kissed me the first time he tied me up. What the hell was wrong with me? This was the worst time to be reliving all those memories.

"Yes, I'm sure." I lifted my head and made the terrible mistake of facing him. God, I had missed the familiar smile in his blue eyes, his strong body, and grounding energy.

"Don't mind me. I was just curious to meet the beautiful Caterina." Santino stuffed his hands in the pockets of his trousers. "I was hoping for a dance, but I can see her card is full tonight. Enjoy the rest of your evening." He winked at me and strode off the dance floor.

"What did he say to you?" Rex stared at Santino's retreating form.

"Nothing. Did he have something to say to me?"

"You looked scared. That was all."

"I was here the whole time. She was fine." Massimo glared in the direction Santino had gone.

"Well, now that the big, bad wolf is gone, can I have this dance?" Rex's sexy grin made my knees buckle.

"No." Jesus, of course, I wanted to dance with him. Mainly because I didn't want him to let go of me.

"You're a terrible liar," Massimo whispered in my ear. "I gotta go find Enzo and make sure he's staying out of trouble. Yell if you need me." He sauntered off.

I opened my mouth to beg him to stay, but the words didn't come out. Instead, I watched him disappear into the throng, while my heart thumped hard against my chest. For all intents and purposes, I was alone with Rex Valentino. After all these weeks apart, he was here with me again.

"It's just a dance, Caterina." Rex reached for my waist and

pulled me toward him. When my body made first contact with his, his breath hitched. "Hmmm." He held me tighter, pressing his forehead to mine. "Did you miss me? Did you miss our sessions? Because I did. I haven't forgotten that you still owe me five months."

"You ruined me." The words spilled out as if they'd been on the tip of my tongue this whole time.

"You ruined me first." He inhaled. "I didn't start this war."

"So I was right. You just wanted to hurt me." I wedged my hand between us. All the nights I spent alone in my room thinking of him reeled though my head. Anger swirled at the pit of my stomach. He had some nerve telling me he missed me while he spent his time with someone else. "I hope you and Donata had a great time. Why are you even here? Isn't she waiting for you in Ibiza?"

"What?" He furrowed his brows at me, then pursed his lips. But I could tell he was hiding a smile. The jerk was enjoying this. "I wasn't with Donata. Where did you get that idea?"

"Lying is for cowards. You told me that." I glared at his impossibly beautiful face.

"I don't lie. And you know that. I haven't seen her since the day she was here to check on my wound. That was the night you left. Remember?" He hissed, shaking his head at me. He opened his mouth, then closed it. Whatever he wanted to say, he knew it would be the wrong thing. "Do you even care if I was with her?"

"Of course not. Don't be ridiculous." I tried to shuffle away from him, but my legs didn't obey me.

Our gazes locked. Yeah, I was jealous of Donata. I was jealous that she got to spend an entire month with Rex at some beach, while I sat at home alone, sitting by the window, watching the rain fall.

"You're killing me." His lips crushed into mine.

As it always did when we touched, the world fell away. I wrapped my arms around his neck and kissed him back. I wanted to taste him so badly. I wanted to prove to myself that I wasn't crazy. That Rex existed. That what I felt when he touched me was real. It felt too real to be a lie.

"Rex." I panted a breath.

"I know." He cradled my neck, ghosting my lips, taunting me with promises of all the things we couldn't have. "Come upstairs with me."

## CHAPTER 4
## No Contracts This Time

Rex

"That's not going to happen. Not now. Not ever." She made to leave then turned around. "You have some nerve. You've been gone for over a month. What did you think was going to happen here tonight? That you were just going to show up, kiss me, and I would immediately jump into bed with you?" She shoved me away and didn't even give me a chance to explain that all I wanted to do was talk.

I smiled at her retreating form, glad that I wasn't the only one who was still hung up on the whole sex thing. Jesus, fuck, our timing couldn't be worse. I fished my phone from the inside pocket of my jacket and called Frank.

"She's headed toward the elevators. Send her upstairs."

"Got it, Boss."

I hung up. When I glanced up, Massimo stepped into my line of sight, shaking his head. "You haven't learned a thing, have you?"

"What?" I rubbed the creases on my forehead, squinting at him to focus. Caterina always had a way to leave me dazed and confused.

"She hates being manipulated. Why do you think she left you before?" He furrowed his brows as if this thing with Caterina was so simple—as if the answer to my problem was right in front of me, but I was too dumb to see it.

"I just want to talk."

"And for that, you need your men to bring her to you? You could've asked."

"I did ask her." I pointed toward the direction where Caterina had left.

He glanced down at his phone. "I have to go."

"Then go."

"Not without my sister." He raised an eyebrow. "Don't make this worse on yourself."

*Fuck me.* Massimo had a point. From the beginning, I had cornered and threatened Caterina to get her to stay with me. She deserved better. I had told myself this time it would be different between us. But I was wrong. All it took was for her to say no once for me to go back to my old ways. I raked a hand through my hair, trying to figure out my next move. I didn't want to mess this up. This conversation was too important.

"Give me five minutes. If in that time she still wants to go with you, I'll let her go."

"You forgot to say please." A smirk pulled at his lips.

The asshole was enjoying this.

"Fuck off." I walked past him and headed toward the grand staircase. The elevator access through the VIP loft was a short cut to my penthouse.

"Don't push her so hard. She's been through enough," Massimo called after me over the jazzy tune still playing on the dance floor.

I stopped to look at him. "I know. But she deserves the truth."

"Yeah, she does." He nodded.

Guests moved out of the way with polite smiles as I made my way upstairs. By the time I stood in front of the elevator car in my private lobby, my heart was beating fast and out of control. When the doors slid open, Caterina greeted me with one of her angry scowls.

"This is kidnapping."

"I just want to talk." I put my hands up in surrender and swallowed. "Please." The gates activated again, and I stepped forward to stop them. If Caterina didn't make the call now, I was going to have to let her go. "Massimo is waiting downstairs. Call him and tell him you're staying. We have a lot of unfinished business. You know we do."

"Rex." She pressed a hand to her forehead and met my gaze.

This was good news. She was at least giving it a second thought. Massimo was right. It wasn't that she didn't want to be here. She was simply tired of being pushed around—first by her dad and then me. Jesus, I was no better than Michael. I had been an asshole. I was lucky she was still standing here willing to give us a shot.

"Call him." I tapped on Massimo's number and offered her my phone.

She took it and pressed the device to her ear. "I'm upstairs with Rex. I'll see you later, okay?" After a while, she glanced down and smiled. "I love you too." She hung up.

"What did he say?"

"He said that if I didn't like what you had to say that I should kick you in the balls and get out of here." She ambled past me and headed for the entrance to the penthouse.

Her perfume trailed behind her. I inhaled it, and for the first time since she left me, I breathed easy. I adjusted my gait to get to the door first and opened it for her. "You look beautiful in that dress."

"Thanks." She ran her hand over it, then her head snapped up at me. "You sent it, didn't you? At first, I assumed Massimo had ordered it for me. But it was you."

"The deep forest green made me think of your eyes. I figured you should have it." I flipped the lock behind me and sauntered to the bar cart near the floor-to-ceiling windows. The view of the city at this time of night was breathtaking. I hoped it would help improve Caterina's disposition. "How about a drink?" I poured wine into two glasses and offered her one.

"You were gone." She stared at the drink in her hand.

"I had a good reason." I reached for her elbow. "And I want to tell you all about it. But first, I want to talk about us. There was so much I didn't get to tell you before."

"Before my brothers paid off my father's debt and took me away from you?"

"Exactly that."

"Why did you do it? Why the entrapment?"

That was a loaded question. I glanced up, trying to sort out my answers. In the end, I opted for the truth sitting at the core of it all. "Because I didn't think you'd want me otherwise."

"Are you serious?" She laughed, shaking her head. "Next

time, how about just ask me out on a date? Like a normal person."

"We're not normal people." I brought her fingers to my lips. Goosebumps traveled up her arm, and something raw unraveled in my chest. How could I want her this much? "There's going to be a next time?"

"Rex." Her eyes fluttered closed, and she leaned closer.

"Tell me what you want, and it's yours."

I braced myself for her answer because, at this point, I had no clue what was going through her head. She was mad at me. That much I knew. But did she love me? Did she want to have a go at whatever it was we had managed to build in the short time she lived with me?

"Against all reason." She fisted the lapel of my tuxedo jacket. "I want you." Her gaze traveled from her hand, up to my face, and then the grand staircase to her left. "All of you."

My breath hitched. "My little virgin, I don't think you're ready for that." I pressed my lips to hers gently. I wasn't saying no. But her brother was right. She had been through enough. Rushing her would only scare her off again.

"You don't know what I am." Her eyes welled with tears.

The hurt I saw in them twisted my insides. She thought I was rejecting her the way I had done the first time she offered herself to me. That night I had said no because as much as I desired her, I didn't want her first time to be a business transaction to save her father, especially when he didn't deserve the sacrifice.

"I'm not saying no, Caterina. I just want you to be sure."

"You said I could have anything I wanted. Don't go and say something mean to make me angry and push me away."

"What happened to the "not now, not ever" from ten

minutes ago?" I picked up a fat curl resting on top of her breast.

"See what I mean?" Her cheeks turned a pretty pink, while she scowled at me with those gorgeous green eyes. "Why do you keep doing that? Why make me love you if you never had any real interest in me? Why am I really here, Rex?"

Now it was my turn to be confused and frustrated because she wasn't making any sense. "You love me?"

"No. Of course... not."

"You just said you did."

"Rex."

My name on her lips was my undoing. I gripped her waist and stalked her back until she was pressed against the cool glass with the entire city at her feet. Her erratic breath came out in puffs and brushed against my face. Reason went out the window, and for the life of me, I couldn't remember why or how sex with Caterina was a bad idea.

I kissed her hard and desperately.

This morning I woke up in an empty bed. My whole body ached from wanting her. It physically hurt to know I couldn't have her. Because even if she didn't exactly hate me before, I knew she would this time. Her dad had crossed the line. There was no coming back from that, not for him, or me.

She slipped her hands inside my jacket and pushed it off my shoulders. A part of me knew that making love to her now was a mistake. But watching her undo the studs on my tuxedo shirt made my cock hard as a rock. I had waited long enough for her. Tonight, she wasn't here to save her dad. She was here for me. No contracts this time. She walked through the threshold because she wanted me.

I stepped back to look at her while I worked on removing my cufflinks. "Take off your underwear."

She cleared her throat as she ran her hands down the skirt of her dress. Her fingers stopped right at the apex of the thigh-high slit, and she glanced up.

"Do it now."

"I can't."

My erection pushed against my trousers when I realized why she couldn't take off her panties. "Were you thinking of me earlier when you put on that dress?"

"I was." She nodded twice.

"Show me."

I had seen her bare pussy more than once. But this was the first time I got to see it because she wanted me to, not because she was lost in a frenzy waiting for me to make her come. Her hand trembled as she fisted the fabric and pulled it up to her waist. My gaze stayed glued to her sex, while I reached behind me, pulled my undershirt off and tossed it aside. Caterina was finally mine.

"You're so beautiful." I pressed my hand to her clit. "Jesus, you're so wet for me already."

I dropped to my knees and touched my lips to her mound. When I glanced up, she was staring at me with her mouth half-open, and she looked like she couldn't breathe.

"Take a sip of air. I promise this part won't hurt." I lapped the length of her seam.

Her folds were swollen with desire. And all I wanted to do was put us both out of our misery, but this was her first time. I had to take it slow. I buried my face in her pussy, nibbling and sucking around her bud. She gripped my hair with one hand while she held on tightly to her dress with the other.

I kept at it until I felt her tense. Then I rose and captured her mouth. I cupped her cheek, kissing her hard, letting her have a taste of her own juices. "You like that?"

"Yes."

"I could make you come like that." I sucked hard on the column of her neck. "I could bury my fingers inside you until you climax. But right now, I want my cock to claim your first time. I want your walls to open just for me."

She nodded, even though I wasn't asking for permission. A shock of adrenaline and desire rushed through me, and I kissed her again. She responded by thrusting her tongue past my teeth while she rubbed against my thigh like she had done on the plane to Atlanta.

That day seemed like years ago now. So many missed opportunities. I regretted every single one of those times when I could've had her and chose not to out of some idealistic sense of duty. The image that haunted me every goddamn night was of her taking off her dress for me in the boardroom downstairs. Every curve of her body was tattooed in my mind's eye.

"I want to see you. Show me like you did before. Take off your dress."

She smiled shaking her head. "That night was a new low for me."

"I hope you know that saying no to you that night was the hardest thing I'd ever had to do. One, because I wanted you in the worst way possible. And two, because I knew my rejection hurt you."

"I wanted you so badly." Her chest rose and fell as she reached behind her to pull on her zipper. She held the bodice in place, biting her lower lip.

"Now."

When she let go, a pool of green velvet gathered at her feet. She wore nothing underneath, as if she had known we would end up in my penthouse before the night was over. Or maybe like me, she had hoped we would finally put our problems aside and give in.

Her nipples tightened until they were nothing more than pink buds. I cupped both of her breasts and brought one to my mouth. She rewarded me with a loud moan right before she called my name. I switched to her other side and sucked hard. Home. She felt like home and hopes and dreams.

"Lie down." I pointed at the upholstered oversized chaise in the middle of the living room.

She did as I asked without question and that made me even harder for her. Caterina was everything I ever wanted and then some. The scene in front of me was like something straight out of one of my fantasies—Caterina naked on her back, tits on full display, and her pussy dripping with desire for me. It was like I had died and gone to heaven.

I reached into my back pocket and got a condom out of my wallet. She watched me with doe eyes while I removed my pants and freed my erection. The smallest of yelps escaped her lips, and then I realized she had never seen me at full mast. I ambled around her, braced a knee next to her head, and pumped a few times. "Take it." I wanted her to get used to my length and girth before I took her pussy. And I'd been dying to see that pretty mouth around my cock.

To my surprise, she sucked me off eagerly, as if she had been fantasizing about this too.

"Christ. You feel too good." I let her hand and mouth work me a little longer, noting she could only take me halfway before her eyes watered. *One step at a time, baby.*

"Last chance to tell me to go to hell." I pulled away and quickly rolled on the condom.

"Rex." She let herself fall back on the chaise.

"I'm right here, love. I've always been here." I pushed her thighs outward and entered her.

# CHAPTER 5
## I Did It for You

CATERINA

Rex braced his hands on either side of my head and lowered himself to brush his lips to mine. His blue gaze stayed on mine as he waited for the initial pain to subside. It didn't exactly hurt. I just hadn't known what to expect to have a cock his size inside me. When I exhaled, he smiled and slowly began to rock his hips to give me all of him. And omigod, there was so much of him. I squeezed my walls tighter, reveling in his length. I didn't want this to end.

"Do you trust me?" he whispered along my neck.

"Yes." A ribbon of desire spiraled from my belly down to my toes, and I didn't catch the rest of his words. He had worked my body into a frenzy, and all I could think of was the orgasm teetering deep inside me. Every time he thrust forward; I inched a little closer. "Rex." I panted a breath, running my nails over the hard valleys on his back. *The man was beautiful.*

"You're already there."

I arched my back, unsure of what else I needed to finish

already. My skin felt hot where his body touched mine. If I didn't find relief soon, I was going to combust.

"Promise me you'll spend the night." He sucked firmly on one of my nipples before he tongued just the tip and flicked it from side to side.

"What?"

When he pulled out, my eyes flew open. The absence of him was unbearable. I hooked a leg over his hip and rubbed against him. That earned me a passionate and desperate kiss, but he kept the shaft of his erection at my entrance, teasing and gliding along my folds. It felt so good, but it wasn't enough. Now that I knew how his cock felt inside me, this clit play was infuriating.

"Don't be cruel," I mumbled on his lips.

"Then tell me you'll stay."

"Where else am I gonna go?" I buried my fingers in his soft hair and brought his mouth down to mine.

With a groan that rumbled deep in his chest, he captured both my wrists with one hand and fixed them over my head. In the next breath, he plunged forward. I quickly found out he had been seriously holding back before. Every muscle in his body bulged up as he rode me hard and without mercy. A slow burn kicked up inside me and then fluttered outward, straight into my clit and the rest of me.

This yearning, this all-consuming desire I felt for him finally made sense. We were always meant to end up together, raw and bare like this. When the air stilled around me and the lights dimmed, I squeezed my eyes shut and simply let go. My orgasm came in waves several times over while Rex continued his fast pace. I had no idea it would be like this.

As Rex found his own release, he tensed on top of me,

whispering against my temple in between grunts of pleasure. "I meant it when I said I loved you. I still do."

"I love you too." The words came from a secret place in my heart, from inside a tiny box I had buried there out of fear.

A pressure lifted off my chest. Saying the words aloud brought down the last wall I had built between us. Because the truth was, I had never hated Rex. I pushed him away because I knew he was dangerous. I knew that if I ever got close to him, I would fall hard and forever.

"I only wish you hadn't taken this long to admit that to yourself." He planted a loud kiss on my jaw and then moved down to both my breasts as his warm hands kneaded each mound. "We could've been doing this all this time."

"Just remember, you were the one who rejected me." I cupped his cheek when his gaze met mine.

"You would've hated me for real if I had taken you up on your offer. You would've hated yourself if I had paid for sex with you. All we have now would've been tainted by greed."

I closed my eyes, so he wouldn't see my tears. Of course he was right. The first time I came to him, I had come to sell him my body in exchange for Dad's freedom.

"Hey." He ran the pad of his thumb along my jaw. "None of that was your fault. You did what you did to protect your family. I'm not one to judge."

"I see anger in your eyes every time you mention that night. If you're not judging me, then who?"

"How about we don't talk about that while my dick is still inside you? Believe it or not, having sex with you tonight hadn't been my plan at all. I really did only want to talk to you." He released a breath and flashed me a charming smile that made my knees weak. "Not that I'm complaining."

He kissed me softly for a long while. Yeah, we had a conversation pending, but for now, I wanted to enjoy this time with him. These past few weeks I had felt so aimless and empty. Now that he was here with me, I didn't want to go back to being alone in Massimo's penthouse.

"Come on." He stood and offered me his hand.

He helped me up, before he bent down to sweep me into his arms. I giggled. I actually giggled out of sheer bliss and excitement as he carried me up the stairs and into the massive bathroom in his suite.

"Do you do this with all your rope bottoms?" I sat on the edge of the tub while he ran the water and added scented salts and bubbles into it.

"Rope play and sex are two mutually exclusive practices." He turned to face me. "For me at least. It's different for everyone."

The smirk that pulled on his lips told me he knew that for me, every one of our sessions had been a major turn-on. I blushed thinking about how things would be different in his rope room now that we had crossed the line. Would he still let me come at the end of our hour? Or would he take me while I was bound?

His amused chuckle yanked me out of my fantasy. Though he was a bit late. My mind had already conjured several wild ideas, most of which included him and a suspension line. I had seen the picture of Violet in such a bind, floating in a dark room with Rex standing next to her. The whole scene was so erotic, it had stayed with me even after I left Rex's penthouse. After the first week of being alone, that particular photo made it into my nightly routine while I pleasured myself.

"Maybe later you can tell me what you were thinking

about. For now, we need to get you cleaned up. Baby steps, love." He pointed at my crotch, where a drip of blood had already dried up inside my thigh.

"Oh. I'm bleeding." Heat rushed to my cheeks.

Not long ago, I had tried to lie to Rex about my virginity. It seemed so old school to still be a virgin at twenty-four. I had my reasons that had all to do with Mom and the years she was sick. That day, he had taunted me, telling me there was only one way to find out for sure. Well, now he had proof of it. Rex Valentino was my first. And it was everything I had dreamed it would be.

"That's nothing to be embarrassed about." He cradled my neck. "Did I hurt you?"

"No, not at all."

"Come on." He stepped into the tub and helped me do the same.

When I sat, he settled in behind me and pulled me into his arms. Who would've thought that a ruthless king would have a caring and loving side? With cheeks still burning hot, I watched as he dipped his hands in the water and rubbed my legs and pussy until they were clean. His hands were pure magic. I didn't care if I was starting to feel sore. I wanted him again.

As if he could sense my need for him, he left my folds alone and wrapped his arms around me instead. "I want you too. But trust me, you're going to be hurting later."

"Fine." I groaned and shifted my body so I could rest my head on his chest. "Can I ask you something?"

"Anything, love." His hands slid up my stomach and onto my breasts.

"Why Kinbaku?"

"Hmmm." He grunted in response. He was silent for several minutes, then answered. "The trust and control that come with it are soothing to me."

His words were hesitant and lacked the imposing tone Rex usually had when he spoke. Was it possible that he'd never uttered those words aloud before? Because he didn't want anyone to know, or because no one dared ask him before? I supposed in his case, it could very easily be both.

"Control?" I asked. "You have an entire floor downstairs full of people who do everything you say. Why do you need more of that?"

"You believe I can tell Signora Vittoria what to do? Control is an illusion. They might fear me. I might be able to force them into doing something I want. But I don't control them. Or you, for that matter. Sometimes, I don't even have full control of my own life. I mean look at how our story began."

"How did you get started with the study?"

"You really want to know?"

"I'm asking." I sat up to look him in the eyes, but I got lost ogling his muscular body. Even sitting here in a tub surrounded by bubbles, he looked manly and sexy as all heck. I pressed my hand to his hard pecs and bent down to kiss him there. "I wanna know. Have you ever been a bottom?"

His head fell back a little as he barked out a laugh. "Jealous is a good look on you." He cradled my neck and brought my mouth to his.

"I'm not jealous. Just curious." And maybe a tiny bit jealous of the person who taught him how to work a rope, how to breathe, and how to get his bottom fully engaged. For some stupid reason, I imagined an older woman teaching young Rex all about binds and gentle touches.

"Admit it. You've been dying to get back in my rope room ever since the elevator door opened and you realized you were in the penthouse again." He gripped both my wrists in his large hand and squeezed just to prove his point.

"You're such a jerk."

"Tell me I'm wrong."

Goosebumps fluttered down my arm. Rex was a master at planting bad ideas in my head. Though if I were being honest, the thought of getting tied down again did cross my mind when the elevator to his floor opened. I shook my head. No, I couldn't tell him he was wrong in his assumption.

"I did it for you." He brushed his wet fingers over my burning cheeks. "I picked up Kinbaku for you."

"Wait. What? How? Why?" I couldn't wrap my head around those five little words. He did it for me?

"Not the practice itself, but what I got out of it. When I realized I had developed feelings for you, I knew I had to change my ways. Learn to control my emotions and be better. For you."

"Kinbaku grounded you."

"It did. Something told me, it would do the same for you. Or maybe that was just wishful thinking. I can't imagine my life without a rope room." A low chuckle rumbled in his chest.

"What would you have done if I hated it?"

"Hmmm. I don't know. Come up with a different agreement. Caterina, I would never make you do anything you don't want."

"What? Like you'd bring in other bottoms? I don't think so." I glared at him. The idea of Rex tying up other women, holding them, touching them—it made my blood boil.

"I really do like this look on you." His deep, sexy laugh

made my clit throb a little. For whatever reason, he found this whole thing funny. He held me tighter and kissed the top of my head. "I guess it's a good thing you like being my rope bottom. I only want you."

"I do like being yours." I rested my head on his wet shoulder.

"I know."

Being like this with Rex felt so easy and familiar. How did we manage to stay away from each other for so long? Did I do that? Did I push him away? Maybe I did, but only because he never showed me any sign that he wanted me, that he loved me.

"You say you've been in love with me for a while." I shifted to meet his gaze. "Why didn't you talk to me? You were always so mean and all-mighty. Ruthless. Like you hated me."

"I did hate you." He tensed, and that usual darkness in his eyes appeared. "At first, anyway."

"I'm not following. What do you mean?"

"I didn't just hate you. I hated everyone and anything that had to do with the Society and being king." He inhaled and hugged me. "I know I was rude to you many times. I hurt you."

Of all the things Rex did and said to me before, only one cut me deep. I had come home from college to see Mom. Her cancer had gotten worse, and it landed her in the ER. That day, he showed up at the hospital where Mom was being treated, he cornered me in a dark room and told me my life was about to change and there was nothing I could do to stop it. "The sooner you get over it," he'd said, "the better off you'll be."

He had meant get over Mom's death. It had been such a

cruel thing to say to an eighteen-year-old. I never understood why he would treat me like that. He barely knew me.

"When Mom got sick—"

"I know what I said that night at the hospital. You have no idea how sorry I am. I had meant it as a warning, and it came out all wrong." He stood and grabbed a fluffy towel off the heated rack. "I think it's time you and I have that conversation." He helped me up and wrapped me in it.

"I went off on you that day. I hated you for telling me to get over Mom's death when she was fighting for her life a few doors down."

"That wasn't what I'd meant to say. That's when I realized you were an innocent bystander in all this, that what was happening to me had nothing to do with you." He wiped my cheek with a facial cloth, then ushered me to the walk-in closet.

When he opened the door, my mouth dropped open. "What the hell?"

"What?" He followed my line of sight and then let out a breath. "Oh, that."

"Yeah, that. A his and hers closet?" I strode to the dress hanging on a valet rod. "I wore this dress the first night I was here. You have a whole closet full of clothes for all your rope bottoms to share?"

"Of course you went there. No, Caterina. I got all this for you. You were always meant to be here with me." He rubbed the creases on his forehead. "I can see why none of this makes sense. But trust me, it will once I tell you the story of the ruthless king who fell in love so hard and so resolutely, he sold his daughter's soul to the devil."

I opened my mouth to speak, but the words didn't come

out. Rex's eyes had the same darkness I had seen in them the night I went to him to plead for Dad's freedom. His words had turned cold and calculated.

"You're scaring me."

"Don't be scared." He pressed his forehead to mine. "You never have to be afraid of me, love. Do you trust me?"

I thought long and hard about my answer because if Rex was about to be honest with me, then I needed to do the same. When I considered all the times I had been with him, I realized that every time he was being cruel, it was because he was telling me a truth I didn't want to hear. I didn't like being around him for that very reason. His reality bit, his candor hurt.

"I trust you to tell me the truth."

"That's all I need."

A soft kiss on the lips made my eyes fluttered closed. When I opened them, Rex was gone. In a daze, while Rex's words floated in and out of focus in my mind, I found a simple sheath dress to wear. I fixed my makeup and then headed out to meet him in his suite.

# CHAPTER 6
## Play the Bad Guy for Him

Rex

"What is it with you and Massimo trying to get me drunk tonight?" Caterina sauntered out of the ensuite bathroom and sat next to me.

She looked good in my home. I hated that we had to have this conversation tonight. We had made so much progress in our relationship—if we could call it that. She had finally admitted to herself that she had feelings for me. Caterina Alfera was in love with me. But was that enough to keep us together? Once she found out what I planned to do with her dad, she would hate me.

"I just need you in a good mood." I pushed the glass of rosé over to her side of the coffee table. "Part of this is all my fault. I should've been honest with you from the get-go. Or at the very least since you came to me to ask for help."

"Just tell me. You're starting to sound like Massimo and Enzo with their half-truths." She sipped her wine, expectantly.

"Remember the contract you signed for me?"

"The one where I agreed to be your rope bottom for six months?" She rolled her eyes as she tucked her legs under her butt. "Yes, Rex. I remember."

"Every mafia favor comes with a price. Everyone knows that."

"I knew what I was getting into." She reached out and squeezed my shoulder.

I took her hand in mine and kissed the inside of her wrist. "Michael signed a similar contract for my father." I grabbed the manila folder off the coffee table and placed it on her lap.

"What kind of favor did Dad ask for?" She glanced up at me. "And what did your dad ask for in return?"

"Read."

While she read, a sense of calm washed over me. There were no more secrets between us. I was done playing by Michael's rules where he always ended up playing the saint to Caterina. I braced my arms on my knees and kept my gaze on the crackling fire in front us.

"I don't know how much you know, but in his time, Michael Alfera was the most ruthless king the Society has ever had. Even the FBI was afraid to mess with us during his reign. Dad wanted something different, but it wasn't up to him. But then, something like out of a fairytale story happened. Michael met your mother. In a matter of months, Anna changed him. So much so that—"

"So much so that he decided to leave the Society. For her." Her green eyes sparkled with unshed tears.

"My father convinced the board to let him step down."

"And I was the price." She sat very still with the contract in her grip.

I swallowed and waited for her to process the pages she

had just read. The minute hand on the clock over the mantle ticked on while she stayed on her side of the sofa, frozen or numb—or too angry to speak. Not knowing what she was thinking was torture. I ached to hold her and tell her everything was going to be okay. I ached for her, for all the times her own father lied to her. I ached for her because there was no going back now. She would finally understand Michael didn't deserve the pedestal she built for him.

Was she even breathing?

"Breathe, Caterina," I whispered and reached for her hand.

She recoiled from me, shaking her head. I deserved that because as much as I'd like to blame all this on Michael, I had to admit, I was complicit in all of it. Several beats later, she released a breath that sounded more like a gasp.

"Tell me what you're thinking. Please."

Her gaze met mine, and surprise registered in her green eyes, as if she had forgotten I was still in the room. "What am I thinking?" She stood, and the crease between her brows deepened. "I'm thinking about Mom and all the years she spent living a lie, loving a man who didn't exist. I'm thinking about my brothers and how different their lives must've been from mine. I'm thinking about all the times Dad could've told me the truth and chose not to."

"It's okay to be angry."

"I'm not angry." She stuffed a hand in her hair and made a fist. "I don't know what I am. What the hell am I supposed to do with this?" She pointed at her chest as if all the emotions she felt right now were trapped in there, threatening to gush out all at once.

"I know exactly how you feel. I read the same contract over ten years ago. It's cruel. I know."

She showed me the papers then tossed them on the floor. "He sold his children like cattle just so he could be with Mom?" She winced, stepping away from me. "The Society got to keep Enzo and Massimo as soldiers. And me, as what? Insurance? So no one could contest your title when it came time for you to step up?"

If she wasn't breathing before, now she was puffing breath after breath. Color returned to her cheeks and her eyes glistened with tears.

"Exactly." I glanced up at her, shocked she wasn't furious with me. I should've told her the truth from the beginning. "It wasn't just you. It was all of us. When Michael chose to leave and signed that contract, I got dragged into it too."

"That's why you hated me. Our parents arranged my marriage to you, the day I was born." She walked around the coffee table. "Who does that?"

"If you asked Michael, he would say— a man in love. A man who wants to keep his family safe." I stood and casually ambled to block the path to the door. She wasn't leaving this room until she heard the entire truth. She was hurting. If she was still here it was because she wanted answers. But who knew how much more of Michael's fucked-up plan she could take? I pressed on. "Dad told me about the contract the day I turned eighteen."

"I bet it felt great to find out you were engaged to a fourteen-year-old?" She fisted her hands.

"I was told I was allowed to date, but if I wanted to keep my sanity, it would be best if I didn't fall in love." I had never said those words aloud. A minute after Dad had that conversation with me, I buried it deep inside me and never gave it a second thought. Though a lot of it manifested itself in the form of cruelty and ruthlessness. "I hated everything you stood for. I was trapped in this life I didn't want because your father wanted to give you a better childhood. In a way, he succeeded, I suppose. You grew up without a care in the world."

"I was clueless. Not sure that's living. How could Dad do this? How could he even think for a minute that this monumental lie could work?" She swallowed and wrapped her arms around her belly, looking so alone and hurt.

"Michael was supposed to give you the speech when you turned eighteen. But then your mother got sick and he postponed the whole thing." Gently, I brushed the back of my fingers over her arm. I didn't know how else to soothe her, to make her pain go away. For me, all of that didn't go away until I found Kinbaku.

She squeezed her eyes shut, but other than that, she didn't move away from me. "That's why you came to me that night at the hospital. To warn me."

"I'm so sorry. In a way, I guess I was looking for a connection, but I wasn't in the right state of mind."

She paced the length of the room from the fireplace to the window and then back to me. "But if I already belonged to you, why the ruse? Why make me sign a different contract to be your rope bottom?"

Shit. Now it was my turn to confess all my sins.

"Because I made a promise to your mother. Your mom found out about the deal Michael had made with the Society. It was right around the time she got sick, four years ago. She came to me and asked me to set you free."

"What? Mom knew?" She pressed a hand to her forehead

while tears streamed down her cheek. "I'm surprised it didn't kill her. To know Dad lied to her for so long, to know her kids were no more than pawns."

"Your mom was much stronger than that. She wanted to fix this for you. She tried really hard to undo it all. She begged Dad, and then me, to release you from the Society contract."

"But it wasn't up to you." She wiped her face.

"No. And she knew that. There wasn't anything Dad could do either. I offered her the next best thing. I told her I would marry you just like Dad wanted. But if you didn't love me, I wouldn't make you be my wife for real." I glanced down at my hands. "I wanted to make good on that promise. It was so important to her. I wanted to give her that. I knew I had to find a way to cope with all my frustration and anger for not having a life of my own."

"That's when you found Kinbaku."

"I had to find a way not to hate you. So yeah, I went looking for it. And it worked. I learned to control my emotions and to see things under a different light." I inhaled and held my breath for a few seconds before I released it. "The next part I didn't see coming. I wanted to get to know you. So I had one of Dad's guys follow you twenty-four-seven."

"You started stalking me?"

I hissed. I wanted to say no, that it wasn't like that. But who was I kidding? It was exactly like that. I thought of all the nights I had spent pouring over her daily reports, memorizing her features, and just falling in love with the light I saw in her eyes.

"Yes. I told myself I just wanted to learn more about my future wife. But then, I became obsessed with you and this insane idea that you were mine. All mine. My birthright."

I stopped to inhale and met her gaze. Her mouth went slack as she stared at me, brows raised in surprise. What was she thinking? I didn't want to scare her off. But also, I didn't want to lie. She was right before—manipulating the truth was the same as lying. She deserved the truth. All of it. No matter how painful.

"Say something."

"Jesus, Rex."

I took a tentative step toward her. When she didn't move away, I wrapped my arms around her and held her tight. A slow burn sparked below my navel. She was still here. "It was Michael's idea to bring you here. He wasn't ready to tell you the truth. Especially after your mom passed away. He asked me to help him."

"Wait? What?" Her voice went up a few octaves. "Dad asked you to bring me here as your prisoner. Why?"

"Because it was time for him to make good on his contract with my father. You and I were supposed to be married as soon as I took over for Dad. That was a few months back. But Michael was afraid to tell you the truth."

"So he asked you to play the bad guy for him."

"I wanted to." No sense in trying to play the hero. I had to be honest with her. I wasn't the hero in this story. "I thought that if you spent some time with me before you found out about the arranged marriage, you would learn to love me. But then, Michael changed his mind."

"He never owed you any money. Did he?"

"That part was real. He did gamble a million dollars at my casino. Except, he did have the means to pay me back." I took her hand and brought it to my lips. "Your dad wants to come back to the Society. He feels that if he does, he no longer owes us anything."

"I'm not a thing, Rex." She pursed her lips. And there it was, the fire and hate in her green eyes had returned. "So what if Dad wants to come back? He's doing it to protect his family."

"It doesn't work that way. No one ever leaves the Society—he did. And you were the price. He has to pay. The only reason he wants to come back is because your mother is gone. I'm sorry, Caterina, he can't have his cake and eat it too."

Her body trembled as she stared at the fireplace. I could see the wheels turning in her head while she tried to put the pieces of the puzzle together. She knew my words were true. And now, all the little details surrounding Michael's actions made sense. He had been using her since he found out he was having a girl.

"In some sort of fucked up Hail Mary, Michael betrayed the Society." I took a long breath to ease the pressure in my chest. "Do you know what that means?"

Her gaze snapped up at me. She already knew where I was going with this. "What did he do?"

"He cut a deal with the FBI. He doesn't just want to return to the fold, he wants to be king. He wants things to be the way they were before he met your mother."

"No." More tears streamed down her eyes. "He wouldn't do that."

"The by-laws are clear on this."

"Rex, no. You can't do this to me. You can't execute him." She hit me in the chest, as if that would change everything her father had done for the past twenty-four years, as if that would make me change my course. I couldn't help her. Michael signed his own death warrant when he agreed to help Clifton. She sighed. "Rex. Please."

"I have no choice." I cupped her face. "Why do you think I stayed away from you all this time? I knew that as soon as I returned to New York, I would have to make an example out of Michael. It's out of my hands."

"No." She slapped my hand away. "You're lying. You're scared because Dad wants your job and you can't stand to lose all of this."

Her breath came out in erratic pants as she searched the room. I raked both hands through my hair and glanced up at the ceiling, looking for answers I knew weren't there. She thought I was doing this to hurt her dad. I couldn't stand seeing her in pain like that. "Caterina, if I could stop what's coming for Michael, I would."

I turned to face her, but she was gone. Son of a bitch. My legs jerked into a run. I had looked away for a second; she couldn't have gone too far. It seemed that ever since I found out about the arranged marriage, I hadn't stopped chasing her.

Out in the hallway, I grabbed her by the waist before she reached the stairs and pinned her to the wall with my body. "I can't let you leave again."

"Why? Because you don't want me to warn Dad? Coward." She scowled at me.

"That. And also, you're not safe with him. Santino knows what Michael did. If he hasn't gone after him, it's because I ordered him to stand down. But if I don't act soon, he'll go after Michael himself. And he'll have every right to do so. You can't be caught in the middle of all that."

"That's what you thought he wanted to talk to me about earlier tonight?"

"Yes."

She struggled against me. "Let me go."

"No. I have a whole house full of rope. If I need to tie you down to keep you safe, I will." I pressed my entire body to hers.

All I had to do was turn the doorknob, and we would be in the Kinbaku room. My whole body ached to take her there, to make her see that I wasn't lying. And that this whole fucked-up situation wasn't my fault. I gripped both her wrists and brought them over her head.

"Rex." The name came out rushed, like a warning, rather than her usual plea.

"Stay. You promised." I kissed her hard, thrusting my tongue past her lips in a desperate need to get her back.

She writhed against me to free herself, but kept her lips locked onto to mine. Our entire relationship had been exactly this. She wanted me, but she didn't believe I could be the man for her. Keeping both of her wrists in place, I gripped her ass with my free hand, rubbing my hard-on over her wet pussy until she stopped fighting me.

The fire in her eyes was all the green light I needed. I yanked up her dress, pulled out my cock and entered her. When I mimicked the same plunging motion with my tongue in her month, she moaned a word that sounded like my name. She wrapped both her legs around me, and I drove deep inside of her.

"I should hate you." She took fistfuls of my hair, rocking her hips forward to take me all the way in.

"But you never could." I slid my erection all the way out and rubbed her own juices all over her clit. "You're so wet for me." I captured her mouth again and thrust into her with all the pent-up desire I'd felt for years, the fear I had of losing her all over again, and this love that no matter what just refused to die. "I want to see you come."

"Rex." She tightened her walls around my cock and let out a sexy moan.

The sway of her warm body dragged me along with her, closer to the edge of the precipice, while waves of pleasure exploded through me. In that moment of unadulterated happiness, I realized there wasn't anything I wouldn't do for this woman.

"Fuck, Caterina."

When her cheeks turned red and she tensed around me, I let myself fall too. I pumped hard as she climaxed with her legs wrapped around me, her hands in my hair, and her heart beating fast against my chest.

"You're mine. Do you understand that?" I kissed her neck and the top of her breasts over her dress. "I love you."

"I love you too." She panted a breath. "Damn you."

I stood there with her body wrapped around me for five whole minutes. We were too afraid to let go of each other and face what we had to do. We were at a standoff. If it were up to me, we'd stay here, just like this, forever.

"Can I ask for one thing?"

"Anything, love." I cradled her neck.

"Give me until the end of our contract to prove my father is innocent."

"Why? He's beyond saving."

"No." She cupped both my cheeks. "Mom tried to save him before she died. She tried to save all of us. I refuse to believe she was wrong in that."

# CHAPTER 7
## Every Favor Comes with A Price

CATERINA

The drumming in my chest slowly came down from the high-octane orgasm I just had. Still trying to catch my breath, I stroked Rex's cheek and then let my hand slide down to his bare chest. The man was chiseled like a Greek statue. How did this happen? When did I become so addicted to his touch and his body?

For Christ's sake, Rex flat-out told me he had plans to execute Dad, and my response was to let him fuck me in the middle of his hallway, outside the rope room no less. If I had been torn about my feelings for Rex before, now my doubts had doubled, quadrupled even.

"Did you seduce me to get a favor out of me?" He grabbed a handful of my butt cheek, nuzzling my neck. "God, you're so beautiful. It's absolutely working, in case you were wondering."

Heat rushed to my cheeks as his semi-erect cock rubbed against my pussy. Before we had our talk, I hadn't realized things would take such a dark turn. Going commando had seemed like a good idea when I was getting dressed. Not that a pair of underwear would have stopped Rex from having his way with me. Or did I have my way with him?

Whatever the case, as soon as he raised my dress, he knew I had hoped to be with him again tonight. In my defense, he had walked out of the bathroom in nothing but a pair of gray sweatpants. I shook my head at him, letting myself get lost in the blue lagoons of his eyes. Rex wasn't the bad guy here. But neither was Dad. He wanted to protect his children. How in the world were we going to fix this?

"I thought you were seducing me to get me to stay."

"Is it working?" He flashed me a charming smile.

I couldn't leave. One, I had a lot of questions swirling around in my head. I needed time to sort them all out. And two, I didn't want to spend the night alone, away from Rex. The minute I pushed away from him and my feet touched the floor, his lips turned downward in disappointment. My insides twisted because I hated to be the one to cause him any more pain. Because of Dad, he had gone through some tough times.

"I want to stay." I placed my hand over his heart. "But I can't let go of this thing with Dad. Do you understand?"

"Of course I do. If I had a better solution, I would've already done it. Don't you think?"

"I believe you're telling me the truth. Your truth, anyway. But I also believe Dad wouldn't do anything to betray the Society. It's not who he is. You have it all wrong. I just need time to show you. To show everyone. Please." I was getting really good at begging Rex for Dad's life.

"You still don't understand my feelings for you, do you?" He cradled my face. "Caterina, I would do anything for you."

"But?"

"If you want time, you'll have to also accept my help. I'm not letting you out of my sight. Not with Santino in his murderous mood roaming the streets. Not while the FBI wants all of us dead. Whatever you're planning, I'm coming with you."

"Thank you." I threw my arms around his neck and kissed him. "I have no idea what I'm doing. But I think we should start with Dad. Let's talk to him. I mean not right now. It's kind of late. But tomorrow?"

"Not so fast, love." He cocked an eyebrow. "Every favor comes with a price."

"Are you serious?"

"You mentioned something about finishing your contract?" A smirk pulled at his lips.

"I should've known you would try to get me back into your rope room." I squeezed my legs to ease my throbbing clit.

"You said it, not me." He braced his hands on either side of my head. "Admit it. You miss it."

Every time I thought of being tied up again, desire gushed through me. And that was before we had sex. Now that we had let our guards down and talked about how we felt about each other, I knew Rex wouldn't hold back during our sessions.

"I did."

He caught his lower lip between his teeth as if considering his options. "Tomorrow. Tonight, I want you in my bed." He took my hand and pulled me toward his suite.

I walked straight to his bathroom to clean up and find sleep clothes. Butterflies fluttered in my stomach as I regarded my own reflection. My cheeks glowed a bright pink. My mussed hair completed the quintessential just-fucked look about me.

"Do you regret it?" Rex came up behind me and met my gaze in the mirror. "Losing your virginity to me?"

"No." I leaned against his chest. "All these years, I had been searching for someone to make me feel alive. But I never found it. I have never wanted anyone the way I want you."

"The feeling is mutual." He kissed my cheek, his gaze glued to mine. "I'm sorry I took you like a savage out in the hallway. I've never had sex without a rubber."

"That's okay. I have an IUD."

"I know that. I still should've asked."

"Of course you know that." I squeezed my eyes shut, embarrassed that Rex knew this small detail about me all this time—when I threw myself at him in the boardroom downstairs, when I practically begged him to take me in the rope room, and when he almost did have sex with me on his private jet on our way to Atlanta. "Why do you know that? I can't decide if that's sweet or creepy?"

"You made a doctor's appointment a few weeks after your mom passed away. I was worried about you."

"So you just stole my medical records?"

"Borrowed. Did your headaches go away?"

"You know they did. You saw the file. What else do you know about me? Was your spy always following me?" Here was another thing about Rex that I just couldn't wrap my head around. He wasn't a regular guy. He was the king of an underground criminal Society. He was my fiancé.

"Yes." He turned me around so I would face him. "Aaron was more of a bodyguard. His job was to protect you as much as it was to report back on your day."

"Aaron. Of course. You know what? It's late. We should go to bed." I ended the conversation before we started fighting again, which at this point, I was sure would lead to more sex. And right now, I needed a clear head, so I could come up with a plan to help Dad.

When I reached the bed, I pulled the sheath dress over my head and climbed in under the covers. The big grin on Rex's face when he joined me made me want to slap him. Why was it always like this with him? One minute, I wanted to tear off his clothes and the next, I wanted to hurt him.

"What's so funny?"

"Here's something I didn't know about you. You sleep naked."

I didn't. I preferred pajama pants and a top. Shit. Again. My brain had decided all on its own that underwear and clothes weren't necessary. I glared at him for making fun of me and this relentless desire I felt for him. The spot between my thighs tightened and desire seeped through my folds in anticipation.

"Every time you look at me like that." He reached over and kneaded my breast. "It makes me want to either tie you down or fuck you hard." He sucked my nipple into his mouth, and I immediately spiraled into a frenzy.

"Rex." I sighed

"I'm right here." He rolled on top of me, keeping his arms on either side of me to support most of his weight. "I can't remember the last time I went to bed this early."

"Don't you have a party going on downstairs?"

"They can manage without me." He bent down and brushed my lips. "I started Kinbaku to cope with the chaos that is my life. I learned to breathe to control my emotions. But when you're with me, I find I don't want air. I only need you to survive this place."

"I always thought you loved being the boss of everything." I caressed his cheek, and he leaned against my hand.

"It's more of a mandate to me. My destiny, I suppose. I can't imagine doing anything else. But I wouldn't say I love it. Though, now that you're here..." he trailed off and kissed me, a long and sweet kiss that lulled all my senses.

Who would have thought that Rex Valentino would be capable of such a gentle gesture? I raked my fingers through his hair and deepened the kiss. Rex pulled away first. "You have questions. I can see it in your eyes."

"I don't know where to begin. It all hurts too much. I don't want to think about it."

Of all the things Rex said to me today, only one didn't hurt. Mom literally used her last breath to ensure my happiness. She went to Rex to beg him for my freedom. Tears brimmed my eyes. They were happy tears. For the first time in the last two years, I didn't feel so alone. Through Rex, Mom was watching over me.

"You can ask me anything." He lowered himself onto his side, before he brought me into his arms.

"Tell me about Mom."

"After she came to see me, I started visiting her at the hospital." His warm fingers slid up and down my arm absently. "She reminded me of my mom. Mom also hated the Society, and what it had done to the people in it. But she saw a different way out. She thought we could return it to its former glory. Fac Fortia et Patere." His chest bounced with a silent laugh. "Do brave things and endure. There was a time when we lived by that code. Mom and Dad wanted to get back to that."

"But *my* dad was standing in the way."

"Michael had his own way of doing things. He wasn't exactly wrong. We live in a world of beasts. Your mother was right to want her family away from all this."

"You got to know her well?"

"Yes. She was a formidable opponent in chess."

"I know. She and Dad used to get in some fierce matches. He hated losing to her." I laughed and something unraveled in my chest and filled it with flutters. Mom's death would never stop hurting, but now I knew it was okay to let go of my grief and try to be happy. "I didn't know you played chess."

"I gave Anna a run for her money."

The crackling fire behind us suddenly died down and plunged the room into complete darkness for a moment while my eyes adjusted to the change. Where before the room was bathed in reds and oranges, now it was lit by the blinking city lights beyond Rex's penthouse window. I thought of Rex sitting high up in his ivory tower, all alone...and possibly reading my files.

"What else did you do?"

"We went on walks around her floor, played chess, sometimes cards. But mostly, we talked about you and me." He held me tighter. "I think that toward the end, she thought we'd make a good match."

"Mom, the matchmaker." I laughed.

Now it made sense why she insisted I focus on finishing college and not worry too much about boys. She knew me so well. I would bet it took her all of two minutes to figure out Rex was the right man for me—she saw the good in him. Even if the circumstances were fucked up, Rex and I did belong together.

"She was going to talk to you. But she knew that would

wedge a chasm between you and Michael. She didn't want that."

"Does Dad know about your promise to Mom? I bet Mom gave him a piece of her mind."

"She never told him she knew. She didn't want to spend her last years fighting over it, being angry at him. On my last visit to see her, Massimo was there, and she told him she knew but asked him not to tell Michael. She wanted everyone to just be happy."

"Wait? My brothers know about the arranged marriage?"

"Of course they do. They've been with the Society since they were children."

"And agreed to keep it a secret from Mom." I pursed my lips to keep the tears at bay. Crying wasn't going to solve anything. "So everyone downstairs knows who I am and they know about us. I feel like such a clueless idiot."

"Only the board members know. Don't feel bad. To them, you're a means to an end. All they care about is that Michael doesn't come back."

Hearing Rex talk about Dad like this hurt. Many times before, he had tried to tell me that Dad didn't deserve my sacrifice, but I didn't fully understand what he meant. The dad I knew wasn't this ruthless king who terrorized everyone around him. He was a family man, a kind man, a loving husband.

"After meeting your mom, I understood why your dad went to hell and back to get her to stay with him. What I don't get is why he would back down from his deal. He, more than anyone, should know that betraying the Society wouldn't end well for him. Why put a target on his back? Why put his family in danger?"

"That's just it. He's doing it to protect us. Mom believed

there was good in him. You're assuming that what you were told is the truth. I'd like to hear his truth."

"I gave you my word. You have five months to prove Michael is innocent. But it doesn't help you to go into this situation with your eyes closed." Rex, as always, had a blunt view of things. He wasn't wrong. "I'll help you. But you have to go into this with an open mind."

I thought of Dad's erratic behavior of the past couple of years—the drinking and gambling. He let Rex take me away and then changed his mind. The dichotomy he was battling inside was something I understood well. Not long ago, I felt this same way about Rex—torn between what I wanted and what I thought I had to do.

"He became the man Mom wanted him to be. Good and kind. She's been gone for so long. Maybe he doesn't remember how to be that guy anymore." I swallowed the lump in my throat. "I have to try. I owe it to Mom."

My heart ached for Dad because, deep down, I knew I was right. But like Mom, I wanted to believe that the good in him was still there. That he hadn't forgotten about all the happy years he spent with his family.

As if he understood what I needed, Rex nibbled on my neck gently while he reached around to rub my pussy. Tomorrow I would have to face the ruthless king, a version of Dad I had never met. But for now, I wanted to forget about the outside world. I turned around to face Rex and then pushed him onto his back. I wanted to feel him between my legs and be in control this time.

"Take what you need, love." He stroked my hair. "But don't forget who's still in charge here."

After another round of mind-blowing sex, I slipped into a

deep slumber. I dreamed of Mom—a mix of the good times we had as a family when we were kids, Rex and she playing chess, laughing like they were old friends, and then Dad with a face that kept changing between the one I knew and a horrible beast.

# CHAPTER 8
## Can I Help You with Something?

CATERINA

The next morning, I woke up startled. For a long second, I couldn't figure out where I was. I had expected to find Rex next to me, but he was gone. His bed felt big and cold without him in it. Even the suite had lost that intimate glow from last night. Had I dreamed it all? Had my mind conjured up a sweet and caring Rex who made love to me for hours?

A smile pulled at my lips as my hand slid down to my sore pussy. Rex was real. Unfortunately, that meant that everything else had also happened—the arranged marriage, Dad's betrayal, and the target on our backs because of it. I puffed out a breath and forced myself to get up. In the back of my mind, I had a short list of what I needed to do today, where I had to go. The thought made a big lump of anxiety churn in my stomach.

I put my hair up in a messy bun and hopped in the shower. The hot water soothed my achy body, but there wasn't much it could do to stop the carousel of bullshit going through my mind. When I finished, I grabbed the towel from the hook. It was slightly damp, and I realized that Rex had probably used it earlier. I wrapped it around my body, brought the excess fabric in front of me, and buried my face in it.

The pressure in my chest lifted, and I inhaled. Where was he? I didn't want to start this day without him. I ambled over to the double sink and the large, framed mirror over it. In the drawer to my left, I found a brand-new tube of toothpaste, brushes, makeup—in short, everything I needed to get ready.

I was happy to see that the toiletries were not the brands I used. That would've been a new level of creepy. And I still hadn't fully reconciled with the idea that Rex had been stalking me—yep, that was the word—for the last four years, almost the entire time I had been in college.

Well, now it was my turn. I put toothpaste on an electric pink toothbrush and stuck it in my mouth. With the vibrating sounds muffling the tiny voice in my head that said I shouldn't snoop, I casually went through Rex's things. This was his bathroom, his closet. All his personal effects were here.

He had an extensive watch collection. Of course a guy who lived to control everything around him would be obsessed with keeping time. His ties, his socks, and fancy leather shoes were all neatly organized. I wished my closet looked this way, but who had time to keep up with this level of tidiness?

I was in the process of going through his tailored suits when I felt his eyes on me. "Can I help you with something?" His deep voice made my knees buckle.

He was dressed in one of his dark suits. Sexy hot didn't begin to cover what he was. With his arms over his chest, he leaned a shoulder on the door frame, and his brow lifted. A few months back, I would've found his stance intimidating and frightening. But now I knew enough about him to see that he was amused—the softness in his eyes and the tiny smile playing on his lips were a dead giveaway. How did I not see that before?

Being in his closet with a toothbrush in my mouth felt very intimate and normal. Adrenaline rushed through me in that moment. When did Rex and I become something normal? Sure, we were engaged, but we weren't a couple. Were we? Our situation was hardly balanced. He was the king of everything. I was his prize.

Pointing at my frothy mouth, I walked past him to the sink. He followed me and stood there while I rinsed off the toothpaste. Of all the years he had been watching me, he'd never seen me go through my morning routine. For whatever reason, that made me feel like I was still in control of my life—that he didn't know all my secrets.

"I was just browsing." I met his gaze in the mirror. "Taking a page from your book."

"That's fair." He wrapped his arms around my waist and kissed my cheek. "You didn't sleep much last night."

"I wasn't exactly looking forward to today."

"I know." He inhaled on my neck and tightened his hold on me.

By now, I recognized that look on his face and the way his body tensed with expectation and something stronger than desire. He wanted control. He wanted me. More specifically, he wanted me under his influence. I knew exactly what he would say before he uttered the words.

"Meet me in the Kinbaku suite." His demanding tone left no room for negotiating.

I nodded.

"Go. I'll be there in a minute."

In a daze, as if his words had hypnotized me, I made my way across the hallway. My heart thrashed in my ears as I pushed the door opened. Jasmine incense greeted me as soon as I stepped inside, and it was like coming home. A whole month had gone by since the last time I'd been here. I was surprised to see how much I had missed being in this room. I missed the serenity of it, the intense energy, and the sense of being alive.

A slow instrumental tune filled the dim-lit space while I snooped around. I hadn't noticed it before, but right over the table with coils of rope, there was a track on the ceiling with rings attached to it. Immediately, I thought of the photos Rex showed me the day he asked me to be his rope bottom. At the time, I had been too shocked to see the beauty in them. But now that I understood the practice better, I longed to see them again.

"Still browsing?" His voice ignited a spark below my navel.

"Were those rings here before?" I pointed at the dark ceiling. "I don't remember them."

"No. I removed them for you. I didn't want to scare you off."

"You used them on Violet." The more I thought of it, the clearer the image was. Violet suspended in mid-air, one leg hanging long in front of her. "I remember the picture."

"Yes, but you're not ready for that. It requires skill and full surrender." He cupped my cheek, surveying my face, as if he were considering my ability to give in to him. "Jesus, Caterina, I've been dying to see you like that."

"I want to try." My voice didn't sound like my own. The

words had come out from somewhere deep inside me. Like Rex, I needed this today. Right now.

He shook his head and pulled the towel off me. "Get on your knees."

I strode nude to the mat in front of the mirror and lowered myself down. My heart beat fast as images of Violet's inked body reeled through my mind. The music changed to a tone that was more alpha waves and meditation beats. I tried to focus on it and let it wash away my worries. But my brain wasn't having it. My body trembled as my gaze followed Rex around the room. It wasn't that I was afraid of him. It was more trepidation—fear of the unknown, fear that I might be going too far, fear that I wasn't ready.

Rex had changed out of his suit. His sweatpants hung loose over his slim hips, yet somehow, accentuated every plane and hard muscle on his upper body. The clank of metal against metal sounded to my left, and in the next beat, Rex's bare feet appeared in my line of sight. I glanced up at the suspension ring, and my body jerked in surprise. He was really doing it.

"Take a deep breath and hold it." He started our session like before by placing a pair of rope shears, an hourglass, and his phone at the top of the mat before he settled behind me.

I sighed when his chest brushed against my hot skin. He went through a few more rounds of guided inhales and exhales until I melted into him.

"Gyaku Ebi. That's what you saw in the picture."

"What does that mean?"

"In Japanese, it means reverse shrimp." He whispered in my ear as he moved my arms to form a box shape over my lower back. "Most people call it Hog tie in English. That's the pose Violet is holding in the picture you mentioned. The main elements of it are helplessness and vulnerability. That requires you to let go completely and let me do the thinking for you." He let out a warm breath. It caressed the nape of my neck and traveled all the way down to my toes. "Are you sure that's what you want?"

"Yes." Again, the word came out before I could think on it. The part of me that wanted this had taken over, pushing away the side of me who still had preconceived notions about the practice. "I trust you."

"Sweet girl." He buried his nose in my hair. "You're stronger than you know."

He dropped several bundles of rope in front of me. My eyes widened in surprise. Up until now, he had only used one length. As usual, Rex anticipated my every thought and need. "We've only done one tie before. This pose requires two more. Are you okay with that?"

His tone and demeanor were so self-assured and in control, they made all my worries float out of my head. I nodded and went back to my breathing, staying with the pace he had set for me. In the one-day long session I had with Violet, I had learned that oxygen makes your muscles more flexible. She also showed me stretches that I continued to do even after I had left the penthouse. Maybe because I missed Rex too much. Or maybe I had secretly hoped that, one day, I would find my way back to him, to this place.

I watched on the full-size mirror as Rex finished the takate kote or TK, which kept my hands tightly behind my back. He then added a third rope to the front that made my tits pop out. His deft fingers perfectly executed every line and knot around me. Fuck me, it was such a turn-on to see him so focused on his task. For him, these sessions were not about sex. But I couldn't say the same about me. Seeing him work the ropes with such skill had my pussy throbbing with need.

When he was finished with the TK, he gently moved my legs around and laid me flat on my stomach. The mat rubbed against my sex in tandem with the hard jute. I would've guessed that would make things better, but it didn't. Desire and need fluttered at my core, but there was nothing I could do to give it relief.

"I'm doing a fast futomomo on both your thighs." He placed his hand on my back. The touch sent tiny flames down to my toes. "And then I'm going to tie it to the TK. The bend in your lower back will be intense. Are you ready?"

"Yes."

The ends of the jute hit the floor with a forceful thud, and my clit tightened a bit more.

"Keep breathing. Even if all you can manage are small sips." He moved to my right side, bent my leg, and started to wrap the rope around it so I couldn't stretch it out anymore.

I was facing away from the mirror now and could only see the dark wall across the way. While I had a view of nothing, I was sure Rex could see all of me. In this position, with my legs spread wide and bent, I was sure he had a pretty good view of my pussy. Thing was, I didn't care. The whole time I wondered if he would touch me there.

"Good girl." He braced his large hand on my chest and hoisted me up a few feet off the floor, so I was partially suspended—not like Violet, but the feeling of helplessness was definitely there. I couldn't move at all. He gently pushed on my shoulder and made me face the mirror. "You look beautiful."

He had a line going from the middle of my back up to the suspension ring. My knees were still resting on the mat, but my upper body was elevated.

"Do you remember the contract? You agreed to hair binding and gagging. Are you still okay with that?"

That should *not* have taken me to a new level of turned on, but it did. Everything he did was a huge turn-on—the way he manhandled me like I weighed nothing, his concentration as he followed the many steps to perfection, and his strong hands.

"Yes."

He wound more rope around my bun. While softly tilting my chin up, he tied the cord to the suspension line, then came back around and ran it through my mouth. My reflection was the epitome of a damsel in distress. He walked away and left me there to stare at his handy work.

At first, I glanced away in shame, even though the gesture required a bit of effort on my part. But Rex was right. It didn't help to go into a situation with my eyes closed. So I followed his advice and faced the woman in the mirror. Our inner strength lived in that tiny nook inside our most vulnerable moments. Mom had said that to me often, but I never understood what it meant. I did now.

A whole minute went by before he returned with a lit taper candle in his hand. He didn't ask for my permission this time. He rubbed oil all over my butt cheeks and wedged the candle in the line so the flame faced my feet. Within seconds, hot wax began to drip down on my toes and my ass.

"I love you." He sat in front of me and petted my hair. "You are so strong."

I squeezed my eyes shut, and tears streamed down my cheek. I finally understood. Sometimes giving in was the strongest thing one could do. In moments of stress, it wasn't about focusing on the predicament, but the abundance of information it provided. I chose to melt into the moment. Not because I had to, but because I wanted to.

"Look at me," Rex ordered. His eyes seemed a deeper blue, more intense and in control. When I met his gaze with all the defiance I could muster, he reached over and pinched my nipple. I squirmed against him and that seemed to please him. "Squeeze my hand as hard as you can."

As soon as I felt his fingers behind me, I did as he asked. Again, he smiled in approval, and that sent a bunch of butter-flies to my stomach because this level of trust and tenderness could only happen between two people who trusted each other implicitly and resolutely. Rex and I were a couple. I had no doubt about that.

He kneeled slightly to my left, leaving just enough room for me to see his face and my face in the mirror. The man was absolutely gorgeous as he sat there puffing out breaths, content from all the work he had just done because I asked him to. Strands of wet hair brushed his temple and brow, and all I wanted to do was touch it and kiss his impossibly beautiful face. But as much as I wanted him inside me right now, I didn't want this moment to end.

Wax pelted on the floor. So much of it was caked on my skin, I didn't feel it anymore. Of course Rex caught on to that quickly. As he fondled my breasts some more with one hand, he scrapped it all off with a knife and let the hot torture continue. He did more things like that, checking my grip along the way while he watched me intently, making sure I stayed aroused and swollen with need for him.

*I love you too.*

I repeated over and over in my head.

We stayed like this, inside his game, until the sands of time ran out. I didn't want it to stop, but not even the all-powerful Rex could keep the real world at bay.

# CHAPTER 9
## Are You Awake?

REX

In all the times Dad tried to sell me on the idea that marrying Caterina was the best thing for our family and the Society, I never considered she would be so perfect for me. Even after I started having feelings for her, I didn't know we could be this.

I unraveled the rest of the rope and cradled her onto my lap. We were both covered in sweat and wax. "I have never wanted anyone in my life the way I want you right now," I whispered on her temple.

Her eyes fluttered open for a beat, but then shut them close again. "Hmmm. Me too."

What Caterina had gone through in the Gyaku Ebi had been intense—even if it had only been a half-suspension. Many of my partners had chosen not to go there. I tightened my hold on her. "Such a strong woman."

"Hmmm." She moaned again, rolling her head toward my chest.

"How about a shower?"

"Okay. Just don't let me go."

"Never."

I let her rest for another twenty minutes. Holding her in my arms like this was a dream come true. The thing about dreams, though, was that they had to end eventually. I didn't want this feeling, the sense of complete and utter happiness, to end. Fuck me. Santino was right. Caterina Alfera was a huge distraction that might get us all killed.

"We have to go." I hooked my arm under her knees and stood.

When she rested her head on my shoulder, I ambled out of the Kinbaku suite. I shouldered open the door to our bedroom and started making my way to the shower. Caterina had another idea though. We made it as far as the sofa before her mouth found mine. So what if this love I had for her was all-consuming? I had waited too long for her to back down now.

As soon as her feet slapped the floor, she wrapped her arms around me, kissing my chest and rubbing her hands all over me. "You can't tell me that after all you just put me through, you're not gonna finish it."

"I was hoping you'd say that, love." I kissed her lips, hard and with all the desire I had kept under control before. At this point, the bed seemed too far away. I couldn't wait. "Face the fireplace," I ordered while I freed my erection.

"Jesus." Her eyes widened as my cock sprung out. "That surprises me every time. I mean, I know it fits, but still." She stroked me, and I almost shot off in her hand.

"Caterina." I cradled her neck and thrust my tongue past her teeth. She still tasted minty from the toothpaste. For some reason, that woke a raw instinct in me. Caterina was mine. She was in my home now, in my bed, and no way in hell was I ever letting her go. To hell with her family and Santino.

Her sexy moan sparked a fire below my navel and that did me in. I gripped her upper arms and bent her over the back of the sofa.

"Rex."

"I'm right here." I entered her and didn't wait for her to adjust to my length before I rocked my hips forward and let her have all of me. She called for me, and that fueled my need for her, sending a shock of adrenaline through me. "Is that the spot, love?"

"Yes." She reached behind her to grip my arm.

She was a vision like this, with her pretty ass high up for me to take. And that was exactly what I did. I plunged into her at a vigorous and fast pace. When her walls clenched around me, I reached around to play with the folds of her wet pussy and her bud, which were already swollen with need.

She widened her stance to give me better access while her pulse beat on my hand between her legs. A few more strokes, and she found her release. I fucking loved watching her fall apart in my arms. I loved the way she struggled to catch her breath. I loved how her skin turned to silk under my touch. I loved all of her.

Panting—this woman had me panting—I wrapped my arms around her and came hard inside her. The lights dimmed, and suddenly, I couldn't see or hear anything. It was as if time had stopped for us. If Caterina was meant to be the death of me, I was fucking okay with that.

"Is it always like this?"

"What?" I puffed out a breath. "The sex? No."

"I never want it to end." She turned around and hugged

me. "I'm so addicted to you. I know I don't have a point of reference for this. But I can't imagine it getting any better than this."

"My little virgin." I stroked her hair. "It's never been this intense for me either."

"Hmmm." She smiled and relaxed against me. "I feel a nap coming on."

"I can see that." I picked her up and walked her to the bed.

Within a minute, she was fast asleep. I climbed in next to her and held her tight. I had cleared my schedule for today so we could go see Michael. But after the night she had after learning the truth about us and her parents, she needed to rest a little longer. A part of me was glad for the reprieve. I wasn't sure if Caterina was ready for the truth.

Every time I gave her an answer that painted her dad under a bad light, she made up excuses for him. Last night, she had made progress accepting who Michael was and the fact that he spent his entire marriage lying to his wife. All so he could have what he wanted. He wanted Anna, but he also wanted this underworld and all the power and money that came with it.

Caterina's slow and even breathing was like a lullaby to me. Before I knew, I had closed my eyes and started dreaming. When I woke again, a whole two hours had gone by. I smiled at the wild curls sprawled on my chest and Caterina's form snuggled around me.

"Are you awake?" I kissed the top of her head.

"No."

"We have to go." I chuckled.

"I know." She glanced up at me with puffy eyes full of dread. "I've put off this talk long enough."

I nodded.

With a sigh, she threw her legs over the side of the mattress and sauntered toward the bathroom, leaving me with a fantastic view of her ass and a hard-on. For a minute, I considered joining her in the shower, but that would lead to another round of sex and possibly another nap. I wanted nothing more than to spend the day making love to Caterina, but duty called.

An hour later, we sat in the back of my Escalade zooming down the Long Island Expressway. Getting to the Hamptons in the spring wasn't as bad as in the summer. Not to mention, Aaron had excellent skills maneuvering the insufferable traffic. If it had been up to me, we would've taken the chopper, but Caterina needed the extra time to hash things out with me.

"Drink some water." I handed her a bottle.

"Thanks." She sipped and glanced out the window.

As it was with everything else between Caterina and me, this situation was fucked up to say the least. For all intents and purposes, I was her dad's judge and executioner. I had agreed to give Caterina time to prove Michael's innocence. But if he confessed, I would have no choice but to call in my guys.

Since we had left the penthouse, Caterina had grown cold and distant. The chasm between us kept getting deeper and wider the closer we got to the Alfera's summer home.

"You don't have to be afraid. I'll be with you the entire time." I met Aaron's gaze in the rear-view mirror, and he nodded. A confirmation that the crew that had left this morning had made visual contact as we had planned.

"I'm not afraid, Rex." She furrowed her brows. "This is Dad, not some heartless mobster."

The way she waved her hand in my general direction was like a kick to my stomach. In my knee-jerk reaction, I gripped her upper arm. "Let's be very clear on this. We're all heartless mobsters here, including your dad."

"I didn't mean it that way."

"It doesn't matter what you meant. All I want from you is to be ready to accept the truth."

Her eyes watered instantly. "We're here to hear him out. Are you ready to accept his truth?"

"Yes." I fucking wasn't. But I was willing to play along so Caterina could have her goddamn answers. And yeah, I was looking forward to knocking Michael off his pedestal. He owed Caterina the fucking truth. "Do you remember the last time you came down to the Hamptons?"

"Rex." Her cheeks blushed, and she avoided my gaze.

"That's a yes." I pointed at her face. "Your mother convinced you to join Enzo at a party. You looked so stunning that night." I brushed the back of my fingers along the smooth skin of her arm. "I wanted nothing more than to dance with you."

"Really?" She flashed me one of her green stares. "Because all I remember was you getting into a fight with Enzo and his friend."

"The asshole was making you uncomfortable. He was all over you. I could tell you were not interested."

"I wasn't. But that didn't give you the right to punch him." Her gaze softened. "Did Mom orchestrate that whole night? So you and I would meet up?"

"She tried." I chuckled. "But Enzo already hated my guts at that point. The minute I walked in, he warned me to stay away from you."

"Did he know then? You know, about the arranged marriage between us?"

"He did. Michael talked to him around the same time Dad talked to me. We stopped being friends shortly thereafter."

"Why?"

Short answer, Enzo realized that if it weren't because of his dad's deal, he would be in line to be king. Instead, he had to forfeit everything to me and lose his little sister in the process. "You can imagine how the whole thing made him feel. Our parents lied to us for many years. In all fairness, he was also pissed off at Michael. Same as me."

"I remember. You hated everyone. God, you were impossible. Acting like you owned everything. Like I was..." she trailed off.

"Like you were mine."

She rolled her eyes. And then it hit her. Why I had acted the way I had when I saw Enzo's friend show up at the party with his grabby hands all over her. "Jesus, Rex. You knew Zack had asked me out before the party. You knew because you were already stalking me by then." She huffed out a breath.

"I wasn't stalking you. The security detail was there for your protection. You do realize that if anyone found out about our agreement, your life would have been in danger. It was a precaution."

"How is that better?" She pursed her lips. I could see it in her eyes. She was still sifting through all the information she now had. It pained her. "I'm your insurance. If you marry me, Dad or Enzo can't contest your status as the head of the Society."

I nodded once.

"So not stalking. Protecting your investment. Your future." She shifted her body to face me. "You didn't have to pry into my private life for that. Zack never spoke to me after that night. He was terrified of me actually. What did you tell him?"

"That you were not interested." I shrugged.

"Right before you punched him."

"He deserved it."

"That's not the point." She ran both hands through her hair and glanced up at me through her lashes. "I wanted to dance with you too. If you had asked, I would've said yes. But no, you had to go all mobster on Zack instead." She shook her head at me, searching my gaze, as if she were trying to really see me and understand my predicament.

"I never said I was a saint. In my line of work, we take and ask questions later. It's how we stay alive." I cradled her cheek. "You need to remember that."

Her breath hitched. Had it really not dawned on her that we had to be married and that once we did, she would be part of my world—part of the world her mother spent all her adult life running away from?

We rode in silence the rest of the way. By the time Aaron took exit seventy, I was ready to be done with this meeting with Michael. Adrenaline pumped hard through me. I had to treat this as any other job. I was here to get answers.

Caterina wiped her hands on her jeans as she stared at her family's beach house. When the tires rolled to a stop on the half-circle driveway, she hopped out of the car and headed for the front entrance.

"Stay in the car." I tapped Aaron's shoulder. "I'll call if we need you."

"You got it, Boss."

I climbed out and joined Caterina while she rammed her

finger in the doorbell. "Maybe he's upstairs." She tried knocking again.

"You don't have a key?"

"No. Dad told me he had to sell the house." She pressed her hand to her forehead then walked toward the window to peek inside. "Let's go around back."

I followed close behind as I texted Aaron. The crew had confirmed Michael was home two hours ago. Where the hell was he? Aaron's reply was instant.

*The crew left. We're alone. Get out.*

My guys had orders to stay put. What made them take off without checking in? Santino's crew was still searching for Clifton's body. For all we knew, he was back in the States too. Shit. This was a setup.

I didn't have time to wait for Aaron or play the guessing game. I darted along the side yard where Caterina had stalked off. This was her home. She knew exactly where she was going and had no reason to think something bad was waiting for her. When I reached the patio, a figure moved from the living room to the kitchen. The steps were too agile for someone who had gone through heart surgery a month ago.

"Stop," I said under my breath as Caterina turned the doorknob and pushed her way in. "Goddammit, Caterina."

I walked right behind her and practically dragged her to the hallway across the way. Sure as fuck, a man stood past the foyer, waiting for us in the next room. I could hear his heavy breathing. He reeked of sweat and fear—just like a pig, a fed.

"You're surrounded Valentino. Come out with your hands in the air. And let the woman go."

"Michael." I scowled at Caterina.

## CHAPTER 10
## *Put Down the Weapon, Princess*

CATERINA

The fury I found in Rex's eyes made me shuffle away from him. Of course his first thought would be that Dad set this up. And yeah, this entire scene looked super sketchy, and Dad appeared to be the only suspect. But I refused to believe that Dad would try and kill Rex. Or worse, that he had Massimo, his own son, help him do it. Because the only reason I had thought to come look for Dad here was because Massimo told me Dad wanted to see me at our East Hampton home.

Shit. This was really bad and didn't help my case at all. I wasn't an idiot. The reason I was still standing right now was because of Rex's feelings for me. What had Rex said before? *Take first, ask questions later. That's how we stay alive.* He was trying really hard not to kill me. But my family seemed hell bent to change his mind.

No, that couldn't be it. My family wouldn't do this to me. Something else was at play here. Someone else betrayed Rex. "Rex. You have to believe me. This wasn't Dad."

"For fuck's sake, Caterina. Look around you. My crew is gone. Even Aaron is not responding anymore. This was an ambush. And the only reason I fell for it is you." He pointed a finger at me, looking daggers at me as if I were his enemy. "I should've known. It was all a lie."

"What? No. You have it all wrong. I didn't know this would happen. I don't even know who's out there." I pressed my back against the wall and peeked around into the living area.

My heart sank. The last time we came here, Mom was still alive. We were all still a family. We were together. The tall window framed in dark wood with the English garden beyond it looked like a Monet painting. Mom loved this house because of the spectacular view. Now my home was about to become one of those murder scenes from the movies.

"Who is that?"

"My guess? FBI."

"He knows who you are." I stole another glance at the stranger in my home. He met my gaze defiantly as if he lived here.

"It's just you and me, Rex. I'm here to take you in." The man called into the hallway. "Come out."

"Maybe he just wants to talk." I reached for Rex's hand, but he stepped back.

"Don't be so naive, Caterina." He raised his weapon and aimed straight ahead. "If he wanted to talk, he would've come to the Crucible. If he wanted to arrest me, he would've brought a team."

Shit. Of course Rex was right. If the FBI had landed a fish as big as Rex Valentino, there would be a news crew and an entire SWAT team outside. Instead, a single guy was asking Rex to kindly step out and let me go?

"Are you saying Dad, or the FBI, sent a professional to kill you?"

"Not either/or. Michael is working with the FBI. He used you to serve me up on a silver platter. I met one of theirs in Ibiza. This is personal to him and he has no interest in abiding by the law. He wants me dead." His gaze shifted from one end of the house to the other.

"We can go out the front door and get to Aaron."

"No. The asshole brought some kind of backup. He wants to do things quietly, but I'm sure if we walk out, I'll be shot down. Maybe a sniper?" He craned his neck to see out the front door. But all I could see out there was his empty SUV.

"Enough with the chitchat," the man called out again, "let's get this over with. The woman leaves now."

"Rex, I swear I had nothing to do with this. You have to believe me." I cradled his cheek. When he didn't move away, I pressed on. "You asked me for my trust. And I gave it to you. Now I'm asking for you to return the favor."

"Fuck me, Caterina. I shouldn't, but I do trust you. Do what he says. Go."

"What? No, I can't let you face him like this. Who the hell knows what he's planning to do? Maybe he has more guys hiding in the house. Maybe he's going to tie you up and set off a bomb or something." My mind was reeling with all the bad things that could happen to Rex. There were literally a million things that could go wrong here. The only thing that was safe to assume right now was that the asshole on the other side of the wall wanted to kill Rex. "You have to come with me."

"How about that?" He brushed his fingers over my cheek

and chuckled. "You actually care if I die."

"What's so funny now?"

"As glad as I am that you're finally thinking like a mobster, I can't let you stay. You have friends in the area. Go find them and get back to the city." He gripped my hair at the nape of my neck and brought me in for a desperate kiss that felt so much like a goodbye.

My chest tightened as tears spilled down my cheeks. This wasn't happening. Rex and I needed more time. We only had one night. I had thought we'd have more time to be together and get to know each other better. I squeezed my eyes tight to clear my vision. It wasn't fair. The FBI couldn't just show up at my home and kill the man I loved like he was nothing, like he didn't matter.

I gripped the lapel of his dark suit and whispered in his ear, "I'll get help. Someone out there should be able to help us."

"Go now." He smiled at me.

I didn't like the resignation in his eyes. I didn't like that he wasn't telling me his plan. Though if he was anything like Enzo and Massimo, I had no doubt he planned to fight and shoot his way out. That plan would work if we knew for sure there was only one guy waiting for him. With my heart pumping hard up in my throat, I did as Rex asked, only because we couldn't stay out in the hallway all day. Maybe Rex could hold off until I found Aaron and the rest of Rex's crew.

"I'm walking out now." My voice echoed in the foyer as I trudged toward the front entrance. I glanced back at Rex and mouthed, "I love you."

I shut the door behind me. In an instant, shots boomed inside the house. As much as I wanted to turn around and go back inside, I forced myself to run to the SUV to look for Aaron. He was the only who could save Rex now. I found him on the driver's side, bleeding and unconscious. The agent inside wasn't alone. For whatever reason, they were very much hoping to keep this whole thing quiet—this was an execution. They were here for Rex. Tears blurred my vision, but I wiped them away.

"Aaron." I placed a trembling hand over my mouth to muffle my sobbing.

*Take a big sip of air.*

I imagined Rex's voice in my head. At first it was hard to breathe, but after a few tries, I managed to get myself under control. Jesus, I had come here to prove Dad's innocence and now I was going to have to fight for Rex's life. But how? I scanned the area around me.

Everything looked the way I remembered—the quiet street, the clear blue sky, and the salty breeze. The lulling whisper of crashing waves in the distance filled the air. And then I remembered one more detail. This early in the Spring, most of the homes around us were empty. If anyone would want to execute a person, this would be a good, desolate spot.

A tiny voice in the back on my head whispered a bunch of incoherent theories. Mainly, that Dad would have known this small detail about our home. I put the thought aside. Right now, I had to focus on helping Rex because one thing was for sure: no one was coming to help us.

I shook Aaron a few more times and gently slapped his cheek. He stirred, and relief washed over me. "Omigod. You're alive."

"Check the pulse next time," he mumbled.

"I'll remember that." I attempted a laugh, but it sounded

more like a screech. "Rex is in trouble." I helped him sit up against the SUV tire. "You've been shot."

"Yeah. Three times." He winced and opened up his jacket to show me his bulletproof vest. "It hurts like a motherfucker. But I'm not dead. Oh, sorry."

"Don't be." I waved my hand in dismissal. Bad language right now was the least of my worries. "Can you see if you can make contact with your crew? Why did they leave?"

"Before I got hit, Frank said he had received a text from Rex telling them to return to the city." He reached for his ribs. He was alive, but I had no doubt he had a few broken bones.

"That's not good." I pursed my lips because now things were starting to look like my brothers had something to do with this. Just last night, they were at Rex's building. "Hacking sounds like an inside job."

"Yes, it does." The look he gave me said he blamed my family. Then his eyes went big. "Ms. Alfera."

"I hear it, too. The shooting stopped. Why?"

"If they don't start up soon, I'd say they're out of bullets." He coughed and cradled his stomach.

"Get your men back here." I made to get up and spotted his phone wedged under the tire. I had a feeling Aaron had hid it when he was shot. Gosh, these guys were always at the ready, always anticipating their next move.

"Where are you going, Ms. Alfera?" He furrowed his brows at me.

He knew exactly where I was going, and he was pissed he couldn't stop me. Rex would be too, but I had no choice.

"Jesus, fuck. At least take a gun with you. Blast everything to hell."

"As much as I like your plan, I don't know how to shoot a

gun. Mom hated guns. I'll somehow end up shooting myself."

"Then what are you gonna do? Kill that asshole with kindness?"

"No. Get us help." I pointed at his phone and strode back to the house.

When I crossed the threshold, it was as if I had gone to another dimension. In the ten minutes I had been gone, Rex and that asshole had managed to tear apart the place. The decorative pillows on the sofa had been shot to shreds, along with all the knickknacks on the mantle. Luckily, Dad's swords were still intact, hanging crisscrossed over the mantle. The sunlight streamed through the window and made the steel sparkle with a sleek sheen. Someone had recently cleaned them. Dad had been here.

The last time I had practiced sword fighting was with Enzo. We had done it to entertain Mom. She had been so happy that day, especially after I beat Enzo. More and more, I understood the reasons behind everything Mom ever did for me—the apartment, my career, training with my brothers. She knew one day I would be swept back into Dad's mafia world. And she wanted me to be ready.

Muffled shots rang out in the dining room beyond the kitchen. Glancing around the chaotic mess they left in the living room, with tables knocked over and glass everywhere, I had to guess they had started throwing punches. All I could hope was that the agent hadn't brought in a full arsenal and that he was truly out of bullets.

I dragged a coffee table over to the mantle and stepped up on it. When I gripped the hilt of the sword, I felt more in control and less damsel in distress. Maybe I didn't have Rex and Aaron's mobster instincts, but I knew how to wield a sword. With my heart drumming, I tiptoed to the kitchen where a cloud of smoke hovered low to the ground.

"Shh." A hand clamped over my mouth.

I struggled until my body recognized the familiar feel of Rex. When he let go, I turned to face him. I had expected to meet one of his furious and intimidating glares, but what I found was a very confused Rex.

"You came back for me?"

"I told you I would."

"You should not have done that. This guy is insane. I'm like some sort of prize for him." He scowled in the direction of the dining room. "What the hell is that?"

"It's a sword." I made to follow his line of sight to find the asshole hunting us.

"Do you know how to use that?" He spoke slowly the way one would talk to a wounded animal—or a deranged person.

"Sure, you point and stab." I meant to make light of the situation because Rex looked like he was about to lose it. "Of course I do. I've been training since I was twelve. I thought you knew everything about me."

"This is curious." He furrowed his brows at my hands. "I didn't know about this."

It had been Dad's idea. An answer to Mom's distaste for guns. At first, Mom hadn't been all that thrilled about it. But then she got sick, and she changed her mind. I had assumed it was because she figured she had very little time left, and she didn't want to spend it arguing with Dad. Now I knew it was because she had found out about my arranged marriage to a mafia kingpin.

"Not so fast, princess." The man's tone and the blade aimed at both of us sent a shiver down my spine.

He'd grabbed Dad's other sword off the wall. Did he know how to fight?

"Stop. I won't fight you anymore." Rex put up his hands in surrender.

"Yeah, we're done here." He snickered. "Put down the weapon, princess."

Like Rex, the jerk didn't think I could fight him. That was the moment I lost it. An avalanche of emotions took over me. I side-stepped his blade, gripped the hilt with two hands and swung, aiming for his head. How dare he come into my home like this? How dare he try to kill the man I love and pin it on Dad? I struck again and again. The surprise in his eyes when he realized I meant to fight him was almost laughable and that gave me the surge of courage I needed to keep going.

I let the anger that had been simmering at the pit of my stomach come to the surface. And yeah, I saw red. The asshole actually thought he had won. I let him have it, setting a fast pace, one I knew I could keep up for several minutes. He had been chasing Rex around the house. He had to be physically tired, and that gave me an advantage.

He backed away, and I followed with one blow after another. Wiping that smirk off his face alone had me reveling in the moment. But I didn't have a killer instinct. For all the hate I felt for him right now, knowing one of us had to die, I still couldn't see myself ending this fight with my blade in his belly.

With one last blow, I knocked the sword out of his hand, and he fell backwards as he tripped over one of the knocked over coffee tables. I had to finish him. I met his gaze. The fear in his eyes told me he knew what would come next.

This wasn't me though.

# CHAPTER 11
## A Deal with The Devil

Rex

"Caterina, let me do it." I put out my hand in front of her to snap her out of whatever trance she was in. The asshole deserved to die, but not by her hand. "This isn't you, love."

"No." She shook her head, glaring at him with a kind of hate I had never seen in her eyes. She stepped closer, adding pressure to make him bleed.

The man chuckled.

I stared dumbfounded at her form. Somehow, she looked taller holding a sword to the agent's neck. I had no idea Caterina could fight like this. Not only that, but she had also fought a trained agent and won. Michael had had to work really hard to keep this little secret from me. What had been his plan? To send Caterina to my bed and then have her slit my throat in the middle of the night? No, she wouldn't do that.

Except now here she was, with a man at her feet, ready to claim her prize. Caterina wasn't a mobster. She was a marketing director at an advertising firm. She had a normal job and a normal life.

Her mother had warned me about it. Practically begged me to never let it happen. Anna didn't want her daughter to become one of us—a ruthless killer with an incessant appetite for power. In the deepest recess of her mind, she must've known Michael would try to use Caterina in this way. I had promised Anna I would never let her daughter go down this path. And yet, here we were.

Two days after she gave into me, she stood in her family's beach house, threatening to take a man's life to save mine. Because even if she didn't understand the rules of my world, she understood this bit. The agent couldn't walk out of here alive. Because if he did, he would eventually come back for her and me. But this wasn't her cross to bear. Caterina wasn't a killer—I was.

I shuffled toward the sword that had landed a few feet from me after Caterina blasted it out of the agent's hands. My mind raced as I plotted all the different scenarios that would get us out of this bind. I had a lot of questions for him. Though I doubted I would get the chance to ask any of them. His men could be getting ready to barge in as we stood here. He had to go now. But what would the agent's team do as soon as they realized he was dead? Maybe there was a way to keep him alive and get some answers from him after all.

"You should've left when you had the chance," he spat.

All the air got sucked out of the room as he punched Caterina in the stomach and took the blade from her. If she had hesitated in delivering the final blow before, he was the exact opposite. In a single fluid motion, he flipped the sword around and went for her side as if he meant to slice her in half. I had never been trained in swordsmanship, but my survival instinct and my need to save Caterina kicked in immediately.

The loud clank of metal against metal pierced my ears. And then everything was on automatic and in slow motion. I had blocked him a few inches before he cut her. From where he lay on the floor, he couldn't match my strength. Hot blood pumped through me as I considered all the different ways he could've hurt Caterina. All the ways he actually meant to. Maybe he had let her go before, but now something had shifted. He considered her a threat.

He had gotten the upper hand before because Caterina was a good person. Because she wanted to give him a second chance. Because she wasn't a fucking murderer. I didn't give a shit if he deserved to live or not. He had gone after the one person I loved the most in this world. I rammed my foot on his Adam's apple and pressed hard until he let go of his weapon.

"You should've left when you ran out of bullets." I thrust the blade through his belly. "Who the fuck sent you? Answer quickly and I'll let your men take you with them. You can survive this."

The blood had seeped through his clothes already and the stench of it lingered thick and heavy in the air. "You know it doesn't work that way." He winced in pain, cradling his stomach.

Caterina walked into my line of sight, just a few feet away. Tears brimmed her eyes, and her brows pinched together. "Who sent him?"

I had a few ideas, and I was sure she did too. Since the moment Caterina walked out the front entrance, the agent had been trying hard to kill me. The asshole knew exactly who I was, and the kind of access I had to crucial Society information. But he never tried to negotiate a deal with me. He wasn't interested in Society member names or in any of our illicit ventures. He simply wanted my head on a platter like some kind of hunting prize.

"I think Michael promised him to let him join our family if he killed me."

"I didn't come here alone." He smirked. It wasn't a confession, more a threat to remind me we had not won yet.

"Caterina." I spoke softly to her while I kept my eyes on the agent. "I know this is a lot to take in right now. But this isn't over. We're not safe. Help me find something to tie him up. Go." I raised my voice and that seemed to jolt her back to reality.

"Aaron is hurt. But he's getting your crew back. Or at least he said he would try."

"Okay. That's good. You did good." I set the sword down and started going through the agent's pockets. "See if you can find some zip ties in the kitchen."

"I know where Dad keeps them." She disappeared into the hallway. When she returned, she had a whole pack of them and set them next to him. "Are you letting him go?"

"I'll have the cleaning crew pick him up." I met her gaze, hoping she would get my meaning. His chances of surviving a stab wound to the stomach or the infection that was bound to set in shortly were zero, which was why he wasn't volunteering any more information. He had nothing left to lose. "We have to go before his men come looking for him."

"Why was he here alone?"

"My guess? Hubris. He thought he could take me on his own." I didn't think she was ready to hear my other theories.

The whole scenario felt like a mobster test—you keep what you kill.

"You came back for him." The agent scowled at Caterina, shifted his gaze to me for a moment while I tied him up, then back to her. "You betrayed your own family. With me, you would've had it all."

Did the deal include Caterina? My insides twisted when I realized there was a one hundred percent chance Michael had offered up his daughter again. Why else would the agent not want to kill her at first? Kill me and keep everything. Fucking asshole, when would Michael stop thinking of his daughter as a commodity?

A tiny fleck of recognition sparked in her green eyes. She finally knew or had accepted what her father was and what he was trying to do. When she advanced on him with fisted hands, chaos broke out as bullets pelted through the windows and hit the wall behind us. The shots were muffled, but the glass blasting across the living room wasn't.

"Get down." I darted toward her and brought her down to the floor. "Where the hell are Aaron and Frank?"

"They should be here by now." Caterina buried her face in my chest, gripping the front of my shirt.

I fished my phone from my back pocket and called Aaron. When he answered on the first ring, I puffed out a breath. "We have the situation under control in here. What's your status?"

"We got snipers. Three. But the cavalry just showed up. Chopper's on the way too. Past the garden, there's a landing pad, can you get to it?"

"We're on our way. We'll need a cleaning crew in here too."

"You got it, Boss."

I stuffed my phone back into my pocket and cradled Caterina's cheek. "We gotta go, love. What's the fastest way to get to the landing pad?"

"We don't have that."

"Aaron says otherwise. Past the garden, is there a large flat area?"

She squeezed her eyes shut and swallowed. I held her tighter. Thinking with bullets whizzing over your head wasn't an easy task. After a few beats, she finally nodded. "Through the kitchen. The way we came. It's a straight shot past the water fountain."

"Okay. When I say go, you make a run for it."

"I'm not leaving without you."

I still couldn't get used to the idea that Caterina wanted me. She loved me enough to risk her life for me. The occasion didn't call for it, but I didn't care. I cupped her cheek and kissed her lips. It was a hard and desperate kiss, a promise that she wasn't about to lose me.

"I'm right behind you."

The room quieted and settled into a low hum, or maybe that was just my ears ringing. That was our small window of opportunity. "Whatever you do, don't look back. Go. Now." I helped her to her feet and sent her off.

On the other end of the living room, by the glass door, the agent lay in a pool of his own blood. Some of it was dry and obviously from his stab wound. But a lot of it was also fresh and still flowing from a new bullet wound to the chest. I didn't know if the guys out there knew their man had failed in his mission to kill me. But it was obvious to me, the agent no longer served their needs.

"You should've known better than to make a deal with the devil," I whispered.

Following Caterina's directions, I darted down the hallway and into the kitchen. Outside, I spotted her hair flowing in the breeze, deep into the English garden that surrounded the house. The snipers weren't shooting at her. She would be glad to know her father didn't want her dead.

The sweet rumbling of the helicopter made me look up and then rush after Caterina. Two steps into the clearing, I was ransacked by a man, just as more bullets flew over my head. Jesus, I was ready for this fuckfest of a day to be over. I rolled onto the ground, but when I made to get up, the man who had tackled stayed in place. It had all happened so fast, I hadn't had time to recognize Frank's eyes behind the mask.

"You're lucky I don't have my gun with me."

"Sorry, sir. The one asshole got away. As much as we would like to keep Ms. Alfera alive, you're our top priority."

"Yeah, I know." I sat on my haunches, glaring at Caterina in the far distance as she climbed onto the helicopter. "I can't get to her. If there's one guy on the loose, he might try to come at me if I join her." I raked a hand through my hair. Suddenly every breath felt like tiny knives in my chest. "Make the call. Tell them to go."

"Yes, sir." Frank stayed low as he spoke fast into his earpiece. "Roger that."

As soon as he uttered the words, the chopper lifted off and quickly disappeared into the horizon. I met Frank's gaze. The concern in his eyes was justified. I had just sent away the only bargaining chip I had with Michael. I had no doubt that if I had shown up to the beach house today on my own, Michael would've given the order to blow up the place, to hell with his neighbors.

But Caterina had come with me. He had no choice but to play the game, use silencers and even send an agent who could handle a sword. Caterina had come back for me. She risked her life for me. And that was something Michael had not anticipated.

We waited another minute hidden in the neatly trimmed hedges near the water fountain. The sweet smell of azaleas mingled with the gunpowder in the air and made me think of Anna and her warning. She was right. This mobster life sullied everything it touched. I hadn't been here for more than an hour and already this place had gone to shit. Caterina deserved better than spending her day literally dodging bullets.

I had to stop thinking about that. Caterina loved me. That meant that my promise to her mother had been fulfilled. Caterina had chosen to stay with me. This incident was on Michael and it had nothing to do with Caterina and me.

"Sir, looks like we have the situation under control." Frank's voice brought me back to the present. "And we have a car."

"Good work." I stood and dusted off my pants. "Any word on where Michael might be?"

"No. He was here this morning. We think he took off right after we received a message to abort the mission." He glanced down at his hands. "Sir, I should've known better."

"This isn't on you." I patted him on the back.

Frank was my right-hand man. I trusted him implicitly. This other thing was orchestrated by someone else. Someone with access to the Crucible and my penthouse.

I had to admit. Caterina's unwavering trust in her father

had made me doubt my own conclusions about Michael. Or maybe I just didn't want to see her suffer like her mother had when she found out the truth about her husband, about all the lies he told her for years, and the deal he had brokered with the Society.

Yeah, Caterina made me wish Michael was a better human being. But the man and the life Anna created for her family wasn't real. The man Caterina called Dad didn't exist. And now that Anna was gone, he had no reason to pretend anymore.

Looking around me, the devastation left behind, I knew one thing for certain—the ruthless king was back. Or he never left. Either way, he was coming for me.

"Where to, Boss?" Frank stood at attention as the rest of my crew joined us one by one.

They were a small battalion, well-trained, and lethal. Why did Michael think he stood a chance today? Right. Because he thought Caterina made me weak. Fuck me. Was he right in that? Of course, he was. I did walk into his trap.

A quick scan of the line of men told me we hadn't lost anyone today. No matter what, I had to make sure it stayed that way. The Society had already lost enough members. Maybe it was high time I stopped thinking with my dick.

"Caterina asked me to bring her here because her brother Massimo told her Michael was staying at the house. How about we pay him a visit? I'm tired of playing the nice guy."

# CHAPTER 12
## Going Crazy with Doubt

CATERINA

I sat back in my seat and let the low rumble of the helicopter soothe my nerves. My whole body hadn't stopped shaking since I left the safety of Rex's arms. Leaving him was the wrong thing to do. With me by his side, he at least had a bargaining chip. Those men didn't want to hurt me. They wanted him. I tapped on the pilot's shoulder, and he turned on my headset.

"Did he make it out?"

The last thing I saw as we lifted off was Rex taking cover. He had let me go because he didn't want the man chasing him to come after me too. If he got hurt, it would be entirely my fault.

"Yes, he did. He will meet you at the penthouse." He tipped his head.

"Thank you."

I wedged my head between my legs and inhaled to ease the harsh thumping in my chest. The helicopter veered left then right, then another round until I felt like I was floating, aimlessly. We were almost back in the city, and I still couldn't wrap my mind around what had happened at the beach house.

Was this how Rex lived his life? In constant danger and bullets flying at every turn? No wonder Mom wanted her husband and children away from the Society and all its lethal drama. To be fair, today's incident had nothing to do with the crime families and everything to do with Dad. Because I had to be honest with myself now, Dad was everything Rex had said. He put a hit on Rex. And what was worse? He used me to get to him.

No doubt Massimo told him how Rex felt about me. I rubbed my temple as I replayed old memories of Dad, like watching a movie on the TV. I saw him teaching me how to ride a bike, his happy face while he watched me open presents on Christmas morning, and then sword fighting with us. He wasn't this murderous mobster. How could he be a dedicated husband and Dad but also a killer?

I hated that I didn't get to talk to him. I hated even more that even with all the evidence stacked against him, I still wanted him to tell me that it wasn't true. That he was being set up somehow. For twenty-four years, he had been a loving dad. That kind of bond was hard to erase or ignore. Maybe Massimo had an explanation for all this. He had wanted me to talk to Dad. He would have to know what the hell happened at the beach house.

Crying and hoping wasn't going to solve much. I had to talk to Massimo. Together, we could find Dad and figure out how to get him to back off.

"How much longer?" I spoke into the mouthpiece.

"Ten minutes." He pointed at the cityscape up ahead.

If Rex took a car back to the city, he wouldn't be home for another hour or so. That gave me enough time to make it to Massimo's apartment, have that talk, and then meet Rex.

As soon as we touched down on the rooftop of Rex's building, a new bodyguard showed up to escort me. I played along and let him usher me to the elevator bay and then down to the penthouse lobby.

Inside, I ambled to the bar cart and poured myself a whiskey. I needed something to calm my nerves, and also, a little liquid courage never hurt. There was a real good chance Rex would be pissed off at me for going out to see my brother. But I really needed to have this conversation in private.

Dad had wanted to talk to me. Didn't he? He asked Massimo to take me to the Hamptons to see him. So why take off as soon as I got there? Because I brought Rex with me? Did I force Dad's hand today? Or was this his plan all along after I told Massimo I was staying at Rex's place? The questions bounced around in my mind as I downed my drink and poured another. One thing was for sure though, I had to stop making excuses for Dad. Massimo would have to tell me the truth, no matter what.

"I'd like to enjoy my whiskey alone." I glanced at the bodyguard standing by the door. He hadn't moved since we had walked in. If he had orders to stay, it would make it extra hard to leave the building. "Or are you to stand there and watch me until Rex gets here?"

"I was just leaving." He nodded and disappeared through the kitchen on the other side of the grand staircase.

He did have orders to stay put, but at least he didn't feel he had to watch me like a hawk. I waited another minute, then headed out the door to the elevator. I pushed the call button several times, but nothing happened. Right. I needed a keycard. Then I remembered Rex had given me the code to use the secret door that led to the boardroom downstairs. From there, I could ride the elevator all the way down to the lobby.

With my heart pumping hard, I darted to the access on the other side of the elevator bay and swung the door open. A rush of adrenaline surged through me as I rushed down the steps. The first time I had been to the level reserved for Society members, I had been trying to escape from Rex. That night, this place had seemed like a maze.

When I reached the boardroom level, I entered the keycode Rex had given me and shouldered open the door. Out of nerves or because I felt like I was running out of time, I took off running down the carpeted corridor. The shimmering chandeliers dotting the hallway pointed the way toward the exit. As soon I got to the street level, I could hail a cab and be in the safety of Massimo's penthouse in less than twenty minutes. It wasn't like the bad guys were waiting for me right outside Rex's building, but I knew I had to be careful.

If I had my phone with me, I could've called my brother to come get me. In my rush to see Dad and clear the air, I had left my phone in the SUV. Making a mental note to ask Rex for it later, I picked up the pace. A door creaked open behind me, and I double-timed it.

I had made it halfway to the end of the corridor when an arm yanked me back by the waist. After the day I had had, I didn't even think about it before I started kicking and screaming.

"Jesus fuck, Caterina. It's me." Rex pinned me against the wall, puffing hot air into my face as he labored to catch his breath. "Why are you leaving?"

"I need to see my brother."

He slow-blinked, pressing his hard body against mine. "Alone? Why didn't you ask me?"

"For one, because you're not my keeper." I glared at him. "And two, because I didn't know when you were coming back. And I didn't have a phone."

"You could've asked any of the bodyguards." He braced his hands on either side of me. "I've had men shooting at me twice in the last week. Caterina, my patience is running thin. How do you think this looks for you?"

"What do you mean?"

"We get ambushed at your father's house. Then I have no choice but to let you leave on your own, because of more assholes shooting at me. And as soon as I get home, I'm told you're trying to leave."

"After everything we've gone through today, you're telling me you don't trust me?"

"I'm going crazy with doubt, I'm not gonna lie." He bit his lower lip as his intense gaze searched mine. "Every time you look at me like that, every time you try to leave me, all I want is to tie you down and fuck you hard."

His mouth caught mine in a sizzling kiss. Suddenly, everything that had happened at the beach—the shootings, the sword fighting and leaving without him—came crashing down on me like an avalanche of emotion. I had come so close to losing him. I threw my arms around his neck and kissed him with all the agony I felt.

I had been so lost in his kiss and the way his body felt against mine that I hadn't noticed he started walking me back toward the boardroom. By the time I had found my bearings, he was already ushering me inside the room and locking the door behind him.

"I'm sorry," I said when I came up for air. "I still can't wrap my head around what happened at the beach house. It's too horrible to think that Dad..." I trailed off. Saying the words aloud would make it real for me.

"You believe me then?" He caressed my cheek. "Michael wants all of us gone. And I'm next on his list."

I nodded.

"I'm sorry." I repeated, even though I knew there wasn't anything I could say to make up for what Dad had done. Not just today, but everything else too. "He ruins your life and now he's trying to take it away."

"Hey." He cocked his head to look me in the eyes. "My life isn't ruined. Not when I get to have you."

He slipped his hand under my top and kneaded my breast. The heated look in his gaze told me he had already forgiven me for the incident from before. My butt bumped against the edge of the oversized conference table, and in the next beat, I was on it with my legs spread open to make room for him. My top came off and then my bra.

"I don't think this is what this room is for." I ran my hands over his shoulders and up into his soft hair while his mouth left a trail of hot kisses from my chest down to my stomach.

"It's for whatever I want it to be." He unbuttoned my jeans and pulled them down to my ankles. "Right now, it's the place where I'm going to bury my face in your pussy."

Desire pooled between my legs instantly. In the back of my mind, I tried to find the words to tell him we should go upstairs, but he was already swiping his tongue up my slit and I couldn't think straight.

The man could work magic with his mouth. He sucked and nibbled and licked around my clit with precision, as if he could read my thoughts and knew exactly how I needed him to pleasure me. He switched between showering my throbbing bud with attention to soothing my swollen sex with gentle kisses and flickers of his tongue.

"Rex." I bucked my hips toward him.

"I know. Be patient." He stood back to remove his shirt.

The whole time, his gaze never left my pussy, as if he were studying it like a map. A half-smile pulled at his lips as he pressed a large hand on the inside of my thigh and continued his sweet torture. This time, though, he slid two fingers down my folds and then inside me.

When he flicked my g-spot, undulating waves of pleasure shot through me. I tried to hold on to that feeling and not come, not yet. I wanted more of this ecstasy. But the spark he had already ignited couldn't be contained. It burned hot under his index finger and slowly inched outward. A few seconds later, I came hard on his hand and face.

I didn't care that we were in an old boardroom meant for important meetings. I didn't care that I couldn't take in a whole breath and that my legs were numb. I just didn't want him to stop. As if he could hear my thoughts, he pulled away long enough to fix his cock at my entrance and plunge in. He thrusted hard into me as I rode the last sensation of my orgasm. Just when I thought it would end, it started up again—the tiny flame at my core and then the big release that made my heart slam fast against my rib cage and throat.

"Jesus, Caterina." He sucked hard on my nipple while he pummeled into me, racing to find his own climax. With a low grunt, he released inside me and then collapsed on top of me.

I cradled his head to my chest, reveling in the weight of him, the hard planes of his abs under my touch, and his hot and sweaty skin on me. He panted a breath on my breasts, and I smiled at the ceiling. I liked knowing I was the reason for his exhaustion.

"I can forgive you for just about anything." He braced his hands on the tabletop to look at me. "But Caterina, if you ever betray me, I don't think I could ever come back from that."

"I would never do anything to hurt you." I touched his cheek. "I didn't know we were walking into a trap. You have to believe me. I'm telling you the truth."

"I know." He bent down and gently brushed my lips with his. "Having you here, it feels too good to be true. I have wanted you for so long."

His phone rang in the pocket of his trousers. He hadn't even removed them, just lowered them enough to free his cock. I sat up and waited as he pressed the device to his ear.

"What is it?" He spoke into the phone and then kissed me again, palming my breast and rubbing my nipple. Suddenly, he stopped and released a long breath. "Yeah, wait ten minutes then send him up." He ended the call and placed the phone back in his pocket before he buttoned and belted his pants. "Your brother's here."

"Massimo? Why?"

"Because I asked my guys to bring him here. I want to talk to him too. I want to know why he sent you to the Hamptons, knowing Michael had sent a crew to kill me."

I raked both hands through my hair and swallowed my tears. He said it all so matter of fact. But this was Dad he was talking about. It hurt to know what he was. "Massimo had nothing to do with that."

"You know that for a fact, love?" He bent down until our noses were almost touching. "I'm done playing this guessing game. Michael is too much of a coward to face me. Now Massimo will have to answer for him."

"Is he on your hit list now too?"

"That's for him to decide."

He stepped back to put on his dress shirt. His gaze stayed on me, but I could see his thoughts drifting away from us to make room for what was waiting for us upstairs. His features hardened too, as if he were preparing for battle.

He hadn't said it, but Dad sealed his fate with the stunt he pulled today. No amount of begging on my part could save him now. But Rex had to understand, that guilty or not, Dad was still my dad and I couldn't let him die.

"Get dressed. I want to get this shitshow over quick."

# CHAPTER 13
## We Were Living a Lie

REX

I pushed open the door to the penthouse and motioned for Caterina to go in. The look in her eyes said she had a million questions going through her mind. But at this point, she knew me well enough to let it rest. I was right not to trust her family.

She shot a glance toward the window. The city lights touched every piece of furniture and cast a blue glow across the floor. When she didn't find Massimo standing there, she went up the stairs and straight into the bathroom.

I did the same. For one, I could still feel her hands on my body and the scent of her arousal tainted every breath I took. I needed to wash it all off and stay focused. Caterina was a dangerous distraction. Today proved just how deadly my love for her had become. I let down my guard for a moment and I almost ended up getting killed.

She stood back and watched me undress and then step under the warm spray. This had to be a record for her. She wanted to lash out at me. She wanted to be angry at me. But she was out of excuses for her family. In a huff, she pulled her shirt over her head and then dropped her jeans to the floor. I averted my eyes and studied the sheen and the different shades of gray on the marble lining the shower stall.

Bracing my hands on the warm stone, I let the water soothe me and wash away the day. Next to me, Caterina stood under the second shower head, hugging a soapy puff to her chest. "Can I at least ask for one thing?"

I slow-blinked and glared at my reflection. "That depends on the request."

"Can you listen to him first? Really listen? I can see you've already made up your mind about him like you did with Dad." Her erratic breath made her chest rise and fall.

Fuck me. Why did I look? I closed the space between us. "Michael put a target on his back himself. He did that, not me. And yeah, I made up my mind about him two months ago. But for you, I took a detour. A detour that almost cost me my life today. I'm done granting requests. Even if it's coming from you."

"Rex." She slipped her hand up my chest and into my hair.

Her tits rubbed against me and damnit if my cock didn't react instantly. She was a tall glass of water in the middle of the desert. And neither my cock nor I cared that the thing to satisfy our thirst might be poisoned. I gripped both her wrists and peeled her arms off of me.

"Not tonight, love." I strode out of the shower and headed for the walk-in closet to get dressed.

When I returned fully dressed in a dark suit, she was just standing there wrapped in a towel, and looking so alone, it made my heart ache for her. "I told you earlier. Massimo is the one who gets to decide if he makes it onto my shit list or not."

"I know. I'm sorry."

I wanted to kiss her. But if I did, my resolve would crumble. And I had to show Massimo that I was done playing games. Brother or not, if Massimo sided with his dad, if he was involved in any way in the attempt against me, he wasn't leaving here tonight. Not alive anyway.

Downstairs, Massimo and his new girlfriend EJ had already been shown to the living room. He paced the length of the sofa while EJ watched him with trepidation in her eyes. She was the key to getting answers.

"So glad you could join us." I sauntered to the bar cart and poured a double whiskey. "Can I offer you a drink?"

"No thanks." She shot to her feet. And for a second, I couldn't tell if she was shielding Massimo from me or the other way around.

"I don't think we've been properly introduced." I offered her my hand. "Rex Valentino."

"EJ Colt." She licked her lips, while her gaze darted between Massimo and me.

"I hear your mother is reacting positively to the cancer treatments. You must be thrilled."

EJ's mom had been admitted to the clinical trial because of his connection to me.

Her eyes watered, and Massimo pounced because he understood the threat behind my words. "That's not how you want to start this conversation, Rex."

"Michael put a hit on me today. So yes, this is exactly how I want to start this fucking conversation."

"It's okay, Massimo," EJ said.

"You shouldn't be here." He pursed his lips and turned to face me.

"No, she shouldn't. But you brought her into this when you and Mickey tried to take over her crew in Atlanta." I inhaled. This wasn't the time to rehash how EJ ended up involved in all this mess. Michael was the real threat here. "Did you have anything to do with the ambush at the beach house? How did Michael know Caterina was coming to see him? How did he know I'd be there?"

"I can't tell if you're pissed off because someone shot at you or if you're going out of your mind because you can't say for certain that my sister had nothing to do with it." He crossed his arms over his chest.

EJ reached for his hand, and he immediately relaxed his stance.

They had only been together for a few weeks and they already had their own silent language. A pang of jealousy spread from my belly up into my chest. Massimo wasn't wrong. I was going out of my mind because everywhere I looked, Caterina looked guilty.

I glanced up the grand staircase and did a double take. Caterina had chosen to wear a cocktail dress that hugged her tits to perfection. Her dark hair spilled in thick curls over her shoulders and somehow accentuated her green eyes. Jesus, how was I supposed to keep my head straight with her standing next to me, looking like that?

"Massimo." She took long strides across the room and hugged him and then EJ. "I'm sorry. I would've come to your apartment, but Rex beat me to it."

"Don't worry about it." He furrowed his brows as he surveyed Caterina's face. "He told you, didn't he?"

"About the arranged marriage? Yes, he did. I know everything."

"And you still want to be here?"

She turned to face me. "I do."

My pulse quickened. I wanted to hold her and tell her I believed she was innocent. But that would be a lie. I sipped from my glass. "Tell me about Michael."

"Dad wanted to talk to Caterina and tell her about what he had done to be allowed to step down. We made plans to drive up to the Hamptons today and have that long overdue conversation with him. That was before the party last night, before we even knew you were in the country. When you and I spoke earlier that day, you were still in Ibiza." He stuffed his hands in the pockets of his trousers and waited for me to digest this information.

Caterina didn't know I was in town. I had hoped to see her at the party last night and talk to her. Not in a million years would I have guessed we'd end up in bed together. The events from last night reeled through my mind. Caterina came to me because she wanted me. I thought of her image in the mirror, all tied-up and in a half-suspension. She did all that for us. Not because she was setting up a trap. No one was that good of a liar.

"How did Michael know I was coming?"

"You weren't exactly covert when you and Caterina left the party last night together. Anyone could've told Dad she spent the night with you." He cocked an eyebrow and shifted his weight from one foot to the other as if he understood what had happened next and why.

Everyone knew how I felt about Caterina. I had never tried to hide it. She was mine, and I needed everyone to know she was off limits. Michael had my job for many years. He was an expert in understanding people's weaknesses. Though he didn't need to be a genius to figure out that if Caterina spent the night, she would be with me the next day too. Michael took a gamble setting up his trap—a gamble that almost paid off had it not been for one piece of information he didn't have.

Was Michael really okay with killing me in front of his daughter? Putting her life at risk like that? He, better than anyone, knew that the innocent always got caught in the cross-fire. I thought of how the shooter tried to get Caterina to leave before he attacked me—a pathetic attempt at keeping her safe.

I met Massimo's gaze. Like me, he was trying hard to do the right thing, not just for EJ but for his sister too. He knew Caterina was in love with me. He knew and he didn't tell Michael, which was why Michael had no way of knowing that Caterina would stay and save me.

"Caterina told you she loved me?" I slanted a glance at her.

"She did." He rolled his eyes. "I don't get what she sees in you. But that's her choice. It was always going to be her choice."

"I promised Anna it would be."

"I did too." He offered me a quick nod and strode to the bar. "Now that my head isn't on the chopping block, I need a fucking drink."

"Massimo, is Dad really trying to get Rex's seat at the table?" Caterina rubbed the back of her neck. "He's not like that. You know him."

"You read the contract." Massimo knocked back his whiskey and let out a breath. "Dad is capable of that and a whole lot more. Over the years, I saw him do some shitty stuff. And then hide it from Mom. He made Enzo and me lie for him. So he could pretend to be a family man, the man Mom wanted. It was all a lie, Caterina. At first, I told myself that we

354

were protecting the two of you. But I'm done. That's the real reason I left after Mom died. I couldn't stand the sight of Dad, knowing all the shit he's done."

"We were living a lie." She glanced down at her hands.

"I don't know how, but Mom found out about the arranged marriage. It broke her heart." He raked a hand through his hair with a look of disgust on his face. "I was done with Dad after that. We're not his pawns to use as he pleases."

She swallowed, wincing as if she had eaten a bitter chunk of truth. "He sold me out, delivered me to the highest bidder, and then, changed his mind only because he wants to be king again."

"I'm sorry, Bells. I should not have left you alone. But I couldn't stay here and watch him do this to you. Rex was your best shot, just like Mom had said. My hands were tied. I'm sorry I couldn't even tell you the truth." He pulled her into a tight hug, and she sobbed into his coat.

"That wasn't your fault. The contract couldn't be broken." She smiled at him, then turned to me. "But Rex was never going to force me into anything."

"He promised Mom. But honestly, I wasn't sure he'd keep his word."

"I'm not Michael."

The only one here willing to betray his own to get what he wanted was Michael Alfera. In the process, he had signed his own death warrant. All I could do was promise his children he wouldn't die by my hand. But there were plenty of Society members more than willing to watch him pay for what he did to us. He exposed our secrets. An entire family was wiped out because of him. Even Caterina had to see that he deserved what was coming to him.

"If you help me stop Michael, in return, I promise to let him go." I put up my hand when Caterina's eyes lit up. "I'm letting him go, but I can't say the same about Signora Vittoria or Santino Buratti. He was with me in Ibiza when we ran into special agent Clifton. He mentioned Michael by name."

"I'm in. Not for Dad, but for you, Bells. You shouldn't start your wedding with your husband's hands stained with Dad's blood." He shrugged.

Caterina blushed and cut her gaze to me. Had she not realized that we still had to consider our pending wedding? I supposed I hadn't either. But that would have to wait a little longer. We still had the small issue of finding the mole in my organization. Santino would handle the rest for me.

"So, if you didn't help Michael." I inhaled and the heaviness in my chest lifted. I was way more comfortable going after a traitor who wasn't related to Caterina. "Someone inside my circle did."

"You're right." Massimo sat next to EJ, bracing his forearms on his knees. He seemed more relaxed, and I could tell he wanted to help me solve this puzzle. Not to save his Dad. We were beyond that. But to do the right thing. "He couldn't have done this on his own."

"Aaron said that someone sent a message from your phone to the crew and told them to abort the mission. That's why they weren't there when we showed up, when we needed them." Caterina tentatively closed the space between us. "He would need someone who's tech savvy. And then there's that guy who wanted to personally kill you." She sucked in her lower lip.

"What happened?" Massimo pinched his brows, while his gaze shifted between Caterina and me.

"When I went back into the house to help Rex—"

"You did what?"

"Relax." She waved her hand in dismissal. "They were out of bullets and I had Dad's sword."

"Oh, my fucking God." He dropped his head in his hands, then glanced up. "You fought him with a sword?"

"And she won too."

"Did you...?" He let the question linger in the air. Did Caterina kill a man?

"No, I killed him."

"Guys, that's not the point." She moved to block Massimo from my line of sight.

"Dad has been planning this coup for a while." Massimo rose to his feet and headed for the bar cart again. "I'm willing to bet it all started when Mom died."

"Or when the feds went after Caterina and you."

I had never seen a man spiral so out of control over his wife's death. Even if Michael had done a half-ass job of changing into a better man, he still did try for Anna.

He gave up his seat as king. That right there told me how much he cared about her. But now that she was gone, every instinct he had suppressed during his marriage had burst out of him. I imagined it to be some sort of avalanche that had been precariously contained by a tiny warrior woman.

I glanced around the room at Massimo, EJ and Caterina. They were on my side. Little by little, I had blocked every pawn Michael had at his disposal. He was done. But I still had to contend with the FBI, their hit list, and those Society members who wanted Michael back. Whatever the number, one or one hundred, they had gone against me, knowing treason was punishable by death. That pissed me off and put me in a very murderous mood. I didn't give a fuck if they had done it out of loyalty to the old king or because they didn't trust me. They would pay just the same as Michael.

"Someone did betray you, Rex. But it wasn't anyone standing in this room."

"I believe you, love." I cupped her cheek. "So how we do catch the snitch?"

# CHAPTER 14
## Mine

CATERINA

"Your dad served himself up as bait. That worked out pretty well." EJ shrugged, looking up at Massimo then Rex.

Massimo brought his drink halfway up to his lips and then stopped. "That's not a bad idea."

"It's not a good idea either." I gripped Rex's biceps. He had crossed his arms over his chest and looked like he was actually considering doing what EJ suggested. I squeezed again to get his attention. "No. I can't go through another day like today. There's gotta be another way." I pointed at my brother. "Massimo can talk to Dad. Or I can try. There's no reason why he wouldn't talk to us."

"I can try." Massimo rubbed the stubble on his cheek. "But Bells, he didn't tell me what he was planning to do at the beach house. He knows I don't agree with his methods. And once he finds out you helped Rex, he'll know he can't trust you either."

Tears stung my eyes. Of course Massimo was right, but it still hurt to know that Dad chose power over his family—over

359

me. I glanced down at my hands, shaking my head in disbelief. "I can't lose any more people."

"And you won't." Rex wrapped his arm around me. "How about we give it a rest for now?"

"Works for me." Massimo set his glass down. "I'll see what I can find out with my crew. Something like the coup Dad is planning requires a shit-ton of people. Someone has to know something."

"Okay, see? That sounds more like a plan." I beamed at him.

"Let's go home now. I think we all need some rest." Massimo offered EJ his hand and then turned to me. "You coming?"

"Caterina." Rex stiffened next to me. "You and I have a deal."

My cheeks burned hot because I absolutely remembered our agreement. Rex gave me time to figure out how to help Dad, and in return, I agreed to be his rope bottom for the remainder of our old contract. That meant I still couldn't leave his penthouse. Thing was, I didn't want to.

"I'm staying." I met Massimo's gaze. His eyebrows went up as he considered the situation. I was a grown woman. If I wanted to stay, I didn't need his permission. "I'll be fine. This is the safest place in the city."

"As you wish." He pulled EJ to him and cocked an eyebrow at Rex. "Does the visit to the mighty king include a ride home?"

Rex chuckled. "I needed to make sure I didn't walk into another ambush. You understand. Take the elevator to the garage level. My driver will take you anywhere you want."

When Massimo and EJ shut the door behind them, a familiar feeling of being home washed over me. "Are we okay?"

"Yes, love. We're okay." He kissed my lips. As with everything Rex did, his kiss was hot and all-consuming. He puffed out a breath and pressed his forehead to mine. "You look stunning in that dress. Why did you wear it? To confuse me?"

"I don't know." I glanced down at the velvet cocktail dress and high heels. "I felt I needed armor for this conversation."

"Why?"

"I was afraid you'd send me away. So yeah, maybe I was trying to confuse you and make you want me." I slipped my hands up his hard chest and braced my body against his length.

His breath hitched. "I want you all of the goddamn time."

His mouth found mine again. I melted into him while he devoured me with a kiss. Every thrust of his tongue laced with whiskey sent a raw charge of pure pleasure down to my already wet pussy. I wanted him inside me again. I wanted his huge cock to fill me up.

"Rex."

"I know, love." He pulled away to look at me.

His blue eyes showed all the desire he felt and all the erotic things he wanted to do to me. My pulse quickened and made me hot and tingly all over. And just like that, I fell into a puddle of want at his feet. When he spoke again, his tone was commanding and so seductive. Oh shit. I was immediately turned on because I knew exactly what he would say next.

"Meet me in the Kinbaku suite." He panted a ragged breath. "Now."

---

THE NEXT MORNING, I sat at my desk smiling like a schoolgirl, staring at nothing in the distance.

"Hello?" Sarah waved her hand in front of my face. "Earth to Caterina."

"Oh sorry. Did you say something?"

"I asked you how your weekend was?"

Jesus Christ. I could never tell her. Ever since Rex barged into my life, every moment was intense and upside down. Rex wasn't your typical guy. He was a mafia king. With him, every minute of every day was about life and death.

"Um...it was good." I squeezed my legs together to ease the ache between them. Last night, Rex had made me come twice in the rope room before he carried me to his bed and fucked me hard for hours. Even though now there was love between us, what we did last night couldn't be called anything else. Our desire for each other was much too strong to taper it down with sweet and slow love making. "How about you? Did you do anything fun?"

"I found this guy on Tinder and we went out. He was nice. We watched a movie. Then he took me to this place that was a hole in the wall but had the best pizza. I'm seeing him again tonight. Maybe I'll get lucky." She bit her bottom lip and let out a long breath. "It's been a while."

"I'm so happy for you." I reached across the desk and squeezed her hand.

A rap on the door jolted her out of her reverie. "Oh my god." She jumped a little in her seat. "I'll get it." She darted to the door and swung it open.

And then it was my turn to startle in my seat. Standing there, wearing his usual tailored dark suit, and looking hotter than he had any right to be, was Rex. I hadn't seen him since the last time he made me come, which happened about twelve hours ago.

When I woke up at six this morning, he had already left for work. So I decided to do the same. Now that we knew Dad was working with the FBI, it was safe to assume I wasn't in any immediate danger. I figured Rex had arrived at the same conclusion because when I asked Aaron to drive me to the office, he obliged without checking in with Rex first, which could only mean one thing—Rex had already told him it was safe for me to come in. My heart melted a little at the thought that Rex would always be there to look after me, even if our arrangement was sort of unconventional.

"I don't think we were introduced before. I'm Rex." Rex's deep voice rumbled just below my navel.

"I know who you are. You're the investor looking to buy our company."

"That's right." A half-smile pulled at his lips. "I'm that too."

"I'm Sarah." She shook his extended hand, while she gawked at him, her mouth slightly open.

Something like petty jealousy twisted in my chest, and I had to remind myself that Sarah didn't know about Rex and me. Hell, I didn't even know. What Rex and I had together wasn't exactly normal or even a relationship. But watching my friend ogle him like he was some kind of juicy steak made me wish Rex and I were a normal couple. The kind that had dates and ate pizza at a dive on a Sunday night.

"Would you mind giving my girlfriend and I a minute, Sarah?"

Wait, what? My head snapped up to Rex.

Sarah's brows shot up in surprise as her mouth formed an

"o." A whole five seconds went by before she snapped out of whatever spell she was under and grabbed the doorknob. "Oh sure. Of course. Oh wow. Yeah, I'll leave you to it." She waved in my general direction and staggered down the hallway.

Rex turned his panty-melting smile my way and slowly shut the door. Before he sat on the chair Sarah had just vacated, a text popped up on my phone.

Sarah: *OMG his eyes. He's like a tall glass of hotness and testosterone. I think I'm pregnant.*

Sarah: *GIRLFRIEND?*

Sarah: *How could you keep this juicy news from me?*

Sarah: *I need ALL the deets. Right now.*

Girlfriend? I stared at the word on my phone. We were boyfriend and girlfriend? The label didn't quite seem to fit what we were. I stuffed my phone in the desk drawer so Rex wouldn't see the flurry of texts streaming down my screen. Something raw and possessive broke loose in my chest. Mine. The word blazed in my mind. I wanted this man to be all mine. I wanted to be his girlfriend. I wanted everyone to know we were together.

"Hi." I blurted out.

"Hi." He unbuttoned his suit jacket and sat across from me.

"What are you doing here?" Not that I was complaining. I loved how he looked in my office, how he took up space. I loved how he filled all the empty spaces in my life.

"I was wondering if you were free for lunch?"

"Lunch?"

After all the kinky things we had done in his penthouse, a lunch date seemed so normal, and so not us. Butterflies fluttered in my belly. I'd never had a boyfriend who stopped by my office just to share a meal with me.

"Last night." He paused to smile at his hands as if remembering something. "We didn't really get a chance to talk about us."

"No, I supposed we didn't." My cheeks flushed.

A reel of images from the rope room popped into my head, and I squeezed my legs together. It was so hard not to want him. I didn't care that we were at work, in my office, where anyone could walk in on us. I wanted him out of that suit. I wanted his hot skin against mine.

"What do you want to talk about?" The air shifted around us, and suddenly, I couldn't quite catch my breath.

"Jesus, Caterina. My cock steels every time you look at me like that." He stood and sauntered around my desk. When I rose to my feet, he pulled me into his arms. "We should've stayed in bed today. You make me want to forget about everything and send it all to hell."

"You were gone when I woke up." I had been so disappointed when I found his side of the bed empty this morning. "I would've stayed."

"I had work that couldn't wait." He took my hand and sucked on the inside of my wrist. "I thought of you all morning though."

My eyes fluttered closed. When I opened them again, Rex had switched places with me. He sat in my chair with his legs spread apart. By now I recognized that hungry look in his gaze. A buzz sparked in my chest and quickly made its way down to my wet pussy. I cut a glance toward the door then back to Rex.

"Take my cock." His tone was commanding, as usual, and

as usual, it was a huge turn-on. "I want to fuck that pretty mouth."

"What if someone walks in?"

"I'll fire them."

With everything that had happened since I left Rex's penthouse a month ago, I had forgotten about the bid he had put in to buy the company I worked for. He wanted to buy it, dismantle it, and then sell it by the pound to make a profit. "Did you buy us out?"

"I did. That was the matter that couldn't wait this morning."

"So is that why you're here? To tell people, you're picking the place apart?"

He chuckled and rubbed the sexy stubble on his cheek. "No, I came to get a blow job from my girlfriend."

"I thought you wanted to talk."

"That too."

"Rex." I shook my head as I searched for the words to refuse him. But as soon as he unbuckled his belt, I knew I was going to do exactly as he had asked. It was as if an invisible force was pulling me toward him, making me kneel in front of him, and guiding my hand to rub up and down his length. "I've never done this."

The only other time I'd had a cock in my mouth, it was the night I lost my virginity to him. I hadn't exactly given him a blow job. I merely lay there and let him slide his erection into my mouth for a few rounds. My pulse spiked and made me hot all over.

"I know, love." He unzipped his pants and freed his erection.

The man had a gorgeous dick. I didn't need real-life

comparisons to know that. I stroked him, and he relaxed in the chair, letting out a low hiss. He was thick and heavy in my hands. Holding him like this, knowing I was the reason for his pleasure, made me feel powerful. The feeling was addictive and so tempting.

"Go on." He gripped the hair at the nape of my neck and brought me down to him.

The droplet of pre-cum at the tip of his shaft touched my lips, and I got my first taste of him. Rex's signature scent, that mix of body wash and woodsy smell, flooded my senses. His hips came up to meet my face at the same time he pushed on my head. He slipped in easily—all the way to the back of my throat.

"Good girl. I knew you could take it all." He pumped into me, making my eyes water from the strain on my neck and my gag reflex.

My entire body ached with need, but all I could do was stay there and let him work his cock into my mouth, in and out as he raced to find his release. After a few beats, I let go of him to rub my hardened nipples, anything to calm down the frenzy that had already taken hold of me. Rex kept the pace for a while longer, fucking my mouth just like he had said he wanted to do.

"Fuck." A low groan escaped his lips just as two buttons flew off and my blouse fell open.

I watched with wide eyes as he pulled down my bra cups, stroked himself a few times, and then came on my mounds.

"I can't believe we just did that." I caught some of his seed with my finger.

"You were perfect." He puffed out a breath. "So perfect." He bent down and kissed my lips. His tongue swirled gently past my teeth, tasting all of me. With a sexy smile, he pulled away and reached for the tissue box. He took my hand and wiped it before he moved on to my chest. The gesture was sweet and soothing.

This was the thing about Rex. He could be so demanding and intimidating, but also tender and kind. No one had ever made me feel this safe and taken care of. How did I ever think I could spend any amount of time with someone like Rex and not fall madly in love with him? Mine. He was all mine.

"I love you." I sat back on my heels and met his gaze.

"Marry me, Caterina."

"What?"

# CHAPTER 15
## I Want You to Want Me

Rex

I probably should've waited until after lunch to pop the question. But after all this time, and now that Caterina had finally admitted her feelings for me, what was the fucking point?

"What?" she asked again. "I'm still trying to process that whole girlfriend thing." She let out a heavy sigh, searching my gaze. After a few seconds, she glanced down at her ruined blouse. "I need to change."

"Okay." I reached for her elbows and helped her to her feet. "I understand you may have questions. How about we have that meal I promised? You can ask me anything you want. But then I'll need an answer to my question."

"Technically, you haven't asked me anything. It was more of a command." She waved her hand in dismissal and walked to the small closet behind her where she pulled out a fresh top. "I always keep an outfit in the office. I spill coffee a lot." She talked fast as her fingers fumbled with the rest of the buttons.

God, I was in love with this woman. I chuckled and rose to my feet.

"Let me help." I reached for her waist and pulled the shirt over her head before I kissed her lips gently. "Don't be nervous, love. We were always meant to end up here. Do you see that?"

"No. I mean, yeah, I knew marriage was part of the contract Dad made with the Society and your family." She pressed a hand to her forehead. "It just didn't seem real until now."

"We're real. Aren't we?" I took her wrist and placed her fingers over my heart. "I want the world to know that you're mine."

Our gazes locked. She knitted her brows and opened her mouth, but the words didn't come out. "Jesus, I'm in the middle of my office in my bra. This is what you do to me. I can't think straight when you're near."

"Is that a bad thing?" I took the silky blouse from her and slipped it on, taking my time with the tiny buttons. "For what it's worth, you have the same effect on me. All the roads in my life, all my thoughts, they all lead back to you. I don't want to wait anymore. Caterina..." I sucked on my lower lip. A rush of adrenaline surged through me with the words I wanted to say next, but she pressed her hand to my mouth.

"Don't say it. Not yet. Let me process all of this first. For example, what happens to my family when we marry? What would the Society do if we don't? What happens to you if we wait? What—?"

I pressed my forefinger to her lips. "Fair enough. Let's have that lunch and we can talk about it. I'm trying here, Caterina. All my life all I've known is to take. In my world, our world, no one will give you anything just because you ask. But with you, I want to ask. And I want an honest answer. I want you to want this too. Does that make any sense?" I puffed out a breath. My heart raced at the idea that Caterina's feelings for me might not match my own. That after all we had been through, she still wasn't ready for me.

"I think it does. Maybe. I don't know."

"Come on. Let's eat first." I winked at her, fixing the collar around her neck.

Minutes later, Frank pulled up to the curb at a high-rise in the upper west side. The whole way there, Caterina had stayed on her side of the back seat, as far away from me as possible. She even kept her distance while we made our way to the rooftop. Pricci's was a contemporary Italian restaurant with a dramatic, modern decor and one of my favorite spots in the city for their creative dishes but also for the spectacular view of Central Park.

"Wow." Caterina draped a napkin over her lap as her gaze took in the atmosphere. "A place like this should be crowded around this time."

"Yes, it usually is. But I wanted us to have privacy."

She furrowed her brows as if asking how the hell did you manage this?

"The owner owed me a favor."

"What kind of favor?" She leaned in. "No, wait. You could tell me but then you'd have to kill me. Right?"

"No." I sat back in my chair and cocked an eyebrow. "He needed a building permit fast tracked. I got it for him."

"Oh. How did you manage that?"

"The commissioner owed me a favor." I poured red wine into her glass. "What you really want to ask is how criminal are we? Go ahead. Ask."

She cleared her throat and took a long sip from her goblet. "Okay. You've never offered information about yourself before."

"It's only fair. I know all about you."

"Have you ever killed anyone?"

"Yes." I braced an elbow on the armrest and tapped my temple. "I could sit here and explain to you how they all deserved it, but none of it will make sense until you fully understand what the Society stands for. We're the keepers of the peace, Caterina. The authorities weren't always around to help us. The Society was created to protect our own. Over time, that mandate expanded to everyone in the city. The police, the FBI, they can only do so much because they're not part of the fabric like we are."

"So you're some sort of vigilante now?" She smiled at her hands. "Violet." She said under her breath. "You saved her from some underground brothel."

I nodded. "We're all criminals here, love. I'm not a saint. And I don't want to be one. But there should be limits. The FBI didn't give a shit that Violet's pimp was into human trafficking, that he was bringing people in from Venezuela and forcing them to work for him. Do you know why?"

She shook her head.

"He was an informant. They decided that these young women suffering was an okay price to pay. All they cared about was catching a bigger fish. Some gun dealer." I smirked. "I took care of them both."

"That's what you do." She inhaled and drank more of the wine.

"We have a finger on the pulse, so to speak. It's a very delicate balance. One that an FBI agent has decided he no longer cares for. If he ever cared. Some of those career agents only care about recognition and promotions." I met her gaze, hoping she would understand my meaning. We were under attack. Everything we knew and held dear was at risk because Michael had decided he no longer wanted to play by the rules. How was I supposed to squeeze a lifetime of indoctrination into one lunch date? "When I was in Ibiza, a man came after me."

"Why?" Her cheeks flushed.

"He wanted to kill me." I pinched the bridge of my nose. "Special Agent in Charge Clifton has a vendetta against the Society. I'm too young to know exactly what our parents did to him. Maybe they made a fool of him one too many times. Who the hell knows? But that's the asshole Michael decided to bring into our midst."

"Rex." She shot me a warning look. Her dad would always be between us. When it came to him, she simply didn't want to know the truth.

"I want to be honest with you. So here it is. Without the Society, the city you know would slowly start to decay. Until there's nothing left. The streets are safe mainly because of us, not them. Michael and his love for your mother threw a wrench into all of it. You asked what would happen if you and I don't marry? The original families would start going at each other to make a play for the highest rank within the organization."

"That's you."

"That would be us."

"When Michael left, he offered you as insurance, so my position would never be questioned by the other families. I didn't steal the throne from your family. Michael surrendered it, willingly. Now we have this agent killing us one by one simply because your dad has changed his mind."

She squeezed her eyes shut. "Okay, I get it. Dad is everything you say. What happens to Enzo? I haven't seen him since he came to pay off Dad's fake debt. I'm sure he's with Dad. Are you going to kill him too? Does he deserve it?"

I had never been afraid to tell the truth until this moment. If I lied now, Caterina would still love me. But if I didn't, where would we be? I refused to start our lives together with lies and betrayal. She deserved better.

"Enzo doesn't get to be king. He can take that up with your dad. If I find out that he's been helping Michael, I'd have no choice but to retaliate. The by-laws are very clear on this. We can't have the Society members killing each other. How does that serve anyone?" Fuck me. Not a lie, but also not a real answer.

"It doesn't matter if I say yes. My family will still be in danger." Her eyes watered. "Dad lost someone important to him. Doesn't he get a second chance?"

"Not like this." I shook my head. "He doesn't just want to come back. I would've welcomed him with open arms. What Michael wants is to be king again. For that, he requires my head on a platter. His agent already tried to get him that when we were in Ibiza and then again at the beach house. He's not playing games here. And he's certainly not asking for a second chance."

I fisted my hands and glanced out the tall windows. The

shimmering glow over Central Park did nothing to stomp down the fury rushing through me right now. What the hell was wrong with me? Caterina's entire family had been hunting me for months, and all I wanted to do was marry her. Santino was right. My love for her made me at best, weak, and at worst, blind.

She sighed across the table, her pretty cheeks still red and her lips parted as if she had a million questions going through her head and couldn't decide what to ask next. "But you're telling me, that in spite of everything Dad has done, you're willing to give me a choice in this?"

"I am. I promised your mom I would. And more than that, I want you to want this. To want me. This life isn't easy. What I'm asking you to become won't be easy. But it's our duty."

"What if I don't want to?"

The question was like a kick in the gut.

"You'd be breaking my heart."

"No, I mean. Is there another way to save the Society from self-destruction? Enzo—"

"I'm not stepping down, Caterina. I've been preparing for this moment for half my life. Michael doesn't get to have his cake and eat it too." I took a deep breath in and reminded myself that Caterina didn't fully understand our world, our rules. She also didn't want to see her family die. But Michael made his bed, literally. Now he had to lie on it. "You can't save everyone."

"I just want to save Dad." She glanced out the window, probably wishing the spectacular view could bring her a bit of solace or a miracle solution to her problem. I was making her choose between her dad and me. She blew out a breath and met my gaze. "How about you? Do *you* want to marry me?

How much of this love you feel for me is about mandates and honor? And how much of it is because of me?" She seemed hurt by the implication of it all.

In her defense I was too, at first. We'd been their pawns all our lives. But now, together, we could be more.

When Dad first told me about the arrangement he had made with the Alfera family, to save the Society, as he put it, I was pissed. I was angry at the idea that my life was no longer my own, that it belonged, and that it was tied, to Caterina's. Over the years, I began to understand why Dad had agreed to Michael's insane proposal. Without someone at the head of the table, without a king, the Society would crumble. By birthright, the Alfera family owned that seat. It was always meant for Caterina or her brothers. I was her king as much as she was my queen.

I rose to my feet and sauntered around the table. "I never wanted anyone as much as I want you. Our union would benefit a lot of people, it would complete the contract between our families. But I don't want any of it, if I don't have your love too. I want you to want me." I dropped to one knee and reached into the inside pocket of my suit jacket.

"Rex." Her eyes went wide as she scanned the empty room.

My heartbeat quickened as I took in her scent and the heat radiating from her body. Caterina was the breath of fresh air I'd waited for, for a long time. Things were finally going our way. The woman I loved, loved me back. We were no longer on borrowed time or against the clock with a fucked-up contract. I could finally ask her.

"Caterina Isabella Alfera, would you marry me?"

She beamed at me, nodding her head.

"Is that a yes or a no, love?"

"Yes." She threw her arms around my neck and kissed me. "The answer was always going to be yes. I just wanted to know you wanted me too."

"I told you." I took her left hand and slid the diamond ring onto her finger. "I'm not good at asking."

Her mouth fell slightly open as she admired the three-carat canary diamond ring. "This ring belonged to my mother."

"It did." I nodded. "She wanted you to have it. She insisted I take it. I don't know why she didn't just give it to you or your dad."

"She wanted me to know she approved of you." She blinked a couple of times, and tears streamed down her cheeks. "So what happens now?"

I had a few ideas. Most of them involved Caterina and I on some far away island, away from all this. But we had a job to do. Those fantasies would have to wait a little longer. I stood and wrapped my arms around her waist, getting lost in those gorgeous eyes that showed nothing but admiration and desire. One of these days, I would get used to that. I would forget how much it hurt to see only hate in them.

"Now you have to plan a wedding. Anything you want, as long as it happens as soon as possible. How about this weekend?"

"That's in five days." She laughed, a sweet and contagious sound that stirred my nerve endings. Jesus, I was putty in her hands. Worst part was, I didn't give a shit.

"Tomorrow then."

"Rex. Be serious."

"I am being serious."

## CHAPTER 16
## I Know, You Know, I Know

CATERINA

"What happens now?"

Rex glanced up at me from his plate of sea bass and waited after the server had placed my seared tuna salad in front of me. A grin pulled at his full lips while he eyed me like I was the most delicious thing.

"Now we go home and fuck the rest of the day."

I laughed. "Okay. And after that?"

"Well." He furrowed his brows as he cut a piece of his fish and brought it to his lips. As with everything Rex did in his life, this small act was controlled and executed deliberately and a with a touch of perfection. When he swallowed, he met my gaze. "We get to work. The threat hanging over our heads is still there. But now we're stronger together. We can beat this."

"Dad's still out there."

"Ah." He dabbed his mouth with his napkin and sat back.

Ah was right. If we were to start our lives together, we

needed to not start it with Dad's execution. Sure, Dad had made a huge miscalculation. Okay, a horrific mistake, but I hadn't lost hope that the man that married Mom all those years ago, that the man that raised me, my father, was still in there somewhere. I knew I could get him back. Dad only needed a reminder of what we were as a family. How happy we were— even if some of that wasn't entirely real. Dad had been a good man for the past twenty some years.

"There has to be a solution that doesn't end with Dad's death." Just saying the words aloud was like a kick to my stomach. I set my fork down and took a big swallow of my wine.

"I promise he will not die by my hand. Santino has strict orders to stand down. But Caterina, once his father decides he's waited long enough, he'll have no choice but to go after Michael. You know he went after the Buratti family, don't you?"

"What?" I rubbed the side of my face. "When?"

"Last month. It's why Santino joined me in Ibiza. He wanted answers too."

The pity in his eyes cut me because he really didn't want to do anything to hurt Dad or me, but Dad wasn't helping matters. Was I being naive in thinking it wasn't too late to save Dad? "What happened in Ibiza? Feel free to skip the Donata parts." I understood that Rex and I were not together when he was in Ibiza. But just thinking of him with Donata, the hot shot doctor with legs for days, made my insides twist with jealousy. Yeah, I was jealous. I never thought I'd be the type, but then again, I never thought I'd ever be engaged to a mafia king. So there.

"I like this look on you." Rex chuckled and sipped from his wine. "If Donata was in Ibiza when I was there, I had no idea.

I spent most of my time on the yacht floating in the middle of the ocean." He shook his head as if the memory of the time he spent abroad pained him.

"Okay, I believe you." I picked up my fork and took a bite of the tuna. I closed my eyes and savored the flavors. Did Rex ever eat a meal that wasn't pure ecstasy? "You were there for a long time."

"It felt like an eternity without you by my side. The island is beautiful and peaceful. I'm sure you know that."

"I'd like to see it with you sometime."

"Anyway, my days included drinking alone by night and chasing clues by day. If I'm being honest, I didn't get anywhere until Santino showed and decided to serve me up as bait."

"What is it with people using you like that?"

"I'm a high commodity. As fucked-up as his methods were, we did manage to get answers. I met Special Agent in Charge Clifton. Apparently, he's the one." He drank as he considered his words.

"Dad made a deal with this Clifton?"

"He did."

My eyes watered. Dad had worked himself into a really tight corner. "What happened to Clifton and Gallo? You obviously made it out alive."

"I killed Gallo. We believe Clifton made it out. We never found his body."

I squeezed my eyes shut, pinching the bridge of my nose. Why were we talking about dead people? Right after a wedding proposal, no less. "Is there anything...?" I couldn't ask again. I couldn't plead for Dad's life anymore. He was guilty. "I don't want him to die. I don't care what he did."

"I know. And if I could help him, I would. I mean that, Caterina."

"I believe you." I smiled at him, though my heart sank as the realization that I was about to lose another parent washed over me.

"Hey." He reached across the table to cover my hand. "How about we talk about the wedding? You still haven't given me a date."

The pressure on my chest lifted just enough to let in a full breath. Why couldn't I have both? Why couldn't I marry the man I love and also keep my family? It wasn't fair.

"Weddings require time. A venue—"

"My building has a rooftop with a backdrop of Central Park."

"Okay. Catering."

He pointed at the wait staff. "They can do it."

"Flowers."

"I know a guy."

"Lots and lots of booze."

He cocked an eyebrow as if saying, "You're not even trying."

The man owned a sex club, and really, an entire building dedicated to debauchery and pleasure. Every night was a huge, fancy reception for him.

"Fine. I just need to wrap my head around all this. Can I, at least, have a day to think about it?"

"I've never been a patient man. You have until tonight."

"You make it sound like I actually won this round. I know, you know, I know I didn't."

He shrugged and continued to work on his lunch. The man was impossible. And I couldn't wait to be married to him.

On the way back to my office, we rode in silence. The lunch date had been an avalanche of new information for me. I hadn't had time to digest most of it. But I was glad Rex was giving me the time and space to sort through my emotions and think about what I wanted to do next. When the car pulled up to the curb of my building, Rex unbuckled his seat belt and shifted his body so he would have me caged in against my side of the back seat.

"Dinner at eight, sharp." He kissed my lips.

I melted into the seat and moaned a yes. He pulled away first, leaving me breathless and gripping his shirt, so he wouldn't leave me so soon.

"I'll need a date by then." He ran a finger from the apple of my cheek down to my lips. "I love you."

"I love you too."

He sat back and nodded to Aaron. "Aaron will pick you up at five."

That was Aaron's cue to spring out of the car and rush to open my door.

"I have work to do, Rex. How about I text him when I'm ready for a pickup?"

"Fine. But if you're not home by six, I'm coming to get you myself."

"I'll see you tonight, Rex." I climbed out and headed for the front entrance. When I reached the building, I turned around and got a glimpse of Rex's profile as the black Escalade pulled away.

As soon as he disappeared into traffic, I glanced down at my watch. Jesus, it was almost three in the afternoon. Time with Rex always went by so fast and it was never enough. I rushed upstairs to get some work done before Aaron returned to pick me up.

On my way to my office, I spotted Sarah and Jill in one of the small conference rooms on our floor. Sarah's eyes went wide as soon as she saw me and waved me over. Letting out a breath, I quickly removed my engagement ring. I wasn't ready to answer questions about how deep my relationship with Rex was, and how far we'd come in just a few weeks.

"What's up?" I asked when she shut the door behind her.

"Rex? Boyfriend? Omigod." She hugged me. "Okay, I gotta get back in there. But when I'm done, you and I are going to talk."

"Yeah, okay." My eyes watered a little. Having someone who cared about me outside Rex's mafia world was comforting to me right now.

"Sarah," Jill called out.

"Shit. I gotta go." She kissed my cheek and went back inside.

I darted to my office and got started on the projects I had pending. The whole time I couldn't wipe the big grin off my face. Rex was mine. All mine. I was in the process of reviewing the last ad concept for the cat food account I had landed last month when my phone pinged with a text. My heart skipped a beat when I saw Rex's name pop up on the notifications.

*Rex: Aaron will pick you up in ten.*

I checked the time. It was thirty minutes past five. Technically, the workday was over, and I was all caught up on the most urgent stuff. Not to mention, I was dying to see him again. Smiling like a schoolgirl, I packed my computer bag. I thought about it for a few seconds, then decided to remove my ring again and drop it in the front compartment.

On my way out, I waved at Sarah who was still stuck in her meeting. She responded by puffing out her cheeks and blowing out air.

"We'll talk tomorrow," I mouthed, and she nodded.

I made it to the curb in exactly ten minutes, but Aaron wasn't there. Traffic at this hour was a bear, so I found a shady spot near the entrance to wait for him. My gaze wandered up and down the street, not really focusing on anything in particular until I zeroed in on Santino across the way. What was he doing here?

My pulse quickened. While Santino, more or less, answered to Rex, he was still the guy who wanted to kill Dad. Had he come here to spy on me in hopes Dad would make an appearance? My stomach churned at the idea that he might use me to get to Dad. Santino wouldn't be as brazen as to kidnap me. Would he? Rex would never stand for that. Santino had to know that.

Then again, he had used Rex as bait back in Ibiza. He'd done it in the name of finding out who was after the Society. Was he here thinking that kidnapping me was justifiable, as long as he got justice for his father?

When I met his gaze, he stepped toward me with a wicked smile on his face. As if saying, I got you now. Shit. I spun around and headed for the door. Two steps in, I stopped. If I went back upstairs, would he put my friends and other co-workers in danger just to get to me? I couldn't discard that idea. Santino Buratti was a mobster.

The only reason he was here right now was because he wanted Dad. I doubted he would care if he killed a few more people in the process. As long as his dad and the Society felt justice had been served, I didn't think they'd care about the small details, like civilians getting caught in the crossfire.

I swallowed the lump in my throat while I scanned the street in both directions, looking for Aaron. Where the hell was he? With trembling hands, I fished my phone out of my pocket. I wasn't used to this living-life-on-the-edge thing. My heart beat out of control and my fingers turned to jelly. One minute I had the device in my hand, and the next, it was flying out toward the curb. I chased after it, but Santino beat me to it.

"How about we hold all calls for a minute?" He picked up the phone.

"I don't know where Dad is."

That was the truth. I hadn't seen him in weeks, not since the night my brothers came to collect me from Rex's penthouse.

"I know." His hazel gaze searched mine. In the natural light, his eyes were almost gold, and I couldn't help but stay frozen in place, as if he were a wild animal and I was his prey. He tilted his head and smiled. "But he knows where you are. Now that Rex is about to get everything he wants, I can only imagine the old man is in a hurry to get to you. If only he hadn't been in such a rush to catch Rex yesterday. You'd be with him right about now."

I furrowed my brows at him. Santino Buratti was a stranger to me, but he knew everything about me and my family. "What do you want?"

"To talk." He handed me my phone back.

"About what?" This peace offering meant nothing to me. I had to get away from him. At this point, it was obvious to me Aaron wasn't coming.

I didn't give him a chance to answer. I spun around and

took off running toward the intersection. Behind me, Santino uttered a string of profanities. I didn't have to look back to know he had decided to give chase. I ran as fast as I could in my wedge booties, which, admittedly, wasn't that fast since I was also hauling a computer bag. I had seconds before he caught up to me.

In my mind, I imagined getting to the traffic light and immediately jumping into a cab like they did in the movies. But this was real life, that would never happen. My only option was to get to a lobby and get the security guard to help me. Of course the next building was all windows. I made it to the end of the street and never saw the next entrance.

"Caterina." A familiar voice called for me. Rex hadn't come for me at six like he had said, but Dad did.

I ran toward his SUV and jumped in. The car peeled away, just as Santino reached the curb with his hand inside his jacket. Did the asshole think he could shoot Dad in the middle of a crowded street?

"Dad." I scooted across the seat and hugged him. "What are you doing here? How did you know I was in danger?"

"I didn't know you were in trouble."

"Then how?" I put up a hand. "You sent that text pretending to be Rex."

"Yes. I wanted to talk to you without Rex hovering over you."

"How were you able to do all that?"

"Kids these days have apps for everything. Hacking a phone isn't a big deal." He shrugged as if tampering with people's phones wasn't a felony.

This was Dad, my own family. So no, this wasn't a kidnapping. But I couldn't ignore the fact that Dad had sent me a fake message, pretending to be Rex, just to get me to leave work early and scoop me up before Rex's bodyguard did. Why?

"Why the ruse, Dad?"

"Because I have someone I want you to meet. It's better if I show you rather than sit here and explain myself." He nodded to his driver.

I met his gaze. The cold stare I found there sent a chill down my spine. Following Rex's advice to talk to Dad with an open mind, open to the truth, I took the time to really look at Dad. This wasn't the old man I had visited in the hospital a month ago. This was the ruthless king Rex had warned me about.

# CHAPTER 17
## You Only Think You Do

CATERINA

The driver maneuvered through traffic until we were well on our way to Jersey. Of course Dad would not want to stay where Rex was still in control of everything. For the past few days, I had been putting off this conversation with Dad. Now that we were here, I could see he felt the same way. Even now as he sat on his side of the back seat, looking regal and as lethal as Rex, there was something in the way he took deep and long breaths that told me Dad wasn't ready to face me, face what he had done to keep Mom.

"I'm marrying Rex." I stared at his profile. "He proposed today, and I said yes."

"You won't have to do that." He pursed his lips, playing with the ring on his right hand.

I studied the raven carved on the crest, same as Rex's. "What did you do? Dad, I know about the contract. I know what you had to do to keep your family together."

Sure, Rex would say Dad sold me out just so he could be

with the woman he loved. But I wanted to believe he had done it for us too. I wanted to believe that everything he had done, he'd done it to protect all of us, not just himself.

"It was a mistake. I never should've let you go to him." He fisted his hand and glared at nothing beyond the car window.

"He loves me."

"He's obsessed with you. Because you're my daughter. Because you're the key to him securing his position within the Society. Nothing more." He met my gaze.

The regret and anger I saw in his eyes punched a hole through my heart. This wasn't the man I knew. "You tried to have him killed. Why?"

"Caterina." He shifted his body, so he was facing me. "I made a mistake a long time ago. But now I see that it's up to me to fix it."

"You set me up to go to him, then sent my brothers to fetch me. Why did you change your mind? What happened?"

"The Gallo kid came to see me at the hospital. He had cut a deal with the FBI. With his entire family gone, there wasn't much he could do to fend them off. He had no choice but to agree to work with them."

"He convinced you to turn against your own family?"

"Not at first. Caterina, I was ready to die. With Anna gone, I just didn't see the point to continue to wander this Earth, alone and without purpose." He stretched out his legs and relaxed his head on the headrest. "But then Mikey sent someone to kill me. And then they went after you and Massimo. I realized my work wasn't done here. The only way I could save you was to be king again. And Clifton was the answer."

"Mikey put us all in danger to save his own neck and you conceded to him?"

"I came up with a better plan. With me back in the fold, I can make the pigs go away, put them in their place." He reached for my hand. His touch was cold and distant as if he were going through the motions, not really feeling anything, not really here with me. "My family comes first."

"You can't kill Rex. I love him."

"You only think you do. But you don't." He shook his head as he surveyed my face. "Everything would be as it should be. If you hadn't intervened at the beach house, we wouldn't be here. Now he knows what's coming for him. It's going to be harder to get to him."

Alarms blared in my head. The idea of Dad killing Rex was as horrifying as Rex going after Dad for treason. I couldn't let two of the most important people in my life go at each other that way. If I lost them both...

"Clifton is waiting for us. I need you to convince him that you're on my side. Because you are. Aren't you?" He placed a finger under my chin and made me face him. "I need your help, Bells."

"The man at the beach house. Was he one of yours?"

"He was the son of a dear friend. There are a few people within the Society that are still loyal to me. When I reached out, they chose to join me."

Rex was right. Someone inside had betrayed him. And it wasn't just one person. I blinked several times to clear my vision. Tears streamed down my cheeks while I considered my options. Dad had, more or less, kidnapped me to get me to work with him and the FBI. And more than that, they wanted me to help them get to Rex. I couldn't do that. Rex didn't deserve it. He loved me, and I loved him.

I scooted over to my side and stayed there for the remainder of the trip. After what felt like hours, the driver pulled into an abandoned warehouse in the middle of nowhere. Was this where they planned to kill Rex? My chest tightened. I didn't want to lose him. I didn't want to live without him. It wasn't fair.

"We're here." Dad nodded to the driver and climbed out.

I followed him because I had nowhere else to go. If I took off running now, I had no way to get back to the city. Not to mention, Dad's men would catch up to me before I made it back to the main road. Instead, I tried to memorize every detail—the colors on the dilapidated walls, the surrounding area, and the slight fishy breeze in the air.

Dad pointed at me, and his driver blocked my way immediately. "You won't be needing your computer for this next part." Without asking, the driver reached for my shoulder and yanked the bag away from.

So much for texting Rex when I had the chance.

"You say you want my help. What do you want me to say to this guy? I know he tried to kill Rex once already." I fell instep next to Dad.

"He acted without my authorization. And now we're here." He said through gritted teeth. By the way his body stiffened every time he spoke of his FBI ally, I could only assume Dad didn't have much regard for Clifton. He was working with him because he had no other choice. "Stay close to me." He gripped my elbow and nodded to his driver.

The guy moved as swiftly as before and opened the small side door for us. Inside, the place was dark and empty, except for the one spot to the left where a man about Dad's age sat at a wooden table piled with folders and maps. His men stood at attention as soon as we walked in. I blinked against the harsh lighting of that halogen lamp overhead. Jeez, was this the FBI war room?

I thought of Rex and the last time he had to mount an operation. He had used his fancy Gulfstream as headquarters. What was this Clifton guy playing at? He had to know Rex had way more resources and men than him.

"Cheap suit, cheap accommodations. Let me guess, Clifton?"

"Clifton is going out on a limb on this one, which is why he needs our help." He motioned for me to go ahead.

When I approached the man pouring over the files in front of him, he glanced up at me, running a hand through his greasy hair. His eyes widened as a greedy smile spread across his face. "Ms. Alfera. So glad you could join us." He wasn't here for his family. He was chasing glory and shiny medals.

"Why am I here?"

"Because, Ms. Alfera, I'm here to make you an offer you can't refuse." He chuckled at his cheesy joke.

I turned to Dad. He rolled his eyes and stuffed his hand in the pockets of his trousers. I'd seen that same intolerance and impatience in Rex. How did I not see it before? How was it that in all my years, I never realized Dad was a mobster? The signs were all there. Maybe I chose not to see it because living the lie was much more comfortable than facing the truth. Rex had shown me how wrong I had been in that regard.

"Ms. Alfera, we need a favor and Michael tells me you're our girl." He walked around his desk and sat on the edge. The guy still wore his FBI badge on his belt. As much as he had gone rogue, I would guess he still held his position within the agency.

"What could a girl—" I put emphasis on girl. If that asshole thought I was too young to be here, why the hell did he bring me? "—Possibly do for you?"

"You can help me catch a killer, a thug."

I fisted my hands, and it was all I could do not to punch him in the face. This was the asshole who put a hit on me and my brother; he didn't get to play the righteousness card with me. "I don't see how."

"The way I heard it, the boy has developed a kind of obsession for you."

Not an obsession. Rex was in love with me.

"You heard wrong." I crossed my arms over my chest and looked at Dad.

"I don't think so. You will bring him to us. And in return, I promise to keep Michael safe. You and your entire family will be under our protection."

"Like Gallo was."

"That was unfortunate."

Yeah, unfortunate that Clifton had used Gallo to go after Rex. Only to have Rex turn the tables on him and kill his informant. Gallo betrayed the Society, just like Dad had. The FBI couldn't protect any of us. "And if I say no?"

"You're willing to let the criminals walk free so they can come after your father? I don't understand why you would do that." He braced his hands on the edge of the table. The bad lighting overhead cast shadows over his face and warped his features. I imagined this was how he really looked on the inside. The agent was a two-faced asshole only concerned with glory.

"What do you get out of this?"

"This is my duty. I get to put the bad guys away and ensure an organization like the Society never rises again."

Except I had it on good authority that Dad had every intention of keeping the Society alive, under new management, of course. "You want a seat at the table, don't you? You get fame and glory from your supervisors, only to turn around and keep the spoils to yourself."

"It's the only way to ensure peace." He smirked.

I got the sense that Clifton was obsessed with the Society and all its members. For too long, he had chased them. Now he wanted to be one of them. I wrapped my arms around my belly tighter. The man was asking me to betray Rex to save Dad. I couldn't do that to Rex, just like how I couldn't betray Dad either. Earlier I had wished for a way to save Dad. Clifton was offering me exactly that, but it was hardly a solution.

"Clifton, give us a minute." Dad's commanding voice echoed in the large warehouse.

Clifton shrugged and gestured for his guys to move out. Dad waited for them to file out the door before he turned to me. "It's not ideal. But it gets the job done. You and your brothers will be safe. I can handle Clifton." He stepped toward me. When he spoke again, his voice was barely above a whisper. "His seat at the table won't last long."

Great. Everyone was more than ready to stab each other in the back, and I was right smack in the middle of it all. "Dad, you made a deal with the devil."

"I did. But not in the way you think." He brushed my cheek.

In his eyes, Clifton was no more than a pawn. Was that how Dad saw the world around him? Chess pieces to move as he pleased, so he could keep his queen? He reached into his pocket and retrieved a weathered picture. In an instant, his features softened, and I saw more of Dad than the ruthless mobster who more or less grabbed me right outside my work.

"I never should've gotten you involved, Bells. I know that now. But I was desperate. Anna was going to leave me. And the Society needed a king."

"So you lied to her. As soon as you found out you were having a girl, you went to Rex's dad and cut a deal with him." I inhaled to calm my voice. "You should've worked this out with Mom."

"She had zero tolerance for the Society. I had no choice."

"Mom, just like you, was willing to do whatever it took to keep her family safe, including making a deal with the mob."

"What do you mean?" The space between his brows furrowed, and his eyes darkened.

"Mom knew about the contract."

"No, she didn't." He shook his head and gripped my elbow. "She would've told me. Hell, she would've left me."

"She went to Rex to plead on my behalf. To beg him to let me be."

"He's lying." Dad raked a hand through his hair and over his reddened cheeks.

Did it mean that much to him that Mom wouldn't find out who he really was? That he sold out his children to be with her?

"Check my computer bag. She gave Rex her engagement ring." I had skipped a huge chunk of the story where Mom and Rex became friends. He didn't need to know just how much Mom had tried to make things better for me. "They eventually came to an agreement. Rex would marry me, but if I didn't want to be his wife for real, he swore he would never force himself on me."

He shot a glance behind him, and his driver jerked into action to show him what he wanted. Dad opened the front flap and immediately found the diamond he'd given her when he proposed. His eyes swelled with tears. Seeing Dad slowly crumble like this—crying over his dead wife and the knowledge that she always knew what he was—was like a kick in the gut.

"I never did figure out how to live without her." He sat on his haunches, pressing a hand to his forehead.

"None of us have, Dad. And we don't have to." I knelt next to him and hugged him. My heart ached for him. He was lost without Mom, just like the rest of us.

"I'm so sorry, Bells."

"All we can do is fight to stay together. I don't know how we do that, but I know that Clifton isn't the answer."

He nodded. And in that moment, I knew Dad was back.

"Would Rex ever make a deal with Clifton?"

"I can ask him."

"I see you've had a nice family chat." Clifton strode to his table, chuckling.

I wanted to punch that smirk off his face. He knew how heartbroken Dad was, and he was using it for his advantage by threatening the only family Dad had left. "What the hell do you want from us?"

"Call Rex. Make him come here." Clifton hovered over us, licking his lips as if he could taste his victory already. "Do this, and your father walks free. He won't have to spend the rest of his life looking over his shoulder, waiting for the Society to find him."

Some choice.

If I chose Dad, Rex would die. If I chose the man I loved, I would lose my family.

I glared at Clifton. The laughter that came out of him sent a cold shiver down my spine.

# CHAPTER 18
## Dead or Alive

Rex

Where the hell was she? I paced the length of the living room. Beyond the tall windows, the city lights had already come to life as the sunlight faded away. Caterina had been away from me for not even three hours, but something didn't feel right. One thing I had learned in the years since I found out I would one day take over the reins of the Society was to always trust my gut.

I grabbed my phone and called Aaron. "Where is she?" I asked as soon as he picked up.

"Not here." He let out a breath. "I've been waiting for thirty minutes. She hasn't left the building. I would've seen her leave."

"She's not answering her phone either." I rubbed the creases on my forehead. "Fuck it. I'm calling her office."

"Should I stay?"

"Stay put for now." I hung up and called Caterina's friend.

"This is Sarah," she answered on the second ring.

"Sarah, it's Rex Valentino."

"Oh." She shuffled papers around. Then a sound like her chair scrapping across the floor blended with the nervous shriek in her voice. "Rex, yes. Hi. How are you? I mean. How can I help you, please?"

"Good. You remember me. I'm looking for Caterina. She's not answering her phone. Is she in a meeting?" I clenched my jaw. I hadn't meant to sound so desperate.

"No. She left an hour ago."

"Fuck me." I braced a hand on the window. "Are you sure? Was she alone?"

"Yes. And yes." She cleared her throat. "Is everything okay?"

"I'm sure it is. Thanks." I ended the call before she asked anymore questions I didn't have answers to.

If Caterina left her office an hour ago, and she didn't come here, where did she go? I texted Aaron and told him to come home. I needed all hands-on deck. At this point, I had no doubt Clifton had decided to make his move. Had he really kidnapped her in broad daylight, off a busy New York City street and right under Aaron's nose? Jesus Christ. How had he accomplished that?

The second I asked the question, the front door swung open. Frank strode in with Santino at his heels. "Caterina took off with Michael."

Well fuck.

"What do you mean?"

"I was keeping an eye on her in case Michael decided to pay her a visit." He glanced upward, pursing his lips. "Which he did. But they already had plans to meet up."

"She would've told me about it. We had lunch together."

"She freaked out when she saw me." His eyes lit up with anger. "Took off running and then hopped into an SUV. I got close enough to see Michael in the back seat. She sure was happy to see Daddy again."

I shook my head to clear all the different scenarios that popped in my head. Caterina loved me. She had agreed to marry me. She wouldn't go behind my back to see Michael. "I'm sure there's a reasonable explanation for all this."

"Oh sure. Let's hear what your dick has to say about it." He raised his voice. "Wake up, Rex. From day one, the Alferas have been playing us. And you can't or won't see it because Caterina has you wrapped around her little finger."

My heart twisted into a painful knot. Caterina wasn't a liar. She loved me. She wouldn't tell me she'd marry me and then take off with her dad. "We don't know the whole story. Let's wait until she calls back."

Santino barked out a laugh, cutting a glance to Frank then to me. "Isn't it obvious to you? Because it's obvious to me. Michael is making a move. She no longer needs you. That's why she's gone."

He didn't know that. He didn't know Caterina either. I pushed all the noise in my mind aside and focused on what I did know. Michael wanted me dead. Plain and simple. He had used himself as bait before but failed because Caterina helped me. Clifton made his move in Ibiza and failed as well.

What was their move now? Band together and try one more time? If they planned to use Caterina to get to me, they had another thing coming because she would never do that to me. She wouldn't sell me out, just like she wouldn't sell out Michael.

"We can't stand around and do nothing." Santino sauntered to the bar cart and poured himself a whiskey. "We have to assume that Clifton and Michael are in on it together. They couldn't get to you on their own. This has got to be their last move."

"She won't help them."

"She's an Alfera. Backstabbing is in her nature."

"She's not Michael." I fisted my hands. "I get that you're pissed because Michael got away from you. But you're out of line here. Stand down."

He knocked his drink back and glared at me.

The silence fell around us like thick smoke while I replayed the last few hours I spent with Caterina. I thought of our time in the restaurant and the ride to her office. All of that was real. Caterina wasn't Michael. Period.

I opened my mouth to tell him to go to hell and to get out of my house, but my phone chimed with a text. When I reached for it, I immediately spotted Caterina's name and beautiful face.

*Caterina: Something came up. I'm dropping you a pin. I'll explain when you get here. Please, hurry.*

I tossed my phone on the side table and rubbed my eyes. Had I read that right? Frank slid into my line of sight. I blinked to clear the bright spots covering his face. He was talking to me, but I couldn't quite hear the words. All I could hear was Caterina's voice in that text.

"Sir." Frank squeezed my shoulder. "What do we do?"

"That didn't take long." Santino crossed his arms over his chest and leaned on the sofa armrest. "The princess is in peril. What do we do now? Serve ourselves on a silver platter or let her rot."

"Enough." I glared at Santino.

"Finally, we agree on something." He shot to his feet and pointed at my phone. "This is a trap."

"I know." I gritted my teeth.

Why would Caterina go along with this? I hadn't realized Michael had this much influence over her. The man sold her out before she was born. He did it to save himself, to get the life he wanted. He threw her into my arms. Not to mention he almost got her killed when he came after me. Now she was on his side? What the fuck?

And because bad news always came in threes, just as I was trying to wrap my head around Caterina's betrayal, Chase Rossi waltzed into my penthouse with Aaron trailing behind him.

"Sir. I found him downstairs. He says he has information you need to hear."

Over a month ago, I had offered the Rossis a seat at the table, given that after the annihilation of the Gallo family, I had an open spot. I had also asked him to use his resources and help me find out who was trying to kill the Society members. Something Santino and I had figured out during our stay in Ibiza. Mikey, Michael and Clifton were all working together.

"You're late on that little assignment I gave you. If that's why you're here."

"I have more than a name." Chase stepped into the living room. "I have a location."

"You're late on that too."

If I were a gambling man, I would bet Michael and Clifton were waiting for me at the location Caterina had indicated. Acid bubbled in my stomach at the idea that Caterina had sold me out without giving it a second thought, or at the very least, thinking about it for more than a fucking minute.

"So you know Clifton is using one of our warehouses in Jersey?" Chase braced his hands on his hips. "We noticed some activity there a couple of days ago. We've been keeping an eye on their movements. I didn't want to come to you until I was sure it was Clifton and until I was sure he was working with one of your own."

"I appreciate that. But you just told us things we already know."

I met Santino's gaze. The asshole had been right about me being blind when it came to Caterina. But now I had a text, and three different people telling me what I should have known since the beginning. The Alfera family was only looking out for themselves. Michael wanted to be king again, and I was standing in the way of that.

"Wait." I took my phone from Frank and brought up the pinned location. "This is your warehouse?"

"It is."

"So you know all the ins and outs?"

A grin pinched the side of Chase's mouth. "I do."

"What are you planning?" Santino's gaze darted between Chase and me.

"I'm going to set off the trap." I was done playing nice with Caterina. It had only put my life at risk, not once or twice, but three times. "You're coming with me." I pointed at Chase and Santino.

"I came here to help." Chase nodded.

"I'll see you there." Santino headed toward the door.

"Would it kill you to be a team player for a night?" I called after him.

"That's exactly the point. I work alone. That's how I stay alive." He shut the door behind him.

"We don't need him." I pointed at Chase. "I can see you already have a plan to get in."

"It was my wife's idea. But yeah. Mia didn't want you to think we were not on the same side."

"Where would I get such a misguided idea?" I raised an eyebrow while I studied his guarded expression. Chase was new to the mafia scene. But this part he picked up on right away. He didn't trust anyone, not even me. "You seem nervous."

"I don't like the shoot first, ask questions later way of doing things around here."

"Point taken." I shrugged. If we weren't about to face the FBI, Chase's visit would've been a welcomed one. "What did Mia come up with this time? Hopefully no more buses filled with angry shooters."

"You heard about that?"

"You did the right thing saving those poor souls. Your grandfather lost his way there toward the end."

"He did, and he paid the price." He fished his phone from the inside of his suit jacket and showed me a floor plan. "No buses needed. We just need a bunch of guys with guns." He used three fingers to pinch the screen and make the image bigger. "This entrance is hidden. It leads to a secret storage room that we used for, you know."

"Illegal guns. You can say it. I'm not the fucking ATF."

Chase coughed several times as if he'd swallowed and it had gone down the wrong way. "Right. Anyway, we can get in unnoticed. Clifton has a small team. We've counted ten men. My guys are waiting for us there. With your guys, we can take him down easy."

"Did you get a sense for how much support he's getting

from the Agency? We can take down ten trained agents, but if he has backup waiting in the wings, I might be walking into an ambush I can't back pedal from." I rubbed a cold hand over the stubble on my cheek and ignored the lump in my throat. Why would Caterina put me in this position?

"If this was an official FBI sting operation, the warehouse would be crawling with agents right now. It isn't." He sat down and braced his forearms on his knees. By the worried look in his eyes, I had to guess he'd had a run-in with Clifton before.

"You and this Clifton have history?"

"We do. Last year, he tried to get me to work with him. He wanted the names of the big 5."

"The big 5?" I laughed at the street name people used for the Society.

"You're the ungettable get."

"I can image the kind of shiny medal he'd get if he brought me in—dead or alive."

"Exactly. That's all he wants. Or it was what he wanted before. Who the hell knows anymore? But I can see things have changed for him. Where before he had a full team at his disposal, now it seems all his resources have petered out."

"You think he's gone rogue?"

"I think he got greedy." Chase rubbed his chest. "Too many years of watching the bad guys win, I suppose."

"We're all bad guys here, Chase. I get how he might feel like we robbed him of the glory he believes he's earned." I strode to the bar cart and poured myself a whiskey. "But I'm not some fucking deer to mount on his wall."

The asshole had been hunting the head of the Society for decades. Just my luck that he would get so close when it was my turn to rule. Images of Caterina floated in my mind's eye.

None of this was about luck or coincidences. If the FBI was on our tail, it was because Mikey and Michael betrayed us. To add insult to injury, Michael saw Mikey's duplicity as a way to get back into the fold.

"If Clifton wants a seat at the table, he's gonna have to go through me first." I turned to Frank and Aaron. "Get the guys ready. We leave in five."

"And the Alfera brothers?" Frank asked.

"Leave them out of this. Sure, they want to do the right thing. But Michael is their father. They'll never go against him."

They all nodded and took off, leaving me to deal with all the rest. The plan was straight forward. Go in, unnoticed, kill the agents and grab Caterina and her dad. If I survived the ordeal, I had one more thing or person to contend with—Caterina. What was I going to do with a traitor? The by-laws were clear on this. I pinched the bridge of my nose to ease the burn in my eyes.

Santino could be a bit of a loose cannon. But I know that when it came to Caterina, he would let me make the right choice on my own. Fuck me. The Society couldn't expect me to kill the woman I loved. Even if she had made it her life's quest to show me just how much she hated me.

I gripped the tumbler in my hand and then hurled it across the room. Was all this a ruse? From the beginning, Michael knew how obsessed I was with her. Did he get her to pretend to love me just so I would let my guard down and become this idiot who would let the enemy sleep in his bed? I had left myself wide open. If I were Michael, I would have done the same. This was the time to strike me down. He had another thing coming, though, if he thought I would just lay here and let him fuck me over.

What about her?

The words flashed in my head in bright red. What about Caterina Alfera? How the hell did I go from her future husband to her executioner in the same day?

# CHAPTER 19
## You Can Drop the Act Now

REX

The Jersey warehouse was about twenty minutes from the marina, practically in the middle of nowhere. Easy place to kill someone and then make them vanish without a trace. This was the place Caterina had chosen for me. Or maybe Michael had picked the location. Either way, they both had decided tonight was my last. I fisted my hands and didn't bother with breathing exercises. What did it matter anymore? Whatever I thought Caterina and I would have one day was over.

"Sir." Frank met my gaze in the rear-view mirror for a moment before he focused on the highway ahead. "Rossi's information checks out. His men are waiting for us."

As soon as Chase had told us about Clifton's location on the other side of the river, Frank had dispatched a small team to confirm our suspicions. "Is she there?"

"She is, sir."

I glanced out the window and squeezed my eyes shut. The heat from the tears in my eyes and the knot in my stomach were a reminder to never again be so stupid, so gullible just because a beautiful woman looked at me with stars in her eyes. It was all a ruse. She never did any of it for me, she had done it to save her dad.

From day one, everything she did was for Michael. If she was going to turn me in, why wait this long? Why not let Clifton's man kill me back at the beach house? Remorse? I found it hard to believe Caterina was a killer. But even if she wasn't, Michael had his hooks in her so deep, she was willing to do whatever it took. She didn't take into account the days we had shared. For that alone, I couldn't forgive her betrayal.

We turned onto a dirt road with tall grass on either side. The night was cold and dark as fuck. When I rolled down the window, a musty breeze wafted inside the car but did nothing to ease the tension in my muscles. My whole body was like a loaded gun—at attention and waiting to spring into action. One good thing came out of all of this—Michael was finally ready to show his true self. And that gave me the chance to make things right. It was high time Michael paid his debt.

"Rex." Chase walked up to the SUV. "Just say when."

"Are they fully surrounded?"

"Yes. I have men up the road as well." Chase nodded, and his eyes darkened with determination.

I got the feeling he wanted this situation with Clifton over and done with as much as I did.

"When." I smirked.

No sense in prolonging it. The asshole responsible for killing the entire Gallo family was inside that building. I couldn't let him get away a second time. Though, technically speaking, the last time we had a face-off, I was the one who got away from him.

In the next breath, my entire crew mobilized, quietly scattering across the field to join the Rossi crew. I followed Chase to the side of the warehouse where the secret entrance was located. He unscrewed a cover made of a composite fiberglass. When he yanked it off the wall, he pointed toward a long and dark tunnel.

"I'll go first." He set down the panel and strode inside.

As soon as we crossed the threshold, one of his men closed off the entrance again and plunged us into darkness. I stayed on his heels, with a tight grip on my weapon. Clifton and Michael had to know I wouldn't come alone. What was their play? Offer me a new deal or simply kill me? Michael's hubris had no bounds. I'd bet he thought that once I was dead, my crew would switch their allegiance to him. He was wrong in that.

Before we reached the end of the tunnel, all hell broke loose outside. Shit. Clifton or Michael's guys had figured out we were here. I darted toward the door and pushed it open. My gaze immediately zeroed in on Caterina. She sat next to Michael staring at her phone. The handful of seconds it took me to recover from seeing her alive gave Clifton and his men enough time to start shooting.

Okay, so they were not interested in a new deal.

Chase had my back, though, long enough to give Santino and Frank time to bust in through the front door, guns blazing. Michael pulled Caterina away from the line of fire and hid behind a table he'd knocked on its side. My gaze darted across the huge space, looking for Clifton's face. But he was nowhere to be found. What the hell was he playing at?

"Stay with them," I yelled over the gunshots, meeting Santino's gaze.

"Don't worry. They're not going anywhere." Santino shouted back, prowling toward Michael. He finally had his prey within reach.

I turned around and headed back the way we'd come in. Clifton couldn't have gone far, even if he took off as soon as he realized I had shown up with a full team. Outside, the shooting had stopped. Far away in the distance, I spotted the taillights of a car getting away. I ran after it, shooting round after round, but it was no use. The asshole was gone.

"Fuck," I shouted into the night.

This was how Clifton had stayed alive this long—by leaving his team hanging as soon as things got out of his control. He had pulled the same maneuver a month ago when he tried to kill me on my own yacht. That day, he had thrown Mikey Gallo under the proverbial bus while he made his escape. Now he had left Michael and Caterina to fend for themselves.

When I returned to the building, Frank caught up to me, while he stared at the faint red lights in the distance, pursing his lips. "Son of a bitch. Nine of his agents are down."

"Okay. Get a cleaning crew in here. And let's move out."

"On it, Boss."

I opened my mouth to ask about Caterina but decided it didn't really matter. Instead, I took in the scene in front of me —the bullet holes on the side of the warehouse, the dents on the cars, and the fallen men. I glanced upward and let out a breath. This was why the Society preferred its anonymity, why we had remained a secret entity for over a hundred years.

If it hadn't been for Chase's inside intel, tonight would've been worse. My chest tightened thinking how we were all here because of Caterina. I rubbed the spot over my heart and sauntered over to the front entrance.

Santino had delivered on his promise to not let our prisoners go. That was exactly what the Alferas were from here on out. I was done asking for their favor, their approval. For my part, I had fulfilled my promise to Anna Alfera. What came after tonight wasn't on me.

Both Michael and Caterina had their hands tied behind their backs with their mouths gagged. I cocked my head and looked at Santino.

"It's better if she doesn't pour honey in your ear." Santino smirked.

I blew out a breath and stalked up to her. "Did you send that text?"

Her eyes brimmed with tears.

"Answer me." I grasped her elbow.

She winced in pain and nodded once.

"Did Michael make you send that message?"

"Rex." The rag in her mouth muffled the word, but I understood it. "Please."

"Did they force you in some way?"

She shook her head as she stepped closer to me. Desperation was written all over her face. Six hours ago, I would've been stupid enough to believe she was worried about me. Her body brushed mine. In an instant, all the anger I felt came crushing down on me. I gripped her shoulders. She winced in pain, but I didn't ease the pressure.

"You can drop the act now. You played your last hand, and it blew up in your face," I said through gritted teeth. "You don't get to plead for his life anymore. We're done."

Of course her reaction was to turn around and look for

Michael. Acid pooled at the bottom of my stomach. Fine. If she didn't care. Neither did I. She made to pull away from me, so I let her go. Losing my support made her trip over her feet and she fell to the ground. I wanted to help her up. But she needed to understand, I was no longer her puppet. So instead, I glowered at her.

"Take her away." I turned my attention to Aaron. "She doesn't leave her room until I decide what to do with her."

"Yes, sir." He gripped both her shoulders and hoisted her up. "And Michael?"

"We have a special place for his kind, don't we?" I swallowed the bad taste in my mouth and strode back to the SUV. Being this close to her made my insides twist in agony.

The next morning, the sunlight bathed my room in a warm glow while I lay in bed fully dressed and staring at the ceiling. I hadn't moved in the last eight hours. Sometime during the night, I had made up my mind about Caterina. Whatever my feelings were or weren't for her didn't matter anymore. I still had a duty to fulfill. The Society still needed a leader, a king.

Numb, I walked to the bathroom and ran the shower. I stood under the warm spray, and mindlessly went through the process of getting ready for the day. When I returned to the suite, Mary Anne stood out in the hallway. The moment I came into her line of sight, she knocked on the door and entered.

"Not now." I raised my hand, and she stopped in her tracks.

"I'm sorry, Rex. I have a few questions for tonight's affair. Unless it's been canceled?" She framed it as a question. The tinge of hope in her tone gave away how she felt about tonight's reception.

"No, it hasn't been canceled." I placed a hand over my chest. "What do you need?"

"Flowers." She took a tentative step toward me. "It would be a nice touch if you at least do something she likes."

I pinched my nose and inhaled deeply. Just thinking of her made my insides quiver. "Japanese Wisteria. I trust you. Do whatever you want." I sauntered out the door and headed toward the dining room. I had a full day ahead of me, and absolutely no desire to get on with it. Breakfast sounded like a good way to pass the time.

The minute I entered the room, I regretted my decision. Caterina sat next to my place at the foot of the table, pushing a blueberry around her plate. I froze in place. My head urged me to turn around and walk out, but my heart beat so fast, I couldn't move.

"Mary Anne," I called behind me, knowing my assistant had followed me. And now I realized she had meant to warn me that Caterina was also having breakfast—or not having breakfast as it were. "Get the cook to make an omelet for her. And make sure it's served in her room."

"Of course." Mary Anne's eyes watered full of pity. At this point, I wasn't sure if her distress was on my behalf or Caterina's.

"I'm not hungry." Caterina shot to her feet.

"I didn't ask."

"Rex."

I fisted my hands and stepped toward her. "Did you not hear me last night? You are not to leave your room until I say so. Go."

"You can't keep me here. Like this. We need to talk."

"I'm done talking. You will finish your breakfast upstairs and then get ready."

She lifted her head, her gaze darting between me and Mary Anne. "Ready for what?"

"Our wedding."

"What?"

I swallowed the lump in my throat and walked off. To hell with breakfast, I needed a stiff drink. Mary Anne stayed behind to explain things to Caterina. Last night, I had come to the conclusion that the only way to keep Caterina alive, after she betrayed me and the Society, was to execute Michael's contract. The only way to get rid of him and secure my place within the organization was to marry Caterina—sooner rather than later. Clifton was still out there and who knew how long it would take him to assemble a new team.

"Good. You're here. You're late, but you're here." Santino shoved a whiskey into my hand as soon as I entered the boardroom. "Let me introduce you to a good friend of mine, Father Esposito."

"Rex." I shook the priest's hand. "I assume Santino explained."

"He did, Don Valentino." His voice quavered as he wiped his forehead with a worn handkerchief he fished out of the pocket of his trousers. "I'm here as a favor to Don Buratti."

"I'm sure you are."

I got the impression the good Father wasn't here of his own volition. Hell if I cared. What I wanted no longer mattered. This marriage needed to happen one way or another. An unwilling officiant was the least of my worries.

"The old man sends his regrets." Santino shrugged and took a big swallow of whiskey.

Last I heard, Santino's dad hadn't fully recovered from the last assassination attempt, which meant Santino was due to take over his family business any day now. Who the hell knew what was holding him back or why he hadn't done it already.

In the next hour, our guests began to arrive. This wasn't going to be a lavish affair, just big enough to include everyone familiar with Michael's contract. Signora Vittoria and Donata Salvatore were the first to arrive. They nodded in my direction and headed straight for the bar cart. Chase and Mia Rossi showed up a few minutes later. Before I knew it, all board members had gathered.

"Looks like everyone's here. I'll go get the happy bride." Santino set his tumbler down and glanced up at me. "Unless you want me to get her brothers too and have the whole family together?"

"Michael is the only one we need here today."

"Right then." He poured himself another drink and left the room.

I met Donata's gaze across the room. She shook her head as if saying, "I hope you know what you're doing."

I raised my glass and knocked it back. This was the only way to restore the peace. The minute Michael realized he had no claim to my title, he would have to back down. If only this solution didn't include the small detail where I had to tether my life to Caterina. How the hell was I going to endure her presence in my home, day in and day out?

Thanks to Santino, I didn't have to do yet another merry-go-round of going through all the possible answers to our fucked-up dilemma. He opened the doors wide and ushered in Caterina and Michael. Both bound and gagged again. Had Caterina put up a fight when she found out she was to marry me in a few minutes?

I stuffed my hands in my pockets to keep my composure. Fuck me if she didn't look absolutely beautiful in that white dress, her hair in an updo of messy curls. Her red pouty lips and smooth cheeks were the perfect back drop to those green eyes. Those eyes that were once again full of hate and contempt for me. A flutter settled below my navel. I took a deep breath in and pushed it away before I turned to face Father Esposito.

"Let's get on with it."

In my peripheral vision, Santino ushered Caterina to my side, then took his place to my left. "It's all you, Father." He gestured for him to go on.

The priest stared at Caterina and Michael, then switched his gaze to the book in his hand. "God help me. We are gathered here today." He droned on about the sanctity of marriage and what it would take to make a long-term relationship work.

He mentioned love, trust, and respect. None of which Caterina and I had anymore. All we had was a fucked-up contract that would soon be complete. I shifted my weight between one foot and the other, growing impatient with the ceremonial bullshit. My sleeve brushed Caterina's bare arm, and she threw me a warning glare.

Of course, my touch was now repulsive to her. I didn't care if she loved or hated me. I had no intention of ever touching her again. So all her warning stares could go to hell.

"I'm sorry, Don Valentino, but I do need to hear her say the words." He motioned toward his Bible. The man was trying to make this fit into his moral arena.

"Do it," I said to Santino.

If I touched her, I didn't know what would happen next.

Santino walked around me and removed her gag. Caterina let out a long breath as tears streamed down her cheeks. For a second, I thought she would beg Father Esposito to let her go. She opened her mouth, but the words didn't come out.

"I'll ask again, dear. Do you accept Rex Valentino as your lawful wedded husband, to hold and to cherish until death do you part?" He furrowed his brows as his eye filled with pity.

"Rex." She glanced up at me.

Our gazes locked.

"Answer him." My heart pumped hard against my ribs.

"I do." She looked away from me.

Father Esposito wiped his forehead again, then proceeded to ask me the same question.

"I do." I nodded curtly.

"By the power vested in me, I pronounce you man and wife." The priest relaxed his shoulder and smiled. "You may kiss the bride."

I turned to face Caterina, sweeping my gaze over her body. After all this time, we were finally married. And yet nothing had changed between us. She still thought of me as her enemy. And I couldn't even bring myself to kiss her.

"Santino," I called over my shoulder. When he patted my shoulder, I side-stepped her and strode out of the room.

## CHAPTER 20
### Enough is Enough

CATERINA

When I thought of marrying Rex, never in a million years did I think it would be like this. And all because of some stupid misunderstanding—or rather for the lack of trust on his part. If only Santino would let me explain. I turned to face him now.

"Mrs. Valentino." He bowed politely, and for a second, the gesture almost felt sincere.

"Why won't you let me talk to him?" I showed him the ties around my wrists. "This isn't necessary. I'm not a prisoner here."

"I recall Rex calling the both of you exactly that."

"So what, you're his watch dog now? He orders you to keep us here and you follow him like a puppy?" I glared at him, wishing I could smack the infuriating calm out of him.

"I volunteered for the job." A smirk tugged at his lips. "The zip ties and the gags are for Rex's protection."

"Santino, please. Let me talk to him." I stepped closer.

He barked out a laugh and grabbed my left hand to show

me my wedding ring. "Isn't it getting crowded around that little finger of yours? I'm not Rex. You may have him wrapped around your little finger, but I'm here to make sure you don't mess with his head anymore."

"I never meant to hurt him. And you know that."

"What I know is that you've been fucking with him since the beginning. You're so wrapped up in Michael's game, you don't care how you're hurting Rex. Clifton, Mikey's death, and all the other attempts are happening because of you. If Rex could just stop thinking with his dick for a minute, he'd have all this resolved." He pointed at Dad.

Translation: if it weren't for me, Rex would've had Dad killed a long time ago.

Santino brought the tumbler to his lips and took a long swig. "But he keeps listening to your lies and making concessions for you. Haven't enough people died already?"

Tears stung my eyes as I considered his words. All I ever wanted was for Dad to be safe. In fighting for Dad, I put Rex and all the Society members at risk. I turned around to face Donata. She stood in the back of the boardroom with a drink in her hand. The dour look on her face told me she agreed with Santino.

"Mary Anne said there's a reception on the rooftop. I'm not going like this, like some prize pig." I showed him my wrist.

"An army of people have been working on this wedding reception since four in the morning. Again, he did that for you. As for being a prize pig, well, you should talk to your dad about that. Either way, you're going to this party and you're going to smile and show everyone Michael delivered on his promise."

"Just take these off then. And Dad's too."

"If you try to leave, my men have orders to shoot Michael."

He fished a pocketknife from inside of his suit jacket and cut the bands. "Stay away from Rex tonight. The man has enough on his mind."

"If you two hadn't shown up last night with guns blazing, Clifton wouldn't be a problem anymore." I let the plastic bands drop to the floor.

I probably shouldn't try to talk to Santino. He had already made up his mind about me. No matter what, he wasn't going to believe anything I said. The only one who I cared about learning the truth was Rex. He needed to know I didn't set him up.

"You were okay throwing Rex to the wolves. But I'm not. We need him at the head of the table." He raked a hand through his hair. "At least you did one good deed today. Because of this marriage, Michael no longer has a way to slither his way back into the Society—not like before any way."

"Good riddance." Signoria Vittoria sipped from her wine glass.

Crossing my arms over my chest, I scanned the room looking for Dad. He had found his way to Rex's high back chair, gagged and with his wrists bound. When was the last time Dad had been in this room? My heart broke in two seeing him like this, lost and in pieces without Mom. Yesterday, I got to meet the mafia kingpin he used to be. But the more time we spent together, the more we talked about Mom and what she wanted for us, and he had managed to, once again, find the man Mom had fallen in love with.

I knew without a shadow of a doubt that once Rex showed up, Dad would have done the right thing and got Clifton to stand down by giving him the only thing he ever cared about— Dad. Santino didn't know Dad like I did. So, in a way, I understood why my plan looked like treason. But Rex knew better. More than that, he knew me.

"Dad, let's go upstairs. A bit of fresh air will rejuvenate you." I reached for the ball of fabric in his mouth and took it out.

"Bells, I'm sorry." He took my hand in his. "For everything. You're so much like her. I don't deserve your kindness."

"I decide who deserves my kindness." I shot a glance over my shoulder at Santino.

"Save us the family drama." Donata joined Santino by the bar cart.

Dad nodded once and offered me his arm, which was an awkward gesture since he still had his wrists bound together. Santino ambled over to us and cut the zip ties before he motioned for us to go on.

"The goal for the evening is simple." He opened the door for us. "Everyone needs to leave the Crucible tonight knowing that the five families are closer and stronger than ever."

Signora Vittoria laughed and joined Dad. "Since when are you such a team player?"

"Since agents started shooting at my family."

His dark stare would've made anyone recoil in fear, but Vittoria held his gaze for a beat, and then smiled. "Let's get on with it then."

"I'd like to think our wedding was any better, but it really wasn't." Mia, Chase's wife, fell in step next to Donata.

Rex had mentioned that Chase and Mia had also had an arranged marriage last year. By the size of her pregnant belly and the stars she had in her eyes every time she looked at Chase, I would say things were going well. My only hope was that Rex and I hadn't missed our opportunity at a happy life together.

"One big, happy family coming up." Donata raised her glass and drank as she followed us out onto the foyer outside the boardroom.

When the elevator door to the rooftop opened, my mouth practically dropped to the floor. Bistro lights crisscrossed overhead with the strands laced with purple lilies that hung low. The wisteria vines and twinkling lights added a whimsical layer to the space. Mary Anne had done an amazing job rearranging the furniture to create separate seating areas along the cement wall that faced Central Park. If I'd had any say in this party, I didn't think I would've done anything different.

Dad played the host to a tee, introducing me to old friends and making it look like my union was a happy occasion, and not the price for his freedom and a life with Mom. As the night wore on, I got better at smiling and nodding at strangers. In truth, the reception would've been a dream come true if Rex hadn't spent the entire time looking at me like I was his mortal enemy, and Santino watching me like a dog every time I got within a few feet of Rex.

True to form, while the party was still in full swing, Rex disappeared. When that happened, Santino joined Dad and me. "I think it's time our lovely bride joined her husband. Don't you think?" He gripped my shoulder. "Michael will stay and schmooze some more."

"Good night, Dad." I kissed his cheek, and he patted my arm.

I didn't appreciate Santino telling me what to do, but I really needed to talk to Rex. With my heart racing, I made my way to the penthouse. The city lights greeted me when I walked in. I had expected to see Rex near the bar cart, but he wasn't. I rushed upstairs and headed straight to his suite.

The room looked the same as it had two nights ago when Rex and I spent a great deal of time having sex by the fireplace. I missed him so much.

"What are you doing?" Rex strolled out of the bathroom in pajama pants and a whiskey tumbler in his hand. The bare chest and wet strands brushing the side of his face made me ache for him—his touch and body heat.

My breath hitched, and I stumbled back at a loss for words. "Santino thought I should leave the party too."

"What part of I don't ever want to see you again, don't you understand?" He tossed the towel on the bed and stalked over to me. "Get out."

"Rex, please let me explain."

"I'm done granting you favors, I'm done listening to your lies, I'm done. Just done. We're done, Caterina." He hurled the tumbler into the fireplace. "Get out of my room. Now."

My body jerked in surprise and I stumbled back. Somehow, I managed to leave without falling on my face. I darted to my suite, shut the door, and leaned against it while my heart thrashed in my ears. Rex truly hated me. How could he not see that I didn't need to choose between him or Dad? Dad wanted me to be happy. He had finally understood that I wanted to be with Rex. Why couldn't he trust me like I trusted him?

I walked to the bed and let myself fall on the covers. This night reminded me so much of the first time Rex showed me the world of Kinbaku. Except, now he didn't love me anymore.

"Good morning, sleepy head. Or I should I say good-afternoon?"

I opened one eye just as Violet pulled back the curtains. Wincing against the shock of bright light in my face, I yanked the covers over my head. "Why are you here?"

"I was in the neighborhood and thought I'd stop and check in on you. Why are you ignoring my texts? It's been weeks." She plopped herself on the other side of the bed and peeked under the fluffy comforter. "Your room smells like you haven't showered in days."

"Probably because I haven't."

"What's going on, Hun?" She stretched out her legs and rested her head on the pillow next to me.

Tears streamed down my cheeks the second I opened my mouth to tell her. "He hates me. A whole month has gone by since the wedding, and I have no idea where he is. I can't even see Dad."

I thought about all the times I tried to reach out to Rex and got nothing but disdain from him. He refused to listen to anything I said. God, he couldn't even stand to be in the same room as me. More than once, he had left the dining room when I showed up for breakfast or dinner. I figured if I kept running into him, he would finally get tired of being so angry and sad and would want to hear me out. But instead, he left the penthouse. I stood there at the top of the stairs and watched him storm out with a suitcase firmly by his side. That was how much he hated me. This house wasn't big enough for the two of us. Shifting my body, I buried my face on the pillow so Violet wouldn't see me cry. I missed him so much; I couldn't stand it.

"Oh, Hun."

"I think he moved out."

"He didn't." She petted my hair. "And trust me when I tell you, that man is still madly in love with you—probably not this version of you. But you know what I mean."

"You say that because you haven't seen him. The first week he was here, he avoided me like I had some sort of weird disease. And he won't tell me what he did with Dad." I squeezed my eyes shut and willed myself to stop crying. I had done nothing else for the past four weeks.

"Is that why you haven't left your room?"

"What's the point? This is my life now."

She barked out a laugh. "Dramatic much? Come on, she pushed on my shoulder. Let's get you in the shower and go out. Well." She bit her bottom lip. "Maybe not out, out. How about brunch on the rooftop? Mary Anne said you go there sometimes to read."

For the last thirty-two days and three hours since we got married, I had become the ghost of Rex's penthouse, wandering between my suite and the rooftop. "I don't feel like going outside. A shower sounds good though."

"Atta girl. You take care of all this." She poked my hair, shaking her head in disapproval. "And I'll get Mary Anne to bring up something to eat. And don't give me that face, you will eat. You look like you've lost weight."

She shoved my legs off the mattress until I had no choice but to get out of bed. I trudged to the bathroom and ran the water. The hot spray soothed my itchy eyes and achy muscles. I made quick work of the shampoo and body wash and then stepped out.

"You decent?" Violet knocked on the door and then strolled in, meeting my gaze in the mirror. "Jeez, when was the last time you ran a comb through your hair. Are you serious with this? Has Rex seen you like this?"

My lips turned into a frown. "I told you he doesn't want to see me."

"Still. Just because your guy is being a stubborn jerk, doesn't mean you can disrespect yourself like this. Girl." She picked up a comb and pushed me down onto the vanity stool before she began to work on the tangled tresses.

"Thank you." I hugged her arm.

"So, what are we going to do about Rex?"

"There's nothing to do. I told you he's not even home." I smiled at her reflection in the mirror, glad that she had thought to come see me. "I've tried talking to him so many times. But each time, he just storms out of the room. He won't listen to a single word I say. He's afraid I'll change his mind. And now, he's gone."

"He is home. I think you should try and talk to him."

I rolled my eyes because I had done nothing else but try to have a conversation with him since the wedding.

"Do it again. And again, until you get through that thick head of his. He doesn't look good. I mean, of course, he's hot as heck, but you know what I mean."

I chuckled. My whole body ached to see him again, to touch him. After she fixed my hair, she left me to finish up on my own. I donned a simple Sunday dress and smiled to myself as I put on a pair of red lacy underwear. When I thought about all the times Rex made me go without panties, a lump formed in my throat.

"Stop it. Crying is not going to fix anything," I scolded the woman in the mirror, then walked out to the terrace to meet Violet.

Mary Anne had brought a tray of sandwiches and little pastries for us to munch on and set up a buffet for us. On Violet's insistence, I managed to eat a few things. She was so easy to talk to and within a couple of hours, she had me laughing again.

"You know what? The rooftop sounds like a good idea. Let's go up there and get wasted."

"Now you're talking." She jumped to her feet and pulled me off the bed. "Let's go now before you change your mind."

As soon as I opened the door, a shock of adrenaline rushed through my body. I stopped in my tracks and stared at Rex standing there, in nothing but grey joggers. Jesus, he looked more beautiful than I remembered. Though that scowl on his face was something I hadn't been able to forget in the past month. The hate in his eyes had haunted my dreams pretty much every goddamn night.

And then it hit me. I turned to look at Violet and the body suit she wore. It was similar to ones I wore when I joined Rex in the rope room. What the hell? I glared at Rex.

"Were you in there with him?" I asked Violet.

"That's none of your business." Rex answered for her.

The first words he'd said to me in what felt like forever and it was to tell me he was with Violet; someone I had come to consider a friend. My blood boiled instantly. He had ignored me all this time. He'd been gone for God knew how long and now that he was here, he was spending time with Violet? In the rope room? My cheeks and ears burned hot. Heart pumping hard, I stomped toward him.

"I'm your wife." I fisted my hands and hit him square in the chest. "It is my business."

"Caterina, it wasn't like that." Violet stepped toward me.

"I'm sorry, I didn't think you'd mind if he guided us through a suspension."

"Don't apologize to her." Rex glowered at me with a searing expression, and then, returned to the rope room.

"What the fuck?" I followed him, ignoring Violet's string of I'm sorrys.

Inside, the familiar place was a shock to my system. Suddenly, I felt alive again. The music and the sweet incense lingering in the air brought me back to a time when Rex and I were happy, when he loved me and trusted me unconditionally.

When I recovered, I scanned the room and found him by the rope table where he was expertly recoiling the rope. Molten lava in the form of jealousy coursed through me. The thought of Violet in his arms had my mind spiraling out of control.

"How dare you?" I stalked toward him.

He released the bundle he'd been working on and braced his hands on the steel table. The muscles on his back strained into a myriad of sweaty planes and valleys.

"If you don't love me anymore, why keep me here?" I asked through gritted teeth. My jaw had clenched so tight, I could hardly breathe.

When he didn't answer, I shoved him, so he would turn around and look at me. I couldn't stand this situation anymore, living here so close to him and yet so far. And now this? The thought of Rex spending any amount of time with another woman, half-naked and sweaty made me see red. I pushed him again, and he stumbled back a few steps.

Our gazes locked. And there it was again, the hot and stormy glint in his eyes. I stepped in closer and hit him again—

really looking for any kind of connection with him—but he gripped both my wrists. "Enough."

"You know what? You're right. Enough is enough." I yanked my arm away, but he tightened his hold and pulled me toward him.

His hot skin brushed my front, and I sighed. I hated that even after the way he had treated me since the wedding, my body still craved him. I hated how he was able to just walk away and throw his feelings for me out the window. I hated how broken things were between us now. He had said it before —he could forgive anything, except a betrayal, which was exactly what he thought I was guilty of when I asked for his help.

Between Dad, Rex and I, we could've defeated Clifton. Not with guns or chasing him to the ends of the Earth, but with a solid plan. The man only wanted his dignity back after all the time he wasted chasing after my dad and Rex's dad.

But Rex couldn't see past my actions. He was never going to come back from this. His chest rose and fell as he inhaled and exhaled. The puff of warm breath lingered between us for a beat before it swirled down to my core like a wisp of smoke. I was at my breaking point, and he still didn't care.

"You got what you wanted. You're officially the king of everything. You don't need me anymore. I'm going home." I yanked my hands away.

The pressure on my chest threatened to split me in half, but I managed to make it all the way to the door before he spoke again.

"Get on your knees and face the mirror."

## CHAPTER 21
### Open Your Eyes

CATERINA

All the air left my lungs. I reached for the doorknob with shaky fingers. Who was I kidding? I couldn't even pretend to want to leave anymore. Rex knew this. Why else would he turn his back to me to lift a rose color coil of rope off the wall? He wasn't forcing me to stay or chasing after me.

I sucked in a breath and ambled toward the mat across from the framed mirror. The gold leaves on the woodwork stood out to me today, probably because of the lighting. The room wasn't as dimly lit as usual.

When I dropped to my knees, Rex sauntered over to me. He dropped a single coil of rope at the top of the mat and then reached for the suspension ring to walk it back toward the table. By now I understood what he intended to do with me— floor play. Unfortunately, I also knew why the ring had been positioned where it was.

I imagined Violet suspended in mid-air with her hips high up in the air and her upper torso tilted forward. Just like I'd seen in one of her photos. She was flawless in her surrender. A lump churned in my stomach again. Yes, I was jealous. Rex had no reason to be with her. In the time we had spent together, I had come to think of Kinbaku as our thing.

I didn't want to share him. But beyond all that, more than anything, I didn't want him to hate me. I didn't want him to think I had betrayed him. Of course, my body had other ideas and as much as my brain had a solid plan to talk to Rex, it was also very much into the idea of being in Rex's arms again.

A sad song began to play on the overhead speakers. The lights puffed out like candles and plunged me into darkness for the few seconds it took me to adjust to the city glimmer streaming in through the tall window. Ignoring my reflection in the mirror, I waited on my knees for at least ten minutes, if not more.

Had he changed his mind? I turned toward the left side of the room, where he stood with his hands firmly planted on the tabletop. Like before, his entire back bulged with layers of tensed muscle. He was still mad at me but was trying to calm down. The knot in my chest unraveled with this new information. Rex still had feelings for me.

I thought of our first session when he tried to explain to me what Kinbaku was for him. The rope was the language, the excuse to interact and have a sort of conversation. I blinked away hot tears when I realized what this session was about. Rex wanted to talk to me, but he didn't know how. Now that I was here, he was willing to give it a try, give us a try. My pulse quickened as I faced forward like he had commanded. I had every intention to wait for him for as long as I needed to.

"Bring your hands to prayer and find your beating heart."

His assertive words startled me. It was as he had said

before—in this room, he was in control. I pressed my palms together and brought them to my chest where my heart drummed with an out-of-control force.

"Match your inhales to your exhales."

I turned to look at him, so far away and so cold. He had to know I didn't know how to do this without him. Sure, he was simply asking me to breathe, but it was difficult to leave all my fears and jealousy at the door. I'd stormed into his rope room because I was angry at him and Violet.

"Breathe, Caterina." He placed his hands on my shoulders, while his hot blue gaze met mine across the way. I'd missed his handsome face, his scent, and his all-consuming presence.

The warmth seeped through my skin and deep into my bones. I leaned back against his hard chest and filled my lungs with precious air. He pressed his mouth just behind my ear, and then a hand on my belly and the other between my breasts. Before I knew it, we were breathing the same, and our hearts thumped fully in-sync.

After a minute, he reached in front of us and grabbed the coil of rope. I lifted my head and stared back at my reflection— my flushed cheeks and bright eyes. When my gaze shifted to him, he dipped his head and began his dance, slow and sweet at first as he tied a single column tie around my wrists. I smiled at him when he brought my hands over my head to settle on the nape of my neck.

And just like that we slid into our comfortable rhythm, where I became his. He was my rigger. And I was his rope bottom. The terms were so simple and yet so vital to what we had. Our lives were complicated, mainly due to the families we were born into and the duty we both had to them. But this, right here, was as easy as breathing.

I stared at him intently, following each one of his movements, letting myself fall into this fantasy. When the tempo of the music changed to a faster beat, so did his roping. He wrapped one muscular arm around me as he wound the jute across my body, and then repeated the process twice more before he gripped my hair and guided me forward. My pussy throbbed in heated ecstasy as I watched him pull my dress all the way up so he could ogle my ass, up in the air, exposed for him to do with however he pleased. I imagined from his angle my butt cheeks looked just like an inverted heart. And in the spot between my legs, he could see my juices dripping inside my underwear. The gleam in his eyes shifted from tormented to that of pure desire.

I moaned in response and that prompted him to change the pace again. This time, he was distant and almost rough as he uncoiled the rope and started on a new bind by doing a single column tie on my right thigh. I stilled as his fingers brushed the hot flesh on the apex of my legs. It was the tiniest bit of pleasure, so quick, I wasn't sure if I had imagined it.

He pushed me forward until my elbows touched the mat in front of me and wound the cord over my back to tie it to my left thigh. When he finished the bind, he picked up my upper body and hugged me tightly.

I stared at us in the mirror—his bulging biceps holding me in a bear hug while my legs were spread wide. My swollen sex couldn't take much more of this. The more he rocked us back and forth, the more my clit ached for his touch or some sort of release. I glanced down and pictured his deft fingers rubbing me there with wide circles and then up and down.

"Stay here. Open your eyes." His voice boomed over the soft music.

Maybe the month of celibacy had something to do with it, or maybe the fear of losing him had me at the very edge, but I had never been this turned on. Before he had offered relief during our sessions, but tonight was about something else. He wanted me vulnerable, so he could control me and even punish me for doing him wrong. Even though I hadn't really.

Just when I thought I couldn't take it anymore, he unraveled the line and slowly brought me down and out of the pose.

"Rex."

He dropped his arms away from me as if I had suddenly burned him or hurt him physically somehow. When I turned around to face him, his breath caught.

"You can see how much I want you." I crawled to him and pressed my lips to his.

"Jesus Fuck, I want you." He cupped my face, and our tongues collided in a desperate kiss.

I pushed him down to the mat and straddled him. Grinding my pussy against his erection felt like heaven. I kept at it, afraid he would get up and leave if I stopped. But what I really needed was for him to be inside me.

He gathered the fabric of my dress and picked it up, so he could see my pussy. His tongue swiped across his bottom lip, and he hissed. "I want to see you touch yourself. Like that night. Do you remember?"

Of course, I did. That had been our first night in this suite. Back then, I had been so confused by my reaction to his touch and the bindings. I had been so turned on, I ran to my room and masturbated to a reel of images where Rex was the main attraction.

"You saw me that night? I didn't imagine it?"

"You didn't imagine it. Do it."

Bracing one hand on his chest, I reached inside my panties and rubbed the way I had done that day. His eyes fluttered closed for a beat as if my pleasure, gave him pleasure. He sat up and pulled the dress over my head. In a swift motion, he took over for me, stroking the length of my slit with one hand, while he pulled and pinched my nipples with the other.

"Rex." I wrapped my arms around his neck.

"I know, love." He slid two fingers inside me and bent down to suck on my taut nipple.

Wildfire sparked deep in my channel as my orgasm began to build right under his fingertips. He sunk deeper and then I was drowning in a sea of heat and rapture. I didn't fight it. Instead, I let him work me until every bit of my release was spent.

"I want to fuck you so badly it hurts." He gripped my waist.

"Then do it."

"If we do, there won't be an annulment. It will make it that much harder for you to get rid of me. Do you understand?" His tone was strained and ragged as he dug his fingers into my hips.

"I understand." I reached for his cock, stroked him, feeling his length and the bulging veins that led up to his wet tip.

"Fuck." He licked his lips as he watched me jerk him off.

I didn't think it could be possible, but his erection stiffened even more. He was hard as rock *for me*. I positioned it near my entrance and tried not to dwell on the fact that up until now, up until I followed Rex in his rope room and told him I was leaving, he had been thinking about leaving me. I thrust down and forward, and was rewarded by a deep, guttural moan. I rocked my hips against him as hard and as fast as I could. Even when my thighs burned from exhaustion, I didn't stop, not even when he tensed under me. His searing expression told me he wasn't in control, I was. A band of pure bliss coiled itself right in the center of my pussy. In a familiar frenzy, I increased the tempo.

"That's right, love. Take what you need." The last bit was more of a groan as he came. Before he was done, he flipped us over, so he was on top and continued to ride me hard, until he spilled every bit of him inside my walls.

That was my undoing. I squeezed my eyes shut and waited for my orgasm to explode. When it did, tiny blue lights sparked behind my eyelids. And then it was all I could do to stop the wildfire from engulfing me all over again.

"Jesus." He panted a breath and rolled off of me. "What are you doing to me?"

Was he already regretting this entire night? I sat up and cuddled against his body. "Please let me talk."

"Why didn't you plead your case with the priest? He was your way out."

"What?" I had not expected that to be his next question.

"Why did you say I do?"

"Because I wanted to marry you." I inhaled to catch my breath. "The circumstances were not ideal, but at the end of the day, there was only one thing I knew for sure. I wanted to spend the rest of my life with you. I still do."

"Then why?" The sadness in his eyes broke my heart. He couldn't even ask the full question—why did you betray me? "Santino's right. I'm a mindless asshole when I'm around you. Every time you open your mouth, I forget about everything else. Even now, I'm laying here waiting for you to tell me a better lie. Anything so I won't have to see you go."

"I didn't betray you, and that's the only truth. I had a plan that would've kept both you and Dad alive. Dad was going to propose a new deal to Clifton. But he needed you there to agree to what Dad wanted to offer him."

"Jesus Christ. And you believed him?" He shot to his feet and pulled up his pants.

"Yes, I do believe him. I know you don't believe Dad has changed. But Mom did change him."

"People don't change. They get old and they change tactics, but at their core, it's all the same bullshit." He braced his hands on his hips.

Okay, this wasn't bad. He was mad at me, but he wasn't sending me away. "Clifton feels that after almost forty some years of chasing ghosts, he has earned the un-gettable get."

"Me."

"Yes, but also Dad. A king to prove he wasn't wrong or crazy. The man is obsessed. And I don't blame him. At this point, if he doesn't win, he'll have to face the crude reality that he wasted his entire life chasing after your dad and mine."

"That part I can attest to. When he had me in Ibiza, he called himself a hero. Who does that?"

"That's why Dad's plan was going to work. Dad was willing to turn himself in. Get Clifton his shiny medals and his dignity back. And in return for him leaving the Society alone, Dad wanted you to offer him a seat at the table. That's how all this situation got started to begin with. Clifton and Mikey killed the entire Gallo family to make sure that when the time came, he would be the one appointed to that spot with Mikey as his second."

"I won't make him a Don." He rubbed the scruff on his cheek. "That's out of the question."

"That's what that night in Jersey was about." I stomped my foot in frustration. "For you to negotiate something with Clifton. That was the only way for everyone to walk away alive—you, Dad, me."

He chuckled, closing the space between us. "You found a third way out."

"That's what I've been trying to tell you. Dad has been going back and forth on what he wants because he's lost without Mom. He doesn't know where he belongs anymore. He's heart broken." My voice quavered, and Rex wrapped his arms around me. "He knows I'm in love with you. He wants to make things right. I know it's a huge leap of faith for you. But I'm asking you to trust me."

"You love me?" He cocked his head, blinding me with a sexy smile.

"Yes." I ran my hands up his hard abs and chest. "Isn't it obvious? I thought I was going to explode when I realized you'd been in here with Violet."

"You never have to doubt my love for you." He placed a finger under my chin and made me look at him. "She wanted me to show her boyfriend how to do a strappado and a suspension. It's tricky, not to mention dangerous, negotiating the two, which is why I agreed to help them. I never touched her. I was here as their teacher. Nothing more."

"You love me?"

"With all my heart." He bent down and kissed me. "So, how do we get Clifton back to the proverbial table so we can talk?"

# CHAPTER 22
## Bet on Love

REX

Caterina didn't betray me. Jesus Christ, I felt like such an asshole. A whole month wasted, wallowing in self-pity, and it was all for nothing. I put her through hell for nothing.

"I'm sorry, I acted like such a—"

"A beast? Yeah, you did." She wrapped her arms around my waist. "How about you make it up to me the rest of night?"

"I can do that." I bent down and scooped her up. "You're so beautiful."

I sauntered out of the Kinbaku suite and headed for our bedroom. Tomorrow, we would figure a way out of this mess. I had no doubt that, together, we could finally put our Clifton problem to rest.

"I need to talk to Dad," she said as soon as I set her down on the bed.

"We both do. But for now, I want to forget about the outside world and spend the night having make-up sex with

440

my wife. A month is a very long time to be away from you. I thought I was going out of my mind."

"Me too." She beamed at me and rose to her knees to pull me toward her. "You're right. They all can wait." She pressed her lips to mine and brought me down with her.

The next morning, I woke up with Caterina curled against my side. I could spend the rest of my life waking up like this. Smiling at her form, I realized that was exactly what was in store for me, a life with the woman I loved.

"When do we get to stay in bed all day?" She turned on her side, and I spooned her, holding each of her perfect tits in my hands.

"As soon as we get rid of our agent problem. I promise." I slipped my hand under the covers and took a handful of her gorgeous ass, making a mental note to come back to it tonight. Before I got side-tracked, I gave her a quick slap and got out of bed. "Michael's been waiting downstairs for ten minutes now. Let's go talk to him."

"What?" She bounced off the bed. "Why didn't you tell me? Omigod, I can't see him like this."

My gaze swept over her nude body. "Probably not."

She rushed to the bathroom and ran the water. I joined her, but faced my own showerhead the entire time. If I turned around, we might never leave the suite. When I finished, I stepped out of the stall and headed over to my walk-in closet. The space looked so empty without Caterina's things in it.

"I'll have Mary Anne move your things today," I said when Caterina appeared at the door with her toothbrush in her mouth.

"Thank you," she mumbled through the foam. "I'll see you in a bit."

I had gotten so used to living with her. The past month had been pure hell. I loved seeing her in our suite again. I loved seeing her this happy. Smiling like an idiot, I got dressed to meet with Michael. At least, this time, we were done with pretenses.

He knew the only reason he was still alive was because I had allowed it. He also knew that Caterina was mine to keep forever. And there was nothing he could do to stop that. For Caterina's sake, I hoped she was right about Michael wanting to do the right thing by her. If I hadn't met her mother and spent all that time with her, I wouldn't believe Michael was capable of doing the right thing. Or that Caterina, like her mom, had the power to bring out the good in him, however small that part of him was.

I made my way to Caterina's room and knocked once. She opened the door instantly as if she was already on her way out. As usual, she looked stunning in a pencil skirt and silky top. Interesting choice of outfit given how we were just going downstairs to see her dad. Or maybe she understood, our meeting was a negotiation.

"Hi." She beamed at me.

"Hi." I offered her my hand, and she took it.

Downstairs, Michel sat on the sofa facing the oversized fireplace. When Caterina stepped into his line of sight, his eyes watered. Was that remorse or something else? "Bells, I worried he was mistreating you."

"No, Dad. Not at all." Caterina met my gaze.

Technically, I had mistreated her, but she chose to let go of that and move forward instead. For my part, I planned to spend the rest of my life making up for lost time.

"Caterina tells me you and Clifton have come to an agreement?"

"Yes and no." He stood and buttoned his suit jacket. "Before." He paused and slanted a glance at Caterina. "Before I had agreed to make him a Don."

"Before when you were trying to kill me, you mean."

"Yes." He nodded once. "Caterina made me see that going back to the way things were wasn't the answer. I'm not going to waste your time with apologies. The deal is this...I turn myself in so Clifton can redeem himself with the agency. But that's not enough for him. He needs you to offer him a spot within the Society."

"You're okay with this?" I cocked my head in Caterina's direction. The last time Michael faced jail time, Caterina came to me for help, even offered sex in exchange for the favor.

"It's better than the alternative."

The alternative being Michael goes along with Clifton's original plan of killing me and taking over the Society. Heat fluttered below my navel. Caterina was agreeing to this new arrangement to save me.

"I'm not making him a Don."

"I know that. Where I was desperate for an ally before, you have no reason to concede." He smiled at Caterina.

She was the key to everything. The reason I was still here listening to Michael's terms and non-apology. The asshole tried to kill me. I inhaled and let that small detail go.

"He's worked himself into a corner. He'll have to listen to what you have to offer." Caterina reached for Michael's hand. The gesture softened Michael's cold eyes. Good, the ruthless king was ready to play Dad again.

"He likes to kill people. Maybe he can join Santino's crew and help us take out the trash."

Michael chuckled. "I can't say he'll be thrilled, but this could be a good conversation starter."

"So make the call." I nodded at Frank who had been standing by the front door since we'd arrived.

He reached inside his jacket and produced a phone for Michel to use. Caterina watched him intently as he typed a message. I got the feeling that she was also betting on the influence her mom had on Michael. It was a huge gamble on our part. But any option where I didn't have to be Caterina's Dad's killer was worth the shot for me.

Five minutes after he handed the device back to Frank, we got our answer. "He's in, Boss. Tonight, same Jersey warehouse." He shrugged. "I guess he doesn't want to waste time vetting a new place."

"Or he doesn't have the manpower." I rubbed the tensed spot behind my jaw. "Get a team ready. And find a bulletproof vest for Caterina and Michael."

His and hers bulletproof vests. Jesus Christ.

"Are the vests really necessary?"

"I trust you. But that doesn't mean I trust them." I motioned for Frank to go on.

"Got it, Boss." He placed his phone to his ear and talked fast on his way out.

"I have to ask. Any chance you can sit this one out?" I crossed my arms over my chest.

"Not even a little bit." She rose to her feet.

I rolled my eyes. "Fine. You'll need to wear something more appropriate."

"You got it, Boss." She winked.

Caterina following my orders outside the Kinbaku suite was brand new territory.

As soon as the sun set in the horizon, a caravan of SUVs headed out of the city. Michael rode with three of my guys. Sure, they were with him for his protection, but also to make certain he didn't bail at the last minute.

Caterina rode with me, Frank and Aaron. They had instructions to remove her from the warehouse the minute things got heated. A little over an hour later, we arrived at the rendezvous point. My pulse spiked, making me wish I had the ability to make Caterina stay home. The tires crunched over the gravel and then came to a complete stop at the front door.

"How does it look out there?"

"He has two men with him." Frank tapped his earpiece as he turned around to give me a meaningful glance.

Clifton was fresh out of resources. Then why did he think he had a way to bargain with the devil? Unless Michael had led him to believe he was ready to double cross me. I could almost hear Santino's voice in my head. *You're thinking with your dick.* I wasn't. Maybe a little. But mostly, I was placing a huge bet on love—Michael's love for his daughter. And his daughter's love for me.

"Let's get on with it." I opened the door, climbed out, then turned around to help Caterina.

Michael and Santino waited in the black car next to ours. When I cocked an eyebrow at Santino, he lifted his chin toward Michael. "I go where he goes until this is done."

Because of Michael, Clifton had gone after Santino's dad,

the Don of the Buratti family. He wasn't wrong in wanting retribution. One way or another, that was bound to happen today. If Michael didn't deliver on his promise to turn himself in, I was more than ready to do him in.

Inside the warehouse, the two agents Clifton had with him promptly intercepted us and patted us down. We didn't need guns for this. My men had the building surrounded. We even had Chase's crew monitoring from a distance. Clifton wasn't getting away from us this time.

"You delivered, old friend." Clifton stood at the opposite end of the large empty space. "What I would give to have my superiors in this room with me." He chuckled as if he had said something funny.

"We're here." I motioned toward Michael. I wanted this charade over and done quickly. "I'm prepared to offer you a spot with Santino's crew. You'll answer to him."

His absurd laugh echoed around us. When Caterina stepped forward, I put out my arm and pulled her behind me. Something was off. Clifton's confidence was the same as it had been on the yacht when he had me tied down with two of his guys keeping guard. Why did he think he had the upper hand? He was completely surrounded.

"You played us?" My furious tone made Caterina grip the back of my suit jacket.

"Yes." Michael turned to face me as he reached inside his coat. "But not in the way you think."

When he brandished his handgun, Caterina made to move, but I held her in place behind me. She squirmed, her breathing shallow. "Dad. Please don't. Think about Mom. What she wanted."

"I never thought someone like me could be worthy of love."

He gripped the handle tighter, pointing the barrel in my general direction. "But then I met Anna, and she made me see what was possible. She made me realize I could have all those things normal people took for granted. She made me yearn for a family."

"Put the gun away," Caterina pleaded. Her words were barely above a whisper. "Rex has the best lawyers. You won't be in jail for long."

Shaking his head, Michael rubbed the creases between his brows. "You deserve to be happy with the man you love. Your mother always knew what was best. It seems, in the end, she got what she wanted. And I will always love her for it." He reached for Caterina's left hand and kissed Anna's ring before he met my gaze.

By the time I realized what he meant to do, he had already turned away from me and pulled the trigger. The shrilling shot rent the air and left a piercing ring in my ears. In the next beat, three more guns went off. And then we were plunged into a familiar chaos of bullets pelting down on the walls and shattering windows. Smoke fueled the air with toxic fumes and made it hard to breathe and see.

"Rex." Caterina's erratic movements shook me out of my trance. "Are you hit?"

"Fuck." As soon as she asked the question, my ribs throbbed in protest. "I think so."

"Omigod." She fumbled with my shirt to tear it open and didn't stop until she had her hands on my bulletproof vest.

"I'm fine. Just shocked. Jesus Christ, tell me Clifton didn't get away." I sat up and squinted my eyes to see through the lingering white smoke.

Across the way where Clifton stood not a minute ago, only

Santino's dark form was visible. He turned to me as the whole scene became clear to me. "You play silly games with the mob. You're guaranteed shitty prizes. I thought everyone knew that." Santino's deep voice truly sounded confounded.

"He's dead?"

"They all are." He pointed at the other agents. "Question is, who else besides them, knows about us and the Society?"

"I'll get my men on that." I stood, wincing. My side still hurt but it felt more like a bruise than broken bones. Thank God for small favors.

"Rex," Caterina called after me.

"Shit." I darted toward her and Michael who was sprawled on the floor, bleeding.

"He's hurt. And he's not wearing his bulletproof vest." She wiped tears from her cheeks. "Dad. Why would you do this?"

"He was never going to be one of us." A slow smile pulled at his lips as he brought Caterina's hand to his chest.

"Don't talk." Her hands hovered over his blood-soaked dress shirt. "We'll get you a doctor. You're gonna be fine."

"They keep poking at me." He made a soft sound like a hiss. "They should know they can't fix a broken heart."

"Dad."

"Don't cry, Bells." He patted her hand, squeezing his eyes shut. "It doesn't hurt anymore. I hate to make her wait."

She cupped his face and kissed his forehead before she looked up at me. I should've known he'd try something like this. Back at the hospital, when Clifton's men went after him, he didn't fight them. He lay there with a pillow over his face as if he wanted to die. He'd chosen the quickest path to his late wife.

"Why would he do this?" She glanced up at me.

448

Contrition? Michael knew he would either leave this place in handcuffs or in a body bag. Those were literally his only two choices. In the end, the old man had done the right thing by Caterina. If we could call it that. This wasn't how she'd hoped things would end.

"I'm sorry." I kneeled next to her.

"We need a doctor."

My gaze shifted from Michael's grayish pale face to Santino. He sat on his haunches and shook his head once before he did the sign of the cross. Whatever Michael did in the past few months, didn't negate the fact that he was once our king. I hung my head and paid my respects too.

"What are you doing?" Caterina fisted my sleeve. "He needs a doctor."

"He's gone, love."

"He can't." She sobbed into her hand. "Why would he do this? I don't get it."

"He's with her now." I wrapped my arms around her. "What the hell happened?" I asked Santino.

"The old man shot Clifton right between the eyes. His agents retaliated. I got them both but not before they hit you and Michael. Jesus, fuck. The old man didn't even move. He stayed there and covered you both." He raked a hand through his hair. "Michael came here to die."

"He came to set things right." I tightened my hold on Caterina. "For you."

# CHAPTER 23
## And All the Nights After That

THREE MONTHS LATER...

Caterina

I braced my hands on the bathroom marble and stared at my reflection in the mirror. Three months had gone by since the shooting, and I still couldn't shake the gory images out of my mind. The same scene reeled through my head over and over—Dad pointing his gun at Rex only to turn around and gun down Clifton. That part was super clear. The rest was a cacophony of bullets whizzing by, weapons being fired, and the thud of bodies dropping in a cloud of smoke. In a matter of seconds, everyone had hit the floor, including me. Rex had shielded me with his body, and then dragged me down with him. He saved me.

As soon as I thought of him, his face appeared in the mirror. Had he been there the whole time? My gaze met his as he bent down to kiss my bare shoulder.

"The guests are asking for you. The memorial started an hour ago."

"Dad's really gone." I turned to face him. We'd buried Dad a few days after the shooting, but Rex opted to wait until I was in a better headspace to hold a memorial for him. I was thankful to have all that time to mourn on my own, without the empty condolences of strangers.

"He is, love." He cupped my cheek. "This is what he wanted. He left on his own terms."

"I know." I gripped the lapel of his dark jacket. "Why am I still angry at him? I can't get rid of this feeling in the pit of my stomach?"

"It's never a good idea to build pedestals for the people we love." He reached for my fur shawl on the counter and wrapped it around my shoulders.

"Black's never been my color." I heard the pettiness in my tone. I didn't care.

"That's not true. You look beautiful." He squeezed my shoulders. "It's okay to be mad at Michael. He put you through hell in the last few months. Cut him some slack. He was lost and afraid too."

"He tried to kill you twice. You forgave him for that?"

He inhaled and exhaled before he answered, "He brought me closer to you. So yeah, I forgive him."

"I hate that he lied to Mom for so long. To me." I stuffed a hand in my hair, searching for the real reason I was mad at him. Was it the lies? The arranged marriage? Or the fact that I spent so much of my time and energy trying to save him when he didn't need to be saved—when he didn't want to be saved. "He only needed me for one thing. I feel like an idiot for all the times I tried to play the hero for him. He was just using me."

"He did love you—in his own way. He could've gone out a million different ways, but he chose to do right by you. Clifton is no longer a problem for us. He can't hurt us anymore. The FBI will have a hard time putting a new team in place. All they have to go on is a morgue full of bodies." He held me close as if he were saying the words aloud for his benefit as much as mine.

The threat hanging over our heads was gone. Thanks to Mikey, his entire family was gone—and with them, all the evidence the FBI had about the existence of the Society.

"It's okay to love your dad in spite of all the bad things. He was your dad. Come on." He took my hand in his and ushered me out of the suite. "He deserves this last gesture in his honor."

I nodded and followed him to the private elevator. When the doors slid open, we were greeted by a server who offered us a glass of champagne. The memorial was more of a reception with members of the Society. No doubt everyone was here to find some sort of closure too. Dad hadn't been the most caring leader when he was in charge.

Rex placed his hand on my lower back and maneuvered us through the throng. "How many people are here?"

"About two hundred. Don't worry. You won't need to make a speech." He chuckled.

"Oh good." I glanced up and smiled at the Wisteria vines and twinkling lights hanging overhead. "These remind me of our wedding. They're my favorite."

"I know. I thought they might cheer you up tonight." He pulled me toward him. His warm body felt so good. "With everything that happened with Michael and the preparations for today, I didn't get a chance to apologize."

"That's not necessary. I understand, Rex."

"I want to say it. I'm sorry. I'm sorry for how I acted. I was blinded by rage. My emotions got away from me when I thought you had...you know." He couldn't even say the word. That was how much he had been hurt by my supposed betrayal.

"I'm sorry too. In my quest to save Dad and keep you alive, I didn't stop to think how things would look from your end."

"I know you did what you thought was right. I know you were trying to save me too." He flashed me one of his panty-melting smiles before he bent down to kiss me on the lips. In an instant, the pressure on my chest lifted.

"Hmm." Someone cleared his throat behind me to get our attention.

Rex opened his eyes but didn't pull away right away. When I turned around and found Santino's broody face, my smile faded. "Thank you for coming." I decided if we were all one big family now, I should be polite. Also, Santino saved our lives back in the Jersey warehouse "And um, thank you for—"

"Saving you?" A wolfy grin pulled on his lips. "Don't mention it. I only wished I'd known the old man was truly wanting to do the right thing." He clicked his teeth, rubbing the back of his neck. "Ah, anyway, sorry for your loss." He nodded once and strode toward the next group of people.

"What the hell was that?" I turned to Rex.

"An apology. I think."

"Right—for the whole gagging and roping thing." I shook my head. "Santino did what he did to protect you."

"He did." Rex lifted his head to find Santino in the crowd and then furrowed his brows.

"They see you as their king now."

"I believe they do. Now that you're here, no one can claim

my seat at the head of the table." He wrapped his hands around my waist. "Just know something. I am your king, as much as you are my queen. This only works because you're here. Because you want to be here. This was always going to be your choice."

"I can't imagine being anywhere else." I stood on my tiptoes to kiss him, but Massimo's voice stopped me in my tracks.

"I see Rex still hangs the moon and all that." Massimo shook Rex's hand and then hugged me. "I've been trying to get a hold of you." He turned a dark stare toward Rex.

"It was all a misunderstanding." I pushed him away and stepped into Rex's arms again. "We're happy, Massimo."

"Yeah, Rex explained. But I wanted to see it for myself."

"Me too." Enzo squeezed Massimo's shoulder and moved in to give me a bear hug.

"You were gone." My eyes brimmed with tears. I couldn't help the reproach in my tone. I missed them.

"I'm sorry. I just couldn't face you." He kissed the top of my head. "I'm here now, Bells. Anything you need. I'm here for you."

I had seen both of my brothers at the cemetery, but we were all in too much pain, seeing Dad go into his last resting place, that words, let alone smiles, felt out of place. I was glad to have my brothers back.

"What happens now?" I asked Rex.

That was a loaded question. What would happen now that Dad was gone? Would Enzo be allowed to step in as Don of the Alferas, even though Dad had walked away? What about the fact that there was a good chance both Enzo and Massimo helped Dad with his whole crazy plan to start a new Society with him as king?

"Enzo has pledged his alliance to me. With Michael gone, the Alfera's seat at the table is no longer frozen."

"You mean Enzo is officially the new Don?"

"He's already accepted my offer." Rex beamed at me. "Massimo will be his second, as it was always intended."

He had finally made good on his promise to save the Society and bring everyone back into the fold.

"I see the newlyweds have found a way to resolve their differences." Signora Vittoria's smoker's voice sent a chill down my spine. But when she spoke again, her words were kind and honest. "I'm sorry for your loss, dear."

"Thank you."

"Let me introduce you to my nephew, Romeo Salvatore." She gestured toward the guy who had joined the group shortly after Vittoria arrived.

"Nice to meet you both. I've heard so much about you." He offered both Rex and me a kind smile as he shook both our hands.

He seemed so out place. The way I felt the first time Rex introduced me to this underworld. By the way Rex surveyed his pretty boy face, I had to assume he was, in fact, new to the Society. As soon as Vittoria, Romeo, and my brothers left, I turned to Rex.

"What's the deal with him?"

"Vittoria is having a hard time finding a successor to train in her footsteps. I helped her find her brother's bastard. He seems capable."

"Why not Donata?"

"She's not interested. And by birth, not actually required

DIANA A. HICKS

to take over. Romeo's dad was the oldest of three. Vittoria only stepped up after both her brothers passed away several years ago." Rex brushed his lips over mine. "I'm glad you're taking interest in the family."

The crime family. He meant the century old, secret Society—my new family.

"I have a lot of catching up to do." I shrugged.

I spent the rest of the night meeting more new people that, in one way or another, were linked to the original families—all but the Gallos who had been wiped out at the beginning of the year because one of their own betrayed them. In this world, trust was everything.

Just when I thought I couldn't handle any more people uttering "I'm sorry for your loss," Violet came to my rescue and pulled me to a quiet corner by the wall facing Central Park. The city view was truly spectacular up here.

"You look good." She pressed a fresh glass of champagne in my hand. "I mean, given the circumstances."

"Thanks." I hadn't seen Violet since my last jealous tantrum. My cheeks burned hot when I thought about how I had reacted when I realized Rex had been in the rope room with her.

"I wanted to apologize." She bit her lower lip. "I honestly didn't think you'd mind if Rex showed my boyfriend a few things." She inhaled, wiping her cheek. "Suspensions can be tricky the first time."

"No, don't. Please don't apologize. I'm sorry for not trusting you. I was in a bad place that day." I hugged her.

"Okay." Her cheeks flushed. "He loves you. Don't ever doubt that."

"I know that now."

She shot a furtive look behind her and then moved closer. "From what he said during our session, I got the impression that you had asked him for the reverse ebi. That's my favorite too."

Heat rushed through me at the memory of that night. Rex had said I wasn't ready, but he obliged with a partial suspension. "He did a partial for me."

She practically squealed as she gripped both my hands. "You're ready. I know you are. Let me help you. I can walk you through a session, how to breathe, how to move."

I hadn't thought about how now that Rex and I were married, I had unlimited access to his skills as a rigger. My heart thrashed in my ears as I scanned the room looking for Rex. When our gazes met, the air shifted with an electric charge. As if he could read my mind or my body, he excused himself and headed in my direction.

"Is that a yes?" Violet squeezed my hands to bring me back to reality.

"Yes. I would love that." I said in a sweet tone, as if we were talking about meeting for afternoon tea sometime next week.

"I'll see you tomorrow then. Nine am, sharp." She winked and strolled in Rex's direction. She whispered something in his ear, then moved on to join her boyfriend, a cute guy who seemed completely enamored with her.

"I think this is the first time you made it through one of your own parties." I sipped from my glass.

"I supposed I did." He furrowed his brows and glanced toward the elevator doors where the last of the guests were making their way out. "I was hoping you still had room in your dance card. We never got to do our first dance." His searing gaze dropped to my lips, and a flutter sparked below my belly.

"There's no actual dance floor." I bit my lower lip, loving how easy it was to forget all the bad when I was with Rex—when he looked at me like I was the most beautiful person in the world. "Or music. And I think it's about to rain." I put my palm up in front of me before I glanced upward. Smiling, I caught a few droplets, while I let him lead me to the center of the rooftop where the glow of the bistro lights illuminated an empty space big enough for us to dance. "Did you send everyone home?"

"I might've mentioned you had a long day." He placed his hand on my lower back and drew me to him just as the speakers along the wall started to play a sensual string-quartet tune.

Rex led me into a turn before he settled in with a pace that was easy for me to follow. The gentle melody should've pacified my need for him. But Violet's words were still in my head. And the buzz between my legs only increased every time Rex's thigh pressed against mine.

"I want you, right here, right now." He panted a breath in my ear as he ran a large, warm hand over my chest where my heart was about to spiral out of control.

"Rex."

He bent down and captured my mouth. His tongue found mine, and I deepened the kiss while my hands fumbled with his belt. A chuckle rumbled deep in his chest as he watched me unhook his tuxedo studs. By the time I had removed his jacket and dress shirt, he had already walked me past the furniture and high tables to a spot where he could press me against the cinder wall.

Raindrops pelted my face as he pulled up my dress, moved my panties to the side, and plunged into me. One day, the desperate need we had for each other would subside, but for now, all I could do was give into it and trust he'd be there to catch me every time.

"I thought you had sent everyone away so you could take me to your rope room." I tunneled my fingers through his wet hair.

"That's later." He ran his tongue along the column of my neck and thrust deeper into me, hitting my sensitive spot straight on. "We have all night, love. And all the nights after that."

## CHAPTER 24

# *Epilogue*

CATERINA

Three months later...

Rex spent several weeks cleaning up the mess Dad had left behind. As it turned out, Clifton had been working on his own for the past few months. The FBI didn't have proof the Society existed. Dealing with actual Society members was more complicated than that. Dad's loyal friends been found guilty of treason. My brothers along with Santino and Rex had to make an example out of all of them. A necessary evil, Enzo had called it.

After the threat hanging over our heads was over, truly over, Rex and I finally made it to our honeymoon. We had spent the last two months in Ibiza, basking in the Mediterranean sun, having sex, and letting the quiet sound of the waves lull us to sleep on Rex's brand-new yacht. A few times, we managed to leave the serenity of his boat to eat in the town center and do some shopping.

Today, the entirety of our plans consisted of staying in bed and catching the sunset later. We were in the middle of nowhere off the coast of Ibiza, surrounded by crystal blue water and a salty breeze. I smiled at Rex's form while he swam away from the boat. I flipped on my belly and closed my eyes hoping for a power nap, but my mind insisted on thinking of Rex instead, his hands on me, his muscled body, and that crazy good cock of his.

Minutes later, drops of cool water pelted on my back. When I rolled over, I met Rex's blue gaze. The man was hot when he wore his tailored suits, but Rex with a tan, mussed hair, and completely naked was a new level of hotness. And holy fuck, butterflies fluttered in my belly with the realization that this was the guy I was to spend the rest of my life with.

"I never want to leave this place."

"Me neither." He lowered down until his body was pressed to mine and kissed me.

Rex was all mine. And I was his.

"But." He nibbled on my neck. "I just received a message and I'm needed back home."

I groaned. "Duty calls, I suppose."

"Sort of. Your wedding gift is finally ready." He shook his head, pursing his lips. "I had wanted it to be done way before now, but negotiations got complicated."

"I don't need a wedding gift. Are you kidding me? This trip has been amazing. Being with you is amazing." I cupped his cheek and rolled my hips to feel the length of his erection. "You're everything I ever wanted."

Just like that, I was hungry for him again.

"Trust me. You do want what I got for you." He beamed at me. "A-List advertising is now all yours."

"What?" I sat up and pushed him off me. "I thought you said you were going to sell it for parts."

"I didn't say that. You assumed that was my plan for it." He shrugged. "I chose not to set the record straight."

I thought back to the day Rex had come to the office. At the time, I couldn't get past the idea that he wanted me to be his rope bottom. I was mad at him for things that weren't even his fault. Of course, when I found out he was buying the company I worked for, I thought the worst of him. But now that I thought about it, he never said he would take apart the firm.

"It was always meant to be your wedding gift." He slid the pad of his thumb over my cheek.

"You let me think the worst of you because you wanted to keep it a surprise?" I laughed.

"I didn't want to lie to you. Not to mention, that if I had told you the truth, you would've told me to go to hell." He licked his lips in that sexy way of his that put all kinds of bad ideas in my head. "I don't think you would've reacted well if I had told you right off the bat that we had to be married as soon as possible."

"No probably, not."

"Are you saying you don't want the company?" He teased.

Of course I wanted it. Who in their right mind says no to owning their dream company? "I mean, you already went through all the trouble of buying it. Jill has been talking about retiring ever since I started working for her."

"She'll never have to work a day in her life. I assure you. She drove a hard bargain." His eyes softened as he surveyed my face. "In that first meeting at your office, she knew I was madly in love with you."

"I'm so in love with you." I pushed at his chest until he was flat on the deck and I could climb on top of him. His hard body felt so good between my thighs. I bent down and pressed my lips to his. "Thank you."

"There's nothing I wouldn't do for you."

"I can't believe you bought me a whole company."

"Jill will stay on for as long as you need her. But she's more than ready to retire, so don't make her wait too long." He cradled my neck and brought me down for a searing kiss. "Now, if you really like your gift, how about you thank me properly?"

His voice turned sinful and full of promises. I felt alive every time he looked at me like that, like I was the only person in the world. How did I ever think I could hate this man? Or live without him for that matter? I was always meant to be his. I loved that my brain and my heart were finally in agreement. I loved that he was my rigger, my friend, my husband. I loved that he owned every part of me.

"For you, I'd do anything," I whispered.

My pussy throbbed with anticipation because I knew what he would say next.

"Get on your knees, love."

---

# Recommended Reading Order

## The Crime Society

Lost Raven - Novella

King of Beasts (Beast Duet #1)

King of Beasts (Beast Duet #2)

Wolf's Lair - Prequel

Big Bad Wolf (Wolf Duet #1)

Big Bad Wolf (Wolf Duet #2)

Once Upon A Christmas - Bonus Epilogue

Dark Beauty - Prequel

Fallen Raven (Raven Duet, #1)

Fallen Raven (Raven Duet, #2)

## Steal My Heart Series

Ignite You

Escape You

Escape My Love - Bonus Epilogue

Provoke You

Unravel You

Unleash You

Defy You

**Desert Monsoon Series**

Love Over Lattes

Love Over Time